Oliver Harris was born in London and now lives in Manchester, where he teaches creative writing at Manchester Metropolitan University. *A Shadow Intelligence* is his fourth novel.

Praise for *A Shadow Intelligence*

'Oliver Harris is always pure quality'
Ian Rankin

'[A] tremendous evocation of modern Kazakhstan and the contemporary intelligence landscape. Scary if true, or even half true'
Sunday Times

'As much a thinker as a doer, Elliot Kane has as much in common with John le Carré's Jerry Westerby, or Lionel Davidson's Johnny Porter, a plausibly multi-faceted old school operator with the skills – physical, psychological, intellectual – to negotiate the geopolitical faultlines of central Asia as Russia and China square up over Kazakhstan's untapped oil reserves'
Irish Times

'A gripping, fast-moving and intelligent novel from new spy fiction star Oliver Harris which will leave readers wanting a lot more Elliot Kane adventures'
Irish Independent

'An intelligent and thoroughly researched spy-procedural giving razor-sharp insight into the particular challenges of twenty-first century espionage'
Big Issue

A SHADOW INTELLIGENCE

OLIVER HARRIS

ABACUS

First published in Great Britain in 2019 by Little, Brown
This paperback edition published in 2020 by Abacus

3 5 7 9 10 8 6 4

A CIP catalogue record for this book
is available from the British Library.

ISBN 978-0-349-14296-8

Typeset in Palatino by M Rules
Printed and bound in Great Britain by
Clays Ltd, Elcograf S.p.A.

Papers used by Abacus are from well-managed forests
and other responsible sources.

Abacus
An imprint of
Little, Brown Book Group
Carmelite House
50 Victoria Embankment
London EC4Y 0DZ

An Hachette UK Company
www.hachette.co.uk

www.littlebrown.co.uk

ONE

The Secret Intelligence Service puts two years and over 100k into the training of new field officers. You're shown how to steal cars, strip weapons, hack bank accounts. There are courses on the use of improvised explosives, two workshops dedicated to navigating by the stars. But nothing about what I had heard one old spy call whiplash. No one tells you how to go home.

You're negotiating with a crime syndicate in Kabul on Thursday; Saturday night you're at a dinner party in Holland Park. Cutlery tinkles. There is something you've forgotten. You lock yourself in the bathroom and call a restaurant on Sadarat Square to speak to a man you know is dead, and when the phone's answered there is the call to prayer in the background. The worlds cannot all be real at the same time. You apologise to your hosts as you leave, blaming jet lag, then sit on the Central Line hearing mourners wail. After the first few times, officers switch to a desk-based role or they find ways of managing the transition. I can't do desks, so I had to learn.

I accumulated rituals, which veered between superstition and procedure. Most of all, I collected places that I could touch as if they were a charm and say: Everything's under control, you know what you're doing. The Premier Bar in Jordan's Queen Alia airport was one of them. Travel between the lucky and unlucky parts of the world regularly enough and you'll find yourself killing time in Queen Alia. The Premier Bar tucked itself away in a corner of the main terminal, a fridge and three aluminium tables, with a clear view across the departures hall. It had Arabic news on a flat-screen TV and bottles of Heineken in a fridge. I thought of it as my local.

I had come to Queen Alia airport en route from Saudi Arabia, and was under strict instructions to proceed directly to London. This in itself was ominous – most of my debriefs were held in third countries. An operation had been pulled suddenly. I had one bag and the clothes I wore, which stank of smoke and petrol. The pale jacket and chinos of a certain type of Englishman abroad are not made for arson.

I sipped a beer and tried to unwind and form a plan at the same time, letting the stress hormones settle, enjoying globalisation at its transient best. A Congolese family in green and purple robes filtered through a charcoal-grey swarm of Chinese businessmen. Two dazzling white sheikhs led faceless wives in gold-trimmed burkas. Eastern European sex workers pulled Samsonite cases, heading to the Gulf, South East Asian ones in denim cut-offs on their way to Europe. The skinny, bright-eyed Bangladeshi and Sri Lankan labourers clutched mobile phones and gazed at the departure boards. Staff of NGOs and media organisations sipped water, restless or exhausted depending on the direction of travel. I watched them move as flights were called: Erbil, Jeddah, Khartoum. There were other solitary individuals like me, meeting each other's eyes but not for long. You found a lot of snapped sim cards in the bins. Private security contractors favoured duffel bags. They looked well-fed, and walked with the stiff swagger of men who'd been heavily armed until yesterday.

Six hours earlier I'd been in an abandoned mansion on the edge of Asir province in Saudi Arabia, close to the border with Yemen. The mansion had been trashed. At some point the previous night a local group of unknown affiliation had stormed the place, looting what they could. The occupant – a notorious playboy, discreet funder of terrorism and precious agent of mine – had fled. I had about ten minutes to clear the place of anything sensitive before a more purposeful crew arrived.

I walked through with an empty rucksack, my footsteps echoing as I searched. I'd never been inside before. It was a fifteen-bedroom, thirty-million-dollar palace: fun to trash, difficult to search. Crystal teardrops from the chandeliers littered the floor among balls from an antique snooker table. There were scattered books, broken glass, trails of blood where the intruders had cut themselves climbing through windows. They'd shot his pets, ransacked his wardrobe, slashed some dubious abstract art and one haunting Fantin-Latour still life. A single word of spray-painted Arabic livened the wallpaper: *Irhal.* Leave.

Which was good advice.

'Are you seeing this?' a voice in my earpiece asked.

The satellite image on my phone showed a convoy of five Toyota pickups heading straight towards me. Unclear who they were, but I wasn't putting my money on Saudi forces. The barrels of the semi-automatics sticking out of the windows were clear enough.

'I see it.'

'Probably time to get a move on.'

I climbed the stairs. The first floor gave a view across the grounds. Most of the buildings I used in the Gulf were built with anti-ram walls, barriers, ballistics window film. This wasn't one of them. It had a defiant lawn, some cacti, date palms and an elaborate sprinkler system. A Ferrari belonging to the man who used to live here remained beside the gates, a white shell of carbonised metal. Silver puddles gleamed in the burnt dust beneath it, which perplexed me until I realised it was the metal of the brake pads, melted and resolidified. That was surreal and beautiful. My own driver leaned against the gatepost, binoculars raised. Two distinct lines of smoke reached up from the suburbs of Abha, the nearest city, 3.4 kilometres away.

'*Eajal!*' Quick, he shouted, turning.

I estimated ten minutes before the men arrived, two more to breach the gates. The Saudi police had vanished, the SAS unit attached to the intelligence services for scenarios such as these was stuck at a vehicle checkpoint on the highway. I was left with three temporarily loyal members of a carjacking gang high on anti-epileptic medication that they consumed by the handful, claiming it gave them courage. Maybe it hadn't kicked in yet.

One of my current allies, Samir, appeared in the corridor behind me: moustache and paunch, antique pistol, bulging eyes.

'We go now.' He was agitated. Beside him stood a cousin or nephew, no older than sixteen, in an FC Barcelona top, barely able to lift his Kalashnikov.

'Five minutes.'

'Two minutes.'

I reached into my jacket, gave the boy my handgun, told him to forget the rifle. 'I'll be back down before they get here.'

I took a breath, mixed some oxygen in with the fresh adrenalin. Nice and alert; let's get this done. The room I wanted to find was proving elusive. I opened doors, looking for electronics and paperwork, finding abandoned Kevlar, fine china, leather-bound encyclopaedias.

One minute.

At the end of the second-floor corridor I located the door I needed. I punched a code into its electronic lock, saw inside, and my heart sank.

Seven or eight crates of material filled the small, windowless space: bank statements, shipping documents, loose cash, bills of lading. I counted four laptops, seven concertina files, stacks of invoices for almost everything but the weaponry he was actually funding. No doubt, somewhere within the mess, were identifying details; lives endangered.

Samir appeared behind me, saw the haul, swore.

'We must leave it,' he said.

It would take half an hour to remove it all. If we had a van. A call came from downstairs: they could see the dust of the approaching convoy. I threw the rucksack into the pile.

'Get a can of petrol from the fuel house.'

'We don't have time.'

'We've got plenty of time. Go.'

I began to sort through, taking the cash, ensuring the hard drives were exposed. A sheet of the *South China Morning Post* caught my eye. It had been folded small, tucked into a box of necklaces. I unwrapped it and saw what looked like two uncut diamonds. Even in the murky room they sparkled: yellow-tinted and unmistakable against the newsprint.

I pocketed one diamond, wrapped the other back in the paper with half the money. When Samir returned with four jerrycans, I gave him the wrap of newspaper and told him it was a present for later; I needed him poor and wary for a few more minutes. We both splashed petrol over the hoard, then he ran down to the car. I took a final breath before dropping a match. Sometimes it's left to you to perform the ceremony alone; to lower the flag. No call to prayer from Abha. There was a deep Sunday peace, which meant that peace was gone.

An hour to the airbase, a flight to Medina, then another Saudi military jet into Jordan. No one had offered me a change of clothes. And petrol smoke sticks to you. Messages kept coming in on the phone belonging to Christopher Bohren, my cover identity: bankers, brokers, a fellow art dealer, a company that specialised in installing infinity pools. All wondering why I'd disappeared.

I had no idea.

I washed the taste of blood out of my mouth with Heineken.

The situation was a mess, I didn't doubt that. My agent had vanished, Saudi Arabia looked like it might kick off, and someone somewhere in Vauxhall Cross was worried about my own potential capture. But I had also been expecting this: the intelligence service liked to keep you moving, stop you building empires and attachments. The longer you were in the field the more vulnerable you became, so the thinking went. As well as the dangers of overexposure, the theory involved some old-school notion of going native. Operations got pulled overnight and you rarely, if ever, got an adequate explanation. I sometimes wondered about HQ's envy of field officers, whether they created their own secrecy just to keep you in your place. Sometimes it was as simple as a budget cut.

For now I wanted to enjoy a last moment of freedom, of being Christopher Bohren. For all the professional setback and geopolitical consequences of my departure, I was pleased to be here. The magic of returning to places never diminished – of finding them still there: the tables, the weary face behind the counter. It was a small victory, as if I'd kept a rendezvous with myself.

On the TV screen: *Militants burn playboy's palace. Is Saudi pact with extremism over?*

That was the question posed by RT Arabic, the Kremlin's new Arabic-language station. They had good footage: a reporter standing beside smouldering ruins, with the carbonised Ferrari visible over his shoulder. I finished my beer and got another.

'You used to show Al Jazeera here,' I said. The owner shrugged. 'You prefer Russian TV?'

'My son prefers it.'

I took the drink to my table, feeling defeated, wondering at the way history creeps up on you. The journey from the counter gave me an opportunity to scan my immediate environment. There had been one man sitting at the Starbucks across from me for fifteen minutes now. He'd taken a seat facing in my direction, although he hadn't looked directly at me once. He had an Arabic paper spread in front of him but his eyes didn't track the text. Not airport security, but I thought I glimpsed a holster.

I finished my beer, watched a group of business people speaking Russian hurry towards the flight to Damascus. After another few minutes my Starbucks friend departed, slinging a laptop bag over his shoulder. I put my phone on encrypted mode and dialled a Saudi number.

'I've had to leave town for a few days. There's a few bits and pieces I left behind which I won't need any more. I'd like you to dispose of it all.'

'Yes.'

'And then I think you should get out.'

'You are leaving us.'

'The situation's become precarious.'

'We are ready.'

'I appreciate that. I have instructions.'

I rested my eyes on a video screen above the concourse: a woman in a field of lavender pressing a perfume bottle to her throat. 'I will be doing everything I can to ensure you have no problems,' I said. 'If you speak to Leyla, will you tell her I'll be in touch as soon as possible?'

He put the phone down. I closed my eyes. The fabled licence to kill is nothing beside the very real licence to die; to walk out of a life and its responsibilities. No farewell, no last confession. I picked up my phone again and called CIA's station in Islamabad.

'Courtesan's a no-show,' I said. 'Everything on ice for now.'

'What happened?'

'I don't know. I'll message when I do.'

I moved a blood-red Swiss passport from my bag to my jacket pocket, booked a night at the Mandarin Oriental in Kensington. Then I went and bought a suit and a clean phone.

I knew from experience that in five or six hours I'd be facing men and women in ironed clothes who would determine, from how I presented myself, the level of mishap they could pin on me. Luckily, routes to and from war zones make for good shopping: Rolex, Ralph Lauren and Prada do their own sleek profiteering. The woman in the Prada concession was elegant, flirtatious, didn't blink at a man who stank of petrol smoke digging out his money belt and buying a three-grand suit.

'You have been staying in Jordan?' she asked.

'Just passing through.'

'English?'

'Canadian. I might get a watch as well.'

I chose a watch.

'Can you wrap this?'

'Of course.' She wrapped it, tied a ribbon and offered me a choice of message tags.

'Just a blank one, thanks.'

Doors of dark carved wood led between potted palms into the Royal Jordanian Crown Lounge. No familiar faces. At the back was a disabled toilet that had served me well over the years. I changed, tore and flushed my receipts, checked my paperwork was in order. Then I took a condom wrapper from my wallet, removed a pouch of duct tape and prised it apart. Inside was a small key, the key to my own life. I rinsed off the glue and transferred it to my pocket.

I shaved, used the corner of my boarding pass to get the dirt from beneath my fingernails. Finally, I tried looking into my own eyes. I was thirty-five, 5'11", 170 pounds, ash-brown hair faded by the Middle Eastern sun. I started operations looking well: groomed, trim but not so worked out that I could be mistaken for military. I ended them haggard, bloodshot, with an edginess that triggered attention.

I eased the tape off the new wrapping paper and removed

the gift box, took out the watch, then tucked the diamond into the velvet lining and rewrapped it. I found the tag and wrote: *Let's quit.*

At the boarding gate, the usual sunburnt crew gripped their Western passports as if they might try to wriggle away. The flight took off at 10.30 a.m. I stayed awake over Lebanon, trying to see how much power was on, caught a glimpse of western Turkey, slept through Europe.

Heathrow was unusually quiet. No issues at the border. I walked into the UK, part of me hoping that there was no one to meet me, but I was out of luck.

TWO

My driver held an agreed name. You could almost believe he was a standard chauffeur if it wasn't for the eyes that scanned the people around me as he took my bag. Square-jawed, broad-shouldered; an army physique at odds with the grey suit.

'How was the journey?'

'Very smooth, thank you.'

The car was convincing too: black Audi, authentic TFL private hire licence in the window. Its bulletproof glass and run-flat tyres weren't easily identifiable to untrained eyes. The sky above was grey, the bite of English winter refreshing.

'Alastair Undercroft apologises for not being here in person to welcome you home,' my driver said, when we were inside. 'We're to proceed directly to the meeting.'

'That's fine.'

He kept his eyes on the mirrors as we drove, watching security and police. After several years living the life of Christopher Bohren, the most likely source of trouble was New Scotland Yard. I let him get going before leaning forward.

'I'd like to go via Marylebone High Street.'

'Sir?'

'I have something to pick up.'

'I've been asked to take you straight there.'

'We have time.'

'Okay.'

He looked uncertain, put a call in to someone announcing our change of plan. Everyone had their orders. But his was the last deference I'd get for a while and I wanted to use it.

London looked solid, fortressed in a thick, impregnable peace. A dream that had congealed. How long was I going to be here? I directed him to a Caffe Nero across the road from Balthorne Safe Deposits and he pulled up.

'How do you take your coffee?' I asked.

'I'm fine, thank you.'

'Go on. Flat white?'

'No sugar.'

I crossed the road to Balthorne. A row of classical columns obscured the front window. Reception was wood-panelled. They minimised human interaction. Four cameras and a smartly suited elderly guard watched you approach the entry gate and place your palm on a glass panel that read your veins. If your veins lined up, you got to enter a six-digit PIN code and walk in.

It became more functional inside: another desk, a brightly lit corridor and finally stairs down to the vault. By this stage the key seemed quaint.

In my box there were a few photographs, some handwritten poems, souvenirs of past operations, and a manila envelope containing a sim card. I unlocked my briefcase and removed a couple of grand in various currencies, depositing it along with a fragment of pottery that might have come from the Temple of Artemis in what was now north-eastern Libya. I kept the diamond. Then I took the sim and placed it in my new phone.

I crossed the road to the coffee shop. As far as I was concerned, the operation had been pulled six months early, I had half an hour for a coffee. And I needed strength for what was to come, whether or not it included re-entering my own life. I took the driver his flat white, with a pain au chocolat, which I felt should buy me ten minutes. Then I returned to the café and sat down.

11

London throbs. You're alert to threats that aren't there any more, and the senses overload. Three young women came in, talking Cantonese. A man in the far corner of the café muttered Kurdish into a Bluetooth headset. I heard the words 'mother' and 'hospital'. The coffee-shop window was bare, no defensive blocks between it and the road. But there would be no attacks. I tried to re-enter the complacency. A copy of *The Times* had been folded on a rack beside the tills so that you saw a strip of flames in a front-page photo, but they were somewhere far away.

My hands looked tanned in the English light. My lips were cracked. I stared at the screen of my new phone. When you charge up a phone, you entertain the fantasy that a life will return. I'd always brace myself for the personal business but forget to brace myself for its dwindling pressure. When you expend your energy maintaining another person's identity your own becomes neglected. In the last seven weeks I'd missed two birthdays, one wedding, several job offers. There was an invitation to lunch from an investor friend who owed me for some timely information; no message from the woman I wanted to hear from. At least, that's what I thought at first.

Emails likewise: irrelevant things or those I was too late for. I checked the junk folder in case that was where my life had been diverted, saw something strange.

It was an email from a TutaNota address with a string of letters and numbers for a name. TutaNota was a German-based encrypted webmail service. This was a procedure I used for agents. Subject line: *Lottery Win*.

The message had been sent twenty-two hours ago. I scanned the email for malware then opened it. The email contained two lines:

HAPPY BIRTHDAY.
CLAIM YOUR PRIZE.

'Happy birthday' meant danger: I was in danger, or the agent in question was in danger, and I needed to initiate exfiltration procedures; i.e. time to get out of town. 'Claim your prize' meant that a file had been uploaded to a message board hidden deep within the dark side of the internet.

When you've refined systems that work in the field, it's good to stick with them. But you make sure each agent has a unique signature, procedural details that identify them so you know who's contacting you in the absence of formal identification. I'd used this particular code with an agent in Turkey codenamed MESCALINE – Khasan Idrisov, a young man I had been fond of, with his pale eyes and thin beard; the frayed handkerchiefs with which he'd mop his brow. His decapitation was still up on YouTube last time I checked.

So the message was a surprise.

I looked around Caffe Nero, sipped my coffee, read the message again.

There was no way anyone should have known the code words, let alone my personal email address as well. Now I looked through my missed calls more closely. Around the time of the email there were three attempts from a foreign landline. 8.12 p.m. last night, 8.14 p.m., then 8.21 a.m. The prefix was 87 172. A check online confirmed it was a landline in Astana, Kazakhstan.

I'd been in the country twice, briefly – both times near the start of my career. There was little MI6 activity there; the service ran a minimal station out of the embassy. It provided some shallow cover for intelligence operatives and electronic surveillance, and enjoyed a moment of inflated importance after 9/11 – Kazakhstan was a supply route to Afghanistan – but in the resource-strapped world of MI6 nowhere retained staff without good reason. The world is big, intelligence operations are expensive and politically complicated. Nothing came up online for the number: no individual or business. I set up GPS scrambling so my location was concealed, dialled the number back. It rang but no one answered.

My driver stood watching me beside his Audi, cigarette cupped in his palm. I needed a clean device with which to access the darknet. That wasn't going to be easy today. As I got up, I wrestled with a thought I didn't have the capacity to process right now. One other person alive knew the contact system, the person I wanted to hear from more than any other – but not like this.

THREE

I considered asking for another diversion, purchasing a laptop, retrieving whatever had been sent. But we were running late, and I was starting to feel any further action needed to be as inconspicuous as possible.

We followed the river east, sank into the Blackwall Tunnel, through the shabby tranquillity of south-east London into Kent; bare branches, a splash of rain, suburban oblivion before the M25 reduced the world to litter-strewn verges.

I rarely got invited into Vauxhall Cross any more. They'd have to disinfect the place afterwards. The ideal of HQ was to remain a sterile domain in which transgressions of men and women like me echoed only faintly. It was a truism in the Intelligence Service that the better you were in the field, the less London wanted to know you. On a shaded lane outside Sevenoaks, the driver stopped, checked his mirrors. When no other vehicles appeared he turned left down a rough track between stone pillars to a gate. Two men in Barbour jackets approached the car, an Alsatian straining at its leash. They let the dog sniff around, checked the driver's papers, peered into the back and gave me a nod. They pulled puncture chains off the track and we continued.

After another minute we arrived at a sprawling red-brick manor house with stables at the side, marshy paddocks at front and back. A Mercedes had been parked in one of the stables. Two armed men in grey suits sat in the main building's flagstoned hallway, breath steaming.

'Home again,' one said, recognising me. 'Phone, please.'

That was new. I handed over my phone. He winked, nodded towards the stairs. 'They're waiting for you.'

Not quite Miss Moneypenny. Still, the familiar environment offered a shred of comfort. I had been here years ago, crafting the Bohren cover in the first, optimistic flush of the Arab Spring.

You have experience with revolutions.

How's your Arabic?

Up to speed with the Muslim Brotherhood?

Rolling coverage on, courtesy of Al Jazeera; me, fresh from Ukraine, still filled with ideas of extending the colour revolutions to Russia itself. Why not? But the Middle East was where the story was happening: freedom blossoming, a chance to remake the world. That seemed a very long time ago. I allowed myself a flicker of nostalgia as I climbed the rickety stairs, breathing the same country air. I remembered the view of low hills and forest. A landscape for deer hunting, I had thought at the time. Tudor country: Thomas Wyatt, Kit Marlowe – men entranced by the power they served, who thought they could borrow some of its glory.

My debrief took place in a large room, a mesh of grey conducting material over the walls rendering it a secure communications facility, but giving the air of dust sheets and decline. Three people got to their feet when I entered: Alastair Undercroft, head of the Global Issues Controllerate; Martina Lansdown, Section Chief: Libya, Syria and Yemen; finally Douglas Mitchell, an adviser to the Foreign Office, though not one you'd come across very often. Undercroft was first to shake my hand.

'Good to see you, Elliot.' The pink ridges of his bald head looked raw under the lights.

'Welcome back,' Lansdown said. Her suit was the olive-green

of military fatigues. Mitchell offered his hand but didn't smile. He sported five o'clock shadow and black hair gleaming with whatever kept it scrupulously parted. The walnut desk in the centre of the room bore two laptops sitting on their secure cases of nickel and silver-plated nylon, plus a Panasonic Toughbook showing satellite imagery. Beside this was a tray of sandwiches, untouched.

Six years ago the Foreign Office had identified an urgent need to bolster our connections with rebels in Libya and Syria. They wanted to know about activists, but also more battle-ready opposition. I was already tuned in to some of the movements from my time in Tunis and Cairo. The plan was to monitor and control the flow of arms, men and communications equipment as much as possible. Prevent massacres, respond to cries for help, without the need for the kind of military intervention that makes news bulletins. Overseeing this was a small, ex-directory unit of MI6 set up in the 1990s after the fall of the Soviet Union, incorporating those familiar with the movement of Islamist fighters, as well as the intricacies of the diplomatic relationships that concerned them: Pakistan, Turkey, the Gulf states. CIA were on board, keen to make it a liaison operation with Six, because liaison operations didn't need to be reported to Congress. MI6 and those Cabinet members in the know wanted it categorised as an Information Operation as these didn't require ministerial sanction. I was needed because you can't do everything with drones.

They wanted me to enter that world, as someone who could befriend funding sources for rebels of all stripes, to map out the web of shifting alliances between Riyadh, Ankara and Tripoli. I thought it sounded like an opportunity to immerse myself rather than run around another desert sticking targets on backs. I would have to win trust, which took time, which was what I'd trained for. I convinced them that art dealing involved as much mysterious movement of funds as any other pursuit, and we created Bohren. I met Rashid Bin Talal six months later at Basel art fair, established that he was setting up a museum of modern art in Riyadh, that he nursed a crippling hard-on for young white men, and that he was shipping over five hundred grand a week to militant Islam. I recruited him five months later. That was quick, but still felt luxuriously gradual by the standards of the modern intelligence service. I codenamed him Courtesan and insisted no more than six individuals knew his real identity. We kept him in play for the sake of his intel, his cash, the cover he gave our own schemes, and diplomatic relations with the Saudis. It was win–win all the way around.

'Courtesan was arrested, six a.m. our time, Saudi side of the border,' Undercroft said. 'Believed to have been taken to Ulaysha prison. Obviously we're monitoring the situation. I know you'll want him out. Intervening now risks drawing attention.'

'So will him talking.'

'It may be too late.'

'Where was E-Squadron?'

'Wrong side of town, it seems. Total cock-up; no one's pretending otherwise. We think perhaps the Turks stuck an oar in. Washington's got its new tunes, as you know, and that's causing pressure. Things were going to come to a head sooner or later.'

Fieldwork sometimes felt like being told to build elaborate and very fragile constructions next to the sea; one day the tide of diplomacy turns and you wonder why you bothered.

'We appreciate the work you've put in,' Mitchell said.

'We're all frustrated,' Undercroft elaborated. 'But those theatres aren't the priority they once were. And there's an additional problem.'

The problem was $500 million worth of weapons supplied to Yemen's interior ministry which had gone astray. The Foreign Office had got jumpy and instructed us to cut all ties before

18

taxpayers' assault rifles turned up on jihadi YouTube. They were very concerned about what 'bore our fingerprints'.

So that was that.

Christopher Bohren had two homes I had decorated, friends, prospects, magazine subscriptions. Obviously, some of this would linger. His work would be reabsorbed by the legitimate art dealership housing him; his personal contacts had been primed for an unannounced departure. Operations Security would fade him out of existence over six or seven months. But it would not be me any more.

When we'd exhausted our thoughts about the events of the last twenty-four hours they brought out lists of names. Mitchell had the air of a man who was about to deal with men even less patient than himself. He wanted me to treat former contacts 'unsentimentally' in order to 'clarify the situation'. It was a phrase the Russians used to mean 'kill someone'.

Every deal I'd made had been cleared with the FCO, yet they had a way of asking about it as if I'd sat alone in the desert wondering how to equip the Free Syrian Army. I existed because of the things the government wasn't allowed to do, and that brought vulnerability. I began to think through the individuals who might have been here but weren't, and what their absence signified.

I cooperated with Mitchell's questioning, but you learned to give London what it needed and not much more. The Foreign Office cannot bear too much reality. When you travel between a world of reports and the one that people die in, intelligence product becomes a dubious thing. You impose order on chaos, give other people a false sense of understanding and authority. It involves the transformation of friends and brothers into agents or targets. That was the border crossing that eventually exhausted you. I wasn't prepared to endanger someone who'd recently had my back just because of a policy change in Whitehall.

As we moved through details – deliveries, payment chains, structures of the Qatari royal family – I kept wondering about the email contact and the missed calls. What was waiting for me on the dark web? The more my welcome home began to feel inadequate, the more this contact seemed the real business. Eventually I let the thought which I'd been fighting surface. The one other living person who knew those protocols was the officer from whom I'd inherited the agent concerned: Joanna Lake. I hadn't seen her in six months, but the thought of a reunion had sustained me.

On a break I went outside, asked for the temporary use of my phone, then took it as far from the house as I could go without attracting suspicion. I found the last number I had for Lake and rang it, but the line was dead.

Kazakh news sites focused mostly on snowfall. There had been a storm for three days, beginning on the night of the calls. Roads were closed, whole villages had been buried. Other than that, the President had made a speech about diversifying the economy. Some industrial strikes continued. Nothing that brought the missed calls into focus.

After lunch I was interviewed by a man of around sixty with the patient, lethal air of Security Branch. He gave his name as Chris. He was curious about why I'd chosen to burn the contents of the secure room rather than bring them home as instructed. Curious about a lot of things, including my visit to the safety deposit box this morning. I humoured him, answering questions accurately, without protest. At one point, I caught him staring at my new watch. I didn't know if he was going through the motions, reminding me of my place, or if he harboured genuine suspicions. Part of me remained in far less comfortable rooms, alongside men and women who'd risked their lives for British schemes and had been left holding empty rifles.

At three p.m., Chris departed. Undercroft and Lansdowne

returned with fresh satellite images. I talked them through the towns and alliances of Syrian Kurdistan, while making my own tour of what survived, distracted by patches of new rubble.

'They've destroyed the old mosque,' I said.

I reached over and enlarged the image. A nineteenth-century mosque I'd been fond of during a brief stay in Al-Hasakah had gone, replaced by a mound of beige stone. It had been bulldozed; militiamen, enraged no doubt by the tiled calligraphy. I tried to imagine that rage. Their iconoclasm was more than just an aversion to beauty and I found it fascinating, even while the results were awful. To them, the sites themselves were blasphemous; not just art or ornament but history itself.

As we were wrapping up for the day, exhausted, I said, 'There's an officer who works in I/OPs: Joanna Lake. Do you have any idea of her whereabouts?'

They said they didn't.

FOUR

We concluded the session at 7 p.m. I was told to proceed to the Mandarin Oriental. Next meeting would be in thirty-six hours at the Mayfair art dealership that provided me with cover.

'Get some rest,' Undercroft said. 'But don't leave the country.' He smiled.

I was driven to the hotel beside Kensington Palace Gardens, Bohren's favourite when staying in London. The place was a cliff-face of red-brick Edwardian ornament facing the darkness of the park. Usual doorman, crinkly smile as I was ushered into luxury. The receptionist smiled too.

'Mr Bohren, so nice to see you again. We've given you the Master Suite.'

'That's very kind.'

'Not at all. No luggage?'

'It's on its way.'

I could feel my physicality adjust as I accompanied a bellboy to the lifts. Bohren was gregarious and slick. Not a man I personally liked, but others seemed charmed. They took to him more easily than I remembered anyone taking to me. The bellboy bowed gratefully as he received his tenner tip. I closed the door and stood among the suite's art deco-inspired features: a chandelier like a starfish stuck to the ceiling, a brass panther on a mantelpiece above the digital fireplace. I turned the virtual fire off, put the diamond in the safe. My phone scanned for electronic surveillance devices.

No detectable signals but it was best to assume you were being watched. I drew the blinds against the view of Knightsbridge. I hated west London, which always made being here somehow comforting; it told me I wasn't in my own life.

I lay down for two minutes and felt the icy creep of depression. Hotel rooms were good for suicides and blackmail, not much more in my experience. Keep moving. Outrun the anxiety. I went back downstairs, walked to PC World and bought a cheap Toshiba laptop, then sat at the back of Starbucks, out of range of the cameras, and used their wi-fi to download privacy software.

Beyond the daylight realms of the internet were the places where people gathered anonymously, and which you could only enter by becoming encrypted yourself. The right technology routed you through a maze of servers, losing your identity in the process. Websites weren't able to track the geolocation and IP of their users, and users couldn't get any of this information about the host. You could talk and meet and share in pitch darkness.

I went to the file-sharing site I had used with my agent, Idrisov, entered the password, scrolled down the board looking for a file named *Dalia*, the name we had agreed.

November 1st, an audio-visual file had been uploaded with the title *Dalia dances*. The thumbnail preview showed a girl in a leotard. It was only if you looked at the file size that you'd notice it was several megabytes larger than it should have been.

Steganography was the art of concealing a message within another message. The Service's technical department had come across a lot of men hiding images of child abuse in apparently innocent jpegs. It was an obvious enough idea to use similar technology for our own purposes.

I downloaded the file, ran it through decrypting software, braced myself for whatever revelation demanded such concealment.

Filename: *Catalyst.avi*

From the opening frame it looked like CCTV or a spycam: black and white, wide-angle lens, high on a wall. The room was plush: white furniture, glass coffee table. I thought maybe a hotel room, but the décor wasn't coordinated enough. Not one I recognised. A suited man stood alone at the window, turned so that his face was obscured.

From the angle I'd guess the camera was concealed in a thermostat or vent. It looked down on the top of a chest of drawers by the far wall and a sofa directly below. There was a window through which you could see an area of roof then what may have been an adjacent wing of the same building.

I cast an eye around the café again, then clicked play.

No audio. There was a briefcase on the glass coffee table, a decanter, a heavy-looking square ashtray. There was a framed picture on the wall: a horse and rider travelling through a mountainous landscape.

He browsed a bookcase at the back, checked his watch. I still couldn't see his face.

Watching people who think they are alone had never lost its attraction. The first few times I expected some secrets to be revealed, but now it was the very absence of secrets that appealed. The fact that humans were all the same, the thrill of their mundanity, our shared solitude.

At fifty seconds he turned, poured a drink, and you saw his face for the first time.

I hit pause. Then I studied the room that he occupied again, then I enlarged the image to see the face more clearly.

It was me.

I was clean-shaven, smart, in a suit similar to ones I owned but not exact. I stood in a room I'd never been in. It was my face, my physicality. I hit play, watched myself sit on the sofa, pick up cigarettes, change my mind and put them down. At one minute forty-five seconds another man entered.

He looked Central Asian, dark hair swept in a heavy fringe, holding an old-school Nokia 130.

I didn't recognise him. The man said something, locked the case but left it lying on the coffee table. I appeared to offer him a drink. He went to a room at the back and returned with a glass of what looked like water. His movements were stiffer than mine. We touched glasses. You could see my jaw muscles tense. Then I checked my watch again.

He left the room with me. A second later the clip ended. The footage lasted three minutes, twenty-five seconds in total.

I remember most rooms, let alone most individuals I've shared them with. I'd never been in that room or met that man. I looked more closely at the shadows cast by objects, the movement of faces and hands: light reflections and skin texture. There was a mirror on a cupboard at the side with a crack across it. The reflections matched. I studied the architecture visible through the window: it looked like we were high up, in a modern skyscraper with a glimpse of an adjacent wing and the roof of a lower tier. The façade was ornamented. Neo-baroque spires fenced the rooftop off from the sky. It didn't look Western, more like something you'd find in a former communist country.

I clicked back, watched myself again as I left. A triangle of light fanned out across the floor, two shadows disrupted it, then both were gone.

FIVE

'Happy birthday.'

I imagined the chain of events behind this. Someone had come across the video file, illicitly or otherwise, and they felt I ought to see it. They wanted me to know I was passing through rooms I'd never been in. There were implications. They chose an ultra-discreet means of communicating: not via official channels; via a dead man's code.

I took the wrapped box from the safe, unwrapped it and held the diamond in my palm. I closed my hand around it, then I tried Joanna's number again. The silence was becoming loud.

Memory erodes from the inside out: beginnings and endings sharpen as the rest grows vague. My last glimpse of Joanna Lake was in a lorry drivers' café on the M1, beside the Newport Pagnell motorway services area. She was following new security protocols. This was one of them: I couldn't be seen within five miles of her workplace, which was a secure governmental facility with unique sensitivity.

We had spent a weekend together, shadowed by its own brevity and the dark unknown beyond it, ruined by a fight of unprecedentedly personal dimensions. I was heading back to Saudi Arabia, to live another life. She was heading back to a UK-based role she couldn't tell me about.

We weren't good at farewells, which aren't easy when both

of you are embarking into secrets. And it didn't help when we tried to rescue the situation with promises we were trained not to believe in. This time, when we spoke about leaving the intelligence service I think we both meant it. We ended with a show of reconciliation but I had emailed twice in the intervening six months without reply.

I had first met Joanna fifteen years earlier, in an anonymous central London building where eight intelligence service recruits had been invited for second-round interviews. They kept us sitting in a draughty room at the back of the ground floor for more than half an hour. I had been working the room, introducing myself to the other candidates, believing it was part of the test and already enjoying the new-found liberty of a fraudster. She spoke to no one. After half an hour she opened a window, perched on the sill then swung her legs over. Seven of us watched Joanna Lake lean into the flame of her lighter before exhaling smoke at the London sky.

When she turned up again at the IONEC – the Intelligence Officers' New Entry Course – I was surprised by how glad I was. And friendships forged on the IONEC tended to stick. They're some of the last you form with people who are allowed to have a foot both in your first life and your life in the service. We got put in different streams. She was more technically attuned, grasped the psychological aspect of operations better: propaganda, information warfare. Part of me still saw intelligence work as a quest for knowledge: to be at the dark heart of things, the one who knew what was actually going on. She found that endearing and naive.

We worked together only twice, briefly, once in Kiev, in 2005, once in Turkey, three years ago, when she handed over the agent, Mescaline.

I imagined her coming across the clip, somehow. Then sending it in the most secure way possible.

I uploaded it to a secure encrypted cloud account, deleted it from my emails, called an operational data analyst at GCHQ and requested a favour. I gave the Kazakh number, asked them to check the databases, see if it came up anywhere. GCHQ processed 600 million call events a day – networks tied to several thousand individuals of interest. It was a big net, finely meshed. I told them I was also going to email a screengrab and wanted to know if the face of the man in it connected to anyone on the system.

I watched the clip again. The room looked real. Was the other individual computer-generated? No books visible, one newspaper on a sideboard at the back – Kazakh; a word, ұлт – nation; ұлтқа шок – nation in shock. The plug sockets took two round pins. The other building, or continuation of the same building, visible from the window could have been anywhere. I enlarged the lighter in my hand. It looked like a dented Zippo given to me by a military officer in Bahrain. When did I last use that lighter? In Ukraine? With Joanna? For good CGI you needed multiple angles, to know the person from all sides. As far as I was aware, there were very few images of me available.

Deepfakes, they were called. Human Image Synthesis. Computer-generated images were being used in propaganda all the time now – Russia's Internet Research Agency generated social media content using politicians' faces superimposed on actors' bodies. It had employed them in online influence operations, mostly domestic politics. You got some sophisticated stuff from Turkey on behalf of the Justice and Development Party: people making speeches they never made, etc. Otherwise it was used for faking celebrity porn. Maybe there were plenty of unknown figures being electronically manipulated as well; we just didn't pick them up. I watched some deepfake porn posted on Reddit, then some of the political videos, and wondered how many teams were currently producing it.

I used the hotel gym, trying to work the acid out of my muscles, ran through some Vinyasa flows, which a former Marine once told me was the only way he got through five months of captivity, then ordered a plain omelette and a carafe of Pinot Noir from room service. I drank two large glasses sitting on the edge of my bed.

I browsed social media. If I'd been allowed my own I would have checked that. Instead I logged in to the Facebook account of a non-existent thirty-two-year-old woman in Afrin: photos of a child's funeral, a glossy meme of a blonde female YPG guerrilla alongside a quote comparing their struggle to the Paris Commune of 1871. I logged out, logged in again as Yuri Cherchesov, a twenty-year-old second-rank seaman in the Russian navy; changed my status to: *restless*. Bohren himself had messages from people who didn't realise he no longer existed: Christopher, I hope you don't mind me writing. I dreamed of you last night. I know you are not superstitious but it made me worried.

I checked a couple of Middle Eastern accounts that always seemed to get news first – one, curiously, with Selena Gomez as an avatar but definitely run by the Electronic Syrian Army, posting content that looked like it came from Iranian intelligence. *China sending troops to prop up Assad.* There'd been another behind-closed-doors agreement between Moscow and Beijing over the future of the Middle East, details to come. European sites were heart-breaking enough: *'You're on your own,' US tells rebels.* I watched the news twice until I realised that the BBC presenter was saying Syrian government rather than Syrian regime. Sometimes a word is enough to tell you the game is over.

I went to the window. I'd had very little sleep in the last three days. The lingering adrenalin of the operation had got me through the debrief, but now I was slowing up. I opened the window, took a lungful of cold air, listened to London hum. The streets were still busy, men and women walking at a measured pace, knowing their home would be there when they arrived. A Porsche accelerated away from traffic lights, radio on news, the words *escalation of violence* fading with its engine.

My phone rang. The GCHQ analyst said she'd run the face through every database she could and no name came up, which was conspicuous in itself these days. The Kazakh landline wasn't on their system either.

I tried it again, and again no one answered.

I called a colleague in the Counter Terrorism section, Linda French, who had worked with Joanna.

'Are you back?' she asked.

'Just in,' I said. 'Quick query: have you heard from Joanna Lake recently?'

'No, I haven't seen her for years. I heard she wasn't with Six any more.'

'Really?'

'Yes.'

'Where is she?'

'I don't know. What happened? Why are you back?'

I tried three other people. None had seen or spoken to her in the last five months.

Intelligence services are labyrinthine and, for obvious reasons, you can rarely see much further than the room you're in. There isn't a human resources department where you can knock on the door and make a polite inquiry. Not for operatives.

The 'happy birthday' code meant danger.

I sent a message to the TutaNota account confirming I'd received the file, asking for more information.

Meanwhile, the insurrection in Saudi Arabia that had ruined several years' worth of my work seemed to have blown over. There'd been some arrests: clerics, intellectuals, activists accused of acting on behalf of 'deviant groups'. Fifteen women had gathered in Jeddah, calling for the release of imprisoned relatives, surrounded by a circle of green-uniformed police holding hands so it looked like a country dance. My pyromania had disappeared from UK news.

Bohren's phone kept flashing. I couldn't bring myself to remove the battery but it was almost dead anyway. I sent a tentative message to the chief of Saudi Intelligence regarding my captured agent, ignored calls from a CIA contact, answered calls regarding the delivery of an artwork to Singapore FreePort, the tax-free vaults next to Changi airport that housed my agent's embryonic collection.

'A delivery has arrived from Christie's New York. But we can't get an answer regarding delivery onwards.'

'Has it been paid for?'

'Yes.'

'Put it in the usual vault.'

'Yes, sir.'

I disguised my IP and logged in to email and bank accounts belonging to my former agent, Rashid bin Talal, browsed the increasing concern regarding his arrest and the swelling of his unperturbed wealth. I had a full suite of passwords obtained over two years by my cybersecurity team. I wondered what they'd make of the CGI clip.

Their chief technician, Stefan Janikowski, technically an employee of Evotec Digital Security, was still stationed in a hotel in Riyadh.

'What's going on?' he answered.

'I've had to go back to London. Are you able to look at a file for me, if I send it over?'

'I've been told no more jobs.'

'Who says?'

'Head office. Apparently payments from your side have been cancelled.'

'When were they cancelled?'

'I don't know. A couple of days ago.'

'Do you know who gave that instruction?'

'No.'

'Stay in place for now.'

'Get them some money or I'll be back in Bucharest.'

That was a setback. Evotec were the legitimate daylight front of a hacking team that had been known to authorities as Hotel California, a motley and lucrative crew combining cybercriminals and former NSA analysts for the most part, based in Romania. Before they had the office and the business cards, they made their money through ransoms: they'd hack defence contractors and major infrastructure and squeeze money for fixing the situation. I liked Eastern European cybercriminals; they tended to work in small teams – not eccentric loners but still under the radar. The criminal background was good cover, and Six weren't the only state agency using them. Outsourcing kept things deniable, which was everyone's favourite word, and a lot of criminals jumped at the chance to work for governments, with the protection it implied. Over the last few years they'd also had increasing employment with big corporates seeking to retaliate against Russia and China over hacks. The legality of fighting back was hazy – which was why the UK government kept arm's distance – but Evotec were good at hazy. They'd received enough work from me to reply fast to my encrypted communication.

I checked with the Evotec HQ in Bucharest and spoke to the boss there, Marius, a charmingly malnourished, unshaven and business-savvy chainsmoker who I had eventually identified as a former colonel in the Romanian Foreign Intelligence Service. The payments for my account with them had been stopped last week, he said. They couldn't process any requests. It looked like Six had cancelled them even before my operation was pulled.

I looked at the message again: *Lottery Win.*

The handover of Mescaline had been as tricky as most

handovers. I could see Joanna, and the venue she'd chosen, dark and sweaty and debased. Where there's a war there's a border, and over the border places like the Lighthouse. It was one of several neon-signed nightclubs on a new strip in the middle of Hatay province, near Turkey's border with Syria – young girls, refugees, forced into the sex trade, wearing sequinned belly-dancing costumes, paraded for local men and bride tourists: men from Kuwait and Qatar, and the richer of the Iraqi refugees. You saw the same phenomenon on the outskirts of Damascus during the Iraq war.

All intelligence officers have superstitions. Joanna didn't like using hotels. She had a nose for the dark corners in which rival agencies rarely ventured. The Lighthouse worked. Joanna kept a room above the club itself. Heat and music rose through the floorboards.

It all felt rushed. She had met me at Trabzon airport a few hours earlier. I hadn't recognised her at first: she'd dyed her hair dark for the job. She wore a blouse and skirt, managing, as ever, to be imposing at 5'4". Chameleon ways; clear, well-bred English features that transformed from glamorous to businesslike with the application of a hair clip. She was skilled at looking like a variety of Western women who made it to exotic places: intense, ambitious, outraged, well-meaning even.

She looked genuinely pleased to see me. That was what I remembered. And even though I realised, in retrospect, how desperate she was to get out of there, I don't believe that was all of it.

'Of course I'm pleased to see you,' she said. 'Elliot, you trust your instincts with other people. Trust them with me.' Then: 'It's been hell the last few weeks.'

She'd been blamed for a questionable bit of intelligence that shouldn't have mattered, should have been dismissed at analysis, but got rushed into the public domain and ended up stalling UN action. It shouldn't have been her thing at all. Joanna was I/Ops.

Information Operations covered a lot, from briefing agents before missions abroad to more covert psychological operations: planting stories, attempts to influence events in another country or organisation in a direction favourable to Britain. Hearts and minds, which wasn't always as fluffy as it sounds. On the wall of their HQ in Basra I'd seen a drawing of someone's brain exploding, above the unofficial slogan: *Because physical wounds heal.*

In Turkey, she was in charge of what she called triage. Hundreds of people were fleeing over the border from Syria each day. Joanna had to identify those with military intelligence, those who might be turned and persuaded to engage in various missions, those with propaganda potential. The morning after the handover we drove to the border and she showed me the big white tents set up with rows of fold-out tables inside: a front line of UN staff, a back line of spooks dividing up the refugees. It looked like a careers fair. She'd spent four weeks collecting horror stories for her own propaganda operation. She photographed what she could, distributed secure phones and laptops to any rebels heading back east and willing to blog, hooked them up with reporters via WhatsApp. She ran workshops with the US state department, tutoring cyberactivists on how to craft their message. Later, in the bar, she'd joke about it: *There's three of them, bandaged to the eyes, and I'm trying to establish if they've used Wordpress . . .*

Then Mescaline turned up. He was meant to be I/OPs only, then started supplying broader intelligence. That was where things went badly wrong. She was putting a brave face on, having been told to step away. I was sent over under the new Bohren cover to assess things. Was he planting disinformation intentionally? Part of a bigger Russian-led psyop? If so, could he be turned again? Tripled? It had been done before.

Joanna briefed me as we drove from the airport. Nineteen years old, Khasan Idrisov had led a turbulent life. Orphaned, adopted by Chechens, he'd headed to Syria a few years previously. Supposedly he wanted out. That was why he'd approached Joanna in the first place. There'd been no one else on hand to receive what he'd described as time-sensitive information on chemical weapons.

'You're going to try to turn him?' she said.

'I'm going to see what he wants.'

'What are they saying about me in the UK?'

'I don't know. But that's what analysts are there for: to catch this kind of thing before it blows up.'

'I was played.'

'It's Russians. Russians fuck with your head.'

The whole thing had the hallmarks of a GRU campaign, at a time when Russia were stepping up involvement in the conflict. The GRU was Russia's largest foreign intelligence agency, more active internationally than the FSB, which was technically civilian rather than military. The GRU's main declared function was military external intelligence, but it also did special ops, and under its umbrella of special ops came some very curious ones. Hence Idrisov might lead to more than just terrorists, I thought.

The handover was awkward and dangerous as ever. Idrisov was evidently traumatised, chainsmoked, avoided looking at me. We were all sweating. Joanna had her headscarf down around her shoulders. He had survived a drone strike twelve months earlier and his badly treated wounds smelled acrid and gangrenous in the heat. We agreed the communication protocol was unchanged. He kept asking when he could move to the UK.

Joanna had been drinking. My bosses said she was being rotated. She said she was being fired, and if she wasn't fired she'd had enough anyway, which is what you say at the end of missions. After the meeting, Idrisov had returned to risking his life – or betraying us – the two of us got shashlik at a place Joanna liked: no glass in the windows, good-natured men with

35

Kalashnikovs guarding the door. She said she was burned out. The way she saw it, all our work had been undone. We'd been outplayed.

When she passed out in the hotel room I sat up watching news until I wasn't watching any more: images of the chemical attack, unblemished corpses, men and women fallen alongside pets and birds as if all nature had succumbed to some over-arching fatigue. Online, Russians were suggesting that the whole thing was arranged by anti-Assad forces to gain US sympathy and airstrikes. As evidence they pointed towards the UK's own footage of rebel groups with missile launchers and what looked like canisters of sarin in the vicinity of the attack around the same time. The imagery was a result of intelligence supplied by Joanna. The Russians were having a field day.

I don't know what was true. No one ever sees the whole picture, but in a situation like that momentum is truth, and we lost momentum. Plans for intervention stalled. The UN froze. Russia walked in.

Twice a week Idrisov crossed over to deliver handwritten messages from IS command, which he shared with me. I moved us out of the Lighthouse to a safe house in the suburbs of Iskenderun. He gave me nothing valuable. Two months later he missed a meeting. An execution video turned up the following week. His confession to camera was that he was a spy for MI6. According to GCHQ, it looked likely the Russians had used him enough and decided to blow him. I wanted to talk to Joanna about it, about this vindication of our theory, but at that time she'd gone off-radar as well, busy with her new role.

Now no longer at Six?

My new anxiety confused the jet lag. It was 10 p.m. here, 1 a.m. in Saudi Arabia, 4 a.m. in Astana, Kazakhstan. Where was I?

I finished the wine, found some English money and went out. The cold November night caught me by surprise, but I couldn't be bothered to return for a coat. Walking felt good. The area suited me: international students, business travellers, tourists. The pubs were small enough to monitor from your seat. I favoured the Queen's Arms. It didn't play music, which meant you could hear conversations, sometimes even relax.

I ordered a pint of IPA and the ease of acquiring alcohol seemed briefly hilarious. Back in the land of the infidel, of personal space, cautious eye contact. Out of the realm of sweet teas and shisha and close, wiry bodies. Reacquainted with the blunt functionality of the pint, solid enough to grip and stop yourself from falling. A TV in the corner of the pub showed Sky news: flooding in Yorkshire, a glamorous awards ceremony. I thought through the stories that weren't there. Someone laughed; a chesty public-school bellow. The man was one of a group of five beside the bar: white shirts, fresh haircuts. The laugher had a cashmere scarf loose around his neck, elbow on the bar, delivering an anecdote about turning up to someone's place in the country uninvited. He reminded me of Christopher Bohren, in the bar of the Belvédère Hotel, in Istanbul's Club 29. I had always been fascinated by people with acts, performers who know that, so long as you make life more interesting, you can commit whatever evil you want. Close by him, a young woman turned in circles. She held her phone in front of her face. I tried to see if she was Skyping or recording. She had strong make-up, a dark fringe, ankle boots with silver studs. A friend with hair scraped back in a ponytail watched her from a table in the corner. I angled my face away and tried to remember if they'd been here when I arrived. They were noticeable and I hadn't noticed them.

When I went up to get another drink the woman with the fringe appeared beside me, clutching a purse.

'Long day?' she said.

She sounded Eastern European, maybe Scandinavian. Neither

of the drinks on their table was finished; the trip to the bar seemed premature.

'Long year.' I smiled and extended a hand. 'Christopher.'

'Anna.'

'Where are you girls off to tonight?' I asked. She named a club a mile or so away. I tried to imagine what route would bring them via the Queen's Arms. It was a down-at-heel start to the night.

'Can I get you a drink?' I asked.

I bought them drinks, joined them. The friend, Inga, was taller and quieter. They were art students, apparently. They had just started at St Martins. I spoke at length about art auctions, private galleries, offered to guide them around London. My persona of the last twelve months was a bon vivant, a war profiteer at ease with his demons. It was a relief to resurrect him briefly.

'Do you both have student ID?' I asked.

'Yes,' Anna said.

'You know the government's trying to persuade universities to put nationalities on a hologram. And then, if your visa expires, you won't be able to get back in.'

'What?'

'Take a look.'

Anna took the purse from her bag and clicked it open. It was thick with cards. She removed a student ID from among them.

'Where?'

'Can I see?' I took it from her and memorised the name and the ID number. 'Maybe they haven't yet. Should be the same technology on the bank card.' I pointed at her open wallet. She slipped a bank card out. Same name: *Ms A. Nailand*. Bank account at Rietuma Banka in Latvia.

'You know a lot,' she said.

'I'm just paranoid about the government.'

Maybe they were real. I took a mental step back; a pause for reflection. Loss of faith in reality was one of the first signs of psychosis. And of being in the game too long. The laugher and his crew moved off, the girls remained. If this *was* something, they knew where to find me. Tailed from the airport? Picked up at the hotel? That would be concerning. If it wasn't anything then I needed to wind down and shake off the tension of the last few months before I made a fool of myself.

After twenty minutes I'd probed as much as I could without appearing excessively suspicious. I checked my watch.

'I've got to run.' I focused in on Anna. 'I know a few gallery openings next week. I don't suppose you'd be interested in coming along, would you?'

'Sure,' Anna said, too readily. I took her number.

'And can I take a photo of us all?' I said. 'Something to make my friends jealous?'

I checked them out online when I got back to the suite. Anna Nailand, Latvian art student, appeared across a few social media sites. So did Inga. How much social media do you need to be real? It was a question I'd spent more time contemplating than was healthy.

I had a message from a contact in Switzerland: Bohren's art dealership in Lausanne was shuttered. So much for a discreet draw-down. Things like that exposed you. Bohren might not have had my name or any other details, but he had my face. When I tried to see if anyone else had noticed this, or anything else odd, I discovered that Bohren's email accounts had been closed down.

And no sign of Joanna.

I watched the road beneath the hotel window, then the park across the road, then drew the curtains again. I felt the clean coldness that came when I was about to act.

I opened my laptop – logged in to my agent's Deutsche Bank account.

Balance $1,792,021.

I'd watched these figures a lot over the last year: debits and transfers signifying arms and alliances. I'd never stuck my hand in before, but it was simple enough. I clicked 'transfer money', went into payees and found the account details for my own Shariah-compliant account with the Jersey branch of the Abu Dhabi Commercial Bank. I set up three transfers of ninety grand, clicked 'send now'.

It cleared in minutes.

I transferred a hundred thousand from Jersey to an account with Union Bancaire Privée in Geneva, then converted the rest of the money to Bitcoin, stored in an anonymous Dark Wallet account. I sent 50k to Evotec's Cyprus account and submitted two tasking requests: information on the TutaNota address that had sent the message – where it had been set up and what device the email was sent from. I also sent the video file and asked for a forensic analysis: what kind of device was meant to have produced it; what CGI software was used in its construction.

I did my own research. The software involved used deep-level machine learning: you fed in images of someone's face and the program taught itself how that face worked, how to generate new versions. It split itself into creator and critic, creating examples and then seeing if it could convince itself that they were real, feeding back errors until it could.

You needed the bodies, though, onto which the faces were mapped. Who was my body double? More seriously: who had the resources for all this? The process required a high-speed graphics processing unit. Supplying it with adequate training data meant having access to hundreds of images of that person. For someone moving around, like I was in the clip, seen from all angles, you might need thousands to be convincing.

I tried to sleep, got up an hour later and watched the clip again. I took a screengrab of my face and used it to set up a recognition alert on Cognizance, the only facial-recognition software that tracked online appearances rather than just CCTV feeds. I did the same for my companion. My sleep-deprived brain was convinced: this was Catalyst, the man who was going to kill me.

SIX

I woke, sweating hard, at 5.30 a.m. There had been no more messages from whoever was using Mescaline's protocols. I checked world news, then found shorts and a T-shirt, ran hard across Hyde Park, outpacing the night's images, one eye out for any surveillance. A mile and a half in eleven minutes. Not bad: would get me into infantry, but not paras any more. I drank a bitter coffee at a cab drivers' shelter, the only place open in the dawn. I had been looking forward to today. To a tentative attempt at being myself.

At 9.30 a.m. I walked to the Maghreb Bookshop on Sussex Gardens, behind the Edgware Road. It was a cornucopia of second-hand books from around the world, most languages represented, forgotten poets gathered in the dust, shelves that squeezed you as you burrowed in.

After half an hour, I took my haul to the counter and the owner studied them. Among others, I had chosen some poetry in Kalmyk – the Kalmyks in Russia were Buddhist descendants of the Mongols – plus a nineteenth-century account of travelling in Kazakhstan. The owner was a small Egyptian man who wore V-neck sweaters and glasses on a chain. He lifted the Kalmyk collection.

'You understand this?'

'A little. I am interested in endangered languages.'

I pocketed the Kalmyk collection and the Kazakh travelogue,

took the rest to a house on Lisson Grove. It was identical to the elegant houses on either side but for a small brass plaque beside the door announcing the Healing Foundation for the Victims of Torture. The door was open. I walked into a long hallway with clients' artwork on the walls, leading directly through to a well-tended garden, where a Sudanese couple were arranging bunting and tables for a party.

'Is Hany around?'

At the sound of my voice, Hany Aziz appeared, grinning, from among the foliage.

'Martin,' he said, because Martin was the name he knew. He clasped my hand. I savoured the sweet incongruity I felt every time I saw him in London, a man I had first set eyes on in Cairo's Tora Prison. That crippled figure had been banished. Aziz's tightly curled hair was now a London grey, but his eyes had grown more youthful. A fine access agent, once I'd acquired his freedom and services, introducing me to the intellectuals and firebrands that passed through his basement. He had established the healing centre five years ago, after arriving in the UK.

I gave him the books and we asked after one another's lives. He told me how he was faring; I lied about mine.

'You must come to the party this afternoon, Martin. Old friends will be there. You remember Sania.'

'Of course.'

'They remember you fondly. And the children.'

'Not today.'

'Then next time.'

'I promise.'

I told him I had an appointment and left him to the garden. Walking back down the cool corridor I thought: I got him out. Even if Egypt went to shit. I don't abandon them.

Café Rakka was nearby. Early in my career I had sought out

43

London cafés popular with various émigré groups, and used them to practise going grey, becoming unnoticed. At the time, I thought maybe I would pick up snippets of information, but people didn't often talk politics and when they did it was usually to parrot the editorials of the popular Arabic newspapers. Still, the food in this one was good, as was the fresh mint tea. You found yourself searching faces. Who might have made it over? Café Rakka had yellowed tourist posters on the walls: the Al-Madina souq, the Great Mosque, Palmyra with the Temple of Bel, all bombed to memories now. Early in the uprising, they had installed a TV and kept it on news, but at some point it had been switched off.

I ordered tea and kibbeh, balls of bread stuffed with ground meat and walnuts. The men wore harsh eau de colognes and ragged moustaches, cracking sunflower seeds with their teeth. Stirring sugar into their mint tea, with the sound of small bells ringing. Sometimes, in Egypt, you would hear that sound as you spoke on the phone: security officers from the dreaded Amn al-Dawla stirring their tea as they listened in. A group of four young Yemeni men entered, accompanied by an older man. I eavesdropped on them, talking about their trips to the Home Office to claim asylum. I tried to ascertain which towns they'd come from, but couldn't glean any details. One of them put in a call to his parents, who had made it to South Korea, by the sound of it, but had experienced trouble of a kind that I failed to ascertain before his credit ran out.

The Royal Mail delivery office on Harrow Road housed the Post Office box to which my own post got diverted, serviced fortnightly by the housekeeping team. The care with which they propped up my clandestine existence seemed suddenly oppressive, dependency-inducing. Currently inside the box was post that had arrived since the last visit: a postcard from a university girlfriend, Laura, showing Marrakech at night: *On honeymoon. We visited Morocco and I thought of you. Did you get the wedding invitation? Don't worry – I know you've been out of the country.*

According to her Facebook, the wedding had been six weeks ago. It looked lovely. Neither the groom's name nor face meant anything to me. For some reason, the image that came to mind was a Saudi facility for returnees from Guantanamo. I had been shown around, as their Chief of Intelligence explained that marriage was central to the programme of deradicalisation: a wife and a job.

I called the number listed on her page.

'You're back,' Laura said.

'Just got in.' I smiled into the phone, wondered why I was faking a smile she couldn't see. 'I got your invitation. Congratulations. I'm sorry I missed it, I wish I could have been there.' I tried to remember the cover story I'd given. North Africa; a posting on behalf of the Department for International Development. 'How are you?'

We spoke about what she'd been up to. She taught French literature at King's; had a doctorate in symbolist poetry. She was poised, articulate, with a life lived locally, with work and interests and friends around her, and now a husband. I found, as I always did upon returning, that without a role to play I suffered from aphasia. I opened my mouth and had nothing to say. There was that icy blankness behind the face. Perform, I thought. Imagine you're trying to recruit her.

'I thought of you,' I said.

'Really?'

And then, because I had backed myself into a corner, because I wanted something to give, I said: 'Yes. I visited the house where Rimbaud lived, in Aden.'

It was true though, I had thought of her then. I had persuaded my fixer to show me where Rimbaud lived when the poet's self-exile led him to this corner of the world. Laura would have been fascinated. And I thought of Rimbaud himself, and the line in his letter from Harar that had always stuck with me: *Je ne compte pas rester longtemps ici. Je n'ai pas trouvé ce que je présumais.* I did not find what I had expected. What had he expected in dusty Yemen? A twenty-six-year-old, picking up exotic languages and diseases and a lot of second-hand Remington rifles, waiting on the edge of the desert as he prepared to head to Abyssinia to sell guns to the king. Poet turned arms dealer. At university, when I first stumbled upon this trajectory, it seemed wondrous and inexplicable. And I had surpassed it without the slightest scrap of insight.

'His house is still there?' she asked.

'Just about. It used to be something of a tourist destination.'

It had been looted, closed down, but I found the old caretaker chewing khat; when I bribed him to unlock the door, he spasmed with a cough so violent he sprayed blood over my wad of tissue-soft rials. Inside, there were empty glass cases, rotting wooden furniture, scattered papers that weren't, to my disappointment, anything to do with Rimbaud but recent governmental directives on agriculture.

'Why didn't you let me know?' she asked.

'I was so busy.'

'Do you have pictures?' she asked.

'I didn't think to take any.'

'And what development work were you doing in Yemen?'

'Water,' I said. 'Mostly. For the refugees. The war's caused a bit of a crisis. Also some education projects.'

'The war,' she said, uncertainly. 'Of course.'

We didn't arrange to meet. I walked out, checked the parked cars, continued back to my hotel.

If Joanna had left Six, I thought, where would she go? Former spies move into banking or private intelligence. She was no more a City person than I was. I called around a few ex-colleagues now working private for the poachers: Stratfor, Kroll, Hakluyt. None had come across her on the scene.

Flax and Kerrigan's had been open two days – a 'soft opening', which meant members of the public couldn't get in but Olivia Gresham could. She was a portfolio manager who had set up her own fund around the time I started working in the Middle East. Like a lot of jobs, 95 per cent of espionage was contacts. Swapping thumb drives in underground car parks can be fun, but a remarkable amount involved simply belonging to a select group of people able to exchange information that others didn't have. Like a journalist, you cultivated a network of off-the-record sources, only for a paper with the smallest distribution possible.

Investors were good. The exposure of several million pounds seemed to sharpen their appetite for knowledge. They, at least, knew where the wars were.

'My favourite civil servant,' Gresham said. 'You look like you could do with a square meal. Go wild.'

Olivia Gresham passed the menu over, immaculate in a char-coal Dolce & Gabbana suit. She had started out trading forex for Credit Suisse, turned down a big position there to set up a fund concentrating on energy commodities. I'd put some cash in but that wasn't why she sought me out. The mutual professional interest was enough to keep the sexual tension productive. She'd chosen the venue, which had just opened, she said. The place was bright, with wood and chrome, high ceilings and white-tiled walls like a butcher's; light glinted everywhere you looked, as if you were inside a bubble. The menu swam in front of my eyes. I kept reading *Experimental Cocktails*. In Saudi Arabia that meant a bag of raw alcohol and a Coke.

We ate duck egg and asparagus, and seafood on ice. She insisted this was a thank you, which meant regularly topping up my glass, the bottle dripping water across crab shell. I'd given her a heads-up on Turkstream – a proposed line pumping gas under the Black Sea – and a Goldman Sachs fuck-up in Libya, which her fund had turned to profitable use if the crustacean still life was anything to go by. I hadn't done it for the sake of a seafood platter but it was all part of the play.

'Who's big in Kazakhstan these days?' I asked.

'Chevron, Gazprom. PetroKazakhstan was bought by the Chinese last year. JP Morgan are trying to get hold of the financial sector. A lot's still bound up in state-owned companies.'

'Got a contact there? Someone who knows the scene?'

'I can make a call. I know a guy building retail units, big box. Tesco's moving in.'

'Is it politically stable?'

'It's a dictatorship. You don't get much more stable than that.'

SEVEN

I picked up a Zipcar Audi from Finsbury Circus, bought a black baseball cap from the Runners Need store beside it, curved the brim and pulled it down towards my eyes. The last address I had for Joanna would take me into dangerous territory, though you wouldn't know it to look at it.

In a sleepy corner of south-east England, a few miles north of Luton and south of Bedford, you find the village of Shefford. There are flower baskets, a winding road past a Norman church, tea shops with white tablecloths, B&Bs with ivy on the walls. Drive out of the village, past fields of barley, and you get to tall fences and razor wire, with cameras every couple of hundred metres. Signs stuck into the ground behind the chain-link warn *No Trespassing*, but they don't tell you it's government property.

Shefford Park was one of the most classified sites in the UK. It housed the experimental wing of the intelligence services. That included technology, but also psychological research. Since 2002 it has housed the Psychological Operations Group, which drew on MI6, GCHQ and the British Army. After the first Gulf war, analysis revealed that a large number of Iraqi surrenders and desertions could be attributed to coalition psyops activity – leaflet campaigns, loudspeaker teams, even a radio station. This success led the UK to create a permanent capability. They took over an old airbase at the back of Shefford previously used by the US Air Force.

The facility was positioned off high-speed roads that didn't let you get much of a look – at what looked, anyway, like any technology campus: modern blocks of beige brick and turquoise glass, arranged around the original seventeenth-century manor house.

It had been acquired by the Foreign Office after the Second World War in order to establish what it described as a 'listening post', a phrase that usually concealed more than it revealed. The radomes and radio masts had gone, replaced by less visible technology. While Bletchley, a few miles away, eventually gained the plaudits, Shefford was happy to stay in the shadows. Which was how you knew somewhere was still important.

It made sense combining technological research and psychological operations. The world moved on from leaflets and loudspeakers at breakneck speed. More recent work included jihadi DVDs that placed trackers on users' computers, and cyberattacks on Islamic State websites, replacing bomb-making instructions with cupcake recipes. Joanna was proud of that one. But that kind of operation barely scratched the surface of what went on at Shefford. There was more to it – sides I didn't hear about – so I was never quite sure what Joanna was working on.

I walked past the church, past a low-ceilinged pub, to the point at which I'd usually leave her, at which she said we had to part. The edge of the village. She said they monitored the village.

I headed for her house.

Joanna didn't explicitly talk about Shefford when we were together. We both wanted to escape thoughts of work anyway. So we just walked, often in silence, amused by the brazen beauty of the countryside.

I don't know what she was doing, but she implied that fieldwork – the basic craft of recruiting human agents in a hostile environment – would become even more irrelevant in the future. That triggered our argument the last time I saw her. I was mentally preparing myself for a return to the Middle East. I wasn't in the mood for someone suggesting that I was wasting my time. She presented her own removal from overseas operations as a conscious choice, which was clearly designed to get a rise out of me. And, I thought at the time, reflected personal bitterness. She had been a better field officer than me. A group of us had been selected to spend two weeks in Brunei learning advanced weapons skills, some abseiling and parachuting. She was in her element, to the extent that there had been talk of moving her to the Special Reconnaissance Service, which they were in the process of setting up, a dedicated sub-unit of the SAS designed for the new era of cyberwarfare. Unlike the SAS and SBS, it took women. Like them it was comprised of an elite with the mental and physical ability to work in small, independent teams under life-threatening pressure. She said she wasn't one for painting her face and lying in puddles.

One fragment of that last, needling semi-drunken conversation had stayed with me more than the rest.

'They have software that can tell you how long a relationship will last,' she said.

'Based on what data?'

'Everything: geographical movement, sleep patterns, conversational rhythms, vocabulary, choices of entertainment options.'

'What does that allow you to do? Marriage guidance?'

'It means, theoretically, if you wanted a relationship to end, you could run the program backwards and see what steps would engineer that outcome.'

That was a somewhat loaded anecdote to share, I thought. I wondered if the ruthlessness was meant to impress me. We were on the third bottle. She looked strikingly beautiful, her eyes large and liquid, as they became when drunk, and which was sometimes a warning sign. Head held high on her long, pale neck, hair escaping its knot to hang around her face, a wildness in her echoing the woodland around us.

'Is that what you're doing? Breaking hearts? People seem able to ruin their own relationships.'

'It's knowledge. It's intelligence.'

'You think that's knowing people?' I stopped myself before saying: attitudes like that led to the mess in Turkey. 'Knowing a community? A culture? When you have software that understands pride, hate and revenge, I'll start job hunting.'

'Is that what you deliver?'

'Sometimes. Not always.'

'A horizon watcher, connoisseur of men's hearts and nation's souls, removed from events, paring your fingernails.'

'You know what I do.'

'You fall in love with foreign places and then destroy them.' She knocked her drink back aggressively, as if this might deflect my own anger. I was beyond anger. I felt something had broken inside her. The comment was in poor enough taste that I barely knew what she meant by it. Five minutes later I was suggesting she get professional help for what she went through. The feeling was mutual, apparently. There aren't many places an argument can go once you reach the imperatives to seek counselling. We were both burned out in our own ways. And how would therapy work? A spy goes to a psychologist. *I cannot tell you what I do, or the precise events that haunt me. My unconscious is covered by the Official Secrets Act.* Obviously, the services anticipated this and wheeled in some shrinks of their own, so petrified of the confessions they received they'd close you down at the first whiff of anything classified. And, of course, they were equally concerned with assessing your risk to Six as to yourself. None of which helped the free and frank revelation of psychological turmoil you craved. If you were lucky you got some MOD psychiatrist on his way to retirement who gave good prescriptions – powerful enough to knock you out, some might say – but little by way of empathy.

And what would that free and frank revelation be, anyway? I can no longer feel the things I once felt. My dreams have become air-conditioned warehouses for the dead. I remember men and women whose fates I am entwined with, but cannot remember which war they are from, and this troubles me, but maybe not as much as it should do. Every night, when I close my eyes I see an egg-sized piece of shrapnel melting the synthetic fibres of a hotel carpet. Every morning when I wake I check the pillow for blood. The problem with trauma is that it's a plughole, and every bad thing gets drawn towards it, towards the thought: *That was where I lost the life I was meant to have.*

Joanna spoke in her sleep. I would listen, of course. An agent of mine in Ukraine used to refuse general anaesthetic in case he let secrets slip while unconscious. I had told him that was unnecessary and tried not to dwell on the lives I was making people lead. Joanna's night ramblings never made much sense, never opened the gates of Shefford Park to me. Sometimes she'd wake up screaming.

We were burned out, and after we'd kissed again we agreed to leave Six. To run away. We joked about hot countries that had no extradition treaties with Britain. I suggested Cameroon, Namibia or Venezuela.

'Caracas has a thriving literary scene.'

'And it would be easier to blend in,' she said.

Neither of us had worked the South American beat. The Caribbean would be our playground: Montserrat, Grenada, St Lucia. I would ignore the drug boats, the private jets from which men emerged with briefcases chained to their wrists, the officials behind high gates. I'd stare out to sea.

We talked about unimaginable things: a home, children, jobs

we could admit to. Our lives would be quiet and apolitical. Love would demarcate our cares.

'We'd need money,' she said.

Six months ago. I had assumed she was still here. I walked past the place she'd been living, one of a cluster of 1940s suburban semis close to the railway station. The front garden had been mowed, then strewn with plastic toys: a tricycle, a slide for a toddler. A maroon Citroën people carrier occupied the driveway. Through the windows, a woman in an apron was washing up.

I went to the end of the street and bought a pair of gardening gloves from the shop opposite the station, tore the tags off. Then I knocked on the door of her old home.

The aproned woman answered, drying her hands.

'I live around the corner,' I said. 'Borrowed these off the woman here, but a while back.'

'She's not here any more.'

'Oh. When did she move out?'

'We've been here five months.'

'I don't suppose you have any forwarding details?'

'None at all. And nor does the former landlord, apparently.'

Joanna's parents were in the phone book. I met them once. They were mannered, English. Father ex-City, a wine trader, womaniser; mother discreetly Christian, frail. She liked me. 'Joanna never brings anyone home,' her mother said. Joanna's personality with them was hilarious; all smiles and self-deprecation. The dutiful daughter with her rising career in the civil service. I wish they'd seen her firing an Uzi.

She was protecting them from herself, I realised. Your closest family members don't have to be completely in the dark about an MI6 career, but you have to ask why you'd give them that to think about. I felt they deserved to know of her coolly walking into a room of Eastern European fascists, enduring enhanced interrogation training, setting up radio stations in the Afghan desert.

'It's Elliot,' I said, when her mother answered.

'Oh yes. Hello.'

'I've been having difficulty tracking Joanna down. Any idea where she is, or how I could get hold of her?'

'We've no idea. I've not heard from her for ages. I thought she was abroad. She never tells me much. Should we worry?'

'No need to worry. I'll tell her to give you a call. When did you last speak to her?'

'Not for a month.'

'Any idea where she might have been?'

'Not in the UK. I know that much. We had another man calling up looking for her just yesterday. He couldn't get in touch with her either.'

This didn't feel like good news. The individual was someone who shared my anxiety or it was a professional hunt. Neither great, but a lead.

'Did he leave a name?' I asked. 'Maybe we can pool resources.'

'Hang on ... Patrick Dolan. He left a mobile number. Do you know him?'

'Rings a bell. Can I give him a call?'

I didn't know Patrick Dolan. I ran the mobile number through Facebook and WhatsApp, then TrueCaller – a search tool that found contact details globally. No sign of Patrick. I drove to an out-of-town Sainsbury's, bought a pay-as-you-go Nokia and messaged:

It's me. Can you meet?

Five minutes later he messaged back.

You ok?
Possibly not. Where can you get to quickly?
New Pag caff? 5.30?

That was our café: the one where Joanna and I used to have

a last breakfast before parting. It gave me a kick of jealousy alongside relief. Was this someone else she trusted? The incautious approach to arrangements told me he wasn't a trained field officer, at least. Unless I was being lured. He'd chosen 5.30, an after-work stop for someone who worked locally – a few minutes' drive from Shefford Park.

See you there, I messaged.

The caff was ageing, in need of a lick of paint, attached to a ten-pump truck stop, with grumpy staff, filthy toilets, and signs advertising beds and showers for thirty pounds a night. I got there early, took a seat at the back, near a rear exit, just in case.

The man arrived cautiously, looking around – which only made him more conspicuous. As did the hi-vis cycling jacket. He was tall, early thirties, clean-shaven with a mop of brown hair. He held a bicycle helmet under his arm, phone in hand.

I recognised him from the birthday of a mutual friend last year. I had a memory of him flirting with Joanna outside a restaurant in Clapham. One of the tech wizards. Tom someone. Tom Marsh.

'Tom.'

He glanced over, eyes narrowed. Then he looked around again, still searching for Joanna, slowly putting two and two together. He turned back to me and walked over.

'It was me who messaged you,' I said. I waited for one final beat of comprehension. 'We're both concerned about Joanna. Get a coffee, take the battery out of your phone.'

He considered this, then put his helmet on the table and joined the queue. At the party, he'd struck me as hyper-intelligent, if a little sheltered. He was working on the technology for mass holographic deception. Talent leads you on strange journeys. At the party he had shown us a photo on his phone: it was Tehran's skyline at dusk, only with a face denoting the Prophet Muhammad rising a mile high over the downtown office blocks. Joanna seemed impressed. I had bridled, ignoring the jawdropping aspects of this and arguing that most Iranians were too secular and astute to care. 'Well, this was what we were tasked with,' he said.

By the time he returned, splashing down a mug of Nescafe, his memory had done some work.

'You're Elliot.'

'That's right. We met at Hugh Stevenson's fortieth.'

'Do you know where Joanna is?'

'No. I'd like to find out. Why did you contact her parents?'

Marsh breathed deeply. I smelled fresh aftershave.

'I was questioned about her, at work. On Monday afternoon. I was taken for what they said was a routine security check. They were very interested in Joanna, whether I'd had contact with her since she left, the nature of our relationship.'

There it was, I thought: the creep of an intelligence agency turning against you. My suspicion was that they knew the answers to those questions. They were shaking him up to see what came out. I had no idea why.

'And have you had contact?'

'No.'

'What's the nature of your relationship?'

'We're friends,' he said, cautiously.

'When did she leave?'

'April.'

'Know why?'

'No.'

'Escorted out? Leaving party?'

'Definitely no party. I don't know if she was escorted. Next week her unit was shut down.'

'What unit?'

'I really don't know much, and I can't say much. I didn't work with her. And ... You know what it's like.'

'Shut down suddenly?'

'Overnight.'

'Do you think it had been compromised?'

'I don't know.'

'Where did Joanna go after leaving?'

'I've no idea. That's what got me worried. That and the interrogation.'

'You'd tried to contact her.'

'Of course,' he said. 'What's your involvement? Why did they think you were connected?'

'What do you mean?'

'The security officer asked about you.'

That gave me a lurch. Something ominous was coming into focus, but it was focus I wanted.

'What did he say?'

'He asked whether Joanna had mentioned you, if I thought the two of you were in contact. I said I had no idea. What's going on?'

I thought of the tension around my recent debrief, the security interview, the confiscated phone.

'Was the man who questioned you someone you'd seen before?' I asked.

'Never.'

'What did he look like?'

'Quite old; maybe sixty or so. No name.'

'Did it seem like in-house security?'

'I don't think so. He didn't sound like he knew the place well.'

'Did he have paperwork? A file?'

Marsh considered this.

'I don't remember seeing any.'

'Was the interview filmed?'

'Not to my knowledge.'

'Anything else strange that you've noticed? Break-ins? Computer viruses?'

'Nothing.'

We finished our coffees.

'Does the codename Catalyst mean anything to you?' I asked.

'No.'

It had been a long shot. But people always know more than they think they do; they have seen or heard things that mean nothing to them but hold the keys to understanding a situation.

'What was Joanna working on?'

'A research group, I think.'

'Researching what?'

'I don't know.'

'When was it set up?'

'Mid-2014.'

After Ukraine, I thought. Russia in Crimea. It had been a febrile time in the intelligence service.

'Targeting anyone in particular?'

'I have no idea.'

'Who else in it?'

'I don't know.'

'Why not?'

He looked around, lowered his voice.

'Strict isolation from all other units. They even had their own canteen.'

'Housed where?'

'The old house. Building D.'

'How many in the building?'

'Hard to say. It had a separate entrance.'

So within the most classified of government sites they had created an enclave of enhanced secrecy. That usually meant the technology involved was sensitive, or the ethics. Often both.

'You must have some idea of what was going on in there,' I said.

'I don't know. She joked it was seeing into the future.'

'Forecasting? Pattern analysis?'

'Maybe.'

I struggled to imagine Joanna cooped up with software all day, no matter how advanced it was. Tom's questioning by unspecified security officers worried me. The security concerns could be real or they could be part of a discrediting campaign. Six and GCHQ collaborated on an 'effects' unit. Its job was using dirty tricks to make life impossible for those it chose to destroy, and that ranged from the manipulation of bank accounts to dropping child abuse images onto someone's hard drive. You didn't want them turning against you.

'What's your hunch?' I said to Marsh.

'Maybe the program they were working on predicted something which they didn't want getting out. Maybe she saw too much.'

He said it deadpan. I tried to disguise my scepticism. Still, if I could keep Marsh out of the hands of security, he was a potentially useful ally. I recommended he set up a new email account for contacting me, one that disguised IP addresses.

'Joanna told me you'd help,' I said. 'If anything happened.'

'Really?'

'You were one of the few people she trusted. See what you can find.'

I walked back to my car and checked a satellite view of Shefford, locating Building D according to Marsh's description. They had partitioned the building off from the rest of the grounds. New trees had been planted, alongside more robust fences. Upper windows and skylights had been blocked.

Shefford village looked cold and empty as I took a final drive through. The first time I visited Joanna here it had been spring. We walked from the farms into woodland with thick carpets of bluebells, everything so simple and bright it seemed to mock us and the barren rooms in which we strategised the world. We picnicked in a clearing, lay back on the grass, an unthreatening English sun above us.

I saw her face with the sun on it, and then her face in moonlight, on our last night in Turkey together, driving along the Iskenderun–Aleppo road. The road was permanently slick with contraband oil dripping from supposed vegetable trucks. The route saw a lot of oil smuggled out and a lot of people trying to reach the refugee camp in Reyhanli. A complex of Byzantine architecture remained close to the border, ruins which had been largely destroyed and reused to reinforce the border itself, but leaving the better portion of a triumphal arch as testament to Rome's north-eastern frontier. Joanna had been amused by my interest in it. In moonlight the arch was ghostly. One wall of a tower remained, so it looked like a tool with a blade and a handle.

We stopped and got out of the car and she took my arm.

'Look,' she said.

Stars blanketed the sky. We lay down to watch them, spotting asteroid showers.

We had kissed before, but not with necessity. Perhaps we had been waiting to become desperate. To prove something. Everything stopped for a moment as I tasted her.

It occurred to me that maybe she thought I was going to die, that this was her last chance. Or perhaps she had decided that she was going to die.

What did she go back to the UK to do?

You're taught to cultivate trusted insiders. What they don't say, but becomes obvious, is you need someone inside Six as much as anywhere. The party where I'd seen Marsh flirting with Joanna was Hugh Stevenson's fortieth. Stevenson was someone I considered a friend. I obscured my caller ID for his sake.

'Hugh, it's Elliot. I wondered if you'd heard from Joanna recently?'

'You're in town?'

'Yes.'

'Can you meet? Now?'

Stevenson shared his inherited townhouse with three dogs, his father's collection of South East Asian memorabilia, and a Nepalese man I had never met. It was a beautiful house on a wealthy Hampstead street. I watched him passing through the golden spotlights of the streetlamps towards me, his silhouette baggy in an oversized belted jacket, his German Shepherd bobbing by his side.

At the end of the street we fell in step.

'Good to see you, Elliot.'

'You too.'

'You've lost weight.'

'It's possible.'

Stevenson was climbing the ranks of Counter Terrorism in Vauxhall. He had cultivated an ageless donnishness although he was only a couple of years older than me. There was a sense of succumbing to class, becoming the person fate had always had in store for him. But he was brilliant in his own self-deprecating way. I had met him in the library at Vauxhall Cross. I used to get in early – in through the double-airlock doors while it was still quiet. I enjoyed the place at that time of the morning: the courtyard with its fountain, the central atrium bathed in cool, green light from the triple-glazed windows – light that always reminded me of the interior of a mosque. I could imagine people removing their shoes upon entering, prostrating themselves towards the Union Jack.

The library was a gem, and underused. In those less digital days, it kept papers from around the world, along with academic publications and the less sensitive reports from rival agencies. It had lamps and leather seats that nodded towards private clubs or the archives of prestigious legal chambers. Stevenson was always there. We developed a friendship based on this convergence. He was curious about my work in the field. I could already see that he was going to rise through the ranks, and knew this would be useful. Also, we liked each other.

'Heard you did pretty well out there,' he said.

'I'm not sure about that.'

'Not your fault it got pulled.'

'Pulled suddenly. Left people exposed.'

'Ours is not to reason why.'

'Fuck that.'

We lapsed into silence.

'How's Sunil?' I asked, remembering his partner's name.

'Fine. Tired. Overworked.'

'And Legoland?' I asked, before he felt obliged to inquire into my own private life. 'What's news in Vauxhall?'

'The current regime's isolated pretty much everyone. Doyle's in the Secretariat now, still obsessed with the Arctic Circle. Ann Swan went to Citibank. Did you hear Etienne had a flap of sorts in China?'

'No.'

'Triad-run billiard halls. The word is: don't mess with them.'

'I'm glad we've established that.'

I momentarily missed HQ: the gossip, the etiquette of careful eyes, locked doors and hushed corridors where you could nod at men and women who you saw every day, and if they didn't know exactly what you did, at least they had an idea, and that was permitted.

'I saw a review I thought would interest you.' He extracted a folded clipping from his pocket: *An Islamic Utopian: the life of Ali Shari'ati.* 'Islam, Marxism, revolution. I thought it sounded like you. Know it?'

'I skimmed a copy when it was in hardback.'

'Any good?'

'Not bad. The usual line: CIA ruined the Middle East, etcetera. Everything's our fault. The publishing house is Kremlin-sponsored.'

His silence made me conscious of my irritability.

'It's worth a read,' I said. 'I have nothing for you, I'm afraid. Ramil Terzi says hello. He's on good form.'

Stevenson laughed.

'House arrest must agree with him.'

We skirted the pond, turned onto a footpath that led into the Heath. Into the trees. Stevenson stopped and crouched, as if to bag dog shit, and we both checked the path behind. No one. When the darkness had closed around us we sat down on a bench. He wrapped the leash around the arm.

'Joanna's a bit AWOL.'

'What do you mean?'

'Definitely not working for us any more, it seems. Stopped six months ago. Not clear why or where she's gone.'

'How can no one know?'

'This is just off a quick check, a personal check. Not many people are being cooperative. Seems she left under a bit of a cloud. Type of cloud unknown. Out of contact since May.'

'She was at Shefford.'

'Yes.'

'I popped in on Tom Marsh.'

'What did Tom have to say?'

'He was questioned about her. And about me. There's been surveillance on me since I returned to London.'

This raised an eyebrow.

'You think it's us?'

'Hard to tell. What do you know about Building D at Shefford?'

'Nothing. Shefford is as much of a mystery to me as to anyone else.'

'Anything codenamed Catalyst that you've come across?'

He shook his head.

'New tech in development? New software?'

'You name it. But I'm not the man to ask about that. I'm still waiting for my pen gun. I can have a sniff, Elliot. But you know what Shefford's like.'

I got my phone out.

'I received an encrypted file three days ago. I believe it came from Joanna. It contained this; the footage is computer-generated.'

Stevenson watched the footage twice in silence.

'It's not real?'

'No. There's something odd about the way we physically interact. That's not my body. And the box at the back, there's no shadow. See how the vase casts a shadow but not the box?'

He looked again, nodded.

'You think she sent it to you?'

'It was sent using a system only she knows about. No one else could have done it.'

'Is there any more?'

'No. I've never been in that room. I've been in Kazakhstan twice, but not for many years.'

'Has Joanna?'

'Not when I last saw her. That was a few months ago. I had three missed calls around the same time I received the video – from a landline in Kazakhstan.'

Stevenson stared at the screen. I could see professional appraisal. He was looking for signs of provenance.

'The reflection's good.'

'The whole thing's impressive.'

'Do you know the other man?' he asked.

'No.'

'The location?'

'The plug sockets are type F, which doesn't narrow it down much. But it looks like there's a newspaper in Kazakh. It's dated two weeks ahead, 13 December.'

Stevenson wrinkled his brow.

'Strange that the date's visible?'

'Seems overdetermined. The message it came with is a duress code. It means the sender needs to get out of the country, that I'm in danger too.'

He sighed and shook his head.

'Why so cryptic?'

'That's what I've been wondering. Maybe the sender was interrupted or in a hurry. It takes time to encrypt files. Perhaps if I'd got the accompanying phone call more would have been explained. Or perhaps the whole thing's deliberately mysterious because it's a trap, a lure. An attempt to play with our minds.'

'By her?'

'More likely someone who's got information out of her.' I regretted saying it immediately. This touched on the world he didn't operate in, and deepened the darkness around us.

'What's going on in Kazakhstan at the moment?' I asked.

'Desert, I imagine. Some oil. Benign dictatorship and shaky post-Soviet nationalism. Why?'

'Who's on it for Six?'

'There's no permanent station. I think the ambassador's Suzanna Ford, but we haven't had cause to use her much.'

The dog barked and we both fell silent. A figure passed up by the pond, male, hunched, hands in the pockets of a short jacket. He continued towards Hampstead Lane.

'How was the debrief?' Stevenson asked.

'They're covering their backs. I'm starting to feel somewhat isolated. What's going on?'

'All I know is there's changes: changes in priorities, in tactics maybe. Heads have rolled, morale is low. Russia's got the wind in their sails, seems to be the common belief. Syria's a test bed.'

'For what?'

'I don't know.'

'Maybe Joanna knows.'

'Maybe.'

'Think Russia's got penetration of Vauxhall?'

Stevenson shrugged – the kind of shrug that says: of course, who can say, what do you think, where does one start?

'They've penetrated people's minds,' I said.

'That's paranoid.'

'No it's not.'

'Why would they isolate you? You're celebrated.'

'As what? Their gun runner?'

'You delivered.'

'That's the problem.'

'What do you mean?'

What I meant: success is never straightforward in intelligence work. You sink deep, you produce invaluable product. It also means people will do deals with you. They prosper, and you become irreplaceable to both ends. You get an aura, a reputation for making things happen. Then you become a repository of other people's guilt.

'It was fun while it lasted, but you know how that goes. You do people's dirty work and it just means you're the last to be cleaned away.'

Six years of work, I thought. This was meant to be the one that went well, that meant I could retire with my head held high, even if no one knew anything about what I'd done. The absurd image that wouldn't go away involved somewhere homely, where I was talking to a child, possibly my grandchild. He held a yellowed clipping while I said something like: I played a part in this. This is who I was, even if you won't read about me anywhere, except between the lines. In this old shoebox is an MBE. No, I don't feel any need to display it. The Queen leaned close to my ear and said she understood I had contributed a huge amount *behind the scenes.*

'I'm moving on,' I said. 'Leaving Six.'

'To what?'

'I have notes for a book: the poetry of Islamic Spain, the invention of love. I want to retrace the steps of the troubadours, lose myself somewhere foreign that I don't have to spy on.'

But as I said it I realised, with a chilling clarity, that I wasn't leaving anything without Joanna. Certainly not with her missing. Stevenson checked his watch, wrapped the leash around his hand.

'Listen, Elliot, I should go. Sunil will be wondering where I am. But will you keep in touch? And not do anything reckless, for anyone's sake?'

'Of course.'

'You've been through a lot. I know it's all a day's work for you, but you deserve a break.'

'Can you sniff around?' I said. 'Keep an ear open?'

'They don't close any more.'

He placed a hand on my shoulder then returned towards the streetlights. I watched for other silhouettes but none came. I stayed on the bench, enjoying the darkness and the sensation of being alone.

AWOL. Where would she go? She was impulsive, a thrill seeker. Given how ill-advised our relationship was, it's a wonder she hadn't initiated it sooner. But I had always thought there was an unspoken agreement, an understanding that this final step would destroy us. We found alternative kicks. We would slip into improvisations while out, snap covers, games we'd developed during training; introduce one another by names made up on the spot, choose ridiculous environments to penetrate:

a meeting of Quakers, a protest against undercover police, a far-right march.

'It will be interesting,' Joanna said, pulling me into the thin flow of marchers, adjusting her hair, her voice, ending up three hours later almost being glassed by a coked-up skinhead in East Ham. All of which was exhilarating and made you feel like you were both special, and deferred the awkward honesty of a relationship.

Two years after training, I was back from Chechnya. She invited me to Christmas with her family. She had always depicted her own life as a home counties nightmare of perfection: Cheltenham Ladies College, parents trying to marry her to stockbrokers, doctors, clergy. *I mean, fucking clergy* . . .

They didn't seem too nightmarish to me. After lunch she showed me how to pick the locked drawers in her father's study, which contained photographs of his lovers, some teenage, some sadomasochistic.

'So which locks do I pick for you?' she asked. 'You don't talk about your background. Is that some stupid Six thing? I don't know how you got here. You were in Cambridge, you were playing soldiers on the side, got a tap on the shoulder . . . '

Boxing Day, we borrowed her father's Aston Martin and drove to where I grew up, a former local authority house in Croxley Green on the edge of London, empty since my mother's death two years earlier. I kept up with bills, never slept there, let the maintenance go. I hadn't been back in a while. Joanna wandered the place, picking up vodka bottles, blister packs. There were few traces of my mother's succession of boyfriends, who evaporated once the pillow needed to be pressed. Most of the bulbs had gone and the winter light was hard.

'Your father?'

'Left when I was four. I don't really remember him.'

'Of course. I should have guessed.'

She lifted an unopened pack of oral syringes and gave me a quizzical look. I filled one with vodka.

'Open your mouth.'

I described my mother's late embrace of alcoholism, and the six months spent feeding her vodka and orange as her body closed down, a scene that wasn't without its own raw beauty. It brought me a cool, enveloping nihilism that later became entwined with what others perceived as courage and determination. I could survive anything after that.

I found a candle, lit it.

'What are you thinking?' Joanna asked.

'It feels like Christmas.'

It took me a long while, taking out the memory of those two days and handling it, before I realised why she had invited me to her parents' place. She wasn't using me to deflect attention. She liked me. She picked through books in my old room – German medieval poetry, critiques of Thomas Mann – found some old photographs.

'P Coy?'

'Pegasus Company. Training for the Parachute Regiment. Playing soldiers, as you said.'

'You look like you've been boxing.'

'They call it milling. It's part of the selection process.'

'What do you do?'

'Punch your opponent in the face as hard and as frequently as you can. One minute, no pausing, no trying to defend yourself.'

'Why?'

'To see if you're as dark and troubled as they are, perhaps. I don't know. It made sense at the time. When they can, the officers pair friends, brothers, get them to knock each other unconscious.'

'Lovely. Why did you choose the Paras?'

'More class-free, less hierarchical.'

'And you ended up in Six.'

'I know.'

Joanna was the only person I had told any of this. I remember, at the time, thinking we were old. We were twenty-four. We survived several years' acquaintance before succumbing to the inevitable. Other partners helped. Joanna used to say: this one had better work or we will end up together. It was a joke and not a joke, brought to comic perfection when we were assigned cover as a married couple in Ukraine.

There was a drunken one-night stand in Kiev, but I think of us getting together in Turkey. And then she returned to the UK, to ignominy, and the distance allowed us to begin a relationship. That we could only see each other every few weeks made it easier. We should have notified our line managers. I didn't; I can't imagine Joanna having that conversation.

It's a mixed feeling when someone's turn for the worse involves agreeing to a relationship with you. I had been worried about her, post-Turkey. Shame can drive people to all sorts of things, and it had driven her to secrecy. And I recognised, in some uneasy way, that it was bound to her desire for me. There was a current of rage and humiliation sweeping her. I understood something of that. Her reputation was destroyed but she had survived, emerged intact on the other side of ruin, and that brings a disconcerting freedom.

We're half-dressed on the dusty ground in Turkey when Joanna's phone buzzes, one of her contacts saying Kurds had tapped into a pipeline beside the camp. It had been going on for weeks, Turkish intelligence claiming the PKK were conducting sabotage operations. We both suspected it was the gangs running the camps. Under cover of night, they'd drill into the line, stretch a hose to a rusty tanker then drive off when they'd finished, leaving the oil flowing into the ground until the place was swimming in it – and the villagers would come out and start scooping up fuel.

'Let's take a look,' she said, already dressing.

We were approaching slowly when a flame danced through the darkness ahead. Someone was crossing towards the spillage with a kerosene lamp. Joanna swore. *That's a naked flame.* I was trying to decide whether to intervene or turn around when the place lit up, sudden as a camera flash, only the illumination held and I could see all their faces, the people who'd been hiding. The fuel was flowing down into the stream, igniting through the trees, the night suddenly wild like a storm. Then there was a scream: a girl with her clothes on fire was running. I couldn't understand where she was running to. We were getting closer, Joanna unclipping her gun hopelessly, and I saw the girl running to the stream to dive in, only the stream was on fire.

Over the past six months I had thought of that night a lot. I had imagined the many places in the world Joanna might be, the many reasons it was best to maintain radio silence. No news was most certainly good news. I understood she would get in touch on her own terms.

Now she had.

EIGHT

When I woke the next morning there was a message from Evotec. They had accessed a recent internal directory compiled by Kaztelecom. The landline I'd been called from came up registered to Nurlan Pokatilov, Apartment 603, 9/1 Malakhov St, Astana 050059, Kazakhstan. It was listed online as a holiday rental.

The TutaNota address used for the Catalyst link had been set up just before the message was sent, on a machine with an IP address that belonged to a PC in Kazakhstan. Evotec had gone one step better: the PC itself belonged to a café going by the initials KS, on Kaldayakov Street, Astana.

The resolution of the clip conformed to several models of concealed camera. The level of compression suggested it had been copied twice. There was no form of watermark on the video clip aside from a time and date stamp. Like the newspaper, it had been set two weeks ahead. In terms of CGI, it wasn't like anything they'd seen before.

I brought up a satellite view, found the street address. The café was on a back street. Nurlan Pokatilov's address was one of many large apartment blocks in the north of the city. I tried calling his landline again but no one answered.

I sent new instructions to Evotec: Kazakh hospital records for the last week, plus recent arrests in Astana, then flight manifests in and out of the country for the days around the contact. My guess was that Kazakhstan's bloated bureaucracy used outdated technology that wouldn't prove too much of a challenge for the hackers.

I looked up routes to Astana.

Breakfast was brought to the suite, which let me spend half an hour browsing Kazakh websites and seeing how much of the language I remembered. Like a lot of the former Soviet Union republics, Russian had remained the lingua franca, but Kazakh still held on strong, especially once you were out of the cities. My Russian was okay; Kazakh itself was a Turkic language, not quite as close to Turkish as some, but plenty of crossover.

Most of my time in Kazakhstan had been spent around Aktau, in the far west of the country, on the coast of the Caspian. My job was to assess routes between Aktau and Baku in Azerbaijan, on the other side of that contested body of water. Aktau was pure ennui and I loved it: I had always sought out places that felt as remote as possible, which wasn't just a question of distance. Aktau had been built in 1962 as a camp for oil workers in one of the world's most lifeless deserts. There were no addresses, just three-digit numbers assigned to each home. The place was dependent on seawater desalinated with the help of a nuclear reactor, and the few trees that clung to existence had been planted using pneumatic drills. The town's main statue was of a Ukrainian poet exiled there by Russia in the nineteenth century, who wrote: *There is only sand and stones. You would gaze around and feel so dreary that you might as well hang yourself.* In the 1960s they briefly named the town after him. I spent most of my time watching oil-service vessels heading for the platforms, wondering when the water froze. Kazakhstan had the biggest extremes of temperature in the world, and this seemed responsible for its stark beauty.

I checked their local news, local bulletin boards, then went to an open-source search tool for videos and skimmed through all recently uploaded footage geotagged to the region. People were filming the snow. Right now it was minus 5 degrees. Workers at a metals factory had gone on strike. Presidential initiatives had been introduced regarding the environment, the economy and social values. I noted what people were wearing, styles of coat and boots and hair.

Perhaps because I knew I was going to go, because I knew this constituted a severance from which there would be no straight-forward return, I went to Croxley Green. I still considered it home although there was nothing much there, and I no longer even felt numb, just a wonder at how emotions fade.

The house was now occupied by a cousin who I had met twice, who was grateful for the space and left my old room untouched. I don't know why I didn't sell the place. There was some superstition around maintaining it, a sense that if I jettisoned this final connection with my own biography the cover lives themselves wouldn't work. What would they be? The centre would not hold.

When I'd been in Kabul, children wandered between cars selling gum and phone cards, chanting 'No mother, no father'. They chanted in English, beelining to the white SUVs of Western organisations, and I had begun to wonder if they even knew what it meant. *No mother, no father.* I still heard them, their small voices, especially in Croxley Green. I got a BMW chauffeur-driven from the Mandarin Oriental to St Pancras, where I walked through the station out to York Way and hailed a black cab.

Croxley was on the north-west edge of London, just inside the M25 but over the border of Hertfordshire. Its low suburban streets constricted around my heart. The historic windmill, the flat common, the interwar high street; a world without a horizon.

Even before she'd seen the house, Joanna had looked around and said: *Do you think every life is a form of revenge?*

Shops and pubs had closed, a new beauty parlour arrived. The public toilets, with their scrawled lists of times for cottaging, appeared to be open for business. The modern, red-brick church had a new notice board carrying photos of refugees.

I walked past my old secondary school where I had fallen in love with languages because they belonged to places utterly different from here. How benign that had seemed, to foster a relationship with places that were not yours. A love of history too, which also seemed to happen elsewhere, and was somewhere to which you might escape. I cleared some broken glass from the children's playground, as an opportunity to check the road behind me. No one there except for a small boy on a bike, who yelled 'Paedo' and cycled off. I had been right at fourteen: this was the edge of the universe.

No one home. I went to the back, climbed into the garden, found the spare keys and let myself in. The place smelled of stale cigarette smoke and floor polish. Figurines crowded the window ledges. I thought of Christopher Bohren's living room, up above Montreux, glass looking out over the Swiss town to Lake Geneva.

The bathroom was unchanged, the strip light harsh. I looked at my hands, the scar in the left palm where a woman extracted from the rubble of Baghdad's police station had dug her nails through my skin. I lifted the blind. There were new locks on the windows, and what looked like traces of powder used by a forensics team.

I went back to the kitchen and sifted the post until I found one from Hertfordshire Constabulary regarding a break-in on 27 November, two days ago. It seemed a strange house to target.

I went to my old room. Books had been taken from the shelves and opened, a file of essays emptied out and hurriedly crammed back in.

I turned on the PC and logged into my TutaNota account. The

coded email wasn't there. I checked the deleted folder, then the junk, then sent mail. All traces of it, including my own response, had been wiped.

A car passed, stopped at the end of the road. It was a van with a ladder on the roof. Parked for two minutes, disappeared again.

I called a contact in Visas and Immigration, read them my passport number.

'What's the status on this individual?'

'Red-flagged.'

'Any details?'

'Instructions are to detain and notify Special Branch.'

I felt a hand grip my arm suddenly. *Step this way, please.* I didn't have the authority to do anything about it over a phone call. I thanked the contact, went to the shed, took a trowel, left through the back gate.

Five minutes walking took me past a postal depot and the first grey-brown fields to a municipal cemetery. I stopped at a clean, new headstone, bowed my head then looked around. No one. I continued to the far end of the cemetery, over the fence, into the woods.

I remembered the forms of specific trees. Ash and beech trees planted twenty years ago. After ten minutes I stopped and began to dig. Just as I was thinking I'd chosen the wrong spot I hit thick black plastic. A couple of moments later I was able to retrieve the canister. The top was stiff but opened eventually. Inside: two passports, papers, hair dye, cash in five currencies totalling ten grand, plus a few basic items of kit: bump keys, skeleton keys, tracking devices. Most field agents organise their own emergency stash: contraband and leftovers. Few entirely trust their wellbeing to anyone else. I checked the dates on the passports, then returned to the house. I sat on the sofa and brought up a map of Kazakhstan on my phone. Vast and blank. The empty centre of the world. I wasn't the first to feel it calling.

NINE

I flew into Kazakhstan on Friday 2 December, a Ukraine Air flight from Kiev. The plane was half full, mostly business people, some families, one or two backpackers. I boarded last so I could walk the length of it and see the faces of my fellow passengers.

I'd asked for a window seat. The desert began a few miles east of the Volga river, Caucasus mountains flattening, a flash of the Caspian. By the time we were beneath cloud again the world looked like Mars: rippled rock, pink then grey, running lifeless to the horizon. I got that ominous feeling I always got flying over deserts. You think you have diminished me, they seem to say, but it is you who are diminished.

Kazakhstan. Eighth-biggest country in the world, over a million square miles of land, and a population smaller than London. We flew over bare planet for three hours then began to descend towards the capital. My neighbour craned to see the window, to witness civilisation erupting out of nowhere. Astana's glass towers burned with the low sun, office blocks of iridescent blue casting turquoise shadows across the business district. In front of the Presidential Palace, two perfectly conical towers of beaten gold stood side by side. The rest was snow.

Twenty years ago there was nothing here but a few crumbling Soviet blocks in a desert flat as the sea. After his country gained independence, the President of Kazakhstan decided to move the capital here. He renamed it Astana, meaning capital, and it appeared: ministerial buildings, business parks, futuristic shopping malls, arising from the dust on his command. Or, more accurately, from the 150-dollar barrels of oil beneath the dust. And it was only when you dropped below 1,000 feet and saw the absence of people on the wide streets that you heard the echo of the old name – *Akmola* – white grave. Hard to forget once you knew it.

It had been sixty-one hours since I left London. Figuring out an inconspicuous route to Kazakhstan was complicated by the fact that UK flights routed via Kiev. Flights from London to Ukraine were closely monitored by more than one intelligence service, so I flew easyJet to Zagreb.

It was when I walked out through Departures that the reality of it all kicked in: smiling at the air steward as he scanned the ticket and handed it back. I felt the carpet beneath my feet as I walked out of my life into renegade status.

I used my own card and passport for the Croatia trip, booking an Airbnb for a week. The flat was up steep stairs, with a view down to a church whose red and white tiled roof formed a Croatian flag. A street beside it filled with people over the course of the afternoon, drinking at the bars that lined each side. I let myself be briefly taunted by that imagined holiday. The paperwork I used for the next leg dated back to a job in Tajikistan and had never been used. The name was Toby Bell. I went to a dark-web site that let you buy Mastercard details for twenty pounds and used one to book my flight to Kiev, and another from Kiev to Astana.

That left me with twelve hours in Zagreb. I called Olivia Gresham and set up a meeting with her property-developer contact in Astana. Then I found a place to print while-you-wait business cards. When I had the cards in the name of Toby Bell, I printed out graphs and spreadsheets concerning the Kazakh economy. My cover was going to be a consultant for investors in Central Asia: something that put me between business and government, with plenty of room for unaccounted cash and minimal infrastructure. As far as I could tell, that was what the word 'consultant' had been invented for. And businessmen were unthreatening compared with other covers: universally explicable, their politics transparent.

I set up Toby Bell's social media, club membership, dating sites. Used the usual company in Hyderabad to stock my new life with friends and contacts. In a shopping mall on the edge of Zagreb's old town I bought thermals, boots, a couple of pre-paid phones. I loaded up the phone with apps – privacy vault, military-grade GPS navigation, police scanner and an app that detected radio signals, including those emitted by surveillance devices. I set the phones to upload data to a cloud account and erase all contents if anyone entered the wrong password.

Hotels in Astana were one-star or five-star. I decided to head for the very economical Lion Hotel in central Astana, but didn't book in advance. December in Kazakhstan wasn't going to be overcrowded.

Evotec sent through passenger lists for all commercial flights in and out of Kazakhstan over the past week. I searched them for any females aged twenty-five to forty, but there were none of the covers I'd known Joanna use. Same with arrests and hospital records. I was going to have to take a look myself.

I marked up a satellite map of Astana with government buildings, police stations and transport options out of the city. Then I added the address of the landline registered to Nurlan Pokatilov from which I'd been called.

At dawn I got up, switched on some lights, tuned the TV to BBC World News, dropped the keys in the lockbox, caught a train to Zagreb airport and flew to Kiev.

*

I had to stay a night in Ukraine, which felt okay. I thought it would sharpen me up. And I had spent time there with Joanna. Some superstition made me want to touch base. I brushed up my Russian and Kazakh on the flight. It wasn't so unusual in Six to have minimal time to immerse in a language before deployment, but this felt rushed. Like turning up naked.

The huge, blocky Hotel Ukrayina had a view of the Maidan. Last time here, many years ago, we were celebrating the Orange Revolution. The hotel served as headquarters of the opposition, which was convenient for spooks and journalists. Ten years later I had seen photos of the same rooms being used as a makeshift hospital and morgue, the square around it divided between protesters and the paramilitary units cracking their skulls.

Quieter tonight, and repainted. The scars of those events were 700 kilometres south in Donetsk and Crimea. I drank in the hotel bar, among the red and gold Soviet-era décor, and rehearsed Toby Bell, his enthusiasm for what he would describe as enabling policy environments, his knowledge of the EU's development cooperation strategy. His sense of opportunity. A man who had never been quite as successful as he wanted to be, perhaps. Who sought approval and had few memories that kept him awake at night.

Two or three days, I told myself. That was all I was going to spend in Kazakhstan. No need for MI6 to know I'd even left the country. Long enough to determine whether there was anything I could do, short enough to remain under the radar. I'd follow the leads I had and ensure discretion while doing it; that was what I was trained to do. If Joanna was there and needed help getting out of the country for whatever reason then a fresh presence could be invaluable. I was wary about crashing into someone else's field of operations, though, if that was what it was. Without even knowing which direction the threat might come from. There's always the opportunity to make things worse.

Around 8 p.m. the bar became a strip club. I tried out Toby. I flirted with escorts, flashed some cash, got in a conversation with an Israeli who owned an IT company, telling him that Kazakhstan was the future. I left at 10 p.m. and spent a couple of hours poring over Kazakh news clippings, identifying useful social media accounts and local journalists. Then I stopped and read some of Frederick Burnaby's nineteenth-century account of travelling in the region, spying for the British state when Tsarist troops were encroaching on the Empire. And I felt the tingle again: entering a country as a spy, your own mystery momentarily equal to the world's.

Few of my fellow passengers looked up to observe the miracle of Astana when it appeared. The Ishim river had frozen – a winding white road through the city – and as we got lower you could see snowmobiles and sledges scarring the ice. Expensive new apartment blocks hugged the left bank, all glass and curves, older Soviet neighbourhoods to the right: sullen, square-shouldered, like individuals who gambled on the wrong future.

Landing was bumpy. Outside it was snow-globe frenzied. Mid-afternoon but that didn't seem relevant. As we left the jet bridge into the terminal gate a woman in a pastel-blue suit smiled and pointed a Sony mini DV camcorder at our faces.

Welcome to Kazakhstan.

At immigration control I chose a line with a young and tired-looking officer who barely glanced at my passport. I got a standard fifteen-day tourist visa on the spot, waited for the official stamp, admired a mural of horses running across the steppe.

The warmth of the arrivals hall thawed the atmosphere as far as the taxis, then the cold bit. Exhaust fumes billowed thick as factory smoke in the freezing air. I chose an alcohol-bloated driver in a dirty Nissan who grinned at me, as if amused to find me in the back of his car. I gave an address a block away from my chosen hotel. The driver grunted as he set off and then the road vanished beneath snow.

'Where from?' he asked, speaking English.

'America.'

'New York?'

'Close by.'

'First time?'

'In Astana, yes.'

He laughed.

'Business.'

'Hope so.' We approached flashing lights that I thought were emergency vehicles but turned out to be a convoy of snow ploughs. 'Quite some weather,' I said, switching to Russian but keeping it unpolished.

'This is nothing,' he replied in Russian. 'Last week, the snow was ... ' He gestured up to the roof lining, which was tobacco-stained. 'Now it will get colder. Less snow, much colder.'

Like most new cities, Astana's roads were broad and straight. We passed large geometric sculptures, positioned around the place in the way you'd try to make an oversized flat look inhabited, then huge new residential developments. The buildings themselves were spread out. I couldn't see many lights on. Very occasionally a human could be seen moving between them, head down against the wind.

One face was repeatedly visible: the Kazakh President. He gazed enigmatically from billboards: Nazarbayev; wise, inscrutable, seventy-eight years old and, given that he'd been running the place as a Moscow-loyal commu-nist when it was still part of the Soviet Union, he'd ruled the country for longer than it had existed. He'd steered a careful path without relinquishing power, keeping Russia, China and the West sweet. Most of all keeping his own people sweet, who voted 90 per cent in his favour in relatively clean elections but still couldn't start a magazine without governmental permission.

A few more of these citizens appeared after we'd been driving for ten minutes. My first impression of them was that they were suicidal. They wove through the cars, which were themselves skidding, appearing from between the grey mounds of slush at the side of the road. I had no idea if somewhere underneath the black ice there were lane markings, but no one would have been able to keep to them anyway.

Astana's icons came in and out of view as we approached the centre: the Presidential Palace with its blue dome, flanked by two identical gold cylinders that contained governmental ministries and the offices of the Sovereign Wealth Fund. Half a mile away, the Bayterek tower soared into the sky, crowned by an orb. To the south – facing the Palace across the city – a glass pyramid lit alternately pink and green. We passed three presidential billboards in a row. Across the last, in dripping red paint, someone had written *Water freedom with blood*.

Two patrol cars sat in front, lights flashing. As if sensing my interest, three men in dark uniforms turned their heads to watch the taxi pass.

'How are things here?' I asked. 'There's a lot of police about.'

'Now, yes.'

'Why's that?'

'Terrorism.'

'Have there been terrorist attacks?'

'No.'

Lion Hotel was in a concrete block that had been painted lemon yellow from the third floor up. The hotel actually occupied the top of the building only. The lift was broken so I walked up, which afforded me a glimpse of a brothel on the floor below, VIP

Massage, with women in dressing gowns checking their phones and waiting for the VIPs.

No one on the hotel reception desk. It was brightly lit, with the city's eager artifice continuing inside: a lot of translucent plastic furniture, an incongruous chandelier spray-painted gold. Tropical fish swam across a 27-inch screen on the wall.

After a couple of minutes I went around the desk and leafed through the reservations book. There was no one else staying here. Eventually a young woman turned up, sleepy-eyed, apologetic, in jeans and a T-shirt; she took my details, gave me a swipe card and rustled up a smile.

'You are here for work?'

'Some meetings.'

'But you will visit Bayterek?'

'Of course.'

'This city has many wonders,' she said. Then: 'Have you been to the old capital, Almaty?'

'No.'

'It is very beautiful. There are mountains, trees. Perhaps you will have a chance to go.'

My room was small, with a painting of a nomad asleep beside a camel on the wall, a view between tower blocks to the business district. I checked the window locks, then the devices currently connected to the hotel's wi-fi network; I logged on and sent an email, unsecured, to the property developer Olivia Gresham had put me in touch with, confirming arrival, saying I was looking forward to our meeting tomorrow. I logged out, connected to a private network and checked my own messages. Nothing from Joanna, one from Six asking me to confirm my current location.

I stood at my window and tried to understand where I was. Across the business district, entire buildings masked themselves in LED displays, others flickering up their height in coloured sequences. A lot of cities can appear utopian from a hotel window at night, but Astana is particularly dreamlike. Flakes cluttering the air added to the sense of unreality, of looking at an architectural model put together by a teenager with ADHD and a love of science fiction. Only the Central Mosque refused to blink, steadfast in its floodlights like an admonishment.

I remembered why I had loved the country the last time I was here: its sense of newness, of gazing out to a future as unencumbered as the steppe. But it wasn't entirely without baggage. The President's excuse for creating a new capital was that the old one sat in an earthquake zone. One look at a map showed you the more pressing threat. Almaty was way down south, tucked into a corner near China. That left a huge tranche of northern Kazakhstan looking lonely and neglected next to Russia, and ripe for the taking. Shiny new Astana was a flag stuck firmly in the north. *Ours*.

I put my less sensitive paperwork in the room's small safe, then found a communal bathroom at the end of the corridor. There were cisterns, vent units, loose ceiling panels. I went for the ceiling, stashing six thousand dollars in cash and the more incriminating equipment up among the pipes. Back in my room, I searched online for car hire establishments and selected the one with the lowest TripAdvisor review, on the principle it would show least interest in me. Finally I mapped a route to the flat the phone calls had come from.

TEN

Snow filled my mouth when I tried to breathe. Skin burned with the cold anywhere it was exposed. Ears were the worst. I pulled my hat down, used the act of turning away from the wind as I zipped up my jacket to check behind, in case anyone had followed me from the hotel. I could see about two feet. My nostrils stung as the mucus began to freeze. I covered my face with my scarf, moved on. I wanted to feel out Astana's energy.

The big, underpopulated streets meant it was a city without cover, which was both a good and bad thing. It made you conspicuous, but also anyone trying to follow you. Anyone crazy enough to be out was wrapped up to the point of anonymity anyway. Locals called it the *buran*, the storm wind that came west from Xinjiang over bare planet, gathering ferocity. Nature had been reduced to occasional thin stalks demarcating car parks. Vehicles were new and high-end for the most part, with little variation: Toyotas, Subarus, Hyundais, usually white or grey. They emerged from underground car parks, driving on compacted snow with the tick-tick noise of studded tyres. They descended again beneath office blocks and shopping malls without anyone setting foot outside.

I got to sightsee alone. In the park that ran alongside the river there was a display of ice sculptures, miniature wonders of the world, the Taj Mahal, the Acropolis, lit by coloured lights. All the older buildings across the water had been painted in pinks and blues and reclad. I walked three more blocks, which was as long as the exposed skin of my face could take, then hailed a gipsy cab. I got into the second car that stopped – I never took the first, as a rule, and I also tended to avoid ones that looked new, with central locking and powerfully built men at the wheel. This was a battered Daewoo, driver maybe twenty years old. I mentioned a dive bar on a street near, but not too near, the car hire. Pronounced it badly so he asked me to repeat before nodding, unimpressed.

Just another entitled foreigner, stupid enough to be outside in these conditions. Easy money. He asked for five hundred tenge, which was comfortingly extortionate, and I got in. The car skidded onto Cosmonauts Street, wheels flailing on black ice, onto the main avenue heading away from the river into the governmental district. The windscreen wipers swept uselessly. A lone figure lost in snow dived out of the way as my driver turned.

A black Subaru Impreza cruised behind us for four or five blocks. I watched until it U-turned at a broad, empty intersection and disappeared back into the storm. We passed some frozen water fountains and began making better progress.

I thought of the graffiti I had seen. *Water freedom with blood.* The line was from a poem, but I couldn't think which. When we were close enough I told the driver to stop, got out and walked. Someone barrelled past, mummified in a parka, scarf over their face. I waited for them to disappear then crossed the road, which gave me a chance to take a good, inconspicuous look in both directions. I was alone.

I found the car-hire place on a back street, and picked up a white Hyundai Tucson. Half the vehicles on the road seemed to be Hyundai Tucsons. The man was indifferent as I'd hoped, hands stained with oil, writing my details with a biro he had to smack on the desk to work. Things felt like they were coming under control. I went for a drive.

Multiple state agencies patrolled the city. Police wore fur hats and long, grey jackets that hid their weaponry. Closer to the Presidential Palace you got military in camo fatigues and sky-blue berets. The elite and more shadowy National Security Committee officers wore black tactical vests and carried Russian-made AN-94 rifles. Alertness was high. I saw two cars being stopped and checked.

The British embassy lay within a block of offices on the edge of the business district. No conspicuous security or aerials. The current ambassador, according to Stevenson, was Suzanna Ford, a career diplomat with previous postings in Stockholm, Nairobi and Brussels. No indication that this was MI6 cover, although one never knew. I memorised the vehicles parked in front of it. The place didn't feel like the sanctuary it would have once represented.

Now I knew the look I stopped at a department store and bought a balaclava, trapper hat, beanie, ski goggles and a reversible down jacket with a hood – which was useful for quick changes of appearance. For the car, I picked up water, food, first-aid kit, two spare phones, a shovel and two litres of vodka.

I drove while I could. Conditions were getting worse. It was time to put a plan into action.

I headed to the address of my missed calls.

The area was all half-constructed new-builds. They looked desolate, the towers haggard. The block I was interested in had a roof, but if it wasn't for lights in some of the upper windows I wouldn't have been sure it had been completed. Up close you saw ill-fitting window frames and protection tape. A courtyard remained half-constructed. This was what happened when oil booms came to a crashing halt: grand projects lurched into ruins before they were fully born.

I pushed the entrance door and it opened into a bare concrete entrance hall, walls covered with protective sheeting. The post box for 603 was empty. I took the stairs to establish their viability as an escape route. They smelled of fresh paint, and I wondered if I was the first person to use them. Then, at the fifth floor, I passed an encampment: a man, woman and two children beneath layers of tarpaulin. They were darker than most Kazakhs; refugees, with a propane gas heater. The man watched me pass, stiff with fear. I nodded, kept moving.

The sixth-floor hallway was freezing. No lights anywhere except for the light under the door of 603. I dialled the landline and heard it ring inside. So I was at the right place, at least. No one answered. I knocked on the door, listened for movement on the other side. No sound.

I didn't know who or what the apartment represented. I wasn't quite ready to draw the attention of a break-in. Not unarmed.

On my way back down I spoke to the homeless family.

'Have you seen anything strange recently? A woman?' I tried various languages, got stares. 'Know who lives in 603?'

'One night,' the father eventually said, in faltering Russian. 'We stay here just tonight. Tomorrow we go.'

I needed to find a cathedral.

Black Mass was Joanna's system, and she'd chosen the name. Her idea was that, even in an unfamiliar city, you could still communicate a location by code. So you had to think what landmarks a city might have: one code for general post office, one for town hall, one for cathedral.

The Assumption Cathedral in Astana was only five years old, though you wouldn't have guessed it. White towers with narrow, prison-like windows supported blue and gold onion domes. A brass plaque announced that it had been funded by Gazprom. The towers looked a bit like distillation towers on a refinery.

The car park was empty, as was the security booth at its entrance. There were few surrounding windows, roofs or ledges with a sight onto the cathedral square. I couldn't see much, but then nor would anyone watching. The cathedral was open. I went in, impressed at the sense of age they'd installed – the incense-darkened icons. I sat in a back pew, thawed out, breathed in.

It would do.

I sent the cathedral code to the TutaNota address, along with a number for my new mobile, then drove on. I should have settled in properly first, I thought, assessed security, familiarised myself with the terrain before trying to set up a meeting, but I didn't know how long I had.

ELEVEN

I filled the tank, got some food at a café with plastic furniture and unshielded neon bulbs, waited for midnight. I checked the exit routes I'd marked on my map: exits from the city, then from the country. The scenario I was hoping for was one in which we had to get out fast. Kazakhstan had China to the east, across mountains. Russia to the north, a long, porous border, the only downside being that on the other side was Russia. Uzbekistan to the south was a strong contender for exit of choice. I had connections there; it led deeper into the 'Stans, into a complexity where you could hide. To the west was the Caspian Sea, boats crossing to Azerbaijan. Shipping routes were always useful: chaotic, bribable, potentially off-radar. Spies like boats. But it was all difficult terrain. All a lot of steppe away.

The café served only one dish: *lagman*, noodle soup, with a few pieces of mutton floating in oily broth, but it tasted better than the Hotel Ukrainya's steak and potatoes, which was almost all I'd eaten in the last twenty-four hours. As customers came in, I studied how people looked at each other – eye contact among strangers, use of mobile phones, hands-free mics. I hadn't seen anyone using a phone indoors yet. People were reserved. Men and women interacted coolly, glances were quick. You could tell someone was unfamiliar to them but only just. I couldn't hear any other foreigners about.

What none of it told me was how much of a mistake I was

making by being here. I sensed I was doing precisely what someone intended me to do. I had made mistakes before. A bad day
at the office for a field operative can be a very bad day indeed.

At quarter to midnight, I returned to the cathedral. Floodlights
around its base caught the snow dancing furiously, seeming to
race back up into the sky. I parked beyond the edge of the light,
with a view in all directions. This was as clear an observation
point as I was going to get. I turned off the interior lights and
watched the snow.

No one showed.

I waited, feeling conspicuous, checking my messages
every few minutes. At 1 a.m. I drove back to the block on
Malakhov Street.

I parked well away from it, covered my face, took a set of
bump keys, which worked on 90 per cent of locks. I used the lift
this time, wary of witnesses. The sixth floor was unchanged.
I knocked again, then went to work on the lock. It gave
after a minute.

The flat contained no personal effects: no books or ornaments
on the hallway shelves, no shoes or coats. Windows had been
left open, dropping the temperature to below freezing. Snow
had blown in. At the end of the corridor I could see a living
room with snow over a sofa. I walked through. A black rucksack
had been emptied across the floor: men's clothes, some money,
painkillers, contact lenses. A bottle of vodka and two glasses
stood on the coffee table. One glass had dark red lipstick smears.

I turned towards the kitchen, saw blood up the wall.

A man lay on his back on the tiled floor. He'd been shot three
times, twice in the face, once in the shoulder. The shots to the face
had been done close up, leaving a bloody gap where his right eye
and the bridge of his nose should have been. They'd removed the
lower jaw entirely. The back of his throat glistened icily, white

knobs of spine among the flesh. Pieces of brain, tooth and hair had frozen to surfaces in all directions.

A few distinguishing attributes remained. He was white; the condition of his skin and hair suggested someone under forty. He wore jeans, civilian walking boots, grey jumper and dark blue puffa-style jacket. The clothes were mostly global brands, neither cheap nor expensive. I felt a draught and saw a doorway in the corner of the kitchen leading into a bin area with chutes for rubbish disposal and a steel emergency door that had been left open a fraction. Beyond the steel door was an external fire escape.

I returned to the living room and checked the glasses on the table. In one, the liquid had frozen, but not the other. The man had been drinking vodka, but the lipstick-wearer had been drinking water. She had been controlling this situation, I thought. It was her safe house.

My mobile swept the place for devices, surveillance or otherwise. Nothing was currently transmitting. I checked the visible realm: the cupboards, the open window and fire escape. No clues. No shell casings that I could see; no prints. A crowd could have come and gone via the fire escape but their footprints would have been obliterated by the snow of the last forty-eight hours.

He'd been moving towards the fire escape, I felt sure. Trying to escape.

No ID on him: no phone, no wallet. I used my own phone to take pictures of what remained of his face, his fingers, then put it in his mouth and tried to take photos of the remaining teeth. Rinsing the phone, I allowed myself a sigh. Thanks, Joanna. I wondered what I was meant to do now. I wasn't in a position to seal the place. I wasn't in a position to stick around.

The lift was in use when I returned to the corridor. By the time it had stopped at the floor below I was already moving down the stairs. The sheltering family were all awake, eating out of tins.

'Excuse me,' I said. 'Apologies.'

The four of them stared at me, new fear in their eyes. I kept my head down and kept walking.

When I looked at myself in the rear-view mirror, I saw why they'd looked scared. I had someone else's blood smeared down the side of my face. I got out, used mineral water to wash, swore again. I sat in the car and briefly shut my eyes. I'd left prints all over the place. I'd be on cameras somewhere. The car certainly would. I had witnesses to my face and voice. The lock of the apartment was now broken and it was only a matter of time before someone walked in.

I parked a couple of blocks away from the Lion Hotel, watched the street for two minutes before going up. The same girl sat behind reception, reading a magazine.

'How was your night?' she asked.

'Excellent.'

'You saw the city? Bayterek?'

'Yes, Bayterek. Has there been anyone here looking for me?' I asked.

'No.' She shook her head. Then, as I moved away: 'Mr Bell?'

'Yes?'

'I've put an extra blanket in your room. Let me know if you need more bedding.'

'Thank you. I will.'

The state of the dead man's face made facial recognition impossible. The frozen temperature made gauging time of death difficult. Nothing on local news about a man missing. I watched the Catalyst clip again and it definitely wasn't the same man. No help there.

I tried the owner of the apartment and got a recorded message about bookings. Online, a calendar showed it was booked for another four days.

I made up an emergency go-bag in case I had to move quickly – spare phone, cash, some first aid – placed it under a pillow. I felt uneasy thinking of the body lying untended in the sixth-floor flat, as if it had become my responsibility, and I was failing obligations to care for the dead. I could call it in anonymously, find a phone box, use my Russian. An ID would surface once media reported it. But did I want to trigger an investigation?

Three days, I thought: in, out. How was that going? I stood at my window and watched the snow, the business district flashing, the river beyond it. The art of espionage involved remembering where you were. This wasn't London, Washington or even Moscow. Mankind, as a whole, had never sunk any flag very deep in Kazakh soil. Frederick Burnaby, passing through one hundred and fifty years ago, heard talk of a Russian expedition against the Khans that set out in midwinter. A thousand men, nine thousand camels, three thousand horses, never seen again. Not even the bones.

You could build a hundred skyscrapers, but you were still in the desert. You had maps and plans but they meant little here.

TWELVE

The storm had subsided when I woke. 5.45 a.m. Astana lay entombed in moonlit snow.

The silence was jarring. My mind spooled through countries I might be in, arriving at Kazakhstan and flicking immediately to the image of a man's destroyed face. I turned the TV on, checked online. No word of a body being found. By the time I was dressed, the sky had lightened a shade. I dressed as I had seen locals do – ski mask first, scarf, beanie, hood up over it, then trapper hat over the hood. Armoured, I went out.

MI6 drummed into you the importance of surveillance-detection runs. They were best performed at times and in places when any possible tail was made conspicuous. Six a.m. in most places was ideal. It felt like starting the day clean. And confirming you were alone converted the loneliness into relief.

The first blast of sub-zero dawn took my breath. I walked as fast as I could over deep, pristine snow, through the last of the silence. I looked for vehicles without snow on the roof, individuals appearing from side streets. There was no one. It felt like the desert beneath the city had begun reclaiming it overnight. In other locations where I'd practised this routine I had felt the imminent life of the city around me, but not here. There was a thin tension to the dawn, an uncertainty as to whether Astana would summon the will to exist again.

Still, it was nice to be able to see it.

Ice had moulded itself around the few branches in sight, around satellite dishes and street furniture as if it was concerned about preserving these things. On east-facing streets, cars had been buried entirely. I saw a man with a shovel carving out a Peugeot 308. Workers in luminescent orange marched behind snowploughs, moulding banks of snow on either side. At the entrance to Nazarbayev Square, soldiers struggled with steel crowd barriers they pulled from an open-backed truck; the barriers had frozen together, and the voices of the men made an angry dawn chorus.

I cut through the park alongside the river and the central mosque appeared, its call to prayer opening up and startling me. Our song, Joanna used to joke. Plaintive as ever, at odds with the glossy, frozen city it appealed to. I slowed, made a rough head-count of those removing their shoes to file in. It didn't seem more than a handful. Unbearded for the most part. Across the road, two stiff-backed men in an unmarked Toyota Land Cruiser also watched.

Terrorism, the cab driver had said. I thought of the evident security tension and wondered what it indicated beneath the surface. Kazakhstan wasn't a hotbed of radicalism. Even if the Soviets hadn't spent fifty years trying to stifle religion, Islam was a relatively late addition, a sheet laid over older creeds involving tribe and land. The Islam that did take root was Sufi-inflected, mystical, superstitious. Still, Kazakhstan bordered the north-west of China, Xinjiang province, where you found 12 million oppressed Muslims occasionally losing patience. Uzbekistan, to the south, had been having its little resurgence. In the other direction was Chechnya. Quite a neighbourhood.

I stopped at the edge of the river, a spot where I could see the embankment and anyone on it in both directions. A few defiant fishermen had carved holes in the ice, huddling under plastic windbreaks that encased them like body bags. No sledgers or skaters yet. No visible surveillance.

I returned to the hotel, collected my hire car and drove to the block of flats on Malakhov Street. I parked across the road and looked up at the windows. They were still open, light still on. No police vehicles around.

I bought a local paper for the sake of blending in, then looked for cafés near police stations.

The one I eventually chose didn't have a name, as far as I could tell. It had a view of the central police station. It was also a block from the grandiose construction housing the Deputy President's office and the Ministry of Oil and Gas. Cheap cafés near important buildings were a potential gold mine: you found cleaners, maintenance staff, security guards, employees having affairs – all sorts of lures to a spy. It had just gone 8 a.m. Inside: ten men and women. Two tables of uniformed police, heads dipping to noodles and soups. A boy of nineteen or twenty continually mopped greying slush from the floor. A gruff man behind the counter took my order of coffee and one of the hard-looking pastries that sheltered beneath clingfilm. I sat for a moment watching the vast Ministry building. It takes three or four minutes to become inconspicuous. I sipped my coffee, waited. Listened.

Eavesdropping brings language alive. You have a few hours on a new posting when your ears are still sensitised. There was that Turkic flavour, the harmonising vowels that preserved the passage of nomads westwards. I listened to the police, then two workers with the faintly Persian edges of Uzbek in their speech, then a woman with splashes of a dialect that sounded like Uyghur, from near the border with China. She had arrived just after me. From her various complaints about work it sounded like she cleaned on most floors of the Ministry building. She lived with an elderly mother. Her daughter's upcoming wedding was a source of grievance. She sat close to a man who did maintenance in the same government offices – he had an identical pass to her, on a key chain. At his feet lay a tool bag containing wire strippers, electrical tape, a socket set.

The newspaper gave some carefully filtered insight into the country I was in. There was a lot about officials launching schemes in rural villages. A wind farm symbolised a possible future; Touch-KZ, a new dating site for Kazakhstan's youth, was taking off. Protests against Chinese companies renting agricultural land simmered in rural areas, but overall there was a lot less hate and a lot less sleaze than in a free press. Nothing about a missing or murdered English woman. I checked what neighbouring devices came up on my phone then logged in to the café's wi-fi.

New dating app popular among Kazakh singles. I found Touch-KZ on my phone, downloaded it and joined with a fake profile.

A minute later I had a match. One girl, two miles away. Tia Zhang, twenty-eight years old, pretty. Catfish pretty. She looked like stock photos, sounded like a robot.

Hey. You look nice. What are you doing?

Camel racing, I messaged back.

Cool! You seem interesting. Check out this site – lots of fun there.

I ran a virus scan and clicked. It was a website advertising pop bands and TV shows. I declined the invitation to subscribe.

Twitter and SoundCloud were blocked but a Virtual Private Network was easy enough to download and allowed you to search the internet without going through government servers. I looked for prostitutes. Prostitutes were often a good first step to finding both the political elite and underworld fixers. There was little information on prostitutes or red-light Astana generally. One gay traveller on a bulletin board asked where he might meet men. Someone mentioned a sauna, someone said Grindr worked.

I checked Grindr. The only men within range currently looking for gay sex were two other Western travellers in a nearby hotel.

I ripped a photo of a young man from the internet – out of courtesy, I chose one safely domiciled in Toronto – and set up a profile on the Kazakh social network, Zuz.kz. Adilbek Antropov was twenty-seven years old, an engineer, loved Italian cars, European football, Kazakhstan. I sent some friend requests, then linked to a piece in the *Washington Post* about kleptocracy in Central Asia. After five minutes it was still up and I hadn't been arrested.

Dictatorship is sometimes hard to put your finger on. People don't go around visibly fearful or furious; you have to attune your senses. *Water freedom with blood.* Now I remembered where it was from: a poem by Taras Shevchenko. *Bury me, be done with me, rise and break your chain; water your new freedom with blood like rain.* 1840s, maybe 1850s. He was Ukrainian, exiled to Kazakhstan when he started agitating for independence. It was a select few who knew Shevchenko's poetry these days, and not many of those painting graffiti.

The door chimed. A man walked into the café: clean-shaven, in his forties, a pale, sullen face – European, maybe English. He ordered a water in passable Russian, took a seat at a table in the corner. Beneath his smart grey winter coat was a pale, slightly crumpled suit. In Europe he would have been a perfect grey man, utterly unnoticeable, but not here. I gave it another moment, then finished my coffee and left.

I crossed the Presidential Park, then doubled back, over a low barrier into the grounds of the Keruen shopping mall. Shopping malls are good for counter-surveillance. It seemed Astana had a fine selection of them. A lot of the world was inhospitable a lot of the time, but that wasn't going to stop consumerism.

I rode escalators up, then down again, with a nice clear view of faces. No indication the pale man had followed. The mall was still quiet. A kiosk at the back sold cigarettes and bus tickets. I bought a packet of Chung Hwa and two lighters.

'And a travelcard, please; something that gets me on buses across the city.'

She slid one across the counter.

'How long does this last?'

'One week.'

'Any bus? Unlimited?'

She nodded, palm waiting for coins.

I returned to the hotel. What I really needed was someone who had access to police files, an ear to the street, a local journalist or detective. Instead, thanks to the kindness and connections of Olivia Gresham, I had an appointment with a property developer. But that was better than nothing. He was local and would be sensitive to political currents, ones that could pull someone under.

I ironed a shirt, brushed my teeth, thought, Toby Bell. Economic opportunity.

We met in the lobby of one of the sapphire-blue towers in the business district. On the walls hung two framed photos blown up to grand scale: one of the governor of the Mangystau district opening the region's first supermarket, the other taken inside a Siemens factory close to the Chinese border, with smiling Kazakhs in white coats and hairnets. Dimash Toreali appeared a minute after I arrived, hand outstretched, black polo neck under a grey blazer, thinning hair gelled back.

'Mr Bell.' He walked me into the lift and up to the office. 'You know Olivia Gresham?'

'Very well.'

'A clever woman. If she recommends you, you are clever too. And lucky. She says your clients are looking to make significant investments here.'

'Hopefully.'

'Worked in Central Asia before?'

'Not as such. I've had some involvement in China.'

'And you studied in England?'

'Yes.'

'Oxford or Cambridge?'

'Neither, I'm afraid.'

'I spent a blissful year at Oxford.'

His office was decorated with two portraits of the President, one with a gold shimmer like a novelty postcard. In between them was a poster declaring: *The City of the Future is Digital.* Toreali beamed at me. I was reminded of Moscow in the Noughties, the excitement of money when it's flowing free and there's no end in sight. But I also got a sense that Toreali ran a tight ship.

He talked about entrepreneurship, a rising middle class, Kazakhstan as a link between China and Europe. As evidence of the country's appetite for modernity he described his flagship development, Khan Shatyr – 'Tent of the Khan' – Astana's biggest retail complex and, technically, the largest tent in the world. Its sloping glass walls were suspended by cables from a central spire. The shopping centre was modelled on a traditional Kazakh yurt, he said, and I gazed across the promotional images and nodded. Gap, Zara, Occitane; an air-conditioned paradise where history came to die. The upper levels were encircled by a jogging track and monorail. On the top floor was a beach with sand imported from the Maldives.

'Did you know Astana had a beach?' He smiled.

'I might have read about it.'

'Open until midnight. You can relax on the sand, minus 40 outside. Locals love it.'

'I'm sure.'

After another twenty minutes the bottle and glasses came out. Ten-thirty a.m. I'd had worse. And I respected the tradition. The vodka in the drawer was like a confession: *Of course, none of this is really bearable.* It made you conscious of its absence in Western offices, and wonder what psychopathy replaced it.

We raised a toast to the unbreakable friendship between Kazakhstan and the UK, then one to peace, understanding and friendship.

I raised a toast to the President, then he said, 'Let's go for a drive.'

Four armed guards accompanied us through the centre of town, in a civilian-model Humvee, as Toreali pointed out the largest aquarium in Central Asia – 'Possibly the only aquarium in Central Asia' – and a new ovoid national archive building under construction. I probed for insight into the political situation, but he was on sales mode and I didn't get anything useful.

'We call Astana city of the future, *gorod budushchego*, and the city of dreams, *gorod-mechta*.'

'Not quite the same thing,' I said.

'Where does the future come from but dreams?' He smiled. We approached the Bayterek monument, its slender tower opening out to cradle a golden orb, and I realised what it reminded me of: the sculpture in Bahrain's Pearl Roundabout, flattened by Saudi tanks six years ago when it became a magnet for pro-democracy crowds.

'This is the centrepiece of the city,' Toreali said.

'Does it do anything?'

'It embodies a Kazakh legend, about a mythical bird that lays a golden egg in a tall tree, beyond human reach. The egg contains the secrets of happiness.'

'And why is it here?'

'Because the President wanted it to be here.'

'If you go up do you discover the secrets of happiness?'

'You discover a cast of the President's hand, and when you put your own hand in it a recording of a choir plays.'

We lunched in the Palace of Peace and Harmony. The Palace was the pyramid I'd seen, sixty metres high, its apex formed of stained glass featuring giant doves. It had been constructed for a World Congress of Religious Leaders, Toreali explained proudly. 'The Palace expresses the spirit of Kazakhstan. Different cultures, traditions and nationalities coexisting in peace and harmony.' It also housed an opera house, a national museum of culture and a projected 'university of civilisation' about which I tried to get information but failed.

We ate in a huge dining area right at the top with sloping glass walls – myself and Toreali and two Korean businessmen with Louis Vuitton bags to whom I was introduced as a successful British investor. The Koreans wanted to build residential compounds in the style of English town houses arranged around duck ponds. They had a promotional clip which they showed on an iPad: Georgian buildings set among trees, bridges, a supermarket. They'd already built two identical villages in Moscow, one near Shanghai. When I asked if the trees were going to be real they weren't sure but said there were some convincing artificial ones these days. I flicked through, past the images of golf courses, Western shops and high-end restaurants, and thought of Egypt in 2011, which had had places like this opening every week and was soon in the throes of a revolution.

'It's going to have the country's first Tesco,' the Korean said.

'The Chinese must love this.'

'They buy five or six at a time.'

We ate sliced meats and an Uzbek-style *plov* of mixed rice and meat. The developer made me study the bottle of Châteauneuf du Pape, and read the label out loud. He filled my glass to the brim but drank Coke himself. His guards stood by the door. I kept thinking about a guy lying in an empty flat with his face shot off.

'I hear the President's daughter likes to sing,' I said.

'She is a beautiful singer,' the developer said.

'I have some connections. If she'd like any bands to perform, to play with her.'

'Oh, she'd love that. Her birthday is coming up. Do you know Coldplay?'

I said I might be able to help. When desserts were done, the Koreans left and Toreali led me to the sloping glass wall. He pointed past a library that looked like a giant contact lens.

'See that railway being built?'

I could see a dark line where earth had been turned, workers in hi-vis orange, small as ants.

'It connects down through the country to the East–West highway, all part of China's One Belt One Road scheme. They are building it for us, connecting up the world. Last week I was having dinner with a couple who have just made the first over-land delivery of laptops from Chongqing in south-west China to Duisburg in Germany. This is the return of the Silk Road.'

I looked past the skyscrapers. Roughly the Silk Road, perhaps; the northern route: Khorgos, Alashankou. Six centuries ago the speed of British ships had drained this route of logic. Within a century or so, some of the greatest cities on earth had withered. Maybe someone then, on the Cape of Good Hope, had seen the galleons sailing past and got the same vertiginous sense of history turning.

'The beauty of the route is it bypasses Russia.' He winked. 'Now that Russia's put up trade restrictions on Western produce people are bringing chickens over the Caspian. Yesterday I had reps from Jiangsu province sealing a commitment to invest $600 million in related projects. So, as you can see, you have come to the right place. Think of Dubai.'

I thought of Dubai. Toreali continued: 'These are places cre-ated on the basis of logistics. It was a small port where they made an economic zone. Now look at it.'

I gazed across the landscape. Almost, I thought. Only, where

Dubai carried a certain regal cruelty, Astana remained more earthbound. It wanted to be liked, which gave the pomp an air of Disneyland rather than Singapore or Manhattan. But both had been built out of oil. I said: 'Someone once described the world to me as countries with long histories but no oil and countries with lots of oil but little history.' I'd spent time trying to divine the lesson in this. Toreali took umbrage.

'Kazakhstan has as much history as anyone else. Just because there are not kings and castles.'

'Of course.'

'Not everywhere can be European.'

'Can I ask you, as one investor to another, how stable you think things are here? A country like this, with its oil, its location, it must be a magnet for unrest and interference.'

'It is very stable.'

'Do the Russians cause any trouble? This is their backyard, right? How do you manage that?'

There was a hesitation that made me curious.

'They know not to push it. The Russians can play a clever game when they want to.'

'Cleverer than the West, perhaps.'

'They have shown that.'

I had the sense, as often, arriving in a country, of waiting for the key to decrypt it: the one that made sense of things and brought disparate pieces together. It was always a shared narrative – not the events that made it into the papers, but the prism through which they were viewed; the stories told at home. The meeting had gone well in so far as proving to myself that I could live my cover. I didn't feel any closer to understanding what I was doing here.

'And the police – are they cooperative? Trustworthy?'

'No more or less than the UK. We are not Nigeria.'

I nodded, gazing across a country that wasn't Nigeria and

considering the world's gradations of prejudice. Then one looming building caught my eye. More than a building, a sprawling residential fortress on the horizon. It stood away from the others, slightly monstrous, centred on a tower with a spire, additional wings of various heights appearing to have conglomerated around it, each with its own battlements. It would have been chilling at the best of times, but it had an extra layer of uncanniness here. I thought of the CGI clip.

'What's that?'

'That building? That is the Triumph of Astana.'

'Know anyone who lives there?'

He laughed.

'I have always wondered who lives there. People making money and people making trouble. It is not a place I have ever been.'

THIRTEEN

When I was back in my hotel room, I watched the clip again, studying the view beyond the window, the glimpse of exterior visible, the shape of the room's own windows. Money and trouble. We were in the Triumph, I felt sure.

I paid it a visit. According to property sites, the Triumph of Astana had 480 apartments, plus shops, restaurants and a cinema. The closer you got the more outlandish it seemed, a fusion of Stalinist and baroque, evidently modelled on the Seven Sisters apartment blocks in Moscow. Stalin had demanded those skyscrapers as a point of pride after the Second World War to compete with Western ones. They were heavier though, and to achieve a scale commensurate with twenty million dead had to expand outwards, mutating as they rose. Their silhouettes haunted the Moscow skyline, and even before I knew their origins I thought they had the cold gravity of war memorials. They made you realise that the scale of other buildings was not born of necessity but a cultural sense of the humane.

Last night the Triumph had been lost in the storm. Twenty-two floors high in the centre, rising to a pointed tower with wings either side, eighteen floors each. Four hundred and eighty apartments. Which one did I appear in?

It felt strange crossing the threshold, onto a polished chequered floor, smiled at by a guard. I felt an urge to ask if he'd seen me before. I headed towards the supermarket, bought a gift box of nuts and dried fruit, registered the various security cameras.

The residential apartments were accessed past a concierge controlling barriers to a set of lifts reserved for occupants. Akhmetov was the most common Kazakh surname. I told the concierge I was here for Mr Akhmetov. Could he call up for me? He said he'd need an apartment number. Behind him was a screen with time and date display. 6 December. The date on the clip was 13 December, a week away.

I found an internet café a few minutes back towards the centre. I wanted to check for photographs of the Triumph's interiors. The café was small, no cameras. Good for anonymous searching. Or so I thought.

A young woman at the counter put down a medical textbook when I arrived. I asked to use a computer and she asked for ID.

'What kind of ID?'

'Do you have a Kazakh ID card?'

'No. I'm from the UK. I'm here on business.'

'Then your passport.'

'Why?'

'It's the law.'

'Since when?'

'Since last year. For security.' She looked apologetic. Her face said: *Obviously this should not apply to wealthy white Westerners, but the law is the law.* 'We are sorry.'

'No need to be sorry. That's fine. That's good.'

Joanna had sent the email from a place called KS. If they were as rigorous as the café I'd just tried, then I had a potential lead to whatever ID she was using. I found KS on Daraboz Street. It turned out the initials stood for Kiber Sports, or Cyber Sports. You had to knock to get in. It was small, with booths divided by plyboard screens. One security camera focused on the door rather than the PCs. The 'sports' in its name presumably related to the old arcade machines at the back.

Two men in their early twenties sat behind the counter, working on a broken hard drive.

When they asked for ID I gave them the Bell passport and watched them make a photocopy on an old beige Xerox. They scribbled down the details in a logbook then assigned me a PC and wrote the number down too.

'Can I see which computer I used last time?'

They looked confused. I took the sign-in book before they could object, leafed back to the date Joanna was here. I ran a finger down the page until I got to the right time. Eleven people signed in that afternoon, one woman: Vanessa McDonald.

The handwriting was Joanna's. Joanna in a hurry. They even had which PC she used.

'I want that one. Number three.'

I got the booth, with a grubby PC and a torn leather office chair. When I clicked into the control panel, the IP matched my records. She'd been sitting here. I checked files on the desktop, then searched the browser history for that date. It had been wiped.

More recent searches involved a lot of porn. The computer was running anti-block software. The country had a blanket ban on adult websites, so a lot of these cafés put on various forms of circumvention and made their money selling access to that part of the web. I sifted through the searches for various sexual practices, through Kazakh sports sites, social media, scrolled slower through news and local politics, but couldn't see any leads.

I went up and paid.

'One more favour. This woman, Vanessa McDonald,' I pointed at the name. 'Presumably you took a photocopy of the ID.'

They found it. The passport matched the name she'd given. In the passport photo she had shoulder-length brown hair. I wrote down the passport number.

'This mark beside it – the star. None of the others are marked.'

'She didn't pay.'

'Why not?'

'She just got up and left.'

'Do you have CCTV footage?'

'No. The cameras don't work.'

'Did the woman seem scared when she was here? In a hurry?'

'In a hurry.'

'She was hurt,' the other one said. He gripped his arm. 'Maybe injured.'

FOURTEEN

I bought a fresh MacBook from an electronics store in the Keruen mall, unboxed it two floors down in Big Ben Coffee, beneath a painting of the London skyline and the dictum *Love Coffee, Love People*. I got on the wi-fi, downloaded a Virtual Private Network to mask my identity and ran a search for Vanessa McDonald.

Plenty on open source, but it was the sixth hit that caught my eye: a *Telegraph* piece eight months ago on blacklisted journalists trying to report from Russia, Ukraine and Belarus.

> The dangers journalists face in Russia have been well known since the early 1990s but concern over a number of unsolved killings has soared in recent months. Now Western writers are reporting threats and obstruction. Those refused entry to Moscow-allied countries this year include Martin Yates, Rachel Hodgkinson and Vanessa McDonald.

I searched 'Vanessa McDonald journalist'. Top hit, curiously, was a right-wing Russian discussion board devoted to media figures deemed unpatriotic. One member had uploaded a crowd photo from the Remembrance Day of Journalists Killed in the Line of Duty, observed in Moscow every December, if not unanimously. Joanna's face had been circled.

Anyone know this bitch? She caused trouble in Warsaw. Looking for address, phone number.

The individual who posted it gave a name that translated as *Russian Truth*. A 'patriot'. It was only their second post. Russian Truth suggested Vanessa McDonald worked for an organisation called Reporters for Human Rights.

This all struck me as the kind of information you put out there if you're trying to build a cover identity: name and photo ID and backstory. Enough to make Vanessa McDonald real if someone was trying to establish her credentials.

The *Telegraph* journalist who'd included her name in the article wasn't one I knew as being a 'friend of the department', in Six's terminology, but the *Telegraph* was cosy with the intelligence services. It could have been slipped in at any level, including source.

So someone had put work into establishing her cover. If she was playing a campaigning journalist that was good reason not to be too visible. But people would run searches. Hits like this would be convincing. The organisation she supposedly worked for, Reporters for Human Rights, had a website on which it described itself as a ground-breaking organisation using documents and video footage obtained both openly and covertly to tell the stories of people suffering at the hands of oppressive regimes. *Our writers and film-makers tap into a network of human rights organisations and workers in the countries concerned, some of them at enormous personal risk, to expose corporate abuse, modern slavery and political violence.* No names came up on the site, for obvious reasons, just an email address and a guide to PGP encryption for those who wanted to get in touch with a sensitive story. It got good dirt, some military documents, governmental papers: Standing Rock, Occupied Territories, water disputes on the border of Uzbekistan.

I clicked tabs of the regions where they worked: Belarus, Philippines, Sri Lanka, Kazakhstan. Under Kazakhstan there were images of prisons and oil pipelines, a quote from a UN report on ongoing detentions, a detailed report on the arrests of individuals associated with a charity called Testimony. That was the most recent story.

Testimony were less cagey. Established 1993, their website listed offices in both the old capital and Astana, which was unusual – most of civil society had stayed in the more attractive, bohemian Almaty. That had been part of the thinking behind Astana, perhaps: no one wants do-gooders complicating utopia. Testimony investigated disappearances, unlawful imprisonment and the use of torture. I checked their address.

The office was inside a crumbling building on the unfashionable right bank. It looked like someone had recently put a battering ram through the door. The wooden sheet that had been hammered over as temporary protection prised open easily enough.

Inside it was dark. The few windows were small and dirty. I left the lights off. The linoleum of the hallway floor was blackened where a fire had been started. Water damage had done the rest.

To the left was Testimony's small office. It had been trashed. Posters, leaflets, ledgers, old filing cabinets opened, one beige PC askew on a desk heaving with paper. There was a sulphurous stink of wet paper and ashes. All the drawers had been opened and rifled, so I took a seat and sifted handfuls of paperwork: it came from lawyers, doctors and journalists, documenting activists who'd been arrested, recording of assaults, threats sent to families. The correspondence gave me staff names and contact numbers.

The director was a woman called Elena Yussopova. I knew the name. She collected evidence of human-rights abuses. A brilliant lawyer and writer, her charity maintained additional offices in Moscow, Grozny and Tashkent, staffed by individuals who'd made their peace, one way or another, with the price on their heads. If you spend your time fighting the violent, powerful and corrupt there are two approaches: be discreet or be very visible. She'd gone for the latter. In truth, neither was going to keep you safe.

A few years ago, Yussopova's husband, also a lawyer, had been found bloodied and unconscious with a fractured skull in the lobby of their apartment building. He died in hospital two days later. Police declared it the result of a hit and run, and nothing to do with the oligarch he'd been investigating. No one went to prison for it, of course. Since then she'd been outspoken. Was she acquainted with Joanna?

I found Yussopova's mobile number among the printed emails. She answered with a brisk, *'Da?'*

'I'm a friend of Vanessa McDonald's. Is this a good line to talk?'

Yussopova sounded hesitant.

'Who is this?'

'My name's John Sands. I occasionally work with Reporters for Human Rights.'

'No, it is not a good line.'

'Can we meet? I am very worried. I cannot locate Vanessa.'

'Nor can I. You are in Astana?'

'I have just arrived.'

She gave the address of a café and said she could be there in an hour.

I swung by my hotel, set up email accounts in the names of Reporters for Human Rights and John Sands. I missed having access to Six's Changeling software which gave you the ability to spoof any email address and send messages under that identity. But sleight of hand got you a long way. The Reporters for Human Rights email address was .org. I set one up at .co.uk. and emailed myself an urgent few lines about tracking down Vanessa. I sent one to myself from Vanessa, backdated to last week, saying everything was going fine and she had spoken to Elena Yussopova. I changed out of the suit into a shirt and jumper.

Unprofessional, I thought. Unprepared. A step closer.

FIFTEEN

Yussopova's café of choice was in Saryarka district, north of the railway line, where the industrial and poorer residential areas remained. Bare parks showed empty pedestals, snow piled up where the communist heroes would have been. The café sat opposite a war memorial. A statue of a grieving mother towered opposite the grate for an eternal flame, which had gone out. Mounds of chrysanthemums and gladioli lay frozen across a slab of pink marble. A bride and groom posed by the memorial, having their photograph taken, a tradition in this part of the world that had always struck me as odd but also in some ways understandable. Life, death, the realm of serious things: the submission of lives to the nation. Her dress was brighter than the snow; the groom wore a scarlet bow tie. After five minutes the newly-weds piled back into a VW people carrier and it sped off towards the next photo opportunity. Elena Yussopova walked in.

I glanced at the street outside. There was a better chance she was being tailed than that I was, but I couldn't see any new vehicles. She was alone. She was unmistakable, lined face accentuating a hard brightness in her eyes. Her hair was dyed dark red and she looked frail, eaten away by fury. She clutched a phone and a packet of cigarettes, studied the place and clientele as she approached. Then she studied me.

'John?'

I shook her hand.

'Thank you for meeting me so quickly,' I said. 'This is obviously terrifying for Vanessa's family. For all of us.'

She took a seat, ordered a coffee. I showed her the emails. Yussopova read them, handed them back.

'You work with her?'

'Yes. But more than that, I'm a friend.'

'When did you arrive here?'

'Yesterday.'

'Have you had any trouble?'

'I don't think so.'

'No one following you?'

'No. What's going on? What's happened?'

'We don't know.'

'When did you last hear from her?' I asked.

'Three days ago. You?'

'She called on Monday afternoon, around three p.m. UK time.'

'And she hasn't gone back to London?'

'No.'

'We thought perhaps she'd just left. It was only when your organisation contacted us, saying you'd lost track of her, that I worried.'

So someone else had called; someone else was missing her.

'Obviously it's sensitive stuff she was working on,' I said.

'Yes.'

'How did she explain the project to you?'

'She said she was making a documentary about Western oil companies in Kazakhstan. She wanted to highlight our work. That is right, no?'

'Yes. We've been amassing evidence of environmental abuses for a long time. Where was she staying?'

'I don't know.'

'When you spoke to her three days ago, did she say she had any plans? Any concerns?'

'No. She was excited. She said the project was going well. I think ... she had something.'

'What do you mean?'

'I don't know. Andrei knows more about it – the communications director, Andrei Nichuskin. He is flying back from Armenia at the moment. Did she not tell you any of this?' Yussopova asked.

'She said she had something. I got the impression it was even too sensitive for her to give us details at this stage. She thought our encryption might have been compromised. She was going to tell me in London.'

My cover was limiting how much I could ask while remaining credible. At the same time, I had no networks to draw upon.

'What happened at your office?' I asked.

'An attack. No one has been caught.'

'When?'

'Two days ago.'

'Do you think it connects to Vanessa?'

'Maybe. But there is no shortage of enemies. Have you told police about Vanessa?' she asked.

'No. I take it you haven't mentioned anything.'

'As I say, until now I wasn't sure. And the police may not be on our side.'

'That's why I'm here. I wanted to assess the situation first. You haven't had any contact with the British embassy?'

'No.'

'Do you have any sympathetic contacts, in police or government? Someone who might be able to help?'

She laughed. 'Sadly not.'

A man and woman came in, took a table one away from us. I checked the street and saw a black Renault SUV outside the café. It hadn't been there before.

'Do you know somewhere more private we can talk?' I said. Yussopova looked around, understood.

'Follow me,' she said.

We walked to one of the old apartment blocks nearby, a five-storey Khrushchev-era block with thick knots of ice spreading from drainpipes across the pavement like tree roots, making the approach treacherous.

Once inside, we climbed narrow stairs to a triple-locked security door behind which was a surprisingly ornate apartment, with crowded bookshelves and a writing desk covered in leaflets and loose papers and copies of *Literaturnaya Gazeta* from Moscow.

I wondered if this was where Astana's intelligentsia gathered. Yussopova went to a small kitchen at the side and put a kettle on. I checked my phone, picked up the emissions of recording devices nearby.

There was a radio on the desk. I put it on to drown our voices. Russian hip-hop. I turned it up. A framed photograph beside it showed a family of four, including a thirty-something Yussopova and her murdered husband. There was an unframed one of Yussopova being dragged away from a protesting group, megaphone in hand. There are good people, then people who will die for the good. It's a different breed, and one that always fascinated me. Joanna used to joke that I spied on them to find out what morality meant. I wanted to know what made them tick, but I didn't idolise them. It was a mistake, as a spy, to think you preserved good conscience through being detached, but at the same time, when your job was following the various strings being pulled in all directions, morality came to seem a question of when you chose to turn away. It was an attempt at simplifying, and could start to seem like a form of defence, if only against the unknown. These were just some of the attempts at self-justification I'd made over the years.

Without getting too close to the windows I checked sightlines: nearby apartments with a view, somewhere you might stick a camera. The same black Renault SUV was on the street below – one man sitting in it. Yussopova came back with tea. Then she noticed the music.

'Did you turn the radio on?'

'I usually do. We've had some serious issues with intelligence companies.'

She nodded.

'Please, sit down.'

I moved papers to sit on a sagging sofa, balancing my tea.

'Who exactly did Vanessa meet?' I asked.

'She met a lot of people.' Yussopova assumed I knew most: fellow activists, lawyers, even some oil-company reps.

'If she had run into trouble with authorities, where might she be held?'

Yussopova shrugged. She listed police stations and prisons. She had no idea where Vanessa would be.

'But there is a precedent for individuals being held in secret, without due procedure?'

'Yes, but usually word gets out after twenty-four hours or so.'

'Did she have a car?'

'I don't think so.'

'Can I see exactly what she was working on?'

We looked through recent campaign material. It covered disappearances, deaths in detention. There were names and organisations familiar to me from campaigns against labour conditions in the Persian Gulf. The biggest file was marked simply 'Saracen'. Saracen Oil and Gas Exploration was a UK-registered energy company. The file contained FOI requests, diagrams of governmental connections, lists of UK figures on the board.

Saracen had been bought up by a British fund billionaire called Robert Carter. They'd drilled a few speculative holes and were now excited enough to be looking to expand their role in Kazakhstan: extraction, transportation and more exploration rights were being sought. I picked up a tattered *Herald Tribune* clipping:

Carter, whose gambles on Central Asia have been increasingly stymied by geopolitics, has made what he describes as a last throw of the dice. Saracen have been in Kazakhstan for six years with little luck, accumulating an estimated 20 million dollars in debt on wildcat drilling. Carter's hope is that new technology will lead to fresh discoveries. But both rivals and shareholders claim he has paid well over the odds on a quixotic and personal mission.

Saracen weren't necessarily who you wanted moving in next door. Campaigning literature contained diagrams of corruption, evidence of lobbying in the UK, Brussels and Astana, evidence of slush funds. Then there was the use of private security, a company called GL5 who protected rigs and personnel, and the use of PR companies to cover up human-rights abuses. Finally there was the use of private intelligence firms to spy on Saracen's accusers.

'Do you know which private intelligence firms?' I asked.

'No. It is very secretive.'

'Do you think Saracen could cause Vanessa trouble?'

'They are a British company.' Yussopova gave another shrug. 'You would think they have more ... British values. But here, everyone becomes different. Now that Saracen has new owners, they are very aggressive.'

I studied a protest flyer depicting a drilling rig spouting drops of blood. Then I looked at the other work lying around: an article about the bribing of local officials, another that focused on online restrictions. Getting shared a lot recently was footage of an incident in which Kazakh police had detained an activist trying to unfold a poster in front of the Presidential Palace. He was expressing solidarity with an independent magazine shut down last month. The editor had been arrested and was now on hunger strike. Testimony were battling governmental censorship to get the story out.

'Things are starting to happen here,' Yussopova said.

'What kinds of things?'

'A revolution. In expectations, at least.'

'To an outsider, this seems quite a solid country.'

'Countries seem solid until they begin to change. Nobody in any of the Arab Spring countries would have predicted those systems could collapse. When there is a powerful police and security service, and a leader who is feared and respected, a lot of people think nothing will change. But systems are much more fragile than we think.'

'The Arab Spring didn't go so well.'

'We are a new country. There are more and more people online—'

Yussopova's phone rang before she could tell me that the internet was ushering in democracy. She took the call in the kitchen. I made a physical search for the listening device: bookshelves were good cover, a lot of visual information to lose a bug in; light fittings work, and mean you can mask the electronic emanations. Finally I knelt, felt under the table and found it. A disc the size of a ten-pence piece, attached magnetically. Inside was a voice-activated micro-transmitter. You wouldn't know what it was unless you'd planted a few yourself. I considered removing it, then heard Yussopova returning and straightened.

'Did Vanessa ever come here?' I asked.

'Vanessa? Yes, several times.'

'Did she help you with equipment?'

'She gave us laptops, phones. All more secure than the ones we had. She recommended software, VPNs.'

'Flash Free?'

'Yes.'

Nice to see Joanna had kept her styles. Flash Free was known among intelligence operatives as inherently compromised software, which meant whichever crew she was spying for would have access to all the activists' computers. I suspected Yussopova's concern was overgenerous.

'Vanessa has been so helpful for us,' Yussopova said. 'She is a brave woman.'

'She certainly is.' I took a final look through the anti-Saracen literature. 'Have you had any direct contact with this company?'

'Only petitions.'

We swapped numbers.

'What are you going to do?' Yussopova asked.

'I'm not sure. Please, please let me know if you hear the slightest thing.'

'I will.'

The black Renault followed me when I left.

SIXTEEN

The driver was European-looking. Tall in his seat, a touch of flab around the face, something very English in a former-military way. He kept close behind me. It was conspicuous: either a rushed job, a lack of training or meant to intimidate. I drove to Khan Shatyr and parked. I went into the mall, to the food court, got a coffee and browsed on my phone while my man sat on a bench on the other side of the court. I looked at what I could find on Saracen. They were headquartered in London, interests in Vietnam, Congo, Angola, Mexico. Evidently they found the Middle East too squeaky clean. Robert Carter had bought the company for £12.5 billion and the inflow of fresh capital had funded its Kazakh forays.

London would be waking up around now. I gave Olivia Gresham a call.

'Saracen Oil and Gas. Any feelings about them?'

'Saracen? Jesus, what are you doing with them? Is that why you're in Kazakhstan?'

'Possibly. What are they up to?'

'They think there's untapped fields still to be discovered under Kazakhstan. The Kazakh government took a lot of money off them for the honour of taking a look.'

'Have they been facing trouble over their activity here?'

'It's oil and gas – what do you think? Trouble from good people, trouble from bad people.'

'Who are the bad people?'

'Rival energy companies, I imagine.'

'Who do Saracen employ on the intelligence front?'

'Probably Vectis. Saracen were using them when they ran into trouble in the DCR. Know anything about this? Why are Saracen so hot for Central Asia all of a sudden?'

'I've no idea, but you'll be the first to hear if I find anything.'

The watcher was still there, still surreptitiously keeping an eye on me. That afforded me a good look at him. He was ruddy-faced under a peaked cap, greying blond, with a slight curl to the hair, blue-eyed, pink-skinned. There wasn't a team – he didn't have surveillance skills. I was definitely dealing with former military.

I made another call to a friend at Kilgariff & Co, a private intelligence outfit big on energy.

'Do you work with Saracen?'

'No, Vectis have the Saracen contract. Why?'

'Following leads. Thanks.'

I knew Vectis Global Insight, as much as anyone did. Boutique, headquartered in Mayfair, crammed with former MI6 of all stripes. The company sold a range of underground services to big corporations. Their website advertised 'strategic advice and analysis for leaders operating in complex environments'. There were a lot of complex environments and the blue-chips paid well. You won't find 'espionage' on their books, but you might well come across 'security consultancy', a trail that led via a listed Georgian building to some less respectable corners of the earth. As a rule of thumb, with PI companies, more wood panelling meant fewer moral scruples.

A lot of them appeared in the 1990s. The intelligence budget was down and taxpayers' money spent on arms and assassinations was a shit-storm waiting to break. British businesses said something had to be done – they needed to compete and had money to spend; why couldn't they just give the money to MI6 and access the desired muscle? That didn't look good either. Companies like Vectis appeared, a whole realm of shadow intelligence agencies with complex relationships to the state. MI6 officers knew them as potential future employers, often useful, occasionally making difficult environments even murkier. The ones we called white-hat companies could advertise their services up front: they relied on a combination of retired police and military with enough old-boy connections willing to check the odd database for them, armies of poorly paid interns stitching together passable reports. Black hats went the extra mile. They solved problems in ways the client didn't want to know about, and their front windows were accordingly opaque. They cost more, and were usually worth it.

Vectis was black-hat. Set up by Callum Walker, former SAS, former SovOps desk in Six. I knew this because he'd tried to recruit me a couple of years ago. We'd met at one of those posturing, closed-shop conferences that spies get invited to, where CEOs and former foreign secretaries mingle. Walker seemed to know a bit about me. Out of curiosity and habit I agreed to drinks at the Special Forces Club the following evening. I figured that an open channel to Vectis would be as useful to me as I was to them. At the very least we could avoid treading on each other's toes.

I wasn't interested in going on their payroll, but I liked Walker. He had a blunt, straight-talking style rare in the intelligence services. He seemed more at home in the private sector. He enjoyed showing me the club, hidden behind an unmarked door in Knightsbridge, photographs of fallen comrades across the walls. Now he was putting surveillance on me.

I called Vectis as Robert Carter's PA and got client levels of deference. I said Carter was heading to Astana and wanted a point of contact. I was told Callum Walker was there now, staying at the Hilton Garden Inn. They wouldn't give more than that but said they'd ensure he got in contact asap. I hung up and began to move.

I paid to go into the spa, reversed my jacket, exited through staff doors. No sign of the tail when I got down to my car.

The Hilton was smart without being ostentatious, stretching the length of a central block just north of Lovers' Park. As far as I could tell, the park got its name from a bad statue of two lovers in its centre. Current conditions weren't going to sustain flesh and blood romance. The hotel gazed optimistically across it. In a few months the view would thaw.

A young receptionist was smiling as soon as I'd cleared the doors.

'Has Callum Walker checked in yet?'

She consulted her computer.

'Yes, he checked in yesterday.'

'Which room?'

'Two zero three.'

I went up. A Do Not Disturb sign hung on the doorknob. No answer when I knocked. I took a glasses case from inside my jacket and removed a device the size of a phone battery that had made my life a lot easier on several occasions. The beauty of globalisation meant that one firm produced 60 per cent of hotel card locks. And every single Onity key-card lock has a DC power socket on the base, a small circular port beneath the lock used to charge up the battery and program the lock with the hotel's own site code. Which means when you plug into the socket, you can read the key from the lock's stored memory, play it back and turn the handle.

I was about to walk in when a voice behind me said, 'Stop there or I'll shoot.'

SEVENTEEN

His voice was calm, semi-automatic pistol held steady as he approached from the end of the corridor. It was my follower from the black Renault.

'Hands out, buddy. Let's see them.'

I raised my hands.

When the gun was at my head, he said: 'What are you after?'

'Joanna Lake.'

'She's not in there.'

'How many guesses do I get?'

He tapped me above the ear with the barrel, directed me along the corridor to the emergency stairs. We descended. I had visions of service levels, basements with bins into which a body could be folded. I was prodded into the first-floor bar.

The hotel had gone for a low-lit, burnished copper theme, which suited the Englishman neatly folded into an armchair, fingers interlaced. The place was empty apart from staff and two expensively dressed women in a far corner. My chaperone had made the gun disappear. We were just three men looking like business.

'Elliot Kane,' Walker said.

'Callum.'

Walker's suit was crumpled. His eyes suggested an overnight flight. He had a moustache that might have looked businesslike to some but said nothing to me aside from former-military.

He looked like a man who had just flown into Central Asia because of an almighty fuck-up. I took a seat opposite him and a waiter appeared.

'Have a drink,' Walker said. 'Warm up.'

I ordered a brandy. Walker ordered a Scotch and a bottle of sparkling water. The guard declined refreshment. He had taken the sofa, back straight, hands clasped between his knees. His top button was tight around his throat. The years since military service could be measured in kilograms. Walker surprised me by pulling out a packet of Rothmans, lighting one with a plastic yellow lighter. He set packet and lighter on the coffee table, beside some pink flowers floating in a stone dish, leaned back, exhaled out of the corner of his mouth. The drinks arrived with a tray of cashews and an ice bucket. I took a sip.

'Where is she?' I said.

'We have no idea.'

'I don't believe that.'

He spread his hands, face grave.

'Vanished. I thought perhaps you lot might be doing better on this than we are.'

'Us lot? I'm not here on behalf of the British government. She contacted me. I came over.'

Walker looked sceptical.

'What did she say?' he asked.

'Not much. It seemed like she might be in trouble, though. I need to know what's going on before I give you any more.'

Walker splashed some water into his whisky. A gold chain rattled on his left wrist. Like his guard, he'd been somewhere a lot sunnier not that long ago; the skin of his ears and nose was still flaked.

'Who have you spoken to?' Walker asked.

'Not very many people.'

'Obviously, it's a sensitive situation.'

'I'm sure.'

Walker hesitated.

I pressed. 'Right now you're in more trouble than I am. You might appreciate my help.' This didn't get an immediate denial.

'You're working for Saracen,' I said. He tapped his cigarette, studied me again. I knew what threshold we were at – either I was going to be permitted entrance or not. In my experience it's the wrong time to push. I took a mouthful of brandy. There had been no suggestion they knew about the dead man. That was a card I held.

'Do Six know?' Walker asked.

'I get the feeling they have an interest. Why would that be? Have you not told them?'

'Vectis's relationship with your employer is somewhat strained, as you can imagine.'

'All sounds very delicate.'

I could relate to his impatience with the well-spoken, well-educated men and women at the top of Six and the FCO and the MOD. There was a no-nonsense edge of grammar school in his intonation, which endeared him to me. When we had last met he had described himself as a scholarship boy like me, army scholarship to Sandhurst in his case. You wouldn't have guessed that, before Six, Walker had spent four years in the SAS – not if your idea of the SAS was unthinking action men. In reality the SAS was defined more by mavericks, especially for Walker's generation. They had a restless drive. It meant their thoughts often ended up turning to making money, and they set about it with gung-ho confidence, a lot of contacts and not always sensitivity to the nuances of a business environment. Walker looked energetic and out of his depth.

'Well, I wish she'd tried to contact us.'

'How long had she been over here?'

'Six weeks.'

'And she went missing five days ago?'

'That's right. Last contact was on the morning of the fourth.'

'What was she doing?'

'Saracen are involved in a big deal over here. They've got a few active fields but want to buy a lot more. But their reputation is somewhat tarnished, shall we say, which means activists were on them before they'd even got going. When Saracen got taken over last year, the new owners hired a company called Piper Anderson Communications to try to clean things up. And Piper Anderson hired us. Obviously they needed to know who was doing what – in the environmentalist community, in rival companies, in the Kazakh government. So we sent Joanna over.'

'How long's she been working for you?'

'Six months.'

'Really? She only left Six in April.'

He saw what I was thinking: Six had a process for those jumping ship. Intel officers were precious and dangerous and sensitive, whether or not you still wanted to employ them.

'We had words. They weren't sorry to see her leave, it seemed.'

'Why not?'

'Falling-outs. Obviously I wasn't privy to the details. We softened her landing financially.'

'What did she bring for that? Intel? Contacts?'

'No.'

'But you headhunted her.'

'She approached us, actually.'

'Why?'

'Why not? We're a good employer, even if you seemed unconvinced. She wanted out of Six quickly, without losing too many pay-cheques. And she wanted a change of scene. We warned her the biggest danger in Astana would be boredom.'

'What did she say?'

'She said: "Good".' He stubbed his cigarette. A waitress tried to swap his ashtray for a new one and he waved her away. 'What did Elena Yussopova have to say?' he asked.

'Didn't you hear?'

'Come on, Elliot.'

'She thought someone might have approached Vanessa with information. Any idea about that?'

'No.'

'Did she have any kind of counter-surveillance team?'

'None.'

'She was here alone.'

'That's right. We agreed minimal contact. She was very much running her own operation. We offered backup, she declined.'

That sounded like Joanna. The bigger the team, the more conspicuous you were. Still, I'd never known her avoid risks. She was someone who liked to step outside the wire, in military parlance. I could see the set-up from Walker's point of view: you've got a pro, she says she can run the operation, you save a lot of money. You've won the contract over more established outfits because you promise the client more for less. And it's only a few eco-activists that you're messing with; not exactly Moscow rules. You're looking at the bottom line and someone's abducting your employees.

'Where was Joanna staying?'

'The Radisson.'

'Had she packed?'

'Yes. We've trawled every border crossing, every airline. There's nothing to suggest she left the country. Which just leaves 2.7 million square kilometres to search.'

'Did she have access to a vehicle?'

'Not to our knowledge.'

'Any hint that she thought she might be in danger?'

'Never. And it shouldn't have been a dangerous job. We gave her a few weeks to get us a picture of Kazakhstan, where it was

133

going. This is about oil in Central Asia, so obviously you're going to be prepared for trouble, but she hadn't reported any concerns. It was mostly planting bugs and picking up gossip: local media, local groups.'

'Was she armed?'

He looked at me, curiously.

'I've been generous. I think it's time you told us what you know.'

I wondered what Joanna was doing risking her life for an oil company. Maybe, after all the smoke and mirrors of Shefford, there was something honest about oil. It was real. Maybe she wanted to cash in on her experience. We'd need money, she had said. I couldn't bring myself to believe she was doing this for us. I imagined that moment of decision: the thought of Kazakhstan, ice and emptiness. The simplicity of it, compared with the hot and complicated places where we had operated on dubious pretexts. When Walker and I met at the Special Forces Club his job offer had reminded me of the conversation that led me over the threshold into Six: offhand, almost childish. 'Fancy a bit of adventure? A challenge? Not many rewards, but you'll have a chance to work off your own bat, explore the world a bit.' I had the sense that he wanted me there in the way we want good friends to share our vices, for both physical and moral companionship. What enticed Joanna to Vectis, of all companies? She wasn't someone who stumbled into things.

'Do Saracen know about any of this?' I asked.

'Our clients aren't interested in operational details. They're looking for oil, not missing investigators.'

'And they won't notice the sudden absence of briefings?'

'That's our problem. Obviously this is an embarrassment.'

'I hope, wherever Joanna is, she's not too embarrassed.'

Walker didn't bother defending the crassness.

'What do you know about her last movements?' I asked.

'She filed a report at nine p.m. on the evening of Saturday 27 November. Dined alone at her hotel. Staff saw her go up to her room, leave again around ten-thirty. That's the last we've got.'

'No pickup on cameras? Card use? Phone signal?'

'None we've got so far.'

The amount of resources not being tapped was agonising.

'Reported this to the police? They might know the terrain better.'

'Vanessa McDonald was supposedly investigating police corruption. Joanna Lake was a private-sector spy. Which of them do you want the police looking into?'

I thought through the legal situation. 'Clear as an oil spill' would be the generous way to put it: a former MI6 agent entering on fake papers, spying on Kazakh citizens, installing surveillance, hacking God knows what, and then Vectis waving guns around when it went wrong. As if sensing this – and keen for an out – Walker said, 'You worked together. Could this be something from the past catching up?'

What he meant was: maybe none of this is our fault. Nor need it be anything to endanger an energy deal. I'd considered this, of course. Most of the people from those days with cause to want her dead were either dead themselves, imprisoned or doing too well to cause trouble. People don't like stirring history up, certainly not off home ground. But it was true, we had worked together – Ukraine and Turkey. Joanna had also done stints in Serbia and Belarus. That's not a CV to help you sleep at night.

'There's no specific operation for which I think someone would still be seeking revenge. Does Vectis deal with kidnappings and rescues?'

'Not directly. We work with GL5 if we need muscle. She has full K&R cover if it comes to it.'

Fully insured for kidnap and ransom. Which could help you rustle up a holdall stuffed with used currency, or even some ex-SAS

135

types abseiling to your rescue. It rarely happened quite like that. I thought through the various options. If she'd been killed straight off it meant she was dangerous alive, that her silence was worth the noise generated by a murder, the obliteration of whatever knowledge she contained. Alternatively, it was a message: stay away. If she was captive, it was a question of what the captors wanted: money, leverage or information. Ninety-five per cent of hostages, the public never hear about: they're diplomatic tools, assets on the balance sheet. Companies have supposed policies on not paying ransoms and states have policies on not dealing with terrorists, but I'd never known either to be ironclad, it just means the press agree not to cover it. But situations got spun out over years. If the captors wanted money it was straightforward, although you'd expect demands sooner rather than later. If they were pressing her for information, the first you might know about it was a body dump.

'Are you monitoring her family?' I asked.

'We're keeping an ear out. There's been no contact. No whispers internationally either. All our offices have been chasing this.'

'I don't think she's dead.'

'Nor do we.'

It was time to get a closer look at Vectis. Walker wasn't telling me much, but I liked a challenge and wanted to know more about his set-up over here. I didn't believe the search for Joanna was being run out of Walker's hotel room. I was also curious about how they'd react to the video file.

'Is the cryptonym "Catalyst" one that you're familiar with?'

'No.'

'Have you come across anything connected to sophisticated technological deception?'

'What have you got?' Walker watched me carefully. I knew the calculation. You can't trust anyone, but you can't spy alone.

'Shall we adjourn somewhere less comfortable?' I said.

*

They knew just the place, it seemed. We took the Renault to an address in the business district, a rectangular block of mirrored glass. Walker swiped us in. The floors housed KPMG, PwC, software and construction companies. Ours apparently belonged to a law firm called White and Chase, with a desk and logo, a smiling receptionist, and nothing else whatsoever as far as I could see. We walked past empty conference rooms to a heavy door with keypad entry, into a windowless office with three monitors and a Faraday cage to block the transmission of radio waves. It was a secure compartmentalised facility: a SCIF, in intelligence community parlance. I was searched before we went in.

Inside I checked the technology – Dell screens, external hard drives, ethernet box on the wall. I produced my flash drive and they unlocked a safe in the corner, withdrew a Lenovo laptop with a USB port. It booted up to an empty desktop and factory settings. Walker inserted the drive. The guard stayed by the door at first. When Walker had watched the clip once he nodded consent and beckoned him over.

They watched it together.

'How did you get it?' Walker asked.

'She sent it to me.'

'No audio?'

'Unfortunately not.'

'Know the other man?'

'No. But I think this may be a room in the Triumph of Astana.'

'What do you mean "may be"?'

'It's faked.'

'Are you sure?'

'Given that I've never been there, it seems likely. Did Joanna assign cryptonyms?'

'No.'

'The video's titled Catalyst.'

Walker shook his head, blankly. 'You may not be the best person to be visible here,' he said.

'Well, here I am. So far I've only had one gun pulled on me today.'

'You say someone approached Testimony, that Joanna might have been in receipt of information from that source?'

'Elena Yussopova suggested as much. I couldn't get any more out of her.'

'Does she trust you?'

'I wouldn't go that far. She's not actively campaigning against me yet.'

Walker reached into a desk drawer and produced a single cigarette. He used a silver lighter with a small blue flame, pressed a button and a fan under the desk sucked the smoke away in a descending stream. Then he continued to watch me, assessing.

'What do you want?'

'Give me access to what you've got so far. I'll find her for you.'

He sighed. 'Do you speak Kazakh?'

'Of course. Who'd try and operate in a country without the language?'

'What's your current status with regard to Six?'

'I'm on holiday.'

'We would have to think how to do this.'

'Sure. It's a sensitive situation.'

Walker sat silently for some time, eyes open and bloodshot. I tried to imagine what he was thinking: maybe it was about the beach he'd recently been on.

'I'd like to send the footage for more thorough analysis,' he said, finally.

'Sure. In return for granting me access to her work while over here, the details of the set-up and information on the search for her so far.'

He nodded slowly, mentally checking through the requests one by one.

'I need to be clear,' he said. 'We're not in a position to go behind the backs of the British intelligence services.'

'You've been managing so far.'

He sighed. 'We're not entirely renegade.'

'Who do you liaise with at Six?' I asked.

'We have a few points of contact. I can't give you names.'

'But you haven't told them about this?'

'No. Why?'

'She came to me, not them. There was a reason for that.'

EIGHTEEN

I gave him my footage to send through to analysts. In return I got a glimpse of the hunt for Joanna so far. Staff in three Vectis offices, London, Berlin and Moscow, were trawling intercepts for any whisper. Walker gave the impression of big data coming in, which could leave you with a lot of haystack and no needle. He had contacts in intelligence companies that had more experience in the region but he was reluctant to go begging for help, as they were all competitors for the Saracen contract.

There were a few more complications. MI6, and the UK government generally, were unhappy about Vectis operating in Kazakhstan: a planned £2 billion sale of BAE helicopters to the Kazakh defence forces meant UK plc were putting a lot of effort into presenting Kazakhstan as a clean place to do business. Neither Saracen nor Vectis were helping.

I got an hour to look through the reports Joanna had delivered. I had to do it in the Vectis office, at an isolated desk, no phone, watched over by Walker himself, passing over paperwork deemed not too sensitive, clicking files for me.

It wasn't worth the effort.

She had spent most of her time monitoring what Vectis called IMGs – Issue Motivated Groups. As well as Testimony, these included the usual suspects: Greenpeace, Amnesty, opposition groups within Kazakhstan in so far as they were allowed to exist. Additionally, Joanna had mapped power structures:

clans, families, regions, departments, all webbed around the presidential family itself; what, in Six, we referred to jokingly as bribe maps. The EU and the UN were concerned about Saracen. Laws were being thrown around by rivals and their lobbyists. Shareholders got jumpy. Alongside the IMGs was what Vectis presented as 'Civil Unrest Analysis': the big picture.

Data, hacked or otherwise, was processed in the UK, analysed, written up and fed through to the PR and lobbying company who had hired Vectis on behalf of Saracen: Piper Anderson Communications. They served as the buffer between a FTSE-listed energy company and people affixing listening devices to coffee tables. I knew Piper Anderson – Lucy Piper used to be head of communications at Downing Street. First time I encountered her she was escorting the PM around Basra, corralling press as they documented a new school for girls. Piper Anderson offered an all-in-one package: lobbying, damage limitation, agenda-steering, legal muscle, cleaning of the internet and subversion of any opposition. If you wanted a think tank promoting the concept that human rights thrived on the discovery of oilfields, it would be blogging by breakfast, academics on-message, with politicians having quiet words to journalists over lunch. They had a lot of former ministers on their board.

Piper Anderson hired spies so the corporates didn't have to.

I read through Joanna's reports on political groups and systems of decision-making in the Kazakh government, and the tone was flat. A quick search revealed that a lot of it was gleaned from subscription to other intelligence companies like Stratfor, which was common enough practice but not for Joanna Lake. Some came straight from the *Oil and Gas Financial Journal*. I could see why Walker wasn't worried about a sudden absence of product.

More useful was a brief summary of those rivals with skin

in the game. The US energy company Chevron had big fields in operation in Kazakhstan and had brought over at least three private intelligence firms. Turkey and China both saw Central Asia as their backyard, fielding fierce resources out of vast and well-practised intelligence services. Russia's FSB loomed large. Then there was Kazakhstan's own intelligence service: KGB remnants, like most post-Soviet states. That was worth remembering.

Between their Sigint and Joanna's inquiries they'd counted eleven other intelligence operations currently active, state and private, all in relation to Kazakhstan's energy sector. Astana was what the Germans called an *Agentsumpf*, a spy swamp. Things heated up in an *Agentsumpf*. The chaos bred a sense of impunity, of minimal blowback. You ended up giving each other cover. It got messy.

Potential threats to Joanna: first up, rival energy companies who knew she was Saracen-connected and wanted to stop the company's expansion. Less likely: activists who'd rumbled her cover and felt aggrieved. Then there were always local political thugs who bought into the cover and might not have liked Vanessa McDonald nosing around. One long-shot involved individuals whose feathers she'd ruffled in the course of her MI6 career and who had chosen their moment to exact revenge. There was the possibility she'd been thrown to them by colleagues for whom she had become inconvenient; there's always someone who'll do your dirty work for you. It would have been quicker to establish those who didn't want to kill her.

I watched some of the documentary footage she'd shot. She interviewed off-camera so I was denied her face. Still, I heard her voice. She interviewed a guy called Craig Bryant. He was a sub-contractor for Saracen; his company, Auracle, had been bought up by Carter around the time he purchased the oil company. It provided tech support for rigs and pipelines. He sat in a bland office with some data pinned to the wall, looking awkward, ingratiating, played. He hadn't expected criticism, starting out on his pitch:

... You've got a thousand kilometres of pipeline – no human's going to be able to monitor ...

Then, when she started throwing around stats on environmental destruction and political corruption he spent some time trying to convince her it was all more eco now and he didn't know about politics.

According to her reports, in the following weeks they went on some dates. You could see from phone records that he'd been trying to call her since she went missing.

'That's bold. She interviews him and he asks her out.'

'Plucky. But it seems he's that kind of guy. Skirt chaser.'

'You've looked into him?' I asked.

'Superficially. He's American, born Sandpoint, Idaho, MIT grad, worked in technology all his life. Been dropped in by Carter to manage drone operations over here. He's done some consultancy work for the NSA and spoken a couple of times at CIA-related organisations like the Brookings Institution, but that's the extent of it as far as we can tell.'

'Know what exactly these drone ops involve?'

'They have high-end sensors – optical, chemical – which help with maintaining pipelines, detecting any leaks or pollution, assessing reserves.'

If Bryant struck Walker as worth pursuing, he didn't show it. I searched through the notes on their investigation so far. There were her recent ATM withdrawals, card payments. The repetitive, unenlightening interviews with hotel staff. A copy of her itinerary as Vanessa McDonald, making her documentary.

I looked through for the detail that could help me and saw nothing.

Then I found it.

11.50 a.m. on 26 November there was a purchase on her Vanessa McDonald NatWest debit card. $11.99 at Zara, Mega Astana shopping mall, followed five minutes later by a coffee at the mall's KFC.

You look for things happening on the hour, the half hour. Gratuitous things. Out of character. Joanna was a coffee snob. Given the choice, she'd risk operations before accepting fast-food coffee. 800 tenge, or just under two dollars, to the Colonel. 11.55 a.m. Before going shopping she'd been at her hotel.

I brought up a map. There were two closer shopping centres. I checked the shops on offer at those and they were pretty much the same. It was a big diversion to buy some earmuffs and an overpriced Americano.

So, according to the map, she crossed town, past two larger malls, to be at Mega Astana as the clock struck twelve.

She was meeting someone.

'Any more from this visit?' I asked.

'No. Think it's significant?'

'I doubt it.'

If I was right, these were strange protocols. Telling nothing to your employer – no pre-contact threat analysis. No post-contact briefing. Maybe this was how they did it in the private sector, but it certainly granted an officer autonomy.

'What are you going to do?' Walker asked.

'Go back to my hotel, shower, think. I'm going to need money, at least thirty grand cash in dollars, tenge and rubles.'

This got little more than a cheek-scratch out of Walker. In my experience, people trust you more when you're pushy. They think they know what you want. Walker said he'd have to clear it.

'Sure. Not with my name attached, though. You're my sole point of contact.'

'Of course. Trust me.'

144

He was nervous about me asking around and suggested that I stay in or close to my hotel until he'd spoken to the Vectis board in London. We agreed that unless there were any dramatic developments we would meet the following day for lunch – I'd be picked up at a specified location and brought to the office. Finally I was dropped back at my car.

I waited until the guard and his Renault had disappeared, then drove away from the Hilton towards the Mega Astana mall.

NINETEEN

It was an unattractive, large grey box that made little attempt at enticing Astana's population. But it didn't have to, it seemed: the car park was full. A giant inflatable snowman shook in the wind, speakers broadcasting 'Jingle Bell Rock'.

I walked in, checked the layout, found the shop she'd been in. The section with earmuffs gave you a clear view to the entrance, across the store; a chance to scan for watchers. She was here for a reason.

Most of the security cameras throughout were basic domes, with a few distinctive box-style cameras at intervals. A company called MicroDigital made a lot of money around 2014 installing security cameras across Central Asia. Cameras were sold with remote internet access enabled, and default passwords that rarely got changed, and even if they were, still allowed infinite password guesses without locking you out – all of which meant you could remotely tap into the video feeds. From there, it was a back road into the whole network, including archived footage. MicroDigital's slapdash approach to password security had opened up plenty to me over the years, from branches of AT&T in Ankara to the Golden Times Bath House in Tblisi.

I opened my laptop, downloaded a port scanner, scanned for the ports. A quick browse gave me cameras and routers. Default passwords didn't work, but they were susceptible to brute force attack. I found the router's IP address and model number, sent a message to Marius at Evotec: I needed Stefan Janikowski. He confirmed that Stefan was still in Riyadh and I was authorised to make direct contact. They gave me a new job code and contact protocol.

I called.

'I hear we're back in business,' Stefan said. 'Your people change their mind?'

'I guess so. I want you to take a look at something.'

Within half an hour Stefan had control of the router and was reconfiguring the network rules. Another fifteen minutes and I was sitting in my Hyundai Tucson with the control board of the security operations centre on my laptop. Twenty-one cameras in total. Archived recordings went back two weeks. I checked for KFC. Three cameras covered the area around the fast-food restaurant. It was straightforward enough to search by time and date.

I didn't notice her at first. She wore a short blonde wig beneath a knitted hat, with heavy-framed glasses. She carried a shoulder bag and the package from Zara. She bought her coffee and sat down, opened a HP notebook, glanced towards the entrance.

No one came.

Five minutes later she was still sitting there, scanning the place from behind her laptop. She checked her watch, then closed the device, got up and left.

I watched it again, disappointed and puzzled. Then I went back to the control board.

Several years ago MI6 realised physical brush passes – an agent handing a file over hand to hand – could be unnecessary in an age of short-range wireless data transfer. They devised technology akin to Bluetooth, using a particular radio frequency to transmit the data. It gained popularity when encryption became strong enough to neutralise the risk of interception, and receivers became small enough to fit into regular-looking devices. Enabled devices needed to be within a range of twenty metres.

Who was around?

We'd been taught that if a hostile party is watching for an officer to make a brush pass they'll check the people in your vicinity. But surveillance teams rarely think – or have the means – to look vertically. And in a shopping centre, twenty-metre radius in all directions can give you a hundred people to profile.

There were a lot of candidates, but after half an hour I had a favourite.

Directly above the KFC, on the upper-level food court, was a Dunkin' Donuts. At one minute past midday a man walked in. He was in his twenties and jumpy. He wore an identical blue puffa jacket to the corpse I'd seen last night.

He bought food and a drink, sat down, set up his laptop. Grey, brimmed cap pulled low, scarf up. As close as you could get to obscuring your face without becoming conspicuous.

The timing synced closely with Joanna's. They left within a few minutes of each other. He got to his feet, looked around, moved off fast. The tray remained on his table, food untouched.

I watched three more times and then I was sure. Her man delivered information. He'd got something. He was a source that required extreme caution, one that she'd decided not to disclose to her employer.

Plenty of potential reasons for reticence. Certainly in Six, where potential agents required a complete risk-profile and managerial clearance before you could engage them, it was worth sidestepping bureaucracy at first. And then, even buried under codenames, they were on the system, and systems leaked.

Who was he?

No news of any individuals reported missing.

I speculated a timeline: the next day they meet at the rented apartment. He's packed quickly, ready to leave. Something's gone wrong. They've been discovered. She tries to call me before leaving. Perhaps they know their phones are compromised.

But only she got away.

She fled, injured, sent me the video file then ran. Where would she run?

I drove out, towards the block I'd visited last night. As I was approaching I saw police parked outside. A full forensics team was active. I kept driving in the direction of the internet café. She'd been heading due north. I stopped and checked a map. I was heading beyond the edge of the city. There was an hour or so of daylight left and I thought I'd make use of it.

Time spooled backwards as you left Astana, shiny buildings becoming construction sites, bare frames, then grey foundations, then rubble. I passed a police car sitting in the shelter of a billboard with the President's face and the words: *Project Astana 2050*. Then you reached the desert.

It took a while to adjust. With the city still in the rear-view, the emptiness stretching to the horizon on either side was less inhuman. You couldn't tell if it was snow or stone or dust, the landscape was just pale grey and lifeless, strewn with loose rocks like a seabed. A sign warned that it was 200 kilometres to the next town. Tufts of grass and the occasional tamarisk bush stubbled the emptiness, then even these died out. The road divided a lunar landscape and was the only thing in it.

Did she run this way?

After ten miles I turned the radio off. The silence was seductive. I stopped the car and felt my soul expand – stretching – searching for other life. The possibility that the rest of existence was a fantasy flickered and grew. I zipped my jacket up and stepped out of the car, turned around. An eagle hung in the air, as still as the landscape beneath it. I crouched and pinched some of the lifeless rock dust, thought of Mongol hordes pouring across it. Lives adapted to the uninhabitable. No wonder, when they reached the civilised glories of thirteenth-century Baghdad, its mosques and libraries and courts, they burned the place to the ground.

When I got back inside the car there was a message from Tom Marsh.

They're looking for you. They know we met.

TWENTY

No answer when I tried to contact him. I sent a message to Stevenson. He sent through an ID for Threema, an app that encrypted voice calls. Plenty did, but Threema was the one that didn't require a phone number or email address. I downloaded the app, entered his ID and he answered in seconds.

'Where are you?'

'I took a holiday.'

There was a long pause. I could hear a soft exhalation that constituted various entreaties. Eventually he said: 'How does it look?'

'She was working for Vectis Global Insight,' I said. 'Under cover as an activist. Client's an energy company, Saracen. Would you ask around? She may have come here because it's a good place to hide. She may have had other reasons. I think she started working off her own bat, recruiting sources. She was on to something.'

'I was about to warn you not to go over there.'

'Why?'

'Astana's coming up high on global risk assessments. The Foreign Office has been debating travel advice. I can't establish the source or details. I don't know what, if anything, it has to do with Joanna.'

'Any word on the trouble in Shefford?'

'I'm still trying to find out. I'm in touch with Tom Marsh. He's been questioned again.'

'Is he okay?'

'Not particularly.'

'Have you had any trouble?'

'Not yet. You've made contact with Vectis?'

'Yes. The boss is over here: Callum Walker. I'd be interested to know if he's ever had anything to do with Russia, and who he's in contact with in Six.'

We agreed to speak again in twenty-four hours. I looked into Vectis, using a combination of open-source research and calls to acquaintances working at some of their rivals. Beyond its oak-panelled façade, Vectis was a global company with a staff of over three hundred analysts and seventy technology special-ists. As well as the Mayfair HQ and some Gloucestershire labs there was an office on Madison Avenue and one in Berlin on the south-east corner of the Zoological Garden with a dedicated cyber-monitoring station. The firm had recently acquired a leading computer forensics and data-recovery company, which meant it had its own hackers.

I knew how it worked. Data would be processed and writ-ten up by a team of analysts in the UK, some with technical backgrounds, some experts in relevant industries or regions. Finished reports could be seen by anything up to fifteen people: there were the founders, who were mostly former MI6, then an international advisory board comprised of senior figures from industry and government. Far too many former spooks for my liking. Several of the names were familiar: an ex-chief of MI6's counterterrorism branch; another SAS man who became Six's head of commercial liaison. Vectis's co-founder, Fergus Chatwell, was former head of station in Germany. Its management board included two Conservative MPs, both whom had sat on the Joint Intelligence Committee.

I called the Hilton where Walker was staying, and inquired about rooms on the floor above his own. They had one which, by my estimation, should be directly above Walker's room. I booked it, then called Stefan.

'I need you in Astana, Kazakhstan. Bring your kit.'

'Kazakhstan?'

'It's peaceful here. And everyone uses Windows 95.'

I confirmed fees for the job and he said he'd be on a flight that evening.

I was left to think about Joanna's double life as Vanessa McDonald. The interview with Craig Bryant had stuck with me. So had the following courtship. Both Joanna and I knew that things happened on operations, through boredom or necessity or both. Neither of us pretended that made anything easy for a partner, or even excusable. Our general philosophy was that sleeping with individuals while under cover was bad form unless really necessary.

She'd interviewed him. Footage showed a keen, optimistic technocrat. Her reports for Vectis suggested a womaniser with a drink problem. They'd had a meal at Le Dessert near Bayterek, drinks a couple of times at somewhere called Restobar, even gone to the cinema.

Then came Bryant's repeated calls and messages:

Drink? I'll be at the usual.

I hope I haven't done something to upset you.

You okay? Let me know you're okay.

I checked his company online. Auracle Geospatial Science was a technology start-up that collected and analysed data from satellite, aircraft and drone platforms. There were examples of their work on the website: locating and surveying leaks, monitoring gas emissions, security, detection of oil spills and damage, the inspection of offshore oil platforms and flare stacks.

The Auracle office was in Astana's Special Economic Zone,

an industrial park in the heart of the capital: ten acres of tax-free start-ups occupying low, windowless units, the whole place surrounded by corrugated fencing and razor wire. According to the list of businesses at the front gate, Auracle shared it with a lot of warehousing and manufacturing plants for everything from pharmaceuticals to diesel engines.

I couldn't get in without the kind of high jinks that were liable to see me arrested, but I suspected Auracle kept most of its business out of the office anyway: the production of satellites and lenses, the drones themselves. They'd need an office to arrange bribes for launch licences, somewhere to shoot the vodka, get the tax benefits.

From what I could tell, a lot of their work involved what, in the service, we called MASINT: Measurement and Signature Intelligence. I first saw the phrase in training, as we were familiarising ourselves with the various acronyms. MASINT was where it got weird. MASINT covered the data that human senses weren't able to receive: ultraviolet and infrared radiation, alterations in the electromagnetic spectrum, variations in the gravitational pull of the Earth. These were monitored using hyperspectral sensors. All sorts of things revealed themselves.

Most of the interest for Six was in relation to collecting data on weaponry and bomb tests. It was only when I saw it being used by BP in Azerbaijan that I became fascinated by the imagery produced. I used to stay behind in the offices, scrolling across the data maps of Central Asia. Oil miles underground showed up as hydrocarbon particles in surface soil and water, but the more recent past was down there too. You could see the outlines of destroyed cities thousands of years old, make out mass graves, the Stalinist ones identifiable by their regular shape, then the fainter sites of what must have been Mongol and Scythian massacres.

Bryant's geographical routine had been mapped by Joanna

first, then Vectis as they searched for her. It didn't deviate much; expats cling to routine and Astana offered few temptations. Office from 9 to 5, then an address on Saryarka Avenue which turned out to be a bar called The Rocks. After eight hours roaming the hyperspectrum, he hit the bottle hard.

I liked the sound of The Rocks. It was the sort of place I would have sought out eventually anyway. A city has currents like any sea. It was useful for a spy to know the places where loneliness swept a man. Whenever I arrived on a new posting I let myself be carried.

It was almost 5 p.m. Bryant would be getting thirsty.

The Rocks had a four-leaf clover in neon above blacked-out windows. Inside it was dim, cramped, walls painted black between mirrors. The space was divided equally between a square dance floor and a darker, UV-lit bar area with stools around barrels. Clientele were nearly all students, starting to trickle in wearing miniskirts beneath fake fur-lined parkas. You could be pretty much anywhere.

Irish pubs were lucky places. The Guinness sign served as a beacon for intelligence agents around the world, looking for corruptible locals and homesick Westerners. My favourites included McGettigan's in Jumeira, The Blacksmiths in Moscow, Molly Bloom's in Tel Aviv – high times, career-defining recruits. You found CEOs and construction workers democratically levelled by alcoholism; local men and women estranged from their own kind for whatever reason, offered refuge by Celtic tat. And locals drinking with Westerners were halfway recruited already. You found prostitutes and pickpockets, just occasionally an actual pint of Guinness. In short, everything you could want.

The young man behind the bar noticed me as soon as I came in. He was tall, muscled beneath a white T-shirt, with sharp eyes and a quick smile, the bearing of someone running things.

'Hello,' he said in English.

'Evening,' I replied, happy to play the foreigner.

'American?' he said.

I laughed. 'Do I not look Russian?'

'Your clothes don't look Russian.'

'English.'

'Pint of beer?' His English was good. Good English in a place like this usually signalled frustrated ambitions. Fixer material.

'You read my mind.'

My beer came in a frosted glass with a puck of ice in the bottom. The barman welcomed me to Kazakhstan. I imagined him in a country at war, where his combination of charm and street knowledge would come into its own. I tipped well and hoped I did not play a part in his life.

A guy beside me with a ponytail was busy on his phone. I saw Twitter, checked his handle, then looked him up on my own phone. He was Dimash Nurtas, a guitarist. Some of his tweets were in English, mostly about music, some politics: retweets about a pro-democracy demonstration by students in Uzbekistan. He had a few international followers.

'Twitter working?' I said. 'I couldn't get it.'

'With a VPN.'

'Which do you recommend?'

'Cloudflare.'

'A lot of people using that?'

'Yes.'

'Do people get angry about the restrictions?'

'Everyone.'

I leaned back against the bar and watched the room. Too early for the dancefloor, but the music was loud. It was Western in style – electronic beats, bassline – with lyrics in Russian and sometimes Kazakh. I tried to hear the lyrics, gauge what the youth of Kazakhstan were dreaming of.

'Been in Astana long?' the barman asked when I got my next drink.

'I've just got here.'

'If you want a bar with girls, you know, a nice place, I can recommend one.' He lowered his voice. 'In London it is like a party town. Yes?'

'Non-stop.'

A suited man at the end of the bar got his attention. I watched out of the corner of my eye as the barman slipped him a small package in exchange for several notes. Then I saw who was buying.

Bryant was tall and too smartly dressed for The Rocks, but younger than he seemed in Joanna's interviews. He could have walked straight out of Wall Street or Silicon Valley. Blue shirt, frameless glasses; bright smile with a touch of desperation. Deal done, he got a round in for a lot of the men at the bar, some of whom knew him.

I positioned myself beside him in the queue for the bar and let him hear me order.

'Someone with the Queen's English,' he said. 'That's music to my ears.' He shook my hand. 'Craig.'

'Toby.'

'What brings you here?'

'To The Rocks, or to Kazakhstan?'

'Both.'

'Kazakhstan for business. Got in yesterday. The Rocks for fun.'

'One day in and you found The Rocks already!' He clapped me on the back. 'You chose a fine time of year to visit Kazakhstan. What's the business?'

'I'm looking around for some investors.'

'Let me guess, hungry for untapped markets. Exploring this exciting new part of the world.'

'Something like that.'

He grinned knowingly, drank deeply. His cufflinks were sand timers.

'How's it working out for you?'

'Seems an interesting time to be here. What about you? What brings you to Astana?'

'I do tech stuff. For the oil industry mostly.'

'Good industry to do that for.'

'It has its moments.'

I bought us more drinks. We grabbed a barrel with stools around it. I wanted to steer him towards revelations, the dark side of this place, his relationship with Vanessa McDonald.

'The oil work ever bring you any issues?' I said. 'I mean, is it still the wild east – gangsters, oligarchs? You get exposed to that?'

'The company I work for does. It's just a question of—' He rubbed his thumb and finger together. 'Bakshish. Whatever.'

'Pretty corrupt?'

He shrugged. 'In the US they only call a place corrupt when the bribes stop working.'

He talked about different nationalities in the city – Saudis, Turkish, Iranians – and about good places to eat and drink, where to find the political class and where to avoid them. He had a story about the President's daughter demanding satellites from an oil company so she could run a TV station. I could see why he was good for background intelligence: atmospherics, as the Americans called it. I could see other reasons Joanna might have taken solace in his company. He was good-looking and overconfident, and a bad choice in terms of her operation, all of which had piqued her interest in the past. There was a wryness to him that I liked, a dark shadow to the optimism. I had come across unadulterated optimism all too often in Iraq and Afghanistan: American men with the same Brooks Brothers suits, fuelled by a faith that the world wanted to grow towards the innocence of their childhoods. It grew sour in the end. Bryant drank with a thirst I suspected had developed since he arrived.

'Is it safe here?' I asked. 'Expats had any issues? That's what a lot of my clients ask.'

'Mostly safe, yes.' He hesitated. Something made him check his phone. He put it away, glanced around. 'There's ten men for every woman here. Are you up for moving on?'

'Sure.'

'Ever been to Chocolate?'

The Chocolate Room was a nightclub by the river, tucked into the base of the Radisson hotel. I drove us there, parked a few metres away from the luxury cars outside the club itself. There was a commotion going on when we got there: the side window of a Porsche had been smashed. I caught a glimpse of figures running across the street, bouncers giving chase while on radios. We were inside before I had a chance to see any more.

The place was large and conspicuously expensive, with a stage and a dancefloor, booths around the side. On the stage, topless women sat in giant gold picture frames that swung on chains. People on the dancefloor paid them little attention – daughters of oligarchs dancing with practised moves as if they were audition-ing for a part. Bryant asked for a table in the corner. For the price of a bottle of champagne and six shots we got a red velvet booth from which you could watch the show and talk undisturbed. He waved away some escorts.

'See that outside?' I said.

'Yeah.'

'Get much of that?'

Bryant shrugged, sipped his Cristal.

'Not yet,' he said.

'What do you mean?'

'This country has a problem: it's called forty-dollar barrels.

The price of oil has sunk. That means the sweetener's running out, economic brakes slammed on. Which is fine for those strapped in.' He gestured at the dancefloor. 'But the people outside ... People start to care about democracy when they can't buy what they want.'

'Right.'

'The government needs a deal from somewhere.'

'There must be room for more outside energy investment.'

'Yeah, maybe.'

'What tech exactly do you do for the oil industry?'

He kept his eyes on the dancefloor as if the question was mildly distasteful.

'Collect data and process it. Data from magic technology.'

'Satellites?'

'Satellites, drones. Sometimes even guys on the ground.'

'For Chevron?'

He smiled. 'Not a bad guess. I'm with one of the littler guys though. Saracen. Know them?'

'They're in Vietnam, right?'

'They've got fields in 'Nam, Mexico. They buy them up, flip them, sell them to the majors for a quick profit. But Kazakhstan's got under their skin.'

'Should I invest in Saracen?'

He hesitated, the smile on his face turning more enigmatic.

'You could do worse,' he said. Then he shook his head ruefully. 'Seriously, I'd be killed for talking about this stuff.'

'Really?'

'High stakes. And not the most gentle crowd.'

'People get hurt?'

'Can do. Will do, no doubt. Why?'

'Just feeling out the landscape.'

'Well, let me tell you: you're going to need a stomach for risk doing any business around here.'

'This place has plenty of oil still to come, right?'

'Sure, oil's oil. But times are changing. The President's not going to live for ever. He's walked a fine line: tight with Russia, but giving us crumbs – oil crumbs, investment crumbs. That arrangement's not going to last for ever. He's, what, getting on for eighty? There's no succession plan. He's kept it that way deliberately.'

'Where do you think the trouble will come from? Islamists?'

Bryant laughed. 'These guys wouldn't know a Koran from a JC Penney catalogue. The trouble will come from the big guys next door.' He tilted his bottle. 'China, Russia.'

'A guy I met yesterday was talking about container traffic from China being on the up.'

'Doubled last year. Only danger is the Chinese don't know when to stop. They're buying agricultural land, housing, you name it. People aren't happy.'

'Better than Russians getting it?'

'They *like* the Russians here. There's an old Kazakh proverb: "To be the captive of the Chinese is a tight noose — with the Russians, it is a wide, open road."'

'Sounds like a Russian proverb,' I said.

'Every country needs protection. You have the US. No one wants to be independent without being strong. Anyway, the Kazakhs aren't so worried about infrastructure. They don't like losing land.'

'They've got enough of it.'

'But it's how they identify. You've got to understand psychology. There's so much of it, it's everything. That's Kazakhstan.'

Another girl came over and he started chatting to her. She looked Indonesian. I went to the toilets where there was crushed ice in the urinals and a guy wearing a tuxedo rapping Kazakh into his phone. The escort had gone when I returned and Bryant was staring into space.

'Why's there ice in the urinals?' I said.

'Why is anything?' He shook his head, then tried to drink from an empty glass. I topped him up. He was drunk now. He asked if I wanted to do a line and I said I was okay. While he was in the toilets, I watched the topless women swinging in their picture frames, skin dusted with glitter. I sipped champagne and imagined being Bryant, stuck out here, living the routine as Joanna had figured it. Every expat is an exile of sorts, looking for something to grip onto. You're free to remake yourself, try things out, which means you end up confronted with who you are. Then you start drinking. I was drawn to these men and women, all on the run from something, not only because my job depended on exploiting their vulnerability. Bound in with their dreams of self-enrichment – bound in, even, with a hunger to see the world – was always a desire to disappear, and I knew how that felt.

Bryant returned and we leered over the dancers, discussing which we found most attractive.

'Are you dating?' I asked.

He pulled a face. 'It's tough. When they hear you work in energy, it's two-hundred-dollar meals for a blowjob. Kazakh women just want to marry you. They want a ring and a visa before you get their number. Funnily enough, the one woman I clicked with was an eco-activist.' He looked at me to check my amusement, and maybe something more, sensing he was on uncertain territory.

'Nice. Maybe she was spying on you,' I said. He nodded philosophically.

'We'd had a few drinks together. You know, I thought maybe she found it kinky. Then she stops returning my calls. Perhaps that was, like, revenge for me working for the oil industry. Maybe that was a protest.'

'Was she Kazakh?'

'English.'

'English? Working over here?'

'Making a documentary.'

'Did she film you?'

'A tiny bit. But she wanted Kazakhstan. I think she had a romantic idea of the place: dudes riding across the steppe, eagles on their wrists. She asked me about oil companies and human rights. You know, liberal. I was the baddie. I fuck up the planet.'

'Isn't it risky doing that kind of campaigning over here?'

'Depends how you go about it. I'm still trying to get my head around this place. There's tensions, around oil especially: workers' rights, people getting moved for new drill sites. I chatted to one old Saracen character about communities they were displacing and he said: "I thought they were nomads."' Bryant gripped my arm. 'Can you believe that? "I thought they were nomads, why can't they just move?" Jesus Christ. Stick around, Toby. It's about to get interesting.'

I helped him finish the Cristal. He had that early-stage alcoholism where inebriation hits sudden and profound. When he leaned in to speak our stubble rubbed and his hand found my knee. The coke didn't seem to have sharpened him.

'You shouldn't drive,' he said. 'We can share a cab.'

It was an interesting proposition.

We got a cab back to his. At a new development behind the governmental district, Bryant told the driver to stop. He clambered out, sank to his knees in the snow, the driver shaking his head as he waited for his fare. I paid, helped Bryant up and got him into the right block and to his door. The flat itself was plush, impersonal, with a lot of grey and white. He sat on the sofa and watched me, a slow, seedy smile spreading as if he'd realised something, then fell asleep in his suit. I searched the place, then searched his phone. 'Vanessa Campaigner'. I scrolled back to their earliest exchanges. She had sent the first message.

It's Vanessa. You were great. I don't know what you were worrying about. I owe you that drink.

To which Bryant replied:

Glad I didn't embarrass myself. Things are crazy at moment. Next week?

I can wait ;)

I had never known Joanna to use an emoji. But then she'd never formally asked me out for a drink. From what I could tell, Bryant wasn't chasing any other women in Astana or anywhere else.

You never know with people. That was what I'd learned in fifteen years manipulating their souls. The closer you look, the more things come apart. One of the big shocks is how readily people will remake themselves for you, shape themselves to your own desires. The power could go to your head.

I saw his dilated pupils in the light of the Chocolate Room. *You're going to need a stomach for risk.* He'd run a long way from Idaho, that was for sure. I took a photo of his door keys, left him snoring.

TWENTY-ONE

I got a cab back to the club to pick my car up. I didn't want to leave it there overnight. And I was still wide awake with champagne and adrenalin.

My Hyundai was where I'd left it, windows intact. I pushed the snow off the windscreen and got in.

A car screeched to a stop in front of me as soon as I pulled out, blocking my way. It gave a brief flash of police lights. I turned my engine off as a man clambered out. He was uniformed. No backup vehicles. One man remained in the police car.

They must have seen me coming. Which was okay, I told myself: letting me get to the car suggested a scam rather than a hit. They'd been loitering where the rich might get caught, expats especially. I didn't know the alcohol limit here but I'd be well over. If that was the worst of my problems I could handle it. I wound my window down.

'Is there a problem?'

'This is your car?' The officer spoke Russian, voice hoarse, eyes heavy-lidded. A functioning alcoholic, forty-something, tall enough that he had to stoop to the window. There was a faded gravity to his jaundiced eyes. A moustache among the stubble seemed like the remnant of a frayed uniform. I spoke Russian back, badly.

'*Ya ne ponimayu.* I don't understand.'

'Your car?' he said in English.

'Hire car.'

'You've been drinking.'

'One beer.'

'You are not in good condition to drive.' He wasn't in good condition to police. His breath was flammable. 'Papers. And keys.'

He took the paperwork and car keys to his vehicle and came back with an old breathalyser, then made a show of tutting when I blew. I went along with this. They hadn't radioed in to base. Whatever performance going on was restricted, which suited me.

'Step out of the car. Come with me.' His English was proficient. The reasonable English spoken by people who needed to fleece English-speakers.

'We can arrange something,' I said.

'Come.'

I followed him to his car, got in the back seat with him. There was a younger officer up front. The car was filled with cigarette smoke.

'Where are you from?' the older officer said.

'The UK.'

'Here on business.'

'Yes.'

'Oil.' He smiled.

'Something like that.'

'You get in trouble here, as a foreigner, it is very bad. Kazakhstan is not England. You would find the prisons very dangerous.'

'Prison?' I fumbled with my wallet and made sure he saw money. 'Tell you what, we can forget this, can't we? My company would kill me if I got in trouble.'

'Four hundred thousand tenge. I give you paper, no more problems.'

Four hundred thousand was ridiculous, the better part of a grand, but who could blame him. This conman was growing on me. There was an air of seniority amidst the vice, a conflict that told a story. I imagined a whole portfolio of petty corruption under his control, which opened more doors than those engaged in it usually realised. He'd have connections above and below, colleagues sheltering him, taking their own skim from nicer offices. I had always been drawn to people with ethical voids at their centre: they were more open to suggestion.

I counted out a few hundred pounds' worth of notes.

'Officer . . . ?'

'Shomko.'

'Officer Shomko, I've got a business proposal. You seem a helpful guy. I was just out looking for somewhere I might get a drink, meet some Kazakh ladies. I don't know this city and I don't want any more dealings with police. How about another few tenge, you show me somewhere I can get what I need.'

I showed more notes. The two men consulted one another, Shomko saying I was his, the young man negotiating his cut. Shomko took the money off me and thrust a handful of tenge at his colleague, who got out of the car with a final glance of disdain in my direction.

We drove to a place with a '24 hour' sign blinking by a small door into the back of what looked like an office block. There was no indication of what was available around the clock, but a vent beside it poured an inverted waterfall of scented steam into the night air.

'You are married?' he said, as we waited for someone to let us in.

'Divorced. You?'

'Divorced. You like Kazakh women?'

'Sure.'

'Do not marry a Kazakh woman.'

'Okay.'

We were buzzed in, hit by the smell of menthol and eucalyptus. A second door led to the front desk of a sauna and massage parlour. A girl lay sleeping on a sofa at the side under a coat. Four men played cards in a side room. A middle-aged woman sat behind the desk watching a Russian reality show. Shomko spoke to her about entry fees.

'What does he want?' the woman asked.

'What do you think he wants?'

'What's so special he gets a police escort?'

They haggled over his cut. Shomko quoted me a price.

'You trust this place?' I said.

'It is the best.'

'Are you sticking around? How do I know I don't get busted coming out?'

He said he'd wait, folding the money into his pocket. I told him to get a girl himself, paid for both of us. The woman rolled her eyes and told Shomko to shower. She gave us towels and keys for the lockers.

Eyes in the steam watched us pass. There were dead branches in a basket by the door, leaves on the floor. I heard the rustle of birch branches against skin as men swiped themselves.

'Go steam. Your girl will collect you.'

'Okay.'

Shomko got changed into a towel and disappeared. I went towards the steam then doubled back to the changing room and prised open Shomko's locker.

His wallet contained some kind of prayer card, Viagra and ID for the National Security Committee, which made my heart sing. Lt Aslan Shomko from the regional department of the NSC, essentially the old KGB with new insignia and less ideology, so it covered a lot of policing, border control, drugs.

There were betting slips and numbered tickets: *Bolim Lombard*. Lombard was Russian for pawn shop.

I put his belongings back, feeling hopeful. Midlife crises were where I stepped in. They came at just the right moment, when an employee was well connected and utterly desperate – you wonder what you have put those years in for, kissing arse. You stumble into me. I'm the pleasure you've been denied. I respect you.

In the end I declined my massage and went for a swim, keeping an eye out for Shomko. When I saw him return I joined him in the changing rooms.

'She give you good service?' he asked.

'Excellent.'

'Sometimes they are—' He made a hand-chopping gesture. Efficiency? Violence? I wouldn't have drawn out an erotic encounter with Lieutenant Shomko. 'Still, I got you a bargain. Usually, Westerners, they make you pay more.'

'Money's not a problem.' I turned back to my things, letting the statement hang in the steamy air. 'So maybe you can help me again some time.'

'Give me your phone.' He punched his number in. 'You get in trouble, you have my number. Shomko.' He patted his chest. We shook hands.

He'd entered his name in my contacts as 'Helping man'.

In my hotel room I considered how best to use him. I thought back through the day, checked for a message from Joanna. Nothing. Just confirmation from Stefan that he was on his way, and the one from Tom Marsh: they're looking for you. It wouldn't be long before they found me. I needed to know how my own country's intelligence service fitted into this.

I shut my eyes and saw the Mega Astana exchange. You get a few bytes of data, travelling through the air like an infection. Shows you something you can't unsee, and turns you into a threat.

Two people in a room in the Triumph of Astana. What could be so dangerous? Was it me or him?

TWENTY-TWO

I tried unsuccessfully to sleep. I was averaging four hours a night. In my shallow dreams, when they did come, I was either in the room in the Triumph of Astana or in my hotel room, Joanna sitting by the bed, waiting for me to wake up.

I was woken by a knock on the door.

'Mr Bell?'

It was the receptionist. When I opened the door she stepped aside and a team of four men pushed their way in, forcing me back into the room and closing the door again.

'Take a seat,' one man said, in English. He wore a suit and holster beneath a grey winter coat. He gestured at the bed. There was another plain-clothes officer and two uniformed police as backup. One radioed confirmation that I was here and they were in.

No badges or warrants shown. The senior officer was tall, the long coat accentuating his height. He had paperwork in his hand: documents from the car-hire company.

'Mr Toby Bell?'

'That's right. What's going on?'

'When did you arrive in Kazakhstan?'

'Saturday afternoon.'

'Passport and visa, please.'

I gave him my passport and visa. He checked these while his colleagues checked the cupboards, moved the curtains, peered inside the bathroom.

'What are you looking for?' I asked. They ignored me.

'The nature of your business in this country?' the senior officer said.

'Why? What am I meant to have done?'

'You have hired a car?'

'Yes.'

'Have you been to Malakhov Street while you've been here?'

'No.'

'Would you unlock the safe please?'

I unlocked the safe and stepped back while he sifted its contents. Then he straightened.

'Get dressed. You come with us, please. It is necessary that we ask you some questions.'

'About what? What's going on?'

'Quickly. Then this will all be over.'

I dressed smartly, knotting a tie. The younger of the suited men took my passport and the key fob for the Hyundai. They led me downstairs to a black Audi with police lights on the roof. I was squeezed in between the uniformed officers.

'Where are we going?'

No answer. We drove north, the rising sun reflecting off the snow and glass, turning the city into fire. After fifteen minutes we arrived at an anonymous, new-looking building, four floors with bars on the lower windows. No state vehicles parked visibly outside, none of the aerials or antennae you'd expect on a police station.

I stepped out of the car. Ten metres of drive led to a narrow, bomb-proof door, with electronic barriers visible inside. Two men in black uniforms stood beside it. It looked like somewhere you went in rather than out. I felt the first stab of real fear. If I was going to run, it was now or never.

Six men against me, at least three carrying small arms, two that looked like they had some pace. Most stood to my left, between me and a six-lane road. Best option would be running towards them – past them – which was counter-intuitive therefore surprising; it meant they'd have to turn, with a complicated backdrop for sighting weapons, plus each other getting in the way. We were still in a public space, and these men were trained, which was sometimes a help: it meant they calculated, and that could slow you down.

There are always worse options than running. I would have the cover of two Land Rovers and then the corner of a building in approximately four seconds. Against a .22 or a .38 from a pistol, a car is going to be an adequate block. But once you start running you can't stop. That was game over. I felt a step closer to finding what I came for in the first place. And I don't really do running while being shot at.

The bomb-proof door led into a tiny security room lined with thick bullet-proof glass. I was searched with cold efficiency. My bag and phone were taken 'for security'. Then the officer on reception duty produced a device that looked like an iPad. He told me to press my fingers against the screen.

'What's this for?'

'Records.'

When they had their records I was directed into a corridor, through two sets of doors with swipe entry, each feeling like another layer of soil above my head, into an office. Not the interrogation cell I'd been braced for. The Kazakh flag was in place behind the desk, beneath a framed photograph of the President, who looked like the Dalai Lama compared to the individual sheltering beneath his gaze. He was small, with dark eyes and a dark suit, handkerchief in the breast pocket, which suggested an ominous amount of pleasure in his role. No computer, laptop or mobile visible. The phone on the desk was a corded black Siemens.

I could tell he was senior. I tried to read the room again,

noticed one other framed image on the wall: three men in traditional Kazakh clothing above a line of text: *If there is no owner of the fire, your motherland will be enveloped in flames.*

The man stared at me, tapping the Toby Bell passport against his desk.

I prepared myself mentally. Keep calm. But Toby Bell wouldn't keep calm, or quiet, and one technique for interrogation scenarios was noise. The more noise you make the fewer questions they can ask, the less chance they have of tripping you up. Outrage was a kind of silence of its own.

'What the hell is this? I've been here less than two days. I have no idea what's going on, but you've arrested a British national for no good reason. I believe your government has close relations with the UK, that a lot of potential investment could be jeopardised if Kazakhstan is seen to intimidate visiting business people at random.'

'You flew in last week.' He spoke calmly, in accented English.

'I flew in two days ago, from Kiev.'

His face was a mask, eyes showing neither doubt nor disappointment.

'The flight number?'

'I didn't memorise it,' I said. The flight number would be a step closer to tracing me to twenty-four hours in Zagreb, and I wanted to delay that revelation. He established my time of arrival and gave instructions to a man beside the door to go and check it. I wondered if they noticed that I didn't ask to speak to my embassy.

'And where were you before?'

'London.'

'But you have been in Kazakhstan previously.'

'Never.'

'Who do you know here?'

I told him about the meeting with Toreali, then asked who

174

exactly I was talking to. He ignored the question, asked for passwords for my phone and laptop. I refused.

'Why do you refuse?'

'Why should I give them to you? I haven't done anything.'

'What would we find?'

'Nothing.'

He asked who I had previously worked for, and then before that, going back years. After a while, as I'd been trained, I just refused, played indignant. I considered making noise about legal representation.

'When did you begin working for Vectis?' he said. So he had that much. Not great, but it made me quantifiable at least.

'I don't know any Vectis.'

'Saracen?'

'The oil company? I've got nothing to do with Saracen.'

He nodded as if he'd expected this disappointment, nodded to one of the guards. I was lifted up and removed from the room. Then things turned nasty. My hands were cuffed behind my back. We reached the top of steep concrete stairs down into darkness. Someone tripped me and caught me before I fell.

'Be careful.'

'Get the fuck off me.'

I felt the rising panic of powerlessness. Then I was slammed face first into the wall. Blood began to trickle into my mouth. The front of my skull throbbed, but I hadn't blacked out.

'Next time you fall down them.' One man turned me around and the other punched me hard in the stomach. I dropped to my knees, winded. There was a voice close to my ear.

'You think anyone knows you're here?'

It was a good question. The Lion Hotel's sleepy receptionist had some awareness of my predicament. Callum Walker knew I was in Astana; he didn't strike me as someone who'd make much noise in the event of my disappearance. Hugh Stevenson might

175

raise the alarm after a week or two. Was I about to find out how Joanna had vanished? About twelve people had witnessed me in the hands of the Kazakh state, and not one of them would remember if they were told not to.

I was uncuffed, given a wad of blue hand towels and taken back to the office. My interrogator hadn't moved, only the papers on the desk had been rearranged.

'You are sabotaging our country. You come here and bring trouble with you. We are peaceful and you create war.'

I shook my head and staunched the blood.

'You think there is no law here?' he asked.

'I've been in this country less than two days.'

'We know who you are, what you are doing here.'

'Apparently not.'

He opened a file and pushed a printout towards me, a poor-quality image of a man walking between a dusty Mercedes and a residential building with steps and an intercom. It took me a few seconds to think where I'd seen him before. It was the man with me in the fake clip. Here, he wore an open-necked shirt and sunglasses.

I tried to see the paperwork that came with it: *Catalyst in Astana*? It was MI6 paperwork, apparently intercepted and now stamped with the crest of Kazakh Anti-Terrorism. I knew that their anti-terrorism was run by a man called Rakim Zhaparov. His name came up in debates over the use of intelligence produced during torture. Identifying him wasn't entirely comforting.

'What is this meant to mean?' I asked. 'Who is he? Why do you think I know him?'

Zhaparov nodded to someone standing behind my right shoulder. A few seconds later a device pressed to my ear. There was a beep and then it felt like a nail gun had fired into my brain. I fell off the seat, temporarily blinded, arms wrapped around my head. Before I could recover, I was picked up and sat back down, ears ringing. I felt sick, and registered the beginnings of dread. What was that device? What kind of long-term effects were we looking at? I really didn't want to emerge from this mentally degraded.

'Tell us what you're doing here.'

'You've just got yourself in a lot of trouble.' My voice came out weakly.

'No, I think you really don't understand who is in trouble.'

I felt the electricity souring my muscles. Everyone has a breaking point, no matter how distant. What did I have to give them, even if I wanted to? What did they want?

The guards lifted me up, one on each arm.

'Have a think,' Zhaparov said. 'See if you remember.'

The doors at basement level were battleship grey with magnetic acoustic seals. The air was freezing. I was pushed into a cell, five metres by five, with a wooden bench along the back wall, uncuffed.

'Your clothes.'

'Fuck off.'

'Then I'm sure you don't mind if we undress you.'

They had restraint equipment – ankle cuffs, fabric restraints, stun belt. Four men, with more behind them. I undressed. They gave me a grey tracksuit, then someone threw a bucket of water over me.

'You have a right to be washed.' The door slammed shut on their laughter. I started shivering uncontrollably. I took the top off and used it to dry myself as much as possible. I tried to keep moving, heart pumping, brain working. I didn't have long before hypothermia set in. Options: I play along, giving fake information, buy myself time. Or I wait it out. They didn't want me dead. If they knew who I was, I'd be too valuable. If they didn't, they might be under the impression someone would care. I could try to scare them with suggestions of Toby Bell's own importance.

177

I knew enough about government and the diplomatic service – maybe get the embassy involved after all. Who knew where that would lead? The next flight back to London, most probably.

The door opened three times in the next hour. Once was a cursory check by the guards, once I was given a polystyrene cup of milky coffee. The next visitor was a man with a Russian accent. He had a goatee, black hair swept back so strands fell around his face, an expensive-looking cashmere coat. He saw me, shook his head and swore at the guards.

'Get him a towel and dry clothes.'

The guards looked disgruntled. A rancid towel was tossed at my face, then my clothes were returned.

'Come on,' my visitor said. 'Let's get you out of here.'

TWENTY-THREE

I wasn't in a position to say no. He led me back to reception, where I signed paperwork that declared my treatment at the hands of the security services had been impeccable. My other possessions were returned. A lot of men watched us leave; I had become quite an attraction.

'Animals,' my companion muttered.

He led me to a dark grey Land Rover with a suited driver at the wheel.

'Are you okay?' he asked.

'I've been better. Who are you?'

'My name is Sergei Cherenkov. Please, get in.' His English was good. The vowels suggested time living in an English-speaking country, maybe some education there. Our driver was thick-necked, shaven-headed.

'Where are we going?'

'Let's get some breakfast,' Cherenkov said.

We drove to a café with no lights on, but my companion appeared to know it would be open. The driver stayed in the car. The café owner turned the lights on for us. Cherenkov ordered teas.

'You drink tea, no?' He took a cigarette from a packet of Kent, looked around for an ashtray. The health warning on the pack was in Arabic. He wore rings on each hand.

'What the hell is this about?' I said.

'I work on cultural matters with the Russian embassy. I know Dimash Toreali. Did he show you the Palace of Peace and Reconciliation? I was advising him on an opera he wants to put on there. To sponsor.'

'And?'

'I was trying to get in touch with you, at your hotel. They said you'd been taken. It took me an hour to find out where you were.'

Toreali didn't know where I was staying, but I let this slide. Cherenkov was Russian intel – he could have surveillance on me or on the people who'd arrested me.

'What did they want?' he asked. 'Your captors.'

'I've no idea.'

The teas arrived with a glass ashtray. Cherenkov looked at them with an air of dissatisfaction. He browsed the menu.

'Would you like some eggs? An omelette?'

'No.'

He ordered himself some eggs. As well as the rings he wore leather bracelets on his left wrist, over a smudged tattoo.

'I am not happy at the way they treated you. They are basic, Kazakhs. They think you connect to a murder. I can see you are not a murderer. Could your embassy not help? Where are they?'

'I've no idea. I'm here on business, not diplomatic duties.'

'And what is the business?'

'I'm looking into some investment opportunities.'

He nodded, sipped his tea. Eventually he said, 'What if we said we knew where she was?' He met my eyes. His were bright. Then he looked away again, as if embarrassed.

I forced myself to say, 'Who?'

'We don't. No one does, it seems. But what if we found out?'

'What do you want?'

Cherenkov scratched his goatee.

'Building D,' he said. 'Shefford. I would like you to give me a glimpse inside. What has been going on there?'

I was transported briefly back to Bedfordshire. He had created the link I had been looking for, even if it led through unknown terrain. Joanna's disappearance connected to her earlier work. At the same time, he'd shown me his cards. When you know what your enemy wants, you're halfway to owning them.

'I've no idea what you're talking about,' I said.

'You'd let her die rather than helping me.'

'You've got me confused with someone.'

He nodded.

'The situation is this, Mr Kane: you are in trouble. You need a friend. Not ideal, a Russian friend, but here I am.'

'I'm leaving now. Don't try to stop me.'

'How could we stop you? At the same time, what are you going to do? I don't want you to be killed. But I think there are people who will kill you, Elliot. If any more unpleasant circumstances arise, we may not be in a position to do much. Then you will want to help us and it will be too late.'

Cherenkov reached inside his jacket. I checked my exit route, potential cover, potential weapons of my own. He produced a silver case, gave me a business card with the Russian double-headed eagle. *Dr Sergei Cherenkov, Assistant to the Cultural Attaché, Russian Embassy, Astana.*

'You're expecting me to work for you?' I said.

'In my experience, you're working for whoever keeps you alive. Help us or leave fast, that is my advice. Give me a call any time. We can find Joanna together.'

'Joanna who?'

He shook his head sadly. 'We'll give you a lift back to your hotel.'

'I'll walk.'

'Wrap up warm.' The eggs arrived and he spread a napkin on

his lap. I left the café, hailed a cab from the next street, took it to the centre of town.

So Russian intelligence wanted to know about Building D. Either Joanna's previous work had followed her over here, or she never stopped.

Stevenson called.

'We've got a small lead.'

'What is it?'

'A codename, issued June 2014. Perfect Vision.' He waited. 'Heard of it?'

'No. It sounds like software, a program of some kind.'

'That may be the idea. It sounds like software, but it's a hell of a lot more. Tom Marsh got a lead from an internal directory. I ran the name against what I could. The budget for Perfect Vision is hidden in Requirements and Production, but it's around seventy million over two years, including the use of Building D in Shefford Park. Building D had 130 members of staff cleared for entry at the peak of the operation last year.'

'That's huge.'

'Huge, maybe compartmentalised. I doubt many of them knew what they were working on.'

'What kind of staff?'

'A lot seconded from GCHQ. Others, from what I can tell, were academics – psychologists, an anthropologist, historians; experts in China, Russia, Central Asia. I've tried to get hold of them but every single one is incommunicado. It was officially designated a research group, but the security set-up suggests it was operational. It wasn't just producing papers.'

I thought back to Marsh's account, the isolation of this unit: separate entrance, separate canteen.

'Who ran it?'

'It bypassed all the usual committees. There was Defence

Intelligence involvement, so clearly the MOD was on board, but no one there has heard of it. Like Tom said, six months ago it disappeared as fast as it had arrived, a few days before Joanna ran away. What have you found?'

I said I had some leads, which felt optimistic. I told him I'd run into some trouble and had had contact from Russian intelligence.

'Surely that's a sign we need to pack it in,' he said. 'Come back. Get yourself killed on home soil, at least.'

The levity didn't conceal his fear. I said I'd take one final look around while I was here. When he'd rung off I found 'helping man' on my phone, memorised the number before deleting it, then went to a phone box and dialled.

TWENTY-FOUR

Lieutenant Shomko answered brusquely. When he learned who it was he told me to wait, and moved somewhere quieter.

'Who are you?' he said.

'We met last night.'

'I know we met. I asked: who *are* you?'

'I've got an offer for you. Meet me and I'll explain.'

'I cannot meet you.'

'Two hundred dollars, just to hear me out.'

There was exhalation, some cursing in Russian.

'Five hundred,' he said.

Good man, I thought. 'Four.'

'Okay. You bring the money. You mess me around, I arrest you on the spot.'

'Deal.'

He named a bar a long way away from the centre, said he couldn't get away from work for a couple of hours. That gave me time to prepare.

I took cash, an amount that would be a couple of months' salary for Shomko, split it between two envelopes taken from reception. I went back to the Mega Astana and bought a hunting knife, strapping it to my calf with a tubular bandage. Then I made a call to a friend who worked for GL5.

There was every chance Shomko would take the money and arrest me, and I'd had enough of that for one day. According

184

to Elena Yussopova's research, GL5 private security were plentiful and up for all sorts. The morning's events had been a wake-up call in more ways than one. I needed backup and I needed options for getting out of Kazakhstan fast and inconspicuously.

I knew GL5 all too well, had people I'd consider friends working for the company, had had my life both saved and endangered by them. At this stage in earth's history, it was hard not to encounter GL5. The GL stood for Global Logistics; the 5 was supposedly the five continents on which they operated, which counted Eurasia as one and suggested they weren't on Antarctica, about which I was sceptical. Most recently I'd helped negotiate two months' work for them in the Saudi desert training Syrian rebels. We'd crossed paths regularly since Libya, when they were the first security company to establish a presence post-revolution. They protected the British Embassy and so, to an extent, myself. Among intelligence officers, their base in Tripoli, behind Martyrs' Square, was known as a place to get a beer and a game of pool. Open the windows and you could smell the Mediterranean through the security mesh.

I called Jim Baillie, a former captain in the Parachute Regiment, now running GL5's cash transportation wing.

'Got anyone I can speak to about your Kazakh team? I need a hand.'

There was a pause.

'Trouble?' Baillie said.

'Not yet. Could do with a couple of bodies this afternoon though.'

I heard him exhale.

'Geoff Purvis is in Astana. He's a good lad, former Welsh Guards. I can make a call.'

Purvis himself called me twenty minutes later. He listened to my request.

'Reckon I might be able to help. Obviously there'll be a price attached.'

'I understand that.'

He asked if I could come to their base, which was in the grounds of the Saracen HQ. I said I'd be happy to pay a visit.

Saracen had taken over a sprawling former Gazprom compound on the eastern edge of Astana, with a helipad used for flying execs into town and geologists out to the drill sites. Purvis met me at the gates. He was tall, fair hair receded to a reserve line halfway back across his scalp, face flushed with what, up close, you saw were spider veins. His trousers were bloused into desert boots, paratrooper style. He gripped my hand and shook.

'So you're a mate of Jim's?'

'That's right. Not seen him in ages though. Thanks for meeting at such short notice.'

'You caught me on a good day.'

Purvis signed me in, gave me a pass. We entered the land of Saracen, past a relief map of the world with coloured lights for oilfields, under ornate ceilings where the raised hammers and sickles showed through new paint, to the GL5 compound at the back.

'Know Jim from Libya?'

'That's right.'

'Ever take you to Mama Tawas?'

'Once. The only brothel I've ever walked straight out of.'

Purvis laughed. 'Jim's one of the finest soldiers I know, but he's a dog.'

We crossed a broad expanse of concrete, past a helipad with a Sikorsky S-70, past a small heating and power plant. There were two hangars and a fuel storage area, then long prefabricated accommodation blocks.

The private security contractors that I could see were

heavily kitted out, if not visibly armed, most heading to and from the canteen.

'They fly in here, get trained, go out to the rigs, drill sites, fields,' Purvis explained. 'Every few weeks they'll come back for some R&R. The kind of places we operate aren't exactly rich with leisure activities.'

The canteen was large, with breeze-block walls beneath arched corrugated metal. Electric bar heaters glowed. Men in various combinations of uniform and civvies sat at long trestle tables. Liverpool played Chelsea on multiple TV screens. A sign at the bar said dollars accepted, and there were plenty around. Pre-9/11, private security contractors all seemed to be South Africans with rotten teeth. The men here were smart, steroid-pumped, with 200-dollar Oakleys protecting their eyes from the neon light. It was a multi-billion-pound industry now. Of the 21 billion dollars assigned for Iraqi reconstruction, over 30 per cent went on commercial security. Contractors came in to defend oilfields, and within a few months they were running aerial surveillance, searching for roadside bombs and staffing quick reaction forces. Politicians found they preferred their coffins without flags on them. The original teams had been built from the best: men from the SAS and US Marines. But you're not going to get 20,000 of those. GL5 swallowed smaller companies, picked up thousands of new personnel each time, then they turned to Peru, Columbia, South Africa, Eastern Europe – anywhere with a recent history of well-trained violence.

It looked like a lot of them had come off night shifts. Most were watching the game, yawning, smoking, drinking towards daytime sleep. I had never liked these places: the willed igno-rance about the surrounding country, the bubble of boredom curdling. But they could be useful. Where there were guns there was a sense of invulnerability, which bred an openness to all sorts of schemes.

The canteen offered a full English breakfast, which Purvis promised me was passable – 'No sheep's eyes. No horse sausage.' We talked football while we ate, then home generally; he wanted to know what was going on in England and I pretended that I knew. He gave me tips about Kazakhstan which amounted to not trusting lap dancers. I dropped a few names and places from Helmand, said I'd been in Sangin in 2006. We both knew Brigadier Rob Clarke and had survived raucous nights at Kabul's Serena Hotel. He got us mugs of lukewarm tea – NATOs, as they called them in the army: white tea, two sugars – and we talked some more about former jobs and then GL5. I studied the old regimental tattoos on his arms, and a fresher inscription: *Si vis pacem, para bellum.* I'd seen this tattoo a few times on my travels: *If you want peace, prepare for war.* Curiously, it seemed most popular with the mercenaries. I was never sure in what spirit it was intended. Over time it had gone from seeming like self-justification to an ironic echoing of the flawed logic that had shaped their lives.

'What do you want us to do?' he asked.

'Just be parked where I tell you to park,' I said. 'And if you see me running, open the door.'

'Straightforward enough.'

'And lend me a gun.'

Purvis sucked in a breath.

'What is this?'

'Jealous husband.'

'And you've only been in the country two days.'

'You know what it's like.'

'Is this jealous husband armed?'

'Hard to say.'

'Does he have his own backup?'

'I doubt it.'

'I'd need to speak to Jim.'

'Of course.'

Purvis wandered outside, phone to his ear, came back ten minutes later with a thumbs-up and an Adidas holdall. Inside it was a well-used Makarov handgun and a box of 9mm ammo.

'Seen one of these before?'

'Once or twice.'

'For every second this gun's in your possession it's nothing to do with us. Never was.'

I released the magazine, counted seven rounds; checked the chamber and reloaded it.

'I understand.'

'Where are you going to meet this jealous guy?'

I took out the address Shomko had given me.

'Casino Zodiak.'

Purvis found two men willing to accompany us. They shook my hand but didn't remove their shades. One drove; both were heavily armed.

The casino was in the middle of nowhere, which must have been what made Shomko feel safe here. It had a post-apocalyptic look, plastic-clad with dribbles of rust over the cladding from the bolts that held it in place. It was deserted. Cacti pierced the snow around the front. Industrial scrubland lay flat for miles around.

We were early enough to recce the place: emergency exit points, potential choke points, sightlines so you could see any vehicles approaching before they saw you. There was a car park at the back which allowed them to wait out of sight.

Inside, deep red carpets absorbed sound and, by the looks of it, a multitude of burning cigarettes. The gambling must have gone on behind the padded doors. No sound of machines or roulette wheels. The only staff member I saw was pushing a trolley of clingfilmed crab.

I found the bar upstairs, one man in a red waistcoat mopping the floor. When he saw me he put the mop down and went behind the bar. I got a bottle of expensive vodka and two glasses, found a back exit, then a window that let me watch Shomko arrive and confirm he was alone.

He slammed the door of his car and walked towards the entrance. I was back behind the vodka in time to watch him arrive.

He looked uncertain, eyes bloodshot. He hadn't shaved since the night before. He felt for his seat before lowering himself down, as if it might make a sudden move. There was ice in his moustache. He removed his gloves, kept his black woollen coat on. I poured the vodka, nudged a shot towards him.

'To the President,' I said, in good Russian. The language caught him by surprise. He studied me, then knocked the drink back, wiped his mouth, fumbled in his shirt pocket for a crumpled packet of Marlboro. He removed a flattened cigarette and lit it. I slid the envelope towards him. He looked inside, left it on the table.

'What do you want?'

'That's just for being here, a thank you. You can take it and walk away now.' I put the second envelope down. 'This is if you want to help.'

He took a deep drag and rested his cigarette in a heavy glass ashtray. I refilled our glasses.

'CIA?'

'No.'

'Take my number off your phone.'

'It's off.'

'Show me.'

I showed him. He sat back.

'They have a picture of you,' he said.

'Why?'

'They want to know who you are.'

'In connection with what?'

'I don't know.'

'I am someone who does a lot of business here and who cares very deeply about Kazakhstan. A man was killed in an apartment on Malakhov Street five nights ago. I'd like to know who he was and why he was shot.'

Shomko drew the envelope towards him and counted the money inside, then he split it, cramming half into his wallet, putting the other half inside his jacket. Emboldened by the currency against his heart, he relaxed.

'I know about it.'

'Okay.'

'There are a lot of resources on this.'

'Who is he?'

'I don't have a name. I can try to get one.'

'Who do people think did it?'

'They are looking for an English woman.'

'Where is the English woman now?'

He spread his hands. 'Gone. She bought plane tickets using a stolen credit card. Lufthansa to Frankfurt then on to Caracas, Venezuela.'

'Caracas?'

'That's right. They were never used.'

'How many tickets?'

'Two; for a man and a woman. Both in fake German names.'

This explained the lack of ID on the dead body. He'd stripped himself of identity before coming to meet Joanna. They were about to run.

'What name do they use for this woman?' I asked.

'Vanessa McDonald. It's believed she stole a car just before disappearing.'

'What make?'

'Chevy Equinox. Grey. There's no sign of it.'

That changed everything. Gave me simultaneous hope

she'd got away and a vertiginous awareness that she could be anywhere.

'Checked car parks?'

'I assume so.' Astana's underground car parks added up to a city's worth of concealment in themselves. No easy way to search those.

'Do cars often just disappear?'

'It's a big country. Could be she headed east.'

'What's that meant to mean?'

'I saw them studying a map, talking about the possibility she went east, that she had connections there.'

'East like eastern outskirts? East like the border with China?'

'I've no idea. Did she have connections outside of Astana?'

'Possibly.'

'Well, possibly that's something you want to look into.'

'Who is in charge of the investigation?' I asked.

'Anti-Terrorism.'

'Rakim Zhaparov.'

'Yes.'

'Why?'

'Fuck knows. Maybe she's a terrorist.'

'It's been kept off the news. I would have thought this was a big story.'

'The news is controlled. This is clearly too sensitive.'

I showed him a screengrab of the man in the CGI clip.

'I think he is codenamed Catalyst. Zhaparov also has a picture of him. Who is he?'

Shomko took a while studying it before shaking his head. I saw him check the newspaper in the background, frown.

'What is this?'

'That's what I'd like to find out.'

He ashed his cigarette nervously, flicking until I thought it was going to break.

'So what do you want?' he said.

'I need you to get closer to the investigation into Vanessa. Recruit someone inside anti-terrorism. They would be rewarded as well. Anti-terrorism comes under the National Security Committee, doesn't it?'

'Technically. But they have their own facilities and security clearances, and a separate network for communication.'

'You must know people inside it.'

'I know people everywhere. Most of them like being alive.'

'What's Zhaparov's vice? Does he like guys? Little girls?'

'He likes power. And he's getting more of it.'

'He's on the rise?'

'Yes.'

I opened the laptop on a map of Astana.

'Which buildings belong to Anti-Terrorism?'

Shomko dropped his cigarette to the floor and pointed out five locations, three in official state buildings, two black sites.

'Which have cells?'

'All of them.'

'Any chance that Vanessa McDonald is in one of them?'

'I don't think so.'

'Where's the main investigation being run from?'

He showed me the main anti-terrorism headquarters on the map. It was housed within the National Security Committee building.

'And the investigative databases – who gets access to those?'

'Senior personnel only.'

'You're senior.'

'Not senior enough.'

'Password-protected?'

'Yes.'

'How often do they change the password?'

'Daily.'

He talked me through the building, the security on the doors, the offices and the integrated IT system.

'Are you searched when you go in?'

'No.'

'Searched leaving?'

'No.'

'You have access to the report that's been circulated.'

'Yes.'

'For now, send me everything that's on the open system.'

'That is simple.'

'Let's start with that then. And find out where she's gone if she's not in Astana, whereabouts in the east people are looking.' I promised him the equivalent of two hundred pounds for every new lead, five thousand if he established where Vanessa McDonald was. The curiosity was too much for him.

'Who is Vanessa McDonald?'

'Someone very valuable.' I gave him the number for a clean phone. 'When you need to contact me, text the number of whatever phone box you're at. I need to know what's going on inside anti-terrorism. In Zhaparov's inner circle.'

He shook his head.

'How much do you want?' I asked.

He retrieved another cigarette but didn't light it. His face bore an expression I had seen more times than I wanted: the discomfort of a man calculating what his life was worth.

TWENTY-FIVE

I let him leave first, then went down to my GL5 escort.

'How did it go?'

'Peacefully.'

'That's what we like.'

I was driven back to their office, where I put a deposit down for any further work. Purvis liked the cash. He didn't ask for the gun back.

'If someone wanted assurance that they could get out of here in a worst-case scenario,' I said, 'one, maybe two people tops, quick and quiet as possible out of Kazakhstan – how feasible does that sound?'

'Informal arrangement?'

'Cash in hand.'

'It's feasible. I'd have to get some names together. I'm guessing it would be a last-minute kind of business.'

'Very. Would you go across the Caspian?'

'The Caspian gets icy, so probably not. We can get to a drill site; there are helis there, a Lynx that will get you to Baku, easy. Five-seater Airbus if the weather allows. We control two helipads in Baku. I'd rather steer wide of Russian airspace.'

'Jets?'

'An Embraer Tucano. But I'd rather not use it for commutes.'

'Where do you park that?'

'Away from prying eyes.' He winked. Embraer was a Brazilian

company. The Tucano was marketed as a light combat aircraft.

'Registered to GL5?'

'Not exactly.'

'What sort of price are we talking about?'

'For a civilian?' He considered. 'The heli's thirty k. Personnel another ten per day, or two grand each. They'd want a retainer, maybe ten up front. For a mate of Jimmy's, call it seven.'

'And how much warning would you need?'

'It depends on the situation. But there's two thousand of us in Kazakhstan. I'm sure I could find some spare hands.'

'Two thousand?'

'That's right.'

'Working for Saracen?'

'Not just Saracen. We've got contracts with the government; border tech. That's the big new market, and we proved ourselves in Israel and Mexico.'

We agreed payments and contacts, swapped some final anecdotes, then began back across the concrete.

'What kind of lads have you got over here?' I asked.

'Everything. Thai, Columbian, Ukrainian. Mostly Brits though.'

'Good kit?'

'Take a look at this.'

He led me to a hangar. Inside, crouching in the darkness, were forms I didn't recognise: thin struts, metal plates, electronic devices that could have been cameras or lasers.

'It's for a virtual fence. Buried sensors and camera towers all linked to central control centres. UAVs, motion sensors. The lot.'

'For protecting drill sites?'

'That's right.'

There was something strange at the back: a rusted COSCO container with Chinese markings. I tried to see it as we headed out; it had been half-obscured by tarpaulin, but I got a glimpse inside and it contained what looked like a military radio system.

Light entered through three bullet-sized holes in the metal. It seemed all sorts of stories sheltered in the hangar.

'Come on.' Purvis moved back towards the daylight.

'You're well equipped,' I said.

'We're doing our job,' he said. 'We own this market. No one's competing right now.'

The day outside seemed brighter. Men had stopped on the tarmac. They stood stiffly as gates rolled back and a black convoy with outriders swept in. Purvis put a hand up to stop me.

An armoured Bentley swept towards the helipad. It stopped beside the Sikorsky and a guard got out, opening a back door as steps lowered from the helicopter and its rotors began to turn.

'Carter,' Purvis said. 'The boss.'

A lone figure moved between the car and the helicopter, head bowed against the wash. Then he was gone, the stairs folded in and the heli took off, sending up gritty snow, everyone ducking. Life in the compound continued.

'Ever used the heli for a search-and-rescue mission?' I asked.

'There was one the other day, actually. A woman. I was never told what she had to do with Saracen. Hunt her down, we were told. Whereabouts? Somewhere in Kazakhstan.' He slapped his forehead and laughed.

'Those were the words used?'

'Something like that. Why? Planning on getting lost? I wouldn't. It's one big fuck-off country.'

'You never found her, I take it.'

'Not as far as I'm aware.'

'And they said "hunt"?'

'Hunt, find her, whatever. Something urgent.'

I was sitting in my hotel room with the gun in my hand when my phone rang. It was Elena Yussopova.

'Elena.'

'John, where are you?'

'I'm at my hotel,' I said. 'What's happened?'

'I need to speak to you.'

'Okay.'

'Can you come round? Now?'

'Sure.'

'Be careful. Extra careful.'

TWENTY-SIX

Yussopova's flat was crowded. It felt like a small, tense cocktail party: cigarette smoke in the air, a pile of coats, dirty coffee cups, and even a bottle of vodka on the table. The computer was missing, books and files over the floor. Her wrists were still red from handcuffs. Dried white cream covered injuries further up her arms.

The crowd shot me hostile glances. I recognised a couple of men and women from the protest photos. One grey-haired man had a case on his lap and was using it as a writing desk, as the group around him talked heatedly about legal options.

Yussopova studied me with a searching intensity.

'You are okay?' she asked.

'Just. Tell me what's going on.'

'I was questioned. About Vanessa. They showed me a photograph of you, from the airport. I was asked if I knew you. If I'd met you.'

'What did you say?'

'I said no.'

I tried not to think of the price she paid for that. I looked across the people and the paperwork in front of them, their plans for a protest; the coffee table with its bug.

'Can we talk in private?' I asked.

'We are safe,' Yussopova said. 'These are good people.'

'I don't know them.'

We went to the kitchen. I closed the door, turned the taps on.

'Do you know who they were?'

'Police, security service. I don't know. It was in the central police station.'

'What did they ask about?'

'They thought I might have documents or information – something from Vanessa. I couldn't understand what they wanted. It wasn't just about our work.'

'It's to do with whatever Vanessa found out.'

'Yes. You should leave.'

'I was also questioned by police this morning.'

A man entered the kitchen before she could react. He was small, middle-aged, with a pullover under a mismatched brown suit. He looked unhappy to see a stranger. There was an argument in Kazakh. *Who is he? How do you know? How do you know who Vanessa was? She brings a lot of trouble.* I gathered this was Andrei Nichuskin, the communications director, back from Armenia. The last one she had contact with.

'John was arrested too,' Yussopova said.

This quietened him. I could see the room through the doorway, responding to the news. I mentioned the treatment I received and a woman in the living room said she was a doctor and offered to check my injuries. I could feel the crowd thinking through the danger and opportunity I represented: a Westerner, an Englishman, someone who couldn't be ignored. I could draw international attention to their cause. That attention could get them killed.

'She spoke to you, before she disappeared,' I said.

Andrei stared at me with small, fiery eyes. Eventually he said, 'She was asking for all those who had helped with previous campaigns. Not just protesters but hackers who have helped us. To capture activism in the twenty-first century, she said. She wanted to know who was local, wanted their contact details. We gave her access to the connections we have.' He said that through gritted teeth.

'Do you have any idea who she spoke to?'

'No. We showed her a list. Now it has gone. Someone wiped it from our system.'

'After you showed her?'

'After she disappeared. Who is she? Who does she share information with?'

I was beginning to understand his mistrust, and why it had turned on me.

'She is one of our best campaigners,' I said.

'When did you last work with Reporters for Human Rights?'

'I'm working with them now.'

'With Anthony Lewis?'

'Yes. But I'm not here to be interrogated again.'

Andrei's phone rang. He stepped back towards the living room, still staring at me, then turned, taking the call.

'I'm sorry,' Yussopova said. 'Obviously the situation is very tense.'

'Of course. I'd be the same. Do you know anything about this list she saw?'

'Just that Andrei believes she approached someone and it created problems.'

'You've no idea who?'

'No.'

'What did they ask about Vanessa today, when you were questioned?'

'They asked what languages she spoke, how long she'd been working for Reporters for Human Rights, what countries I knew she'd been in. They were also suspicious of her. So, you see ...'

Yussopova trailed off. She was still in shock. She ran a glass of water and in the light from the kitchen window I saw her injured arm more clearly. They were burns; cigar burns. I lifted her coat off the back of the chair and smelled it.

'Who questioned you?'

'A Russian. I don't know who.'

'Could you describe him for me?'

'Smart, clean-shaven. He had grey hair, parted.'

'Glasses?'

'Yes.'

'Tall?'

'Certainly not small.'

'What else do you remember about him?'

'His nails were neat, like a doctor's, a surgeon's.'

'Did he do this?' I gestured at her burns.

'What do you think?'

The intercom buzzed. Everyone fell quiet.

'It's Irina,' someone said. A woman entered a moment later, indistinct beneath layers of clothing but visibly pale, with bright, scared eyes.

'Timur and Natalya have been arrested. We should not be here. This place may be bugged. They know about our plans.'

'Bugged or penetrated,' Andrei said.

'You should go,' Yussopova said. She meant: before the crowd turned against me. 'This is not your problem. It is not safe for you here, John. Leave Kazakhstan as quickly as possible. In England, tell people what is going on. We will try to find out what happened to Vanessa.'

'If anyone asks about me again, don't try to protect me, okay? You are in more danger than I am.'

'I don't know if that's true.'

I called Walker when I was back in my car, asked him to compile a list of Russian visitors to Kazakhstan in the week Joanna Lake went missing.

'There'll be thousands.'

I gave specific names to check. After less than ten minutes he came back with a result. It was one I had hoped not to get. From air traffic control: a Russian-registered Gulfstream G280 jet had landed at an airfield a few miles north of Astana two days before Joanna went missing. It had an armed security licence for four passengers, including the jet's owner: Vladislav Vishinsky.

TWENTY-SEVEN

A hotel room in Turkey: Joanna pacing, cracking pistachios and flicking the shells towards the bin.

'You think I gas kids? For a psyop? You think that's what we do?'

'No.'

'This is what they want: we turn on each other, we destroy ourselves from the inside.'

'I know.'

'Doubt everything. Everyone's as bad as each other. Everything's fucked.'

I could see Joanna, later that night, sitting on the narrow bed, her back against the roughly plastered wall, eyes closed, TV muted on Russian TV: *Irrefutable evidence attack was staged. German reporter says incident was false-flag.*

'Is that why you were really sent here?' she asked. 'You're over because they don't trust me?'

'They don't trust anyone.'

That was the start of her fixation. Fixations were dangerous in intelligence work. Five months later we were in Shefford. It was the first time I'd seen her after Turkey. We were in her Shefford home, before she got paranoid and reluctant to have me over. And I still wasn't sure if that was about security or what was going on inside, which was her own little research project: notes and clippings in carefully locked drawers, which she checked upon entering, refusing to tell me what they concerned.

I picked the locks when she was asleep, knowing that she would do the same to me. Kept the anglepoise low, moving the sheets silently so as not to wake her.

Russian news: female faces – birth and death dates for each face. None were older than twenty-three. Then pages of interactions on social media, screenshots, photos of wounds. All were young women who had jumped off buildings in Russia in the past three months, all of whom had self-harm scars.

The main light came on. Joanna stood in the doorway.

'Jesus Christ, Elliot.'

'What is this?' I said.

'A game.'

She put on coffee. We talked for the rest of the night. Joanna had connected the suicides to participation in an online game linked to the Russian-based VKontakte social network, Russia's answer to Facebook. The game consisted of a series of tasks assigned to players by an administrator over a fifty-day period; one task per day, innocuous to begin with, ending with them killing themselves.

'The idea is to desensitise them, to test the limits of what can be achieved remotely, through online control. It originates with a unit set up by this man, Vladislav Vishinsky.' She brought up a photo, a mugshot, early Nineties. 'It was him, the one we saw in Ukraine. He was behind the whole thing in Turkey as well.'

'You're sure?'

'I said you were paranoid about Russia. I was wrong. We're getting the structure and operations of their Cyber-Cognitive Warfare unit. Vishinsky set it up. We think he was a qualified psychologist before spending time in prison, though it's not clear what his offences were, as the record's been wiped. His name appears in a document from 1993 called "How to Win Wars with Children's Tears". It's a strategy proposal paper, possibly written while he was locked up, drawing heavily on America's experience in Vietnam. He argues that Russia can't compete on defence expenditure and they should fall back on psychology, use targeted psy campaigns to bring Russia together and to defeat their enemies abroad, move away from war in the physical environment towards a war in our minds. Or, as he puts it: from direct annihilation of the opponent to their inner decay.'

Joanna spoke calmly enough, stopping to sip coffee. She had the file in her brain, and relayed information as if it was as native to her as childhood memories.

'Vishinsky draws on what the Soviet General Staff call reflexive control theory. It means feeding an opponent specially prepared information so that they make a decision of your choosing; owning their thought process. Vishinsky says the digital era is a gift, in this respect. Using these tactics, they can reclaim Greater Russia. The paper must have reached some influential people. He's released early, sent to Moscow, given resources within the National Defence Control Centre. In documents, his unit is referred to as Unit 19.

'By the early Noughties, Vishinsky's being referred to as *Volshebnik*, the magician. We had a Russian defector walk into the British embassy in Istanbul, back in 1998. They were able to describe, in very vague terms, something originating in Unit 19 called ALKHIMIYA – Project Alchemy – which involved the control of populations. That was 1998, for Christ's sake. Nothing was done.

'On 22 February 1999, the eve of Russia's annual Defenders of the Fatherland holiday, the Defence Minister Sergei Shoigu announced the creation of a new information operations force combining cyber troops and propagandists. They had sophisticated means of tracking the morale of rival military forces. The internet allowed them to extend this to entire nations. Their sensitivity to national psyches allowed them to craft tailor-made psychological campaigns. Vishinsky's GRU textbook even advised different approaches to waging psy warfare on different NATO members: "abstract-logical" propaganda for the Germans, visuals for the French and Americans, etc. Around the turn of the millennium it stopped being simply a tool of Kremlin policy and began to affect the policy itself. Vishinsky was advising Putin directly.

'It was around this time Putin changed his tone. No longer a pragmatic realist when it came to world affairs, now he became Mr Nationalist. He got an ideology: reclaiming the former Soviet Union. Vishinsky produced speeches and propaganda along these lines and it played well. It was a narrative, a national goal: make Russia great again. It secured access to a lot of oil and gas. And he had persuaded Putin that they could compete, thanks to this new unit.'

Joanna talked through the dawn, but never told me what she intended to do about all this, or who she was working with at Shefford and what they had to do with Vishinsky. So I had no idea how a man shot in Astana might or might not connect to it all.

Budget hidden in Requirements and Production, but huge. Staff size one hundred and twenty. Some definitely came from GCHQ. Others were academics ... The security set-up suggests it was operational. It wasn't just producing papers.

Closed down. Someone inside Six saw to that. I was curious about where their sympathies lay.

The report from air traffic control gave us Vishinsky landing at a military airfield in Koyandy, north of Astana, at 10 a.m. on 22 November. I opened my laptop, checked what had been trending on Kazakh social media in the last twenty-four hours. The President's daughter had been chalked up as judge on SuperstarKZ; the regional governor of Mangystau had proposed bird watching as a potential tourist attraction; a Russian woman had been raped in northern Kazakhstan, close to the Russian border.

Several news sites carried high-definition photos of the victim's face, bruised and tear-stained. Her name was Yulia Vectisishina, and she lived in Schuchinsk. A lot of people with Russian surnames were sharing the story across various platforms, connecting it to an attack a few miles away in Petropavl, a majority-Russian village, where a cultural centre had been burned down.

The woman was Russian, the rapists were alleged to be ethnic Kazakh. People were posting photos of angry crowds. They held signs that said: *Kazakhstan is Russia.*

TWENTY-EIGHT

'How directly does the Kremlin direct this unit?' Walker asked.

'Arm's length. But Vishinsky is close to Putin. Nothing's going to happen without approval.'

'And it dates back to Ukraine?'

'It pre-dates Ukraine. It's drawn from psychological work the Main Intelligence Directorate was doing in the Sixties. But we started getting a concrete picture of how it functions in 2014. I think Joanna was working on it before leaving Six. I need you to back me and redirect resources. I think she's alive. She found out something about Russia and Kazakhstan.'

We were in the private room of a canteen inside the White and Chase building, away from other suits, a platter of sushi going to waste between us. Walker had collected me from reception, dropped some unspecified paperwork off in his temporary office, which gave me another view of the keypad and the electronics set-up. He'd been hungry so we went up to the canteen, which he'd assured me was secure. I'd decided not to mention my own arrest, or run-in with Sergei Cherenkov, partly to see if Walker knew. So far there was no suggestion he did.

'Vishinsky represents an expansionist, hawkish, ultra-cynical circle at the heart of the Kremlin,' I said. 'They push a narrative that NATO is seeking to encircle Russia. When they wanted Crimea annexed, Vishinsky had to assure Putin it could work. He masterminded the combining of cyber warfare, kinetic attacks, propaganda and what the Russians call *Maskirovka*: masking, military deception. He was on the ground, coordinating it. Now he's here.'

'Why now?'

'I don't know. I think Joanna knows. She tried to get out. Look.'

I showed him the file Shomko had sent through. Walker studied the plane tickets to Caracas, the fake names. I wanted to see how he'd react. If this didn't get his support he either knew where she was or he didn't care.

'How did you get this?' he asked.

'I bought it. The investigation concerning Joanna has been moved away from the units you'd expect to be handling a murder. This is from anti-terrorism. Chief of Kazakh anti-terrorism is Rakim Zhaparov.'

Walker nodded as if this made sense. He pincered some sashimi.

'It fits the picture we're building. There's Kremlin ties.'

'What do you know about him?'

Walker chewed, considering. 'Relatively young, ambitious. Supposedly waging a war against militant Islam. Close to Moscow. Not a pleasant creature if certain reports are anything to go by. And he's caused us problems before. He wants Saracen out of Kazakhstan. Wants all US and European companies out.'

'Has he got the muscle to do that?'

'The only muscle in this country is the President. The President thinks that kicking out Western oil companies will jeopardise other business. He's keen for Kazakhstan to seem international, competitive, independent. Zhaparov's a Moscow puppet. Whenever the President gets too cosy with the West, Zhaparov suddenly has resources from Russia, usually in the name of counterterrorism, keeping Kazakhstan a buffer between Russia and Islamists. It was Zhaparov who banned praying in public, and installed pro-government imams. But it's obvious he's also a buffer against the West. Moscow's nervous about Galina, the President's daughter. She's pro-West. When Putin annexed Crimea, she encouraged her father to start diversifying military purchases away from Russia. When Moscow tried to get Kazakhstan to join in with counter-sanctions against the West, she pushed her father to decline. And she hates Zhaparov. A few years back, when he was Chief Prosecutor, he went after one of her boyfriends for money laundering.'

'And we're tight with Galina?'

'We shower her with gold.'

'How much?'

'Millions. A lot of it is property, mostly for family members. It's a big family. But she's our best chance. Lucy Piper always says that the way to a president's heart is through his daughter.'

'Cute, but she's not in charge yet,' I said. 'What's the President's own relationship with Moscow like?'

Walker considered before responding, dipping a maki roll in soy sauce.

'Kazakhstan's always been a staunch Russian ally, but Ukraine made them uneasy. Nazarbayev walks a tightrope. A few years ago, they started limiting Russian broadcasting over here. Russian officials complained and now it's an offence to even think along those lines. A lot of Russians came here in Soviet times. Most of those remaining are in the north of the country, close to the Motherland, and the main government policy seems to be not to antagonise them.' He ate, then looked at the police file again. 'What did Joanna stumble into?'

'I'm not sure she stumbled. I think she walked purposefully towards the obsession she's been nursing for years. That's what I'm worried about.'

'Wait until Robert Carter hears about this. Moscow's scuppered big deals of his before. He had plans for a pipeline in Turkmenistan; closed down at the last minute as a result of political pressure from China and Russia. Billions written off.' Walker shook his head. But even as he expressed his concern for Carter's traumatic experiences with Russia, I could see his eyes glinting. He saw opportunity in crisis, in traumatised billionaires.

'Has anyone in the UK discovered that you're here?' he asked.

'Not as far as I'm aware.'

'How long do you think you need to find out what's happened to her?'

'Five days.'

'Wait there.'

I watched the main restaurant through the doorway: white-shirted men with chopsticks and Breitlings and thick windows between them and the world. Lives lived thirty floors up. Downstairs I'd got another look at the entry procedure for the building, the cameras and stairways; Evotec had managed to access an original planning application for the block including architectural drawings that gave us the server room in the basement. All this was habit, but so was distrust.

I checked my phone. Online a story had started trending: two young Kazakh men who'd fought in Ukraine on the pro-Russian side had been sentenced to five years each. *Heroes jailed*. They'd actually been sentenced last year, but the story had gone viral again. Meanwhile someone had painted 'This is Kazakhstan' on a hillside in the north of the country in white letters ten feet high. I was wondering how much effort and paint that would take when Walker returned with a laptop case branded 'Astana 2018'.

'This is what you asked for,' he said. Inside was thirty grand's worth of paper money divided equally into plastic wallets of dollars, tenge and rubles.

Like most cases of money, it felt dirty, dangerous and very useful.

When I was in my car I called Stefan.

'Are we playing?' he said.

'I've got the money in cash.'

'Okay.'

'I want you in the Astana's Hilton Garden Inn. I've booked a room. Target will be directly below. His name is Callum Walker. He may be running counter-surveillance, so move gently. I'll give you more when you get here.'

I called Geoff Purvis and we established procedures for a quick escape.

On my way back to the hotel I stopped at a hunting shop and bought bullets and cold-weather gun lubricant. I drove out to the desert to test-fire the gun but struggled to find anything to aim at, eventually firing once towards the horizon before my fingers went numb.

TWENTY-NINE

I checked out of the Lion Hotel and into the Ramada Plaza. It was more in keeping with the Bell cover, and I had a superstition about sleeping where I'd been arrested. The Ramada put a lot more grey-carpeted corridor between me and the world, even if I knew it was a false sense of security. An eager bellboy, no older than nineteen, helped me with my cases.

'Where'd you learn English?' I asked.

'Here. I like to talk to people.'

'Follow the football?'

'Of course. My team is Chelsea.'

'Abramovich.'

'Yes.' He grinned.

'Know Astana well?'

'Very well.'

'Where did you grow up?'

'Shymkent.'

'Deep south. Isn't that what they say? I heard it's like the Wild West down there.'

'It is different. The jobs are here.'

'Well, you've earned this.' I folded a couple of notes into his hand. Loyal bellboys were a godsend.

I set up a wireless camera, smaller than my fingertip, positioned so it faced the door: motion-sensitive, high-definition, straight to my phone. I locked the Makarov in the safe.

The hotel's bar was a cavernous, Hollywood-themed place with a lot of young staff and few customers. It served food through the night: Happy Hour was 8 p.m. to 2 a.m. For a city with no evident desire to party the night away, Kazakhstan had a lot of places that never closed. I drank a beer and thought of the lines by Thomas Mann: *In an empty, unarticulated space our mind loses its sense of time as well.* He was describing a sea crossing but it fitted Astana. *Our mind loses its sense of time and we enter the twilight of the immeasurable. Dämmerung des unermesslichen.*

I planned my next move.

Joanna had acquired information and possibly contacts through Testimony. That had evidently got her in trouble. It coincided with the appearance of Vishinsky. A psychological war had begun. Did it involve fake videos of myself? She saw what Vishinsky had planned, tried to warn me. Here I was.

Stumped.

Cherenkov wanted Perfect Vision. I tried to imagine a piece of forecasting software effective enough to inspire the envy of hostile governments. A crystal ball. Or it was something else entirely, some means of defeating Russia's psyops. A truth machine. Perhaps the attention on me was a bluff and they already had penetration at Shefford that meant the project had been compromised, the whole thing falling apart in time for them to make a play for Central Asia.

I needed cyber capabilities, and was keen for Stefan to arrive. I had a strong lead in terms of the Chevy Equinox, but no easy means of pursuing that beyond what the police had already attempted. If Russia was preparing for action, there would be big changes inside Kazakhstan's state apparatus. Shomko could map structure and sympathies. I could inform Six by some back channel. But why hadn't Joanna done that? Stevenson's words haunted me: *changes in priorities … Russia's got the wind in their sails … Syria's a test bed.*

The men who had attacked the Russian woman had been named on social media. I typed their names into Google to see if they really existed. It was hard to say without a photo. Meanwhile, two other Kazakh men had been hospitalised in what sounded like revenge attacks in Schuchinsk, a house set alight.

I called the hospital mentioned in reports and eventually got through to a doctor who sounded young, stressed and tired.

'Can I speak to the men who were admitted?'

'No.'

'But they are there?'

'We can't give you any information.'

'I'm family.'

'Makes no difference.'

'Can I just check – were there any men admitted at all?'

He confirmed that two men had been brought in but wouldn't give any more details.

I found the number for a bar in the town owned by a woman called Olga Sergeeva, which was a Russian surname. Sergeeva herself answered.

'This is Dmitry Zubkov from the *Moscow Times*,' I said.

'What do you want?'

'How are things there? We in Russia are worried. How are people feeling?'

'People feel there is a lot of bullshit around.' The woman hung up.

He is beyond cynical, Elliot. That is what we haven't understood.

I know.

You say you met him.

I thought I had. 2001, Baku, Azerbaijan.

I hadn't realised until later that Vishinsky was the individual concerned. At the time he'd been just one strange encounter in a series of them. Baku had been an *Agentsumpf* for sure, a baptism of oil and fire. By the time I got to the place there'd been five years of dark-side operations. MI6 had scrambled to help British business mop up what they could of the former Soviet oil industry. When the wrong man got into power, backed by Russia, MI6 was tasked with sorting out a counter-coup. My predecessors set up ratlines: backdoor arms channels from dumps in Turkey via Armenia. They got a more amenable dictator in place. Three months later, £5 billion worth of energy deals were signed.

The whole project had been set up by men and women with experience of Bosnia, of drugs for arms networks. Intelligence doesn't have a rule book, which means people fall back on what they know, which isn't always sophisticated. I arrived to help deal with the fallout. It was one of my first operations for Six, running an agent close to the deposed dictator and trying to anticipate blowback. I was twenty-four, out of my depth, and excited to be there. The experience should have left me feeling disillusioned, but I didn't want illusions anyway; I felt only delight at getting the chance to see geopolitics up close. I think Vishinsky sensed that: the vulnerability of appetite.

The old Soviet Intourist Hotel was the only place foreign oil execs were allowed to stay, a five-storey brute on Neftchiler Prospekt, oilmen's avenue. The lack of facilities didn't keep anyone away – middlemen, warlords, oil execs. Reps for BP, Amoco, Pennzoil, Unocal. Then mercenaries from the US and Afghanistan fighting in Azerbaijan's war with Armenia who added to the squeeze and the ratio of guns to guests. The US, Turkish and Russian embassies were all in the hotel itself. The UK embassy was in the offices of BP down the road, which told you all you needed to know. Azeri security services had the hotel wired from top to bottom. If you needed to talk to a politician you could say their name in an empty room and they'd turn up an hour or so later. People chained cases to their wrists to move down corridors. No one left the place. Deliveries of paper and whisky came in each morning. If you were curious about what the world looked like you could open your curtains and gaze across the derelict rigs crumbling into the sea.

I may have been the only one to get out and about. Daily, mid-afternoon, I'd walk past boomtown Baku, dutifully checking reflections in the windows of Bulgari and Armani to see if I'd been followed, but also spying on the shops themselves – capitalism as impossible dreams. I'd walk through Bibi-Heybat, a suburb where the first-ever oil well had been drilled, to an industrial zone called Black City where refinery chimneys coloured the sky grey with smoke. Offshore rig platforms looked like churches floating on air, the spires of the drilling towers hazy in mist. Someone told me they'd sunk seven ships to form the foundation for the offshore platform, one of which was the first oil tanker, *Zoroaster*. I admired the scale of the gesture, like a sacrifice, and the historical link it created. Once upon a time the burning gas just leaked from the ground and Azerbaijan was known as the shrine of fire, a place of Zoroastrian pilgrimage.

When the weather was good, I'd walk to a spot on the coast from which you got a glimpse of *Neft Daslari* – Oil Rocks – a town on stilts in the sea with two thousand rust-bitten drilling platforms joined by a network of bridges. That particularly day was clearer than most, and I was trying to make out what remained. I didn't notice the tall, elegant Russian approaching, cigar in hand.

I was sure I hadn't been followed, yet I could see no reason for someone else to be there. And he seemed content to appear as if he had sought me out. It was Vishinsky, although I didn't know that then.

We fell into polite, mutually curious conversation. He told me that when the Tsarist regime began to crumble in the early twentieth century, the oil workers of Baku went on strike. One of their leaders was a young Joseph Stalin. Vishinsky gestured to the city behind us and described the whole place in flames, even the waves of the sea, covered in oil from the burning wells.

'And what did Stalin seize first? The printing presses.' Vishinsky's eyes gleamed. I remember thinking he was intelligent, that he liked the sound of his own voice, that he appeared to have crafted his speech for me personally.

'Stalin gave us a destiny,' Vishinsky said. 'And then it went. You have not felt that. In the West you are children, easily scared and with few memories. You do not know despair. But perhaps you will learn.'

I wondered why he was interested in me.

The following week, back in Vauxhall, I put together a case for engaging with him, playing along. I was willing to play double. The operation was turned down as too risky. In the chaos of the next few years I almost forgot about that meeting. Then I saw him in Kiev. Or, at least, Joanna saw him.

'He nodded at me,' she said. 'As if he knew who I was.' She showed me the picture she'd got later that night. It was the man who had approached me in Baku.

'What do you know about him?' she asked.

I told her: he seemed hyper-nationalistic, believed in regaining lost Soviet territory.

I thought of him as we witnessed the Orange Revolution ignite, feeling the euphoria spread through Ukraine, a demand for fairness and freedom being heard for once, opening the future through the will of the people. And I thought of him nine years later when the first Novorussiya accounts appeared – 'New Russia' – with dedicated websites and domain names. Novorussiya was what Russians called the Crimea in the eighteenth century, when it was annexed by Catherine the Great. Someone was conjuring a political entity back into existence. Two weeks later, Russian troops took control of the main route to Sevastopol. Men in anonymous uniforms occupied the Crimean parliament building. In Six there was a sense of disbelief. But they got away with it because the psychological groundwork had been laid.

'They're playing a bigger game than us,' Joanna had said then. 'We don't have a vision.'

Ten years later, her concerns about Vishinsky were more personal. Over dinner at an Italian restaurant in Milton Keynes she said that he had a file on us: the two of us, a supposed team.

'We triggered him; we're on his radar.'

She got me access to a copy of the relevant GRU report. It included a picture of us in Kiev's Navodnitsky Park, together with attempts at establishing our real identities and the nature of our relationship. *Not believed to be sexual partners.* Yet he had coupled us, before we were together.

'He's convinced that we were involved in a US-led coup in Ukraine. Refuses to buy genuine democratic yearnings. I think we've found his own paranoia.'

I felt his shadow over us.

You met him. What did he say?

He said: People who believe in nothing still believe in oil.

The rape story had been picked up internationally from one local news site. The originating website was called InformAsia: it was big on graphics and pop music, and drew heavily on social media. It had been set up a year ago, and seemed to survive without much advertising. Some rudimentary searches gave me ten Vkontakte accounts that appeared to have linked to the story almost simultaneously, mostly women, mostly young, with several thousand followers each.

Where had I seen that website? I found the dating app on my phone, checked the first match.

You seem interesting. Check out this site – lots of fun there.

I clicked through to InformAsia, which had put a photo of the victim on its landing page.

THIRTY

I spent too much of the night browsing, until I started to believe the region's entire internet had been gamed. Stories fuelling Russian resentment came up everywhere you looked.

Fired for speaking Russian. Statue removed. Beaten up on the way to school.

People in public services were being forced to speak Kazakh rather than Russian; a politician who resisted the new language laws had been assaulted at a rally. Alongside those kinds of stories was a low-level hum of outrage and titillation: mother shamed in Kazakh restaurant; teacher beats pupil; child crucified by Muslims. Meanwhile, on the same sites, the epidemic of homosexuality in the West got good coverage, as did Europe's spiritual bankruptcy in general. NATO was heading for extinction, Russia ready to bring peace to the Middle East.

I logged in as Yuri Cherchesov, my Russian sailor, and clicked Like on pictures of 'Kazakh militias' targeting Russians in northern Kazakhstan. They posed with horse bows apparently looted from a museum. They urinated on a portrait of Putin from behind blurred pixels.

Vishinsky's great insight: propaganda didn't have to be believed to be effective. No more than pornography had to be believed to make you come. It just had to keep you staring, feed you fantasies.

Women's tears, women's shame, everywhere I looked.

There were various ways sophisticated cyber operations could enhance information warfare: devices and websites can both be infected so you get steered the right way, websites look real but aren't, pages shoot up the rankings. I looked for the same phrases or links appearing simultaneously; big waves of people piling in to comment immediately, then repeating the process at regular intervals. I amassed fifty accounts, ten blogs and six websites that struck me as suspect or just heavily anti-West and sent them through to Evotec to see if they could get me anything: matches with previous cyber operations, source IPs, syntactic patterns to see how many people were producing this. Every major military power had units running social media now. NATO and US Central Command had poured millions into it in the last couple of years, but they were playing catch-up. The West couldn't compete with the office blocks in Moscow and Shanghai filled with young men and women operating their distant personas. You used to be able to watch the syntax: the Chinese skipped plurals; Russian's a phonetic language so spelling tended to be a weak point. But it was getting more sophisticated on all fronts. Bots came fleshed out, with face shots scraped from Picasa and Flickr. The software existed to create hundreds of these a minute, inserting them into comment threads and forums, interacting with people just like a human. But software couldn't do everything.

I called Walker at 8 a.m. and talked information warfare. He said social media was monitored for Vectis by Piper Anderson, the PR company hiring them. Piper Anderson's CEO, Lucy Piper, was on the ground in Kazakhstan, currently with a trade delegation. I said it could be useful for me to speak to her and he said he'd put a call in.

'Does she know about Joanna?' I asked.

'Unfortunately.'

*

I caught up with the delegation at a Saracen-sponsored School of Business, Law and Management. It had a glossy new visitors' centre attached, its creamy imitation marble engraved with the message: *Energy awakens ancient history*. A lot of men circulated with branded name badges: BAE, Glaxo, Whitbread; then some junior ministers, journalists, a university chancellor. I caught a glimpse of the British ambassador to Kazakhstan, Suzanna Ford, slightly dishevelled in a grey skirt suit, laughing and drinking white wine. She turned, met my eyes before I could look away, gave the smile of someone having to smile at everyone. I couldn't see Piper.

The new centre displayed fragments of pottery they'd dug up, alongside bad watercolours of a traditional nomad community. At the end was a display regarding wildlife protection, signed off by an organisation I'd never heard of called Clean Caspian. The ribbon had already been cut and hung limply on either side of the entrance. Four silver minibuses waited to transport the delegation back to the Marriott once a group of schoolchildren had finished burying a time capsule for an unspecified future generation to pore over. The capsule was a Tupperware box, and the hole into which it was being deposited had been created in the icy courtyard with the help of a blowtorch and pickaxe. The ceremony was being filmed.

I introduced myself to a man directing proceedings, with cropped ginger hair and a waistcoat, his name badge identifying him as Neil Graff from Piper Anderson Communications. He said Lucy was at the Marriott dealing with a last-minute emergency but I could hitch a ride back to the hotel with them.

At the Marriott I was directed to a restaurant, dim and low-lit and almost empty, with tables set for the next day. Empty apart from one person.

Lucy Piper stood alone at the windows, phone to her ear. She wore a white suit, hair up, eyes cool. The screen of a MacBook glowed on the table behind her. She was having a bad day.

'No ... I don't know ... It's worse than we thought.'

In the low-lit comfort it took me a second to connect her to the figure I'd seen stepping among the former Taliban like some mascara-laden angel of history. There was a lot of paperwork on the table, pinned down with a vape the size of a Colt .44.

She hung up, put on a professional smile.

'Hey there.'

'Lucy Piper? I work for Vectis. Toby Bell.'

Her smile turned cooler. She extended a hand. 'Callum mentioned your name. Another former Commando?'

'Something like that.'

No suggestion she recognised me. I scanned the visible documents. They had the day's analytics: Google results for 'Saracen', 'Saracen in Kazakhstan', 'Kazakhstan oil', 'Kazakhstan corruption'. Critical social media accounts had been mapped geographically. She had a photocopy of a petition launched by Testimony – *The lavish trade mission is a green light to political oppression* – along with a strategy to quieten it, which looked like it might involve an organisation called the Kazakhstan Business Alliance whose contact number was a London landline.

Her company was well connected in Westminster, of course, with a muscular lobbying operation involving former politicians and diplomats, and direct lines to the EU and the UN. But it was their dark arts that kept the clients coming: managing Wikipedia entries, controlling their own astroturfed NGOs, manipulating Google results so that the first thing you saw when you searched 'Saracen Kazakhstan' wasn't a woman being dragged from a court room.

Against this, photos of the local kids burying their time capsule to mark the opening of the Saracen-sponsored law school. *British Secretary of State for Industry leads largest-ever trade mission seeking to cement UK–Kazakhstan ties.*

I took a seat.

'Any news?' she said. 'On the ... situation.'

'We're working hard. We may have something of a Russian influence operation on our hands.'

Piper sighed. 'Russian influence.'

'Have you had issues with any unusual online activity?'

'Issues? Reality is melting. That's an issue. That's new terrain. How long have you got?'

She clicked on a video, turned the MacBook towards me. Five guards in black uniforms surrounded a Daewoo Nexia on a narrow road. They pulled the doors open and dragged three men in T-shirts and jeans out of the car, forcing them to lie face down on the ground. There was a rocky escarpment on one side of the road, a fence on the other. One of the uniformed men pulled a handgun and fired at the men's legs.

Title: *Saracen Oil's private army.* Posted today, 7,324 views.

'Genuine?' I said.

'We're checking. There's quite a lot of GL5 in the country. The views have doubled in the last couple of hours and it's just been reposted by a big name in the US. All of which shows you why a story about a woman who turns out to have been spying for a British oil company and got herself caught up in fuck knows what could give us a lot of fires to put out.'

The source was an account called Miss_P, with a picture of a Disney princess as an avatar.

'They've spent eight months tweeting diet tips and inspirational quotes: *Count your age by friends, not years. Count your life by smiles, not tears.* Fine. There are make-up tips, a guide to Astana, then, 23 November, Miss P goes in heavy on abuse by Private Security Contractors. She posts on various platforms and gets big amplification.'

A quick glance at the analytics told me it was the system Vishinsky's unit had developed. You establish shepherd accounts – active and influential people who kick off a trending topic. For that you need a large number of followers and interaction with high-profile players. Those are difficult to establish, and had to be run by humans, but you only needed a few. Sheepdog accounts follow and are also run by humans. They retweet the stories and riff on them, turning up the heat, making the whole thing go viral. Then come the sheep – the zombie army of bots – helping to amplify it and spread the stories across platforms.

Up next on Piper's tour of melting reality was the still image of a young woman sitting in the snow, crying, forked tributaries of blood down her face.

'What happened to her?' I asked.

'Attacked by police during protests in a town called Semey.'

'Connected to the rape?'

'I don't know. I don't think so.'

The picture came attached to a report on a citizen journalism website called InfoVillage, apparently hosted in Armenia. *Tensions simmer as protests continue.*

Semey was in the north-east of Kazakhstan, close to the border with Russia. Its central square had been occupied, which at minus 10 degrees suggested a serious level of commitment. Origins of the protests were unclear – the report alluded to ongoing refusal by local authorities to allow environmental campaigning or union activities. Last week, three students had been arrested for inciting discord. Rather than quashing things, the situation blew up. Locals were now out in force with photographs of the students and banners demanding justice.

It didn't vibe ethnic conflict, more anti-oppression. People were singing. Some of the elders wore traditional Kazakh clothing.

'The signs say things like *Put the People First*,' I said. '*Protect Workers' Rights*.'

'Okay,' Piper said.

They looked genuine: home-made, not mass-produced – varying handwriting, different paint and ink. Someone lifted up a

Styrofoam model resembling the Goddess of Democracy statue erected by protesters on Tiananmen Square.

I clicked back to the men being dragged out of the Daewoo.

'Who filmed this?'

'A member of the public.'

'Just passing by? It's not filmed through a windscreen.'

'That's true.'

'Have the British press picked up any of this?'

'I'm managing to keep them at bay for now.'

'This is a DV camera, not a phone.'

'You reckon?'

'I know. The lighting's off a camera light.' I listened to the voices in the background, checked the uniforms, then some of the other videos posted which purportedly documented GL5 malpractice: a man in his underwear on a concrete floor, someone on the ground with their head between their knees, someone handcuffed to a trough. 'At least two of the other videos are from Georgia,' I said. 'Shot five years ago at least. You can hear the voices in the background, the accents.'

Piper nodded slowly, eyes lighting up. 'Interesting,' she said. 'You're sure?'

'That's a Georgian number plate in the background.'

She grabbed her phone and stood up. 'Get yourself a drink.'

Piper wandered over to the window and made a call, touching her forehead to the glass as she spoke.

'We may have some ammunition ... Yes, I'll send that ... No, we don't want to drive more traffic unnecessarily ...'

I went through her bag. In a thick Gucci wallet I found a swipe pass identical to the one Walker had used to access the Vectis office block. I pocketed it. I went to the bar and helped myself to a beer. She came back thoughtful.

'Do you think your missing colleague connects to all this?'

'Maybe.'

Piper took a hit on the vape, disappeared briefly behind an apple-scented cloud.

'Shit,' she sighed. Then she turned to me again, flapping a hand at the steam. 'You've been here awhile?'

'Why?'

'You seem to understand this place more than most people.'

'I wouldn't say that.'

'How do you see it?' She brought up footage of the crowd in Semey. 'Is this a revolution? That's what I'm worried about. A Central Asian spring?'

'No. People like the President. They like what he's done.'

'These guys?' Piper pointed at a clipping on the table: *Kazakh Police Break Up Strikers*.

'They aren't protesting about the President. They want a pay rise. We have strikes in the UK.'

She nodded. I felt her warming to me and pressed on, trying to imagine what Toby Bell would have said.

'This region's got failed states all around, and here's one that's doubled its GDP, that hasn't been at war. The population's generally happy. It's got religious pluralism.'

'That's what we tell people.'

'Churches, synagogues. It's a secular Islamic state: modern, open-minded. Isn't that the holy grail?'

'Where's the synagogue?'

'Almaty. There's even close ties to Israel. You don't have to draw too much attention to that, but it's true.'

'Like Turkey used to be,' Piper said.

'Sure, but less complicated. A young, optimistic Turkey without Kurds.'

'What are you doing tomorrow morning?'

'Why?'

'Some of the delegation are unconvinced about British involvement here – they see it as high-risk. I could do with them meeting someone articulate, with a few facts at their fingertips. A little brunch to get the British government onside.'

'Brunch is good,' I said, conscious that I was being swept along by my own acting ability. We swapped numbers. Piper took another suck of vapour, and sized me up.

'You should meet Galina. She'd like you.'

'The President's daughter?'

'She likes English men.'

'Why not? I'm a sociable guy.' We shook hands. I stood up. 'Can I ask a weird question?' I said.

'Sure.'

'What was in the time capsule?'

'Time capsule?'

'At the ribbon-cutting ceremony.'

'I don't know. An iPhone, a football shirt, I think. Some poems by local children, their hopes for the future. Why?'

'What are their hopes?'

'Their hopes? I have no idea. It was all in Kazakh.'

THIRTY-ONE

Stefan messaged that afternoon: Eagle landed.

I checked that there was no lookout in the Hilton's lobby, then walked through to the back stairs, up to the room I'd booked for him, and knocked.

'I'm going to get some food,' I said, using our usual code.

He opened the door in shorts and a hoody, headphones around his neck. It was good to see him.

'Elliot,' he said, when the door was closed, gripping my hand. 'Where the fuck am I?'

'Winter wonderland. I appreciate you stopping by.'

Stefan kept his hair cropped military-close, a neat beard with the first touches of grey that made his cheeks look more sunken than they were and brought out the blue, insomniac intensity of his eyes. His room already smelled of energy drinks, a chemical undertone to the pine-scented toiletries; curtains closed, TV on Formula One. He had three computers set up in total, a MacBook on the bed, two Panasonics on the bureau: rugged, magnesium-alloy-encased laptops of the kind used by the military. A separate 2 TB hard drive stood on the bedside table, fan whirring, connected to a Wave Box – a portable device that generously bestowed strong, password-free wi-fi to all those within five hundred metres or so. It gave us all of the internet traffic flowing through it – email, instant messages and browser sessions. There was also an array of outfits: workers' overalls, hi-vis vests, a toolbox.

'What's going on?' Stefan asked.

'Why?'

'I placed a wall-contact mic near the room you're interested in. The occupant makes and takes calls on a dedicated satphone; deep encryption. Plays white noise from an audio jammer.'

Stefan showed me images he'd taken with an under-door camera. Walker's room was neat. You saw the audio jammer on the bureau, a black box barely bigger than a cigarette packet. A suitcase had been lifted to the bed, which was made. There was a suit over the back of a chair and a bottle of whisky beside the bed.

'Is he in there now?'

'He left ten minutes ago. So who am I spying on? What are we doing here?'

'A woman's missing. She was working in Astana for Vectis, the private intelligence company. She's vanished. We need to know what she got.'

'Who is she?'

'A former colleague of mine. Her name's Joanna Lake. If you see or hear anything mentioning that name, let me know.'

'How long's she been missing?'

'Seven days now.' I talked him through the mall swap, the email she'd sent from the IT café. Stefan checked the locations on a map, then sat back and sipped his Red Bull. It was a relief to have someone I trusted around. Stefan had been a teenager when I first met him, ten years ago. He came to my attention in a dusty office belonging to New Scotland Yard's cyber crimes division. Seventeen years old, born in north London to Polish parents, he'd been arrested for hacking his school's system, promptly hacked into the police unit investigating him, then crashed the Home Office website. He already had a criminal record for breaking into electronics stores. He'd tried to escape the country but was picked up at Dover with his brother's passport. I got him released the next day. A year later he was helping GCHQ develop battlefield capability, and a year after that directing cyber ops in Afghanistan. If he ever wished I'd left him on the run, he was polite enough not to say so.

A couple of years later I was in Dubai when I heard that someone at the Burj Al Arab was wiping minibar accounts from the hotel system. I found him locked in his room, war-fatigued, drinking a cocktail of Mountain Dew, tequila and Zopiclone, and gambling heavily. I paid off his debts and put him in touch with Marius in Romania, who regularly asked for contacts on the ground: people who could infiltrate delivery chains or break into places covertly. Stefan was trained in all that. He had the rare combination of skill and greed that made men return to conflict zones voluntarily. I got him a six-figure salary, knowing he was worth twice as much.

'You think she's still in the area?' he asked.

'I think it's a possibility. I think she discovered something that was dangerous for her. Look out for the words "Perfect Vision",' I said. 'And "Catalyst".'

Stefan nodded. He'd heard enough cryptonyms in his time, and knew not to ask for more knowledge than he needed. The more you knew, the more people wanted to torture you.

I showed him the map I'd marked up with cafés and restaurants near the buildings I was interested in, anywhere targets might gather. Often the secret was not to try and directly hack the offices themselves, but find where staff congregate with unprotected smartphones and laptops. Stefan had a Polar Breeze – a remote data-sucking device for tapping wirelessly into nearby computers – and a Stingray, which was able to mimic a cell tower and force all phones in a 200-metre radius to connect to it. From there, it could extract contact information, dialled numbers, text messages, calendar entries. It could give you a stepping stone into an entire network.

'There's a range of places I'd like to know more about: Kazakh security services to start with, then Gazprom offices and the Russian embassy.' I pointed out the internet café Joanna had used and asked him to see if there were any traces of her activity there. 'Callum Walker in the room below us heads the company Joanna works for: Vectis Global Insight. I'd like to know why she's working for them, and anything they might be keeping from me.'

Then I showed him the plan of the Vectis office.

'All their computing's on a closed network but I reckon we can establish a physical breach.' I handed him the swipe pass from Piper's bag. He turned it in his fingers. 'TensorCo electronic gates at the front,' I said. 'Dozy security, two dozen different companies across the building. The swipe will work the lifts as well. Office entrance is pincode; possibly 3579 or 3570. Facilities maintenance for the building is done by a German company called Apleona, and that includes tech. Server room's in the basement.'

'And this is a job for Six?'

'It's a job for me.'

'How are your diplomatic relations with the Kazakh government when I end up in a cell?'

'We use the usual contingency plans. There's a big security team here; you don't have to worry about that.'

He looked uneasy. I was leaving when he said, 'What do you want me to do about the bots?'

I stopped. I'd almost forgotten my request to Evotec regarding the psychological war being waged online.

'Have you got a lead on it?'

He typed in a password. The face of a young woman appeared on the screen of the MacBook. She was pale, in her early twenties, Caucasian with a touch of Kazakh; streaks in the hair and a certain force in the dark eyes.

'Who's that?'

'The enemy. You wanted to know about online activity. This

has just come through from the team. She connects to pro-Russian blogs. You'll be pleased to know you're right: there's a massive online information warfare operation going on.'

They'd identified over two hundred accounts, a lot simply amplifying a core of ten or twenty with original content, 'hand-written', so to speak. The handwriting meant you could compare phrases and grammar to open-source social media.

'She runs this site,' Stefan said. 'Aliya in Astana. Favourable to Russia. Favourable to the fight against Islamist terrorism. Anti-Western oil companies. She posts heavily on Vkontakte.'

I studied the face again. There was something haunting about it; someone you'd find yourself watching without meaning to. I wondered if it was computer-generated.

Stefan showed me a cartoon on the Aliya in Astana site: a drawing of Zhaparov stamping a polished shoe on a bearded mullah. I recognised the style. It looked like those produced by an outfit called Infosurfing, which posted pro-Kremlin graphics on Instagram. Quotes from Zhaparov's speeches had been put into calligraphic fonts, sometimes alongside pictures of eagles or faded-out photographs of balaclava'd special forces.

Aliya also reposted Testimony reports on Saracen malpractice. Only she beefed them up with images: a photograph of Robert Carter and CEOs in what Aliya claimed was a lapdancing club. It was set alongside a photo supposedly showing workers at one of the drill sites, malnourished Chinese and Indians squatting around a pan of rice in something resembling a shower block.

She was good: skilled at counter-argument, quick at sourcing memes, often using Western or Asian celebrities. She addressed other commentators by name, engaging in four or five debates simultaneously across various platforms: about the barbarism of traditional Kazakh customs like 'bride kidnapping' – in which a groom abducted his wife-to-be – about increasing use of the veil in rural communities to the south and east of the country. She debated the economic benefits of oil exploration. She originated hashtags: #KZFreedom. #StopSaracen.

I clicked #StopSaracen, got a photograph of a woman burning.

A forty-year-old woman had set herself on fire outside a Saracen compound in Shymkent. It was the second self-immolation in a week. The only footage that had surfaced showed a Kazakh police officer rushing towards her with a coat in his hands to smother the flames. The woman herself was barely visible, lying on her side next to an electronic gate, hands to her head, flames consuming her torso, which wasn't easy to achieve and took a lot of accelerant. Apparently the woman had longstanding issues with the company over compensation for the death of her husband, a rig worker. People were debating whether it counted as terrorism, whether it was even political or just tragic, some belated *sati*. Others pointed out that there were no corroborating sources.

But there was an interview with her brother, weeping tearlessly on a sofa in a low-ceilinged front room. I tried to figure out what felt strange about it. Finally, I enlarged the prints on the wall behind him, then I brought up the clip of myself in the Triumph.

'Look,' I said to Stefan. 'The prints on the wall behind him.'

'What about them?'

I showed him the Triumph clip. Both rooms had the same print of a horse and rider travelling through mountains. The rider was bending down asking directions from a peasant with a staff. The path behind him meandered from the woods into a rocky landscape.

'Even the light reflecting on the frames is identical,' he said. 'What's this clip of you about?'

'I don't know. But someone somewhere is crafting fake videos. Maybe several people, maybe a factory of them.'

'Maybe an algorithm.' Stefan was still staring at the screen.

'What do you mean?'

'These days they can create their own imagery. Places, faces, whatever.'

'Whole scenarios?'

'Sure. If an algorithm can predict a scenario it can create an image of it easily enough. Deep learning's a step away from deep dreaming, where computers become imaginative, start generating their own content.'

'They could produce scenarios then produce imagery to fit them?'

'Why not? There could be a thousand videos of you being produced every hour, a thousand parallel universes.' After another moment, he said: 'The fire's good.' He tapped a knuckle against the image of self-immolation.

'You don't think it's real?'

'No. But I think someone's got their effects working nicely.'

We watched the burning woman again, then the grieving brother.

'Has Aliya posted fake videos before?' I asked.

'I haven't checked. And it's not as if it's easy to tell. The US defence department has tried to develop tools for detecting computer-generated material, but no silver bullet yet.'

'Any more information about her?'

'We located her personal social media,' Stefan said. 'The name behind the more glamorous persona is Aliya Savinova, a postgrad student at Nazarbayev University. Syntax gets a ninety-seven per cent match; so does vocabulary, even typos.'

'Address?'

'There's no address online but we got her IP and wi-fi connection history. Every morning her laptop connects to home broadband. Records suggest there are four people living at that address: one is Ms Savinova.'

I took a look at Savinova's personal social media. Pre-2017 she'd been a lifestyle blogger: recipes, fashion, music, also cultural happenings. She posted poetry, talked about her short stories as well. The poetry was good, covering urban ennui, romantic longing, thinly disguised erotic musings.

She liked modernism, eye shadow, drinking alone. I wondered if she liked starting wars.

'Think her account's been hijacked?' Stefan asked.

'I don't know. Think she's definitely real?'

'According to her Facebook page, she just checked in to a gallery opening two miles away. So I guess you've got one way of finding out.'

THIRTY-TWO

I drove to the gallery, a new glass box beside the river, sponsored by Credit Bank of Moscow and Emporio Armani. It was already crowded when I got there, with high security for a wealthy turn-out. I tried to see the guest list, began to blag my way in, then the voice of Craig Bryant reached me from the throng.

'He's with me.'

Bryant drifted into view with a woman in heavy make-up and heels that raised her a couple of inches above him. He ush-ered me in.

'I told you it was a small town at heart.'

'Small town with big money.'

The smell of paint mingled with expensive perfume and canapés. The crowd was mostly business, the power circuit, a few sharper, younger Kazakhs. The art was modern, one room darkened for video installations, one involving bean bags and headphones. The stated theme of 'Nostalgic Futures' was offset by models in tight black T-shirts distributing Armani goodie bags. The Russian bank co-sponsoring the show kept a lower profile.

If Bryant felt any sheepishness about our last encounter he didn't show it. He introduced me to Dr Zyabkina. Zyabkina, Bryant explained, was a psychologist working with the Health Minister to tackle the problem of radicalisation.

'How interesting,' I said. 'The Health Ministry.'

'It is a public health issue like any other,' she said. 'That is how it must be treated, like an epidemic.'

I glanced around for Aliya Savinova as I fell into conversation, found myself studying the crowd. The white-painted space was still novel enough to inspire deference. Older attendees circulated obediently; the middle-aged recognised it as a new kind of fun like fast food and rock music. A lot of the young were checking their phones.

'Think they've got an epidemic?' Bryant said.

'Things are certainly febrile.'

'Maybe I was wrong in my judgement of this place.'

'Places change.'

'If the heat online spills into the real world, the region's going to be getting a lot of attention fast.'

'Think it will?'

'It's tense times ahead either way. As if this place didn't have enough going on.'

'Right. You would have thought a fear of Muslims could bring Russia and the West together,' I said.

'That's the real enemy, right? That's the happy ending they can agree on: kill some terrorists.'

Then I saw her. A young woman with black hair, magenta lipstick, glasses. It felt like seeing a celebrity, with an extra frisson of shared secrets. There was a poise to Aliya that made her seem, on first impression, older than her twenty-three years: cool, sceptical eyes, black jeans, white blouse. She took photos of the exhibits. Twice, she checked her phone and typed something.

She was accompanied by two female friends. I waited for her to move away from them, saw which way she was circulating, then told Bryant I'd be back. I took a fresh glass of wine and placed myself two works ahead. A semi-abstract painting incorporating symbols from Kazakh rock art. A sign on the wall said that the artist grew up in Mongolia, completed her education in Utah, where she became interested in a new idea of nomadism involving fluidity.

Aliya Savinova browsed a few metres away: a wall-hanging woven from fragments of sportswear; a vitrine of old ID cards. I watched her reapply her lipstick, checking her face in her phone. She was someone with layers, I thought; hidden aspects and desires, which was what you looked for in a potential agent. Espionage, like any vice, is a weapon against mundanity, against being unnoticed or unworthy of notice. Contrary to expectations, you sought the attention seekers.

Finally we were side by side.

'Can I ask – do you think this is patronising?' I said. I spoke Russian. She looked at me, then at the work we'd arrived at: a pastiche of Soviet realism: heroic workers holding games consoles.

'Slightly.'

'I don't imagine this means much to anyone now,' I said, as we walked past. 'It's a concept, well executed. Not much more.'

'Yes.'

I introduced myself as Toby. She told me she was Aliya. We walked on, in step, casually. I saw her friends turn, look. She glanced at them and gave a wry smile. I struggled to discern the personality she projected online. But then that was the point of an online personality: you could be different. I wanted to know how the operation was being coordinated. Did she work in a centre of some kind? Did she receive instructions remotely? Was Joanna on to this? She reminded me a little of Joanna.

We walked past glossy portraits of militiamen – Kiev, Zagreb, Georgia – into a final room devoted to a triptych of large black and white photographs. The central one showed the Cathedral of Christ the Saviour in Moscow collapsing in clouds of dust as the Soviets dynamited it. To its right, less dramatically but more hauntingly, was a mosque in Uzbekistan being used as a warehouse for cotton. To the left was a Ukrainian synagogue converted to a centre for communist youth. A banner hung across it with the old communist slogan: *Peace to the World*. This was the title of the artwork.

Aliya studied each image in turn. An older woman with an Armani badge arrived at our side, beaming.

'It is good they are showing this, no? A lot of people still think it was better in those times. Young people too. They don't know about this.'

'Do you think that's what it's saying?' I asked.

'Yes,' she said, less certainly. Someone caught her attention and she wandered off. Aliya looked sceptical. I leaned closer.

'I was in this country a few years ago,' I said. 'Further east. I met a man who was ninety-four years old. He used to be a travelling merchant, carrying gold into China, then returning with his camels loaded up with silk. Anyway, he became a butcher in Almaty, settled there, and a friend of mine introduced me to him. I asked what he thought of Kazakhstan now and he said, "Everything was better in the time of Czar Nikolai II."'

Aliya smiled.

'He said that?'

'Czar Nikolai. Yes, in the 1900s. Downhill from there.'

'Maybe he was right.'

'Are you an artist?'

'A writer. And a student.'

'What do you write?'

'Various things.'

'I've always wanted to write,' I said, ignoring her opacity. 'It must take dedication.'

'Not so much what I do.'

'Do you write fiction?'

'A little. Less so now.'

We arrived back at the militias. One thing they had in common, it occurred to me: all had been fighting Russia or Russian proxies in the last few years. I wondered about the Credit Bank of

241

Moscow's involvement. Last year, a show of photo-journalism in Berlin got taken down when it turned out to be put together by the Kremlin.

'Going to write about this?' I asked.

'Maybe.'

'I've always wanted to find some *young* Kazakh writers, people writing about now. Can you recommend any?'

'Of course.' She recommended a writer and said she knew her personally. I repeated the writer's name to memorise it. Aliya's friends were wrapping up for the cold, eyeing the outside in a way that made me think of sniper fire. Craig Bryant drifted into view on the far side of the room. He saw me, lifted a glass. I saw him consider approaching.

'You should get back to your friends,' I said.

'Yes.'

'It's been a pleasure to meet you.' We shook hands again. I began to move away, then stopped. 'Aliya?' She turned. 'I'm fairly new to this place. Would you possibly meet me again? Chat some more?'

She pulled a face, as if this was distasteful, or awkward.

'Perhaps,' she said. 'I'm very busy.'

'Of course. I understand. No obligation.' She made a final appraisal of me, then gave me her number.

'It's been a pleasure, Aliya,' I said. She nodded, and was gone by the time Bryant made it over.

'Get lucky?'

'It's nice to meet some locals.'

'I can find you more. What are you up to tonight?' Bryant asked. 'There's a bar just opened in Yesil district called Insomnia.'

I might have ended up accompanying him to Insomnia if my phone hadn't buzzed with a text: a landline to call.

Lieutenant Shomko answered.

'The woman you are looking for,' he said. 'I've got something.'

THIRTY-THREE

We agreed on the sauna.

'Room 303,' the woman said when I got there.

'Security cameras—'

'Already off.'

The room was dimly lit; candles, a bowl of condoms. He was standing beside the window. He had a laptop and a flash drive. He stank of cigarettes. A TV showing a music channel, on mute: Russian hip-hop, silent pool parties. I put the sound on.

'I can't do any more for you after this,' he said.

'What have you got?'

'I need money.'

'I'll give you money.'

'Now.'

I handed him his envelope. He transferred the notes to his wallet, inserted the flash drive, opened a file. It was CCTV footage: a static shot of a broad, black Mercedes S-Class on a six-lane road. The backdrop looked like Astana: tower blocks and snow. Next shot you knew it was Astana because the car turned in through the gates of the Gazprom office. Time stamp: 11.31 a.m., 25 November. One day before the wireless dead drop in the mall, two days before Joanna went missing.

'Who is it?'

He clicked to another shot, seventeen minutes earlier. The car was parked on a back road, someone in a parka with the hood up approaching it. He zoomed in. You could just about see a face beneath the hood. It was Joanna.

She appeared to climb into the car. It pulled out while the door was still closing.

Shomko went over to the window and checked the street outside.

'The car's registered to an individual called Aleksandr Kolobkov,' he said. 'He's a fixer for a man called Vladislav Vishinsky.'

I looked again at the images, starting to feel uneasy.

'A fixer?'

'The driver has been identified as Viktor Trunenkov, former special forces soldier now working for Vishinsky.'

'You're sure about that?'

'This is why you are hunting her, no?'

A car door slammed outside. Shomko peered down.

'Customer,' he said.

We both listened to the customers arrive, and kept listening until the showers came on.

'Where does the car go?'

'We don't know. Did you know she was working for the Russians?'

'That's not what this says.'

'I deserve a bonus, no?'

'There's a lot of ways of forcing someone into a car. They don't all involve guns.'

'Blackmail.'

I clicked back to the car shots. 'What cameras are these from?'

'The earlier pictures are from a police security camera. The ones on the alleyway are from a camera belonging to the Keruen shopping centre.'

'You took them from the systems yourself?'

'No. Someone else did.'

'Seen the original footage?'

'This is original footage.' He took the envelope out of his pocket and counted the notes.

'What about the man who was shot on Malakhov Street?' I said.

'I don't know. Maybe he found out what she was really up to.'

'What does the investigation say?'

'I have heard nothing about the investigation, except that people want to find the English woman.'

'I told you to get information from the investigation.'

'I got you information about the woman you want. Five thousand dollars, you said.'

'Who gave you these? I need a name, otherwise this means nothing.'

'He is trusted.'

'Not by me. I don't buy this.'

'You don't pay?'

'I don't believe.'

'So you were fucking her and she deceived you. Now she's fucking some Russian.' He spat. 'I am sorry for your heartbreak. Don't fall in love with spies.'

THIRTY-FOUR

I locked the door of the room when he'd left. If there was any truth in his theory it was too much to contemplate; it would be the universe inverted, and I resisted opening the door on that possibility because it would be overwhelming. If this was some sophisticated attempt at framing her then I felt sick at the efficiency, and deeply wary of my involvement. It would explain the suspicion on me and Tom Marsh, on anyone she was close to or came into contact with. It might explain the closing down of Building D's operation, and her running to Kazakhstan.

I looked again at the stills.

Images are powerful because they suggest you don't have to think. Here's truth. But there's always a story behind them. In the story behind the disappearance of Joanna Lake there was an email to me. *Catalyst.*

One woman getting into a car. I enlarged it on the screen as if an answer would appear. It was her; no force, everything to suggest she knew what she was doing and wanted to make it discreet.

You recruit someone to the intelligence services because of their confidence and cunning, and then train them to lie for their country. They elect to transfer these skills to a private company working for the energy industry. You ask: could they ever lose their moral bearings? Go rogue?

But not for Vishinsky. Not in a million years. Surely.

In my experience, you're working for whoever keeps you alive. I found Sergei Cherenkov's card, wondered what he knew about all this. I was still holding it when I noticed the music videos had been replaced by grainy footage. People stampeded through a shopping mall. Behind them walked a calm, young-looking man, strolling with an automatic rifle.

People dived into shops, pulling doors closed. The man strolled past abandoned benches, fountains, potted palm trees. It cut to a news presenter reading an autocue: *Sunlight shopping mall, St Petersburg.*

I clicked through channels. Most were showing the same footage. Initial reports said eight people had died, twenty wounded. The attacker had been shot by police. He was Kazakh.

I left the sauna, returned to my hotel and went online. A video by a group called the Islamic Movement of Kazakhstan had gone up, claiming responsibility. It showed five Kazakh-looking men in combat fatigues with Korans and AK-47s. The landscape was semi-arid, a low chain of dusty green mountains in the background. Could have been Iraq, could have been Syria. Could have been southern Spain. It was turning up everywhere, along with their statement: *We demand that Russia ceases all activities in the Middle East and Central Asia. Until Russian troops and their proxies withdraw from all Muslim lands we will wage war against you wherever we find you. You come to our land, we will come to yours.*

The leader spoke calmly, directly to camera, in Kazakh-inflected Russian. A black flag billowed slowly behind him. Shadows lined up. His lips synced with the words.

Kazakhstan was secular, but there were 16 million inhabitants, and at least some were unemployed young men with access to YouTube. One hundred and fifty or so had headed to Syria over the last couple of years. Wars leak. One or two were going to make it back. I'd come across Central Asian fighters, though not as many as from the UK. I'd come across fighters from most countries, from the land of YouTube: men and women who'd walked out of their homes, out of work, taking in the drab surroundings a final time as the words of a video echoed: *Look around as you sit in comfort and ask yourself if this is how you want to die.* I should know something about walking out of your life into someone else's war.

Once you've gone, you've gone. For most jihadis, returning home meant prison and torture. Life is different when you can't go home. You start dreaming of new things, changing the world so it fits you again. It's an all-or-nothing situation. And when you've been a commander of armed men, saluted and cheered, it's hard to go back to being a mechanic or a hairdresser.

Walker called. 'Seen this?'

'I'm watching.'

'Know anything about IMK?'

'Why would I?'

'Thought it was your side of things.'

'No.'

'Did you get any more from your contact?'

'I'll let you know when I do.' I hung up, deleted the incriminating footage of Joanna, then I walked to the screen and stared at the grainy shots of the mall shooting. The incident happened around 4 p.m. in St Petersburg, 7 p.m. in Astana. Broke 8 p.m. Now experts had appeared, nodding over videolinks: 'ISIS has been down on its luck in the Middle East, so it's going to move its attention to those nations that have tried to defeat it. We're going to see increasing numbers of these incidents.'

I clicked to Twitter. The attacker had been named as Bakhtiyar Ibraimov, twenty-one years old, born in Aktobe, Kazakhstan. He'd travelled to Syria in July 2015, where he'd fought with a unit attached to Al-Nusra. Arrived in Russia on a Saudi passport that might or might not have been fake.

Aktobe was an industrial city; grim prospects. Should have been wealthy with oil, but the lowest incomes tended to be around the oilfields. The disjuncture bred wild and angry dreams. These were the places to watch. There are always two capitals, the one with the power and the one with the resentment: Benghazis, Aleppos.

From Aktobe to the Al-Nusra Front was far from implausible. Al-Nusra were a tight, effective force in Syria, operating as conventional military or clandestine cells according to need. We'd tried to distance them from Al Qaeda for the sake of some tentative collaboration, but that was a push even for us. They'd been designated untouchable. Their promotional clips usually came through a media outlet, The White Minaret, which posted to a jihadist web forum called Shamoukh al-Islam. This video wasn't on either.

Aliya Savinova's take on events had just gone out: *Did the Sunlight attacker have contact with British intelligence?*

That gave me a chill across my back. I clicked the link to her blog. Under an old cartoon of imperial powers gathered around a map, she went to town.

Experts have no doubt that the events of 9/11 were the handiwork of the CIA. The so-called 'terrorism' in the Middle East is also the handiwork of the CIA and Mossad. Therefore why should Kazakhstan doubt other possible crimes of the West?

It is known that MI6 sent fighters from terrorist groups to Libya and Syria. One insider has said: 'The dangers of "blowback" were raised but never fully taken seriously.'

It is Russia that lies exposed to take the brunt of this 'blowback', having led the fight against ISIS while the West wavered. Perhaps certain heads in Western intelligence find this convenient.

The first thing that struck me was the mix of registers. Aside from the quote, which I recognised from an *Observer* article, the vocabulary wavered. 'Brunt', 'certain heads' – that wasn't the style of English I'd seen her using elsewhere. Second thing was the nature of this material, which felt a little close to home.

Now I watched the IMK videos again. The guns looked like Chinese-made copies of AR-15 assault rifles. China had supplied a lot of knock-off AR-15s to rebel groups in South Sudan. When the Sudanese economy tanked, their government offloaded hundreds to Qatar. Qatar had them airlifted straight to western Turkey for smuggling into Syria. Wars exist in hard-wearing materials, and these circulate. Sometimes that was convenient; Bohren understood all this. But his weren't the only shady AR-15s around.

Two hundred and forty IMK videos had been uploaded in the last two weeks. That gave me a lot to trawl. None more than two weeks back, as far as I could tell.

It looked like they were either trained by IS's media team or working directly with them. They shared the same slick production techniques: good lighting, careful composition, multiple camera angles. They minimised the colour palette, which made the end result sharper. It was textbook – if anything, it was too textbook. Then there was the music. I had a secret love of *nasheeds*, the a capellas accompanying every IS video. There were companies deep in Iraq tasked with nothing but churning these out. Over the last couple of years I'd collected examples in Turkish, Uyghur, English, Bengali, French and Chinese. I'd never heard one in Kazakh before.

They had shiny Toyotas and new body armour. I tried to remember details of the missing cache I'd been questioned about by Alastair Undercroft: vehicles, assault rifles, body armour. I thought through my chaotic exit from Saudi.

Blowback.

Aliya's blog had been featured on Russian TV: *My blog featured on TV!!* An obscure Christian Orthodox channel had lifted a map from her website, black arrows indicating the flow of Islamists from the Middle East into Kazakhstan. The channel ran it alongside video of right-wing activists chanting in a Moscow suburb.

It wasn't immediately clear what they were protesting against: Kazakhstan, Central Asia, Islam, an influx of Central Asian migrants trying to outrun a collapsing economy. The protest crowd was 90 per cent young men in Adidas and jeans, some sporting black balaclavas or blue medical masks, often football scarves pulled up over their faces; they had esoteric flags involving swords and eagles, fists and crosses. The yellow of Russian nationalism. Moscow, but outskirts. I remembered those places: Yugozapadnaya, Petrovsko-Razumovskaya; vast high-rises and little else. I turned the sound up. There was the predictable chant of 'Russia for Russians'; one I liked: 'Sport! Health! Nationalism!', which sounded slightly less bizarre in Russian, but only just. Then the occasional rendition of 'Fuck the Jews' thrown in for good measure. One from the repertoire.

I called Alexander Turbayevskiy, reporter on Moscow's *Kommersant* newspaper, but also closely involved with the Sova centre, a Russian NGO that monitored ethnic hatred. He'd been a corduroy-clad oasis of humane intellect during my stays in Moscow.

'Are you watching what I'm watching?' he asked.

'How did they get organised so quickly? How did they get permission?'

'It's the tip of the iceberg. The nationalist parties are suddenly loud and everywhere, especially Rodina.' Rodina, meaning 'Motherland', had been vocal about Ukraine – and even Syria – an anti-West voice set up by Vishinsky's team. 'Rodina leaned on the city authorities. Nationalists get to march, it seems. All seventy or eighty of them. There were some attacks afterwards: three men beaten up badly.'

'Online activity?'

'Massive. With an increasingly clear narrative: Kazakh terrorism is a threat, shadowy forces are using Central Asian Islamists to attack Russia.'

Aliya's MI6 conspiracy theory appeared on Russian platforms – LiveJournal, VK, the website of the Young Guard of United Russia – alongside stories about the dangers of Islam. One story repackaged accusations from Ukraine: a Russian boy crucified on the side of a building. In some versions the victim was still alive when he was pinned up, in others locals gathered to collect the blood. References to Odessa had been converted to Karaganda. Slightly more grounded in reality were images of broken gravestones from the west of Kazakhstan. A court in Atyrau had just jailed eight followers of a purist Wahabi sect for destroying a local graveyard. The followers believed that Kazakh traditions of ancestor worship transgressed the rules of Islam. They were shown receiving their sentence in a court of dark green and beige, a line of five men, heads bowed.

I watched more clips on Vkontakte. A kid no older than fifteen, cheeks red from the cold, said: 'I came here today because there's an occupation going on by people from Central Asia. They steal, they're violent and we need to get rid of them.' Another interviewee, an older man, called the Kazakhs a terrorist threat and said he'd support any Russian intervention – there was a right to self-defence. I watched him five times, convinced that the shape of his head morphed at the edges as he spoke, the mouth somehow detached from the rest of his face. Authorities in Moscow were looking into how the shooter had got a Saudi passport. Saudi officials denied any form of collusion.

Aliya had tweeted: *They will attack Astana next.*

I looked at the tweet for a long time. Then the comments: *Don't tempt fate. Keep telling it, Aliya. That would wake these jokers up.*

It could have been dismissed like any other online prophecy.

Only, she'd been blogging about the dangers of an attack on Russian soil forty-eight hours before Bakhtiyar Ibraimov walked into the Sunlight shopping mall.

I was building a conspiracy theory of my own.

I picked up the phone, dialled a number I'd hoped not to use again. Mohammad Reza Nikfar answered promptly. Not many people had this number, and if he'd given it to you it was because he valued your acquaintance.

'It's me,' I said.

'Don't tell me: you're putting the band back together.'

'I'm curious to know what you've heard recently.'

'I've been trying to contact you,' he said. 'Are you back in Turkey?'

'Not right now. What do you know about St Petersburg?'

'There's a possibility he connects to our network. Maybe distantly, maybe not so distantly. Can you shed some light?'

I felt vertigo, standing over a pit of my own making, with difficulty discerning the knot of connections at the bottom. Nikfar, or Reza to friends, was Iranian-born, CIA-trained, Peshawar-made. He'd been in the dark corners of the CIA long enough to have helped build the Taliban and take it down again. He was the hinge between Langley and Pakistan's Inter-Services Intelligence, the largest intelligence agency in the world. It was called Inter-Services because it drew on all branches of Pakistan's armed forces, but I always felt the name described a bigger crossroads, the intelligence equivalent of the arms bazaar in Pakistan's north-western mountains, where every gang came, no laws applied and you could get pretty much anything for a price. Aside from being a reckless visionary, Reza was one of the few intelligence officers who operated at the heart of things.

'Do you have the name on the Saudi passport?' I asked.

'Yousef Shaheen.'

I had arranged a few Saudi passports in my time: they were

gold dust, welcome almost everywhere. I didn't remember a Yousef Shaheen.

'Know when it was issued?'

'No. But something's going on. All the grapevines are whispering: Central Asia, Kazakhstan, the game's moving. I heard Bakhtiyar Ibraimov, the shooter, was involved in drafting up Central Asians to fight in Libya. He has phone connections with UK recruitment networks.'

I fought against mounting disquiet. 'Heard' wasn't a strong verb in intelligence circles; phone connections extended as far as you wanted them to. I stored Reza's conjecture for later reflection.

'IMK a thing?' I asked.

'Possibly. Remnants of Al-Nusra and Abu Uzair's men. It's very hazy at the moment. If it exists it's a splinter cell. I'd take the black flag with a pinch of salt, but they did come up in a JIX report yesterday. Where are you?'

'Kazakhstan.'

'You had a heads-up on this?'

'Not as such.'

'What have you got?'

'Some leads,' I lied. 'But I need your help.'

'Are you on usual channels?'

'Personal ones. They'll do for now.'

He sent the information through: a report from Joint Intelligence X, the secretariat at the heart of Pakistan's security services. The time and date put its distribution twelve hours ago. It was one page, light on detail, collating information from sources in Uzbekistan and Afghanistan.

Intelligence had suggested that a group identifying as the Islamic Movement of Kazakhstan was in possession of detonators and 4,000 kilograms of C-4 explosives. The load originated in Afghanistan: it had been packed in crates on an articulated lorry travelling from Hairatan in Afghanistan to Termez in

Uzbekistan. Uzbek intelligence had tracked it by satellite, with the intention of identifying the insurgent cell. Somewhere along the line things went wrong. The artic was stopped but it was empty. The load had already been transferred.

In the twenty-four hours after the failed seizure, sixteen homes and businesses were raided across Afghanistan. The lorry driver's brother was cooperating. Police had seized a laptop containing research on fuel-air bombs along with a detailed satellite image of Astana and surveillance photographs of public squares.

I called Reza back.

'Have any more details surfaced since this report?'

'Nothing. They came out of nowhere and vanished into nowhere.'

'I'm going to need you to update me if you hear anything more about Astana or the IMK.'

'Of course.'

'What put you on to them?'

'A woman from your end, the one you introduced me to.'

'Joanna Lake?'

'That's what I was trying to contact you about. Is she kosher?'

I felt a stab of adrenalin.

'When was this?'

'About six days ago.'

'What did she say?'

'She'd seen plans of some kind, relating to those explosives. Wouldn't give me a source.'

'I need to know the exact contact time.'

He checked, came back. It was 11.02 p.m.

'11.02 in Islamabad?'

'Yes.'

Then it was a few minutes before she contacted me. In the very narrow window between fleeing the safe house and vanishing.

'She's missing,' I said. 'Went missing in Astana last week.'

'Shit. No one's chased me about that.'

'What device did Joanna call on?'

'Cellphone. We've run a check: it was clean, it's now dead. Been dead for days.'

'I'm going to need your help.'

I sent through a still from the Mega Astana, in case Reza could ID the man in the cap, the probable source for her intelligence. He couldn't. I promised I'd pass any further information his way, took a final look at the anger raging online, then closed my browser.

Where are you, Joanna? What have you led me into?

She'd called Reza. She knew him as one of the only individuals plugged into terrorist networks in all directions. She put him on to an attack, shared intel. Did that give me some frayed thread of a narrative to set against the one in which she sold us out to Gazprom?

I had my eyes closed, the sunlight red through my eyelids.

'When was the last time you kissed someone you weren't trying to recruit?' she asked.

'A long time,' I said, although it wasn't strictly true.

'Did you know some people do it because they enjoy it?'

'Perverts,' I said. If she was making an accusation of coldness on my part it was neutralised by the summer afternoon. I heard the splash of wine in her cup. Then she said, as if it followed from her previous thoughts, 'Do you ever think about all of that probing they did when they recruited us? All that cross-examination, interviewing friends and family behind our backs, setting us tests: we thought they were weeding out the corrupt, but what if that was what they wanted? We were chosen because of our flaws.'

'I don't think they're that imaginative,' I said.

'They chose us because we were already halfway corrupt.'

*

I turned Cherenkov's business card in my hand again and wondered what light he could throw on Perfect Vision, and what I'd have to do to get it. Be careful, I thought. Exhaustion had begun to fog my judgement. I wasn't going to sleep, so I went for a walk.

The roads had iced. I took my gloves off and touched the hard snow. It was what Mongolians called a *harin zud*, a black freeze, when snowfall was followed by another sudden drop in temperature. The earth became inaccessible. Out on the steppe it spelled the death of livestock in their thousands. I'd been told of horses eating their own hair. People died but it was impossible to dig graves, so they were mummified until summer, organs replaced with pine needles and larch cones. In Astana it meant drivers kept to 10 miles per hour, like a city-wide funeral procession. Near Bayterek I saw three crashed cars, one on its side, strands of emergency tape fluttering.

The colours of the office blocks changed from green to blue. There was an unearthly metallic ticking sound that I eventually identified as streetlights agitated in the wind. I got the war-zone feeling, where everything seems provisional, and when you look at buildings you see their destruction too.

Who else was chasing this imminent attack? I didn't feel in a position to take responsibility for stopping it. Reza was good, but he had more allies in Peshawar than Washington. When Joanna needed access to northern Syria I introduced them. We met in the closest he had to an office – which was someone else's office behind five walls of concrete and barbed wire. There was a poster of an imaginary Kurdistan on the wall, a photograph of a young-looking Reza with Bill Clinton. Joanna was all charm and only gave me her opinion of him on the flight back: she said he was well connected and borderline insane. The CIA, she felt sure, kept him active in the hope that he'd get himself killed.

I'd first bumped into him in Tajikistan, the most lawless corner of Asia at that time, controlled by a circus of Russian soldiers, Islamist guerrillas, warlords, bandits and deserters from all sides. It was 90 per cent mountain rock. The only way to make a living was by trading weapons or narcotics. Russia had established outposts along the border, then manned them with drunks and criminals, whiling away long hours as they waited to be decapitated by insurgent Afghans.

I was in the country ostensibly to learn who controlled its mountain passes. Someone in Vauxhall had identified this as important – China was using Tajikistan as a bridge to the Middle East – and I was happy to spend a couple of weeks based in the capital, Dushanbe, heading to the mountains when I could. On the way back to Dushanbe one time, I decided to return through the Yagnob valley to see if I could find the isolated village of Yagnob itself. People there were said to be descendants of people from the ancient kingdom of Samarkand. They spoke a language that hadn't changed significantly in five thousand years. When they prayed, it wasn't towards Mecca but in the direction of the highest mountain peak, the stepping stone to heaven.

I didn't find any Yagnobi. I ended up deeper into the valley than I probably should have done, especially on a raw February night. When I bumped into a crew of Russian soldiers, I was low on food and water, and almost relieved to see them. I still had vodka and cigarettes, and this, combined with the fact that they were strung out on heroin, saved me from summary execution. They invited me to their camp.

The camp was a dirt-walled hole in the ground. I was led between sandbags into something resembling a First World War trench, where everyone was wasted and they were using fuel barrels to make moonshine. Reza sat among it all, serene, pupils constricted to pinpoints. I thought he was one of the locals, in his filthy kaftan and turban and beard. Then I heard his accent.

He reminded me of pictures I'd seen of British special forces in Yemen in the 1940s, looking as if the desert wind had whittled them down to a foreign core.

He spent a long time assessing me, trying to establish which intelligence service was operating on his territory. We ate around a table with a carpet on top and embers burning beneath it. They melted snow for water. Every few mouthfuls someone would raise a toast and we'd knock back another fifty millilitres of vodka. When the Russians sank into oblivion, Reza proposed we borrow their motorbikes and go up the mountain. That was fine by me.

I remembered him howling into rain at the peak.

'This is it, right? This is what I call getting off base.'

Next day we drove along the border with Afghanistan. I'd earned his trust. We skirted the most beautiful and dangerous scenery I'd seen, mountains folded around poppy fields. We followed a two-lane road towards China. When we were a hundred miles or so from anything, Reza sat me down and we talked networks, funding programmes, his plans for the region. He wanted to know what I thought, and what support I could get. It seemed a bit crazy, knocking around foreign policy on a mountainside littered with smashed cars, although it doesn't seem so crazy now. On the way back he stopped in at a mud-walled village, 'dropping off provisions'. While he chatted up locals, I looked inside the remaining parcels on the back seat of his car. They contained encrypted radios and body armour.

By the following week we were solid friends. In 2013 he began making noises about support for rebel militias: Libya initially, then Syria. *Asked for you by name, Kane.* Kurdish-led Syrian Defence Forces, he said: they're our men. They've got the fighters, Saudis have the money. Boom.

He linked Joanna up with some Kurdish cigarette smugglers based in Qamishli, a Syrian city near the Turkish border. She had been suspicious before meeting him, then disarmed by his charisma – and more suspicious. I had mentioned him the last time we met, a conversation the three of us had had about emotional manipulation. I'd used him as an example of what you can't do with computers. 'He's mad, but he understands grievances.'

'There's software for that,' she'd said.

Joanna and I argued, in a fairly civil way at first, about psychology: a nation's psychology and the limits of computing; historical and cultural sensitivity – trauma, resentment – how would a machine learn that? Feed in artworks, school lessons, poetry, I suggested, jokingly; dreams, nightmares.

'Why not,' she said.

GCHQ had a program called XKeyscore which had already hoovered up data for entire populations, including medical records. It consisted of over 700 servers at approximately 150 sites. The data came from satellite intercepts, telecoms access, and what they called overhead: pickup from planes and drones. There was third-party product from twenty-seven countries, content and metadata. Like a lot of industries, the challenge facing the intelligence services wasn't getting all this information, it was figuring out what to do with it. You've got every word used in phone calls, emails and messaging services in Georgia over a twelve-month period. How do you turn that into knowledge? How can you accept that it doesn't tell you the future?

'So what's next?' I asked. Part of me was getting sucked in, wondering if maybe Joanna and her secretive Shefford unit really had glimpsed something ahead.

She said there would be another incident like the Crimea. Russia wouldn't sit still. We argued about that. I said the risks were too high.

'You don't think they would?'

'I'm not saying they wouldn't *want* to. They want secure

borders. Russia's idea of a secure border is one with Russians on both sides. But there are limits. Think of the potential consequences.'

'Nations aren't rational actors,' she said. 'They're bitter old men.'

'But you think you can predict what they're going to do.'

'You don't need to be rational to be predictable.'

Sometimes it seemed as if the entire intelligence service had become obsessed, chasing an infinite meteorology. It had started out simply enough, with a search for algorithms that could warn us of attacks, identifying digital landscapes that had previously led up to terrorist incidents: communications activity, social media, financial transactions, geographical movement. Then it turned to visual patterns: how someone moves around a city, their posture, their silhouette, whether they have a bag, how the bag is carried. All the messages you write without intending to.

This is mankind's eternal quest, I'd argued. To protect ourselves from randomness. To know everything. The machines allowed fixation. In the old paper archives you could see the sickness of an obsession, the visible mess of paper, stacks and annotations. One click of a mouse could deliver three hundred lifetimes of obsession.

At five past midnight my phone buzzed. Reza had sent through a message.

This her?

I opened the attached file. It was a photo of a group: four men, three women, wrapped up for a hike. They were outside, in the snow, a boxy concrete building behind them. One of the women's faces had been circled. She was standing at the back of the group. Almost as if she hadn't wanted to be picked up.

It was her.

She wore a woollen hat and hiking boots. Some of the other

members of the party had walking poles. Was this Joanna as Vanessa? I didn't recognise any of the other individuals. There was no geographic tag to the image. I was left with the blurred face, some trees that looked like pines breaking the deep snow, the building behind her. A faded sign said Кинотеатр. Kinoteatr. It was a derelict cinema: 'Miners' Cinema', according to signage grown encrusted in icicles.

Reza's analysts had retrieved it from a computer in Berlin they were monitoring, which had received it on Facebook in a posting originating in Kazakhstan. Eco-activists. It had been posted a couple of months ago. The activists connected to various campaigns against pollution, but had been careful to remove geotags and any reference to a location. It wasn't Astana. Behind the cinema, a wall of coniferous trees clung to a steep white hillside.

What was Joanna doing here two months ago? According to Walker, she'd been in the country six weeks. I asked Reza to get any more details he could, studied the image again. Well away from Astana, by the looks of it. I thought of what Shomko had told me: *There's a possibility she headed east. She had connections there.*

I tried to call Stevenson but he didn't pick up. In the hotel's business suite, I printed off a story by the writer Aliya Savinova had recommended. I pulled the chair away from the centre of my hotel room so I'd see anyone entering a second before they saw me. Then I removed the handgun from the safe, cleaned it, oiled it, rested it on the arm of the chair.

THIRTY-FIVE

I woke up in the chair, listening for the layered sirens of an attack. The city was silent. It was 6 a.m. No smoke on the horizon, just the steam rising out of the top of Khan Shatyr.

I checked jihadi sites, then social media, then global news. Cellophane-wrapped flowers piled high outside the Sunshine mall. The first victims had been named, photographs of them placed alongside candles and rosary beads.

No news of any man found shot in Astana. No news of an English woman missing.

I studied the eco-activists' photo of Joanna again, partly kidding myself I could derive more clues from it, partly because she looked happy in the photo, and I hadn't seen her like that for a while.

Lucy Piper messaged: she'd pick me up for a breakfast meeting at eight, heading to a restaurant on Nurzhol Boulevard.

'Is Callum going to be there?' I asked.

'He's on his way. Why?'

'Just checking.'

I messaged Stefan and suggested that it was a good time to recce the Vectis office. He confirmed intent.

Aliya Savinova's story had fallen to the floor. I picked it up and thought about what I'd read the previous night. It was well written. A lonely woman fears she is going mad; she contemplates the way in which we believe in unreal things when real things cease to help us, 'when a limit is reached and only darkness lies ahead'. Lost in fantasy, she succumbs to an ill-judged relationship. The writer's name was given as Salima Qupiya. In Kazakh, *qupiya* meant secret or mystery. There were few traces of her online; a poem in an Almaty magazine, a reference on a literary website from two years ago. No photos. According to a biog, she was the same age as Aliya Savinova. She wrote with Aliya's laconic scepticism. Began studying at Nazarbayev University, it seemed, when Aliya did.

Piper picked me up in a chauffeur-driven Bentley. We drove fast. There were cars sticking close behind us.

'Whatever's being thrown at us online is part of a concerted operation,' she said. 'It's at scale, and individuals within UK intelligence are interested. I don't know if that works in our favour or not.'

'Are the intelligence services going to be at the meeting today?'

'Not to my knowledge.'

We approached a group of people outside a police station. I saw, too late, that they were holding placards, and that Elena Yussopova stood to the front. Our eyes locked as she stared through the Bentley's windows. I turned away, swore.

What were the consequences of that? I didn't have my identities clean, that was the problem. I was floundering.

We stopped on Nurzhol Boulevard before I had a chance to attempt any more questions. Cafestar was a restaurant on the grand avenue running between ministerial buildings and elite apartment blocks. It was encased in snow. In season, no doubt, the café's terrace would be shared between high-end escorts and ministerial wives showing off Paris fashion and international school English. All that seemed to relate to another world right now.

'Ms Piper.' A big grin from the young waiter on door duty. He beckoned me through. A GL5 guard stood inside like a sullen maître d', jacket fastened over his gun. A nod at Piper, a hard look at me. Callum Walker sat with a man and woman at a circular table in the centre of the room: white napkins, heavy cutlery, bowls of fruit and cafetières. There were no other customers; either the place had been cleared especially or it wasn't popular with the morning crowd.

I was introduced as a Russia expert assisting Piper Anderson. No one seemed to want to mention Vectis by name. The man beside Walker was Tom Chambers, former foreign secretary, now lobbying for Saracen. I could have done without active Westminster around. He was silver-haired and freshly shaved, in a tailored navy suit, silk tie and handmade Italian shoes. With him was Lynn Cook from Saracen in a blue Chanel suit. We all shook hands. I took a seat next to Chambers. On the table, among croissant crumbs, smashed blueberries and bowls of granola, were copies of yesterday's media coverage of the trip and a timetable for today.

Chambers took an iPhone from Walker, glanced at the screen, passed it to Cook. She raised an eyebrow, passed it to me. It showed a dead man on a mortuary slab, face blackened with bruises, mouth a mess of broken teeth. His left ear hung on by a flap of skin.

'He was arrested last night at the protest in Semey,' Walker said. 'Died in the police station. His brother got the photo.'

Piper took the phone.

'Has it gone international?' she asked.

'Not yet.'

She shut her eyes, opened them, passed the phone back to me.

'What do they want, these protesters? No drilling? Human rights?'

'I don't know,' Walker said. 'I'm more concerned by who's retweeting this image. This one's a troll. Scroll down.'

I scrolled down to a clip of Putin giving a speech. It concerned his favourite theme: the break-up of the Soviet Union as the greatest geopolitical catastrophe of the twentieth century, leaving millions of Russians stranded outside the Russian Federation. A minute in, he dismissed Kazakhstan as a recent invention: 'The Kazakhs have created a state where there was never one before.'

'Is that true?' Chambers asked.

They looked at me. I paused it.

'Technically,' I said. 'I've not seen this speech before. Where's it from?'

'It's hard to confirm if it's genuine,' Walker said. 'Our Moscow office isn't aware of it either. It's got over eighty thousand retweets in Kazakhstan alone.'

'How many people are even online here?' Chambers asked, looking puzzled. A waiter approached.

'Please,' Piper said, handing me a menu. 'Everyone, eat. The croissants are amazing. They fly in the pastry.'

I ordered coffee and a croissant, double-checked the staff folding napkins in the shadows. The lighting was soft, a lot of it coming from a tall glass box filled with bottles of wine, like a trophy cabinet. Chambers speared the remains of his eggs Benedict.

'You say this is a concerted operation?' he said. 'Kremlin-based?'

'I suspect so.'

This provoked a deep breath. Chambers looked to Piper. 'You're keeping Jack in the loop?'

'Daily.'

Jack, I thought. Jack Burrows at the Foreign Office.

'We may want to make that hourly.'

Piper said: 'For now we want to neutralise this as far as possible. It may be that attack is the best form of defence; whack-a-mole isn't working.' She looked at me, eyes wide, waiting. 'Toby?'

'Kazakhstan's independent,' I said. 'Whatever Putin might say, this is a strong, proud, independent country. We've got nationalism on our side.'

'Nationalism,' someone said, as if testing the word.

'If they're peddling a "Kazakhstan belongs to Russia" line, you want blogs promoting Kazakh independence, authentic Kazakh identity. A secular one, modern, outward-looking. Nationalism not nationalisation.'

'Nationalism not nationalisation.' Piper wrote it down.

'There's Kazakh warriors you want to bring into play.'

'Got any names?'

'There's one called Raiymbek, eighteenth-century. That could be the pseudonym of someone writing a blog called Kazakh Independence.'

She scribbled furiously.

'And the independence stuff: like anti-Putin?'

'Deeper than that. You've got plenty of history to draw upon. Kazakh servitude to the czars; legends in which they brought together all the clans to fight against Russia.' We had a look on her MacBook, found a romantic oil painting by some Englishman showing the hordes gathering with incongruous spears. 'The Bolshevik invasion saw hundreds of Kazakhs fleeing south. They call it *Aktaban Shubryndy*, running to the bone.'

'I like that.'

'Get people talking about historical injustice: the famine introduced by collective farming; Kazakhs burning their grain and slaughtering their cattle rather than letting them fall into Russian hands. You could have a Pinterest board of famine pictures.'

'I'll get our team on it.'

'And keep Galina onside,' Chambers said.

'We've booked the Marriott's thirty-eighth-floor bar for her birthday celebration,' Piper said. 'There's a catering team coming from Paris. It's under control.'

My coffee and croissant arrived. Both were good, as promised.

'Toby,' Piper continued, 'I'm told you read Kazakh.'

'A little.'

'Can you check this?'

She pushed the draft of an article towards me. It talked about all the good work Saracen was doing. Accompanying the piece was a photograph of the Caspian refinery, its vast metalwork lit against the night. It had a Union Jack flying.

'Is this for local readership?'

'Yes.'

'The piece is great. I wouldn't stick a Union Jack on the Caspian. And I'd get the word "land" in there,' I said. 'Land is the main treasure. You're helping them be prosperous so they can keep their land.'

'Clearly no one's told them what's under it,' the woman from Saracen muttered.

'It's symbolic. Oil will go, not the land.'

'But it's oil they're against.'

'They're not against it; they just don't think they're getting dividends. Tell them poverty here's dropped from around fifty per cent to four per cent in the last fifteen years. That's people not dying. It wasn't because of NGOs, it's because companies got the black stuff out of the ground.'

'Hear, hear.' Chambers pushed his chair back and rose. 'I've got to run. Toby, been a pleasure.'

Chambers and Cook had to return to the trade delegation. They were late for a tour of a factory manufacturing asthma inhalers. Stefan had messaged. He said we had a problem; he'd explain if I could suggest somewhere safe to meet.

THIRTY-SIX

I found a motel on the edge of the city's industrial area. Migrant workers smoked together in the overheated lobby, hi-vis vests steaming on radiators. There was a shop beside reception selling alcohol and microwave food. I booked a room, checked it, closed the curtains and returned to the car.

'Meet at the lorry park on the Alash Highway,' I told Stefan. 'Ten p.m. Pull in. I'll flash my lights, then follow me.'

I drove back to where the road forked, then pulled off behind the rusting frame of a disused petrol station, hidden from the road but still able to see the vehicles passing. At five minutes to ten Stefan's rental BMW passed. No other vehicles around. I pulled back onto the road, overtook him.

Inside the motel room he removed his laptop from its aluminium case, opened it. The screen showed a photo of the Vectis office. Then a second picture, closer to floor level – the junction box for the ethernet.

'Someone's already done it.'

'Done what?'

'Hacked them.'

Stefan changed windows, logged into a discussion forum. Halfway down a black screen filled with monospaced text someone had posted an almost identical picture: same office, same junction box.

'The forum's called Abysm, probably the smallest, most select

269

hacker community on the net. Eighty or ninety members, a lot of them pros. The US Department of Justice has tried to take it down on several occasions. The set-up is invite only: you have to show how you're going to be useful for the other members, so there's a culture of bragging, a lot of sharing tips, trading tools. On Monday 20 November, a guy calling himself nomad9 says he's been approached for a job; talks about somewhere ultra-secure that he's been asked to get into.

'"Been asked to do a thing", were his exact words. It's an isolated systems network, behind multiple firewalls. The target organisation's clearly sensitive. All data's encrypted when it's transmitted, so he needs to get access internally. He posts some details; there's a conversation about potential vulnerabilities, a joke about it being banking or military.

'First he thinks about replacing a keyboard with an identical one containing a keylogger, thereby getting all the passwords. He says his client would be able to make the swap and then retrieve the memory chip.'

'Which suggests his client is someone already inside the organisation.'

'Right. This is the make of keyboard in the office: Corsair K95.'

'That's right.'

'Then he says his client reckons the target's too savvy for that. So he sources a replica ethernet box and puts a device in it that can sit on the Local Area Network, between the target and the server, grabbing all the traffic as it passes through. It's a classic man-in-the-middle attack. From what he describes online, the device involves a crossover cable and a wireless card: the data he or his client wants to see is transmitted wirelessly and he'll have picked it up easily enough. Gets in, does all the things I did, except then he disappears off the face of the earth.'

'What happened?'

'His messages stop. Rumours start a few days later: he's either been killed or arrested. Someone says they think he was in Astana, but there's nothing on the news. Someone knows his family and they say he's disappeared. A few friends drop into the forum to say he's not contactable in the real world either. The last they heard, he'd stumbled across something crazy, something way bigger than he expected. The whole thing's become news in the community, people circulating the pictures he posted, trying to figure out what he was on to. There are rumours that maybe the British intelligence services were involved, then CIA, Mossad, FSB.' Stefan turned to me. 'Now I've just tried to hack the same organisation.'

'Do you know who he is?'

'Nomad9 is a guy called Ruslan Batur. Pretty shit-hot, worked for the Kazakh government on cybersecurity between 2012 and 2014, but fell out over some of the things he was asked to do. He's got a history of using his skills for political ends: hacktivism, connections with human-rights groups.'

'Got a picture of him?'

'Mugshot, from an arrest in 2015.' Stefan clicked the mouse and brought up Ruslan Batur's mugshot. Batur was twenty-two in the photo: with shoulder-length dark hair, large eyes and a wispy attempt at a beard. 'According to people online, at least ten individuals have been questioned about him over the last few days, in six different countries.'

I showed Stefan the CCTV footage of Batur in the Mega Mall on his way to pass what he'd found to Joanna, and then the shots I'd taken of his corpse.

'You knew it,' Stefan said. 'You knew he'd been killed and still sent me in.'

'I didn't know who he was or what he'd done. I've been trying to find those out.'

'Jesus Christ. You said Joanna Lake was working for Vectis.

Now she's spying on them. So who was she actually working for? I'm trying to figure out who's most likely to kill me.'

'No one's going to kill you.'

'This is something big, isn't it?'

'What makes you say that?'

'There have been attempts to wipe even *talk* of the hack from message boards,' Stefan said. 'Look.' He brought up a page of code. 'One hacker site, Black Hat, published a report, nine a.m. US time, connecting the disappearance of Batur to the conversations on Abysm, suggesting he may have stumbled into information to do with an intelligence service. It gets blown offline an hour later. By their own account they were hit by a DDoS attack – they posted a grab of their server log.'

DDoS: Distributed Denial of Service – a technique used by criminals, bored teenagers and intelligence services alike to derail a target website by bombarding it with communication requests until it goes into meltdown.

'The style is distinct,' Stefan said. 'Most attacks piggyback on multiple computers to get scale. This one just fools the host into thinking it's receiving excess communication. It's trying to put together the fragments of data being sent, but getting the wrong information, so thinks it's overloaded when it isn't. The beauty of this technique is that it leads to buffer overflow. The host starts to wipe the data it already has.'

'Seen it before?'

'I helped devise it.'

'What do you mean?'

'It looks like what we called Slow Clap. The bosses at GCHQ were queasy about piggybacking civilians' PCs to get their mass of attackers, so I helped develop techniques using software errors and security gaps that could be run off one PC only. Pretty ingenious, if I say so myself. You can take a target down solo.'

'Are GCHQ the only ones with it? What about you guys?'

'Not from me. But these things catch on fast. Like I say, what's going on?'

'Do you have any idea what Batur got?'

'No.'

'Is there any chance of us repeating the hack?'

'There's no way. It's locked down now.'

'Do you think there might be a copy of the stolen data anywhere?'

'I'm not sure I'd go looking for it if there was.'

'I need malware for Aliya Savinova's phone: an exploit for Androids, one that would work on an LG G5.'

'I can get them to send something through. But you're not going to crack this alone.'

'You think I can just drop it?'

'No, I think you're in trouble. That's what this is about. I can't stick around.'

'I'm not asking you to.'

Stefan sighed. 'What's Aliya Savinova going to give you? She won't know who she's working for.'

'Everyone knows something. And she interests me.'

'She hates the West.'

'She likes hating the West. She'll enjoy my company.'

THIRTY-SEVEN

Evotec sent through the malware a few hours later, along with a 'pattern of life' file for Aliya, including professional and friendship networks, educational history and financial records for both her and her family. She had some extra money coming in, a personal account with Halyk Savings Bank of Kazakhstan that received monthly transfers of 300 dollars from a business account at the Asia Credit Bank in the name of ACT Strategic Communications. No ACT Strategic Communications came up online.

I dialled the number she'd given me. The way someone answers a call is usually informative in itself. Are they in the environment you'd expect? Any suggestion of a delay while devices are initiated? My call was killed after five rings. I sent a text.

It's Toby. Can you call me?

Aliya texted back. In five minutes. She called in three and a half. She sounded happy.

'Toby, hello.'

'Can you speak?'

'Yes, briefly.'

'I read a story by the writer you recommended.'

'Already?'

'"The Edge of Things". I found it online. I began reading it last night and couldn't stop. I think the writer is hugely talented.'

'You do?'

'Do you know them well?'

'Quite well.'

'I have a friend who edits a literary magazine in London. I think they would be very interested in doing something with her work. He is very interested in literature from other countries.'

'Really?'

'Yes. Are they contactable?'

'I think so. I will find out.'

I gave it a beat.

'It's very nice to hear your voice. There's not many people here I've met who I have much in common with.'

'Me neither.'

'Would you meet me for a coffee?'

'When?'

'Today.'

'Okay,' Aliya said. 'A quick one.'

'Do you know Café Corso on the corner of Bayanaul Street? I can be there at seven.' Corso was far enough away from the governmental district for discretion without it being impractical for her to get to.

'Seven? I think so. I will try.'

'I will be there.'

'Okay.' She hung up.

Too easy, I thought. The doubt was drilled into you over time: no one simply took your hand when you reached out.

I sent an encrypted email to Hugh Stevenson, informing him that Joanna had hacked into Vectis. I asked him to see whether Vauxhall had any previous concerns about the private intelligence company, but suggested he move carefully.

I bought a new shirt, checked my phone for news. Semey had

kicked off in a serious way. News of the young man's death in custody had spread fast. Another protester had been injured and was critical in hospital. The square was filled with chanting, braziers lit, flames promising violence of their own.

Is this a revolution? Piper had asked. A Central Asian spring? I took a brief look at inflation rates and average incomes. These were the ones to watch, short of being able to watch the silent majority itself, the weather creeping through its heart, approaching that magic point of collective rage when risking your life became a rational act. That was what I had prided myself on assessing in CX reports. A horizon watcher, as Joanna had mocked. There were several online tools for calculating the likelihood of civil unrest, but I didn't feel any of them took enough account of people like Aliya.

I pocketed the Makarov, and wondered what I was trying to protect myself from.

Café Corso was over the top for a first date, but I wanted somewhere with front of house as a line of defence. They did Russian-inflected dishes, heavy on cream and pastry. The interior decoration involved doilies and cross-stitch cushions decorated with children sledging. Somewhere a sleazy expat might think was discreet, but not so high-end that you'd run into government men and their mistresses. I chose a seat out of earshot of other diners, but with a sightline to the door.

These situations are never my favourite: the fact is that at least one of you might be risking your life by turning up. And yet the appearance of relaxed confidence is all. Nine people inside, five staff, four customers: two men talking Italian at the counter; a man and a woman in dark suits at a window table, poring over designs for what looked like a nightclub. Lace curtains on a brass pole divided the window in half. Above them, the sky was getting dark. Streetlamps caught fresh flurries of snow in the air.

She entered a moment later. The fur of her hood framed her face, sparkling with tiny diamonds of ice. I got up and hugged her, feeling for wires or weapons. Then I kissed her cheek. It was cold.

'I'm so glad you could come. You must be freezing. Sit down.' She placed her bag in her lap, looked around.

'Been here before?' I asked, in Russian.

'Never.' She spoke English. That was fine with me. You didn't truly get to know someone unless they were speaking their first language, but if English made her feel safe, or want to show off, English was fine.

'It's okay, a little eccentric. Forgive the cushions.'

'I forgive them. You have the word "kitsch" – is that right?'

'Borrowed off the Germans, yes.'

'Kitsch.' She tried the word in her mouth. Her make-up was fresh, her drop earrings caught the light.

'How was your day?'

'Fine.'

I passed her the menu. 'Go wild.'

'You take all your women here?'

'Only the ones that write such superb fiction.'

She considered this. 'Is it obvious?'

'To me.'

Aliya ordered hot chocolate with cream. I ordered *sbiten*, a Russian drink with honey and spices. When the waitress left I said, 'I thought the story was quite brilliant. The way you used such clarity of language to describe confusion, both lucid and utterly at sea.'

'At sea?'

'Lost. You say, in the story, there is clarity in being lost. That is the heart of it, for me. The magazine I've mentioned it to – *The Walbrooke Review* – are very interested. I know the editor there, Jack Morley. He's a nice guy. The magazine's small but read by influential people. They've published Anna Starobinets, Guzel Yakhina, I believe she's of Tajik origin.'

'Really?'

'You know her work?'

'Of course.'

'What do you think?'

'It would be amazing.'

'What are you working on?' I asked. 'At the university.'

'My thesis.'

'Tell me about it.'

'I don't think you'd be interested. It is not to do with business.'

'I have interests beyond business.'

'I am looking at the idea of authentic literatures, the invention of folk cultures. A lot of it is fantasies, sometimes made by the communist party. Many of our heroes were selected by the Soviets – secular poets and thinkers.'

'But is it not true that you had "bards" here?'

'Yes, singers. An oral tradition. But now they are gone. I am not sure people will bring them back, or should try.'

'That sounds a provocative angle.'

'In a Western university it would not be provocative.'

'Do you get funded?'

'Very little.'

'But enough to survive on?'

'Just.'

Our drinks and cake arrived. She ate the cream off the hot chocolate first. I sipped the *sbiten* and was transported back to a winter in Moscow, when I had decided Russia was the country I loved the most: the stark, magisterial beauty of the place, the cautious friendships, the writers I had met.

'And what exactly do you do?' she asked.

'I advise people investing money. I'm here to do some research. It is very dull.'

If I embodied the West she hadn't attacked me yet. Perhaps her politics were a private matter, to be preserved in fantasy.

'Will you go back to England for Christmas?' she asked.

'I'm not sure yet.'

'What about your family?'

I was momentarily thrown. The image that flickered into view was of Croxley Green. It was replaced by Toby's parents: richer, more glamorous.

'They are dead,' I said.

'I'm sorry.'

'A long time.'

'Are you married?'

'No,' I said. She raised an eyebrow quizzically. I changed the subject.

'What do you make of recent events here? The ethnic tensions?'

'I think a lot of it is exaggerated.'

I managed to stifle a laugh at her audacity.

'Your family is originally from Russia, no?'

'My father came here in 1970.'

The Virgin Lands campaign, I thought: Khrushchev trying to turn the emptiness into agriculture, importing Russians by the thousands to summon wheat from the steppe.

'What did he think of moving here?'

'He felt he was doing his duty. At that time a lot of Russians came, to farm. It was an adventure. That is what they told them. Building the socialist future. My grandmother was furious when she learned that my mother was marrying a Russian. But I solved everything when I was born. I am harmony.'

I laughed. 'You are exceptionally harmonious.'

'Thank you.'

'So your mother is not Russian.'

'No. My father rose quite high in agricultural work. Under the Soviets, he would have been looked after. Now, ethnic Russians can only rise so high. They are made to feel uncomfortable. Sometimes people refuse to serve them.'

'Does he think about going back?'

'He loves this country.'

'Of course.'

'And my grandmother is with them. She is not well. Home is not such a good place to be. But I am saving money.' She wiped cream from her lips.

'Do you feel free here?'

She shrugged. 'You are free until you want to criticise the government. People are not used to thinking for themselves anyway. Do you like it here?'

'Very much so.'

'You preferred Almaty to Astana.'

'No.'

'It is nicer.'

'It is pretty. I like places that don't entirely work, though, the less pretty ones.'

'Why?'

'I don't know. They are just themselves. People are surprised you are there. I like places that haven't been expecting me.'

She drank her chocolate, considering this. 'Does England work?'

'Sometimes. Have you been to Europe?'

'No.' She hesitated as she said it, which made me curious.

'Really?'

'What do you mean, "really"?'

'You sounded uncertain.'

'I have never been out of Kazakhstan. It is not easy for us. Why don't you have a wife?'

'I'm never anywhere for long – not in England.'

She waited for a proper answer.

'I haven't found someone I want to be with. I am a very private person.'

'You date Kazakh women?'

'No.'

'A rich English businessman in Astana and you have not found a wife.' Her eyes held a wry glint that reminded me of Joanna.

'I know,' I said. 'I can't have been paying attention. Still, I'm not being sent home yet.'

'You think you will be sent home?'

'It was a joke. I'm very much my own boss anyway, and I would happily stay here. Perhaps I will.'

She looked sceptical. I felt the lightheadedness that comes as you begin to enter your cover and believe the things you say; when you are most convincing and most vulnerable. Stay sharp, I thought. Maybe it was too hot in here, sudden comfort after the cold. The Italians left, a family of four arrived. It was 7.15 p.m.

'May I ask,' I said. 'Is there a special man in your life? A boyfriend?'

She shook her head, stirred the remains of the cream into the chocolate. 'I do not have time. A man will want me to stop working.'

'All men?'

'Kazakh men.'

'Marry an Englishman.' I turned my cup in its saucer. 'I mean, I have heard this is still a very traditional society.'

'More than ever.'

'What do you mean?'

'Traditions are returning. People's idea of tradition.'

'Why is that?'

'Now we have some independence, people want Kazakh identity. We have Russia above, China next to us. Both big powers.'

'And how do you feel about this?'

'I don't know. You have a lot of questions, but you are the one who has seen the whole world. What do I know?'

'I've seen very little of the world.'

'I don't mean to be angry. It has been a stressful week. Do you know where the bathroom is?'

'Downstairs, I believe.'

'Excuse me.'

She went, taking her bag. I searched her coat pockets: headphones, receipts for lunch, blister pack of Pipofezine, an antidepressant. The life report placed Aliya's home twenty minutes' drive away, but I'd checked the bus routes and they were slow. And, in this weather, unpredictable. I thought I could find a way to accompany her.

Aliya returned, appearing more composed. I needed to get her out of here.

'You are interested in my politics?' she said.

'I'm curious.'

'We won't be a serious country until we have democracy.'

'But people approve of the President.'

'Of course. He is all we know. He has kept us out of war.'

'Perhaps that's all you can ask.'

'For now. Soon things must change.'

'The people I have met here are good people. I think maybe your country can remain peaceful. Advance, and remain peaceful.'

I called for the bill, paid in cash. 'I'll drive you home, if you like. I've got a feeling the buses might be difficult.'

'Where are you going?'

'Well, I was going to go towards Koyandy. There's a supermarket out there that stocks some European things I can't get anywhere else. It's open late.'

'Really? That's quite close to where I live.'

'Perfect.'

'You have a car?'

'Yes. I'm parked just around the corner.'

A home visit was good due diligence. She would invite me in. Hard, if not impossible, to fake a family.

282

'No. It is not necessary,' she said suddenly.

'I am driving you,' I said. 'No arguing.' I was surprised by a burst of adrenalin. I watched her wrestle with something that evidently needed to be said.

'You must understand,' she said, finally. 'My home is not rich.'

THIRTY-EIGHT

I'd left the car a street away. She climbed in without comment. I kept the headlights off for as long as possible, in case someone was looking out for them, only switching them on once we were on the main road. She looked at me curiously.

Night had settled, with a quarter moon sharpened by the cold. Her directions led us into older eastern suburbs, in the process of being brought into line with the architectural look of the capital. All the surrounding villages were meant to be put in order by 2020. Right now it looked like a construction site: concrete plants, steel frames, tower cranes with aviation warning lights.

'A city changes faster than a human heart,' I said.

'What is that?'

'Baudelaire.'

'Oh, I know Baudelaire. *Les Fleurs du Mal.*'

'He's one of my favourites.'

'Do you think it's true, about the city?'

'This city, for sure.'

Digital visions of the paradise to come decorated the hoardings of building sites. Faceless people moved through an imagined world: hotels, shopping centres, residential compounds with their own golf courses. Build it and they will come. Oil dreams. Aberdeen, Houston, Kuwait City, Baku. Crude trades at over $100 and cities appear. You can make any ideology seem successful. But it's not the future, it's just money. It runs out.

I put the radio on. *Semey on a knife edge. Nazarbayev on his way to address protesters' concerns.*

'Have you heard about this?'

'No.' Aliya looked as shocked as I did. 'Really?' You could hear the crowd on the radio, chanting. When would he appear? The protesters weren't going anywhere. Now even more people would join them. Maybe it was a stroke of genius. If anyone could pull it off, it was Nazarbayev.

'The President knows this is it,' I said. 'This is how things start.'

'Yes.'

'Think it will work?'

'I hope so.'

'He'd better have something good to say.'

'It is Nazarbayev. He just needs to appear.'

We crossed the city's ring road. A minute later Aliya directed me left, into a cluster of low, plain houses. Her home was set back from the road, lights on. I stopped the car.

'Have a good night,' I said.

'You should come in,' Aliya said. 'They'll be amused.'

'Wonderful.'

'In a nice way.'

The entrance was set back, no windows overlooking. No cars parked up.

'I won't stay long.'

Aliya's mother answered the door. She looked like her daughter: tall, dark-eyed. Her father appeared behind her with a grey moustache and two days' stubble.

'This is Toby,' Aliya said. 'He is English. He gave me a lift home.'

'A guest!' The father shook my hand and pulled me in. The living room was low-ceilinged, warm. Filling one end was a dresser whose shelves held Soviet china. The grandmother lay on a couch to the side, face folded towards her toothless mouth and small dark eyes.

We sat on cushions around a low, lace-covered table. The mother produced a loaf of home-baked *shelpek*, Kazakh flatbread. The father opened a bottle of vodka and found two glasses. I looked around. A rare thing, access to ordinary homes. The people who are not bad or powerful and so rarely worth spying on but can sometimes change history. Cable TV box, television tuned to Europa Plus, the non-state news station, showing reports from Semey, the crowd outraged in the snow, waiting.

The mother switched it off, as if this were a private concern. I had a quick look at the local wi-fi connections on my phone, preparing to email malware to Aliya's mobile. That was the goal I'd set myself, although it was feeling more uncouth by the minute. They had KazakhTelecom broadband, connection speed 5 Mpbs. Decent enough.

The father offered me vodka. His right arm was artificial, the hand prosthetic.

'To the friendship of our countries – two great empires, once upon a time.' He had the Russian habit of smiling with the eyes alone. I imagined him forty years ago, arriving in this part of the world, in the southern reaches of the Soviet Union, full of wonder about the life ahead of him. Astana was an administrative base for the agricultural project. A land of travellers soon to be extinguished by Soviet wheat farming.

Aliya's mother fussed over having company, fetching bowls of pilaf, saucers of sweets. Aliya knelt beside her grandmother. There was a transparent flash of pity, a genuflection. She kissed the old woman's hands and the grandmother ran a hand through her hair. Then she stared at me.

'Who is he?'

Aliya spoke Russian. 'He is English. Visiting.'

'A prince?' The grandmother cackled.

'She thinks you might be royal,' Aliya called over. Her parents laughed.

'I'm the next-best thing.'

I felt that lightheadedness again. You get moments on a job – especially after a drink – when you're in a life, a home like you imagined a home might feel like. Enclosed in a moment. You're welcome there. But it's always someone else's home, and no one knows who you are.

I watched the grandmother and imagined her surviving the decades, passing through famines and ideologies. Her speech was inflected with something neither Russian nor Kazakh, almost Chinese. Aliya joined us, declined her father's offer of vodka.

'Where's your grandmother from?' I asked.

'Karakol, even further south than Almaty.'

That made sense. I was hearing traces of Dungan; she was a descendant of refugees from Northwestern China, Hui traders who knew the routes west. A rare linguistic treat. Aliya turned to her parents. 'She is worse.'

'Today it is bad,' her father said. He asked me about England, how much flights and houses cost; if I was anti-European. He had read on Russian sites that Britain and America were not friends any more. Asked whether I shared concerns about immigration, and what I thought of Kazakhstan.

'It is beautiful,' I said. 'The landscape.'

'Have you been to the national park at Burabay?'

'Yes.'

'You are here at an interesting time.'

'Really?'

'You say *honeymoon*? The honeymoon is over. Many of my fellow Russians returned to the motherland after independence. Others enjoyed the oil boom. But now, without the oil prices, no one knows what will happen. But don't believe this is the next Afghanistan. These are good Muslims. Not like the ones you have wars with. People like my wife.' He smiled at her. 'I am more Muslim than her.'

When we had eaten, the parents cleared plates away. Aliya and I were alone with the sleeping grandmother.

'Let me email you the details about the magazine,' I said.

'Please.'

I emailed them, the links directing to malware instead.

'Have a look. I've been having difficulty with sending documents.'

'It opens but the link doesn't work.'

'Hang on, I'll try again.'

'Okay. This one works fine.'

'Great.'

The bathroom was upstairs. So were the bedrooms. I took the opportunity to explore. The parents' room had bare plastered walls, a bed and single dresser. A framed wedding photograph stood on the dresser. I listened to the voices downstairs, questioning Aliya: where she met me, what my work was.

I opened the dresser – costume jewellery, bills going back years. Beneath them was a display box with a clasp. I opened it. On one side was a black and white photograph of an unsmiling man in the fatigues of a Soviet Tank Division commander. Her father. I recognised the Darul Aman Palace behind him, still intact, and felt a momentary shiver, as if overhearing a stranger discussing your own dream. Kabul, maybe 1979 or 1980. He could have been no more than twenty-one years old. Pinned opposite it was a Soviet Valour Medal with a red, white and blue ribbon.

Sent to farm, sent to fight. Lives picked up and dropped down. I put the box back, returned to the hallway. The plasterwork here was peeling. All the furniture was old. Military pensions never stretched far. I thought about the medical treatment for her grandmother, and imagined the life of a bright daughter, a lucrative daughter. Responsibility like that could corrupt more effectively than anything else.

Her room was at the end of the corridor. Single bed, clothes draped over a single chair. No PC, but a laptop on the desk. On her shelves: old Russian translations of the English and American writers considered revolutionary enough to be published under the Soviet Union, a canon about which I'd always been curious – Shaw, Hemingway, Shakespeare, Ford Madox Ford. Then newer editions: Orwell, Fielding, Proust. A collection of Shevchenko's poems, the revolutionary currently sprayed across Astana's walls. I took that down, leafed through to 'My Testament', the poem in question, in case it was marked in any way. It wasn't. I put it back, read the other spines: *Rewriting the Nation: Elites and Narratives, Modernising the Kazakh Alphabet*. On the desk were more current affairs: *The New Imperialism, The Globalisation of NATO*. On the wall above the desk was a list of time zones and public holidays in different countries. A key had been left in the top desk drawer. I was approaching when I heard her steps on the stairs. I took a book from the shelf.

'Auezov,' Aliya said, when she arrived beside me. She was smiling. 'He is a good playwright.'

'When I was in Almaty I saw a procession of men and women all dressed in white,' I said. 'I couldn't imagine what was going on. They didn't look like any particular religion. So I followed them all the way to the central cemetery. Do you know it?'

'Yes.'

'They went to Auezov's monument and took turns kissing the statue. Then they sat down nearby and read from his works.'

'It is a tradition, on the anniversary of his death.'

'I thought it was beautiful. And the cemetery itself was so overgrown. I loved all the headstones together: crescents, orthodox crosses, Stars of David, Red Stars. They all seemed very equal and comfortable together. But only one had worshippers that day.' I put the book back. 'I should go.'

She nodded but didn't move except to tilt her head. I kissed her. She took hold of my wrists and kissed me back with raw, clumsy enthusiasm. When we drew apart she glanced at the stairs. The grandmother could be heard, complaining that I had not eaten. Aliya rolled her eyes. She moved closer so that I was against the wall and kissed me again, her fists against my stomach.

'I'm trapped,' I said.

'You are not the one who is trapped,' she said.

The family protested when I tried to leave. The father gripped my shoulder with his good hand. The mother gave me some *shelpek* to take home. At the door, Aliya said, 'Thank you for the lift.'

'No, thank you. For everything. It was an honour to meet your family. I hope to see you very soon.'

'Send me a message.'

'I will.'

'You are a kind man.'

'Not really.'

She smiled. 'You don't like it?'

'This is nothing. Really.'

'No, it is something.' She glanced behind her, then came out to kiss me once more in the snow. 'You are kind, whether you like it or not, Toby.'

THIRTY-NINE

I stopped at a workers' café on the way back, heated by an oven in the centre of the room, the lighting mostly supplied by headlights coming and going in the car park. More *lagman*, Silk Road comfort food. You could measure where you were in Central Asia by the noodles, which thinned as you approached the Altai mountains and China. The clientele looked and sounded like rural migrants, *kolkhozniki*, on their way to night work at the construction sites.

Lights swept the room as a lorry pulled up outside. The driver came in: a fat man with a swaggering, loudmouth look on his face. He knew most of the people, saw I was out of place. I could feel him watching me, waiting for the opportunity to stir some entertainment out of a turgid night. In the end I turned and nodded. 'Come far?'

'You are Russian?'

'English.'

He said a name. It took me a moment to realise he was saying *Oliver Cromwell*: 'Oliver Cromwell, he was a man of the people.' The revolutionary Cromwell loomed large in Soviet accounts of British history.

'Some of the people,' I said.

'How much does a lorry driver earn in England?' he asked.

'Lots. You're a driver?'

'Thirty years.'

'Where have you come from tonight?'

'Balkhash.'

'Via Karaganda?'

'Yes.'

'How are things there?'

'There's people out, you know—' He mimed the waving of placards. 'Angry.'

'A lot of them?'

'Maybe.'

'Checkpoints?'

'North and south, yes.'

'What about Balkhash?'

'Quiet. But always too quiet. No women.' He laughed, turned to the other men and they laughed too.

A country in transition. I thought of Aliya's declaration: *soon things must change*. Kazakhstan was a beacon of hope. But states live miracle to miracle, utopias need cash. You have to keep the faith in progress going or the bad dreams start.

I thought of her grandmother's dialect. Not many Dungan speakers remained. My old supervisor at Cambridge would have been fascinated. I saw myself flying Astana to Heathrow; the train to Cambridge. It's chilly but bright, Hertfordshire passing by, a winter day that looks like spring. Straight to the college library. The security guard remembers me, nods. I find Victoria Fell's *Literatures of Central Asia* on the shelf. My bookmark is still there. I sit down.

In fantasies we can be still. Yet that library was a place I had scavenged for means of escape. Linguistically, I had moved outwards from the European tongues into the disorientation of Russian and Arabic, then south, to the strange ones in between. In my second year I won a prize to be spent on travelling, so I hiked down to Tehran. That was in 2002, two months after Iran joined the Axis of Evil. It didn't seem particularly evil. A man who ran a pub near where I grew up had told me that in the

1970s they used to drive double-decker buses from London to Afghanistan and on to India, searching for pot, opium, mysticism. That was before 1979: before the Iranian revolution, the Soviet invasion of Afghanistan. He had faded photos of himself in tie-dye, the bus painted orange. It felt like learning of an old land route between continents that had become submerged.

But, with the low profile of a solo traveller, I re-created much of the route. The mid-Nineties were tranquil compared with now. With every step away from home I felt lighter. My mother was on her third partner since my father's death, but any anger I had carried from my childhood was becoming counterbalanced by a sense of guilty relief; I could escape.

After Iran, the closest I could imagine to a future was some kind of fieldwork that kept me travelling, so I proposed a thesis on Persianate culture in the time of the Mongols. The violently expanding empires of Genghis Khan and Tamerlane had thrown scholars and poets together, some seeking refuge, others collected by the emperors themselves: trophies and treasuries of knowledge. I was interested in the illiterate Khan, collecting scrolls as he conquered, haunted by the knowledge they promised. *Hunting truth like the enemy*, my supervisor had said. Here, I thought, was a corner of history obscure enough to hide in.

My supervisor was a brilliant woman. She'd spent time in Sudan and Yemen and had written the definitive book on Arabic poetry. Her husband had been a 'diplomat', as she described it. In retrospect, of course, it was all quite obvious. She was waiting for people like me. The whole place was a honeytrap.

When she first suggested work for the government, I was still recovering from an exercise with the 4th Battalion, Parachute Regiment. My feet were swollen and blistered to the extent that I was forced to wear flip-flops. I remembered sitting in her office like that, my PhD proposal in her hands, wondering why she seemed uninterested in it.

'This is all fine and I think you would do it well. I wondered if you'd thought about other options.' She put the sheets down as if they'd left her unsatisfied and would do the same to me. 'You volunteer in the reserves,' she said.

Even while I sat there with bare feet and a bruised cheekbone, it surprised me that she knew this.

'Yes.'

'Do you enjoy that?'

I had joined as a gesture against the comfort of the college, the equation of learning with physical ease. And because it seemed an entirely unlikely thing to do. The training felt like the shedding of skin, which reminded me of learning a language. I had spent my first months at the university impersonating those around me, fascinated by their ready-formed personas, their postures and ensconced positions in networks that appeared to have arisen spontaneously. I had practised stretching my vowels, relaxing them as if I too was relaxed, letting my voice sink back in my jaw. I borrowed the grandeur of the college itself like a costume.

But, to my surprise, it was the army reserves where I excelled. The Brecon Beacons, where most of the training took place, was beautiful and desolate. Ten-kilometre runs became 20 with packs, became 50-kilometre marches with strapless carbines, two hours' sleep in a damp bivouac then 50 more. It became clear that they were not interested in your strength so much as your weakness. To know someone well enough to stake your life on them, you needed to know where and when they'd break. But you could only break if you were whole to start with. The art was to divide yourself in advance – from pain, primarily, your own and others', and then from fear. The training, which had seen two men die in the previous five years, was both a border in your life that you were challenged to cross, and an ineradicable partition within you once you had done so.

I enjoyed map work, and even weapons training, which I

approached as you'd approach a class on Japanese wood carving – an intriguing skill you would never actually need. I remembered the meditative way in which a visiting commander with sunburnt cheekbones and sun-bleached hair unrolled a black and white keffiyeh which held an MP5 rifle, and arranged the pieces on the scarf, cleaning them, slotting them back together. When he had finished there was the faintest scatter of sand on the Cambridgeshire floor. I looked up. He was watching me looking at the sand. He winked.

'Yes,' I said to my supervisor. 'I enjoy it.'

A delicate first interview overlooking St James's Park two weeks later, training at Fort Monckton eight weeks after that. All spies have these stories: being chosen, steered. No one wants to believe they sought this profession out.

The car's interior still smelled of Aliya's perfume. I sat in the back seat, opened my laptop, brought up a control board that replicated the home screen of her phone. I opened contacts and address book, recent messages, check-ins. I went in to her emails, deleted the first one from me with the infected link, then closed the laptop and drove back into town.

I was in a shop attached to a petrol station, buying soap and a new toothbrush, when I heard a sound like popcorn. It came from the phone held by a man beside me. He stared at the screen. The crackling sound was semi-automatic gunfire. The man looked around, put the phone away, embarrassed.

Someone moved past, at the end of the aisle, talking on a mobile, an urgency in their voice. I walked back to my car.

Footage had been uploaded to YouTube showing protesters in the central square. It was hard to tell what was going on. The crowd became ragged, individuals running, turning; some people had fallen. There were voices close to the camera, a man and a woman. *Where are they? Get out of here ... Where is she? Go up Baiseitov Street.* Then a ripple of tinny gunfire joined, after a second, by three sharp cracks from a rifle. Then a woman wailing some distance from the camera: hoarse, repeated cries of 'No'.

The woman close to the camera spoke again: *Oh my God, look. Look. They shot him. Oh my God.*

There was no way anyone could bury this. It was going to be a question of how it was used.

He's hit – they shot him.

The clearest footage came from a window overlooking Semey's floodlit square. The voices were in the room where it was being filmed. *They shot. They're shooting.* The camera phone remained steady. Two or three hundred protesters were trapped in the square. They began running away, found themselves blocked. More shots.

Eventually most scattered, leaving the human debris: the dead and the injured, dark forms against the snow, then those trying to move them. The person filming focused on one man, shot in the leg, dragging himself across the ground. You could see he was young – just the exertion suggested he was young, wearing glasses and a black baseball cap. Then he shook as if electrocuted as someone fired another round into his body.

It didn't sound like the standard AK-74s. A more modern assault rifle. At least three individuals firing, one from a height. You could see the crowd running right to left of the screen, then a louder report, closer to the camera, and they moved in collective panic towards the back.

I felt their shock. You think you're protected because something special is happening. And there are hundreds of you, standing side by side: people who've never fucked with power before and can't imagine that it's as desperate as they are.

It was online for around ten minutes, then disappeared. I had three missed calls from Piper.

'Nine, ten dead,' she said, when I eventually got through. 'Confirmed. A lot critical.'

'Who opened fire? Police? Military?'

'No idea.'

'Where was the President?'

'We think he was stuck on the runway. Maybe weather. Maybe sabotaged.'

'Jesus Christ.'

'It's localised. It's a local dispute that got out of hand. That's how we're framing it.'

'You can go further. Make it about elements in the Kazakh government close to Russia. Connect it to Zhaparov.'

Piper sighed.

'Say there's stuff under the surface; people investigating him. The President's an experienced dictator; he hates mess. This is an opportunity to move Zhaparov out of power once and for all.'

'We can't afford to inflame things.'

'It's not going to blow over.'

'If you've got ideas of what we might get out there, send them my way.'

I drove into the centre. Khan Shatyr was open. I headed past Tiffany and Hugo Boss up to the food court, the Kyoto Bar, where I ordered an overpriced Japanese whisky. Screens in the café showed sport. It looked like Semey had gone blackout. The staff were watching their phones. I found a number for a couple of businesses there, hotels and restaurants, dialled them and the line didn't connect.

Joanna had talked me through the principles of psyops: the essential ingredients of a political scandal are that it should be shocking and not immediately refutable. The best lies are built on truth. All you had to do was make people look; things came apart by themselves.

I had a platform. Piper's team had been hard at work. Raiymbek now existed – complete with a picture of himself on horseback with spear and helmet. He worked Twitter hard, posting almost hourly in Kazakh, Russian and English. The content was eclectic, ranging from footage of Russians abusing a Kazakh prostitute, to repeated links to a blog called Kazakh Independence, which had been up three hours and already boasted 800 subscribers. Its first post, on the Bolshevik invasion of Kazakhstan and its atrocities, had been shared more than 120 times.

I lifted an image of one of Zhaparov's elite anti-terrorist troops and identified them as the men firing at protesters, emailed it to Lucy Piper and suggested Raiymbek might circulate the idea that the shooting was on Zhaparov's direct orders.

'Use the phrase "Putin's puppet".'

Piper approved. I called a freelance journalist contact, one who was always keen for tips, less keen on fact-checking, and got pieces fast onto a reputable site that frequently fed into the national press.

'Want an angle on this shooting in Kazakhstan?'

'What shooting?'

'I'm sending you something over. Take a look.'

She stayed on the line.

'Okay, I'm interested.'

'Can you get it up asap? I think there's rivals of yours here trying to break the story.'

'I can try. I appreciate this.'

A man walked in, stared at me, lifted a phone. I paid for the whisky, walked out.

I walked fast. Up the escalators. The artificial beach was open for another three-quarters of an hour, according to the boy taking my money. I said that was fine, and he gave me a towel. It was quiet inside – a long stretch of sand and sunloungers alongside the water. Snow tickled the glass roof above the artificial waves. Most of those remaining were drinking and eating at tables set up in the sand beneath palm trees. No one followed me in.

I got a smoothie, checked the gun, calculated escape through the staff exit, watched the entrance. A message came through ten minutes later: the story was up.

They'd run it as I'd written it. Added the images, a clip of the shooting that I'd saved off YouTube. I used a couple of my social media accounts to broadcast the link. Tagged in a selection of anti-Russian figures: Polish, Ukrainian; some Washington-backed organisations, some human rights, some teenagers in bedrooms.

I waited.

Eighty views. Then up to 100 as I watched.

Sites in the US and Poland were linking to it. Then the first pickup from mainstream media in Turkey and India.

My phone buzzed. I thought at first it was response to the story, but it was the alert I'd set up on anyone attempting to break into my hotel room.

Footage from the hidden camera showed me a team of three methodically sifting my possessions – two men and a woman, gloved, using what looked like a portable X-ray scanner. They were searching for something specific. They had a SEEK device – a Secure Electronic Enrollment Kit – used by CIA and US special forces to collect biometric data. Useful if you want to ID someone after you've killed them, check you've popped the right insurgent.

I looked around. If it was an intelligence operation they'd have someone keeping an eye on my movements.

Sure enough, two men were coming in. I saw a third I hadn't noticed before, beside the water. All were conspicuous. The two arrivals looked thuggish, with clothing that would conceal arms – one in a brown leather jacket, one, taller, in a black anorak. The one beside the water wore a baggy grey suit. I finished the smoothie, wrapped the glass in the towel and smashed it beneath my heel. Then I got up and moved towards the exit, retrieving a good-sized shard as the men began to follow.

The larger of the two gripped me by the arm. 'We'd like to speak to you.'

It wasn't clear what happened next. I removed the shard, then it seemed that the man beside the water fired at my assailants. There was the fizz of a pistol with silencer. Glass smashed. They turned, releasing me. A girl screamed. I threw myself through the doors and kept running.

A BMW pulled out behind me when I got to the road. I headed to the riverbank, then down the bank to the ice, heard the car stop and saw its lights above me as I crossed the river. The left bank had police driving past. I kept to the darkness, clambering up snow to dry land, wondering where to lie low. I needed somewhere badly placed for murders, with the cover of other people. I looked around and saw the neon sign for The Rocks.

The doorman nodded me in. The young barman came out from behind the bar to shake my hand. I took my drink, moved into the darkness at the back, leaned against the bricks and watched the door. It was filling up, the first tentative forays onto the dancefloor. Green lasers cut through the artificial smoke like targeting systems.

'Rahmat says you're from England.' A girl's voice startled me.

'Rahmat?'

'The barman.' She was twenty, maybe twenty-one, made-up like an advert. Training told me not to trust her, but instinct suggested she was genuine. She spoke English. She was drunk, eyes narrowed.

'That's right.'

'You look serious. Do you think my English is good?'

'Very.' I saw her friends giggling in the background.

'I am a television presenter.'

'I bet you're a good one. Where are you from?' I asked.

'Astana.'

'Really? I didn't think anyone was born here.'

'Yes. I wish I could go to London.'

She bumped a hip drunkenly against me. I watched the room reflected in the mirrored walls.

'Let me ask you a question,' I said. 'Who would you choose as President?'

'Nazarbayev.'

'I mean after Nazarbayev.'

'Someone modern.'

'Is it important to you to vote?'

This was funny to her. 'Loosen up. It's, like, a party here.' She disappeared into the smoke. I looked around. The man with the leather jacket sat at one of the barrels, staring at me.

There were enough bottles and glasses around, if I needed weapons. The club had only one exit and he'd positioned himself between me and the door. I was outnumbered but we were in a crowded bar and people would pile in sooner rather than later if a fight broke out. Then I saw Sergei Cherenkov, Assistant to the Cultural Attaché, Russian Embassy, walking out of the dry ice towards me.

He wore a waistcoat over a white T-shirt, hair gelled back. He held two bottles of lager, gave me one.

'Was that one of your people? With the gun?'

'No.'

'Well, someone's protecting you.'

'Maybe.' I had no idea, but if Russian intelligence thought I had an armed guard I wasn't going to disabuse them of that notion.

'We're not the threat, Elliot. For fuck's sake.'

'What are you looking for in my room?'

'The question is what the CIA is looking for in your room, and why they have contingency plans to assassinate you.'

This struck me as over-dramatic but not implausible.

'Have you found Joanna?' I asked.

'Really, Elliot. I'm serious. One of my best men just got

attacked, when we're trying to help you. I suggested that you keep in touch with me or get out of Kazakhstan. Can you see the problems you're causing?'

'I'm not sure I introduced the problems here.'

'Can we sit down?'

We took a booth. It was dark, and Cherenkov sprawled on the leather seat opposite me. 'I haven't found her,' he said. 'No one's found her. People found the body of Ruslan Batur, of course. Tomorrow the story's going to come out. He was working for a gang: organised crime. That's what they'll say. Shot by a Makarov pistol, like the one you're carrying.'

It was possible, and would raise some interesting questions regarding GL5. More possible was the idea that Cherenkov was trying to disorientate me, force me into a position of desperation.

'Your prints are there, Elliot. Either you killed him or Joanna Lake killed him.'

'Or someone else with a Makarov.'

'I haven't found Joanna, but I found this.' Cherenkov took his phone out, swiped down videos and played one. It was a couple having sex. They were in what looked like a hotel room, bed sheets tangled. None of the flamboyance of porn, just two bodies, naked and entwined. The shot was static, low-quality, from a camera that must have been high on the wall. It looked like surveillance. Cherenkov gave me the phone. It could have been my back. The hair was right. I had to wait another minute before my face was visible. Joanna's was clear enough.

'Is it real?' he said.

'No.'

'I don't want to see this,' Cherenkov said. 'Why do I have this?'

'You tell me.' I gave the phone back, disguising my mounting desire for violence.

'I have it because some guy in the GRU got it from a friend in the CIA who got it from Six. One way or another they wanted it to land in Moscow. Why is that? You and Joanna Lake, apparently at a hotel in Pakistan last month. But I know where you were last month, and it wasn't there.' He sipped his beer, put his phone away. 'Can I ask: how does it feel, seeing that?'

'It looks like a rushed job. Are you working with Vladislav Vishinsky?'

'No. I work with the consular section of the Russian embassy. I've told you this. I wish you'd really talk to me. This is a question we've asked ourselves: can you blackmail someone over something they didn't actually do? Perhaps the question is, can someone feel shame over something they didn't do? What do you think?'

'I don't feel ashamed because someone is trying to play games with me.'

'Are you ashamed of the things you do while you are someone else?'

'Shall we cut the philosophy? I thought you wanted to know what's going on. Perfect Vision.'

That got him attentive. 'Indeed.'

'First tell me: is Joanna Lake working for you?'

'Not for me personally. Whether she's working for anyone else, I'd like to know.'

'If she's in Russia, just tell me and I'll clear off.'

'Not as far as we're aware. What she was working on?'

'Next time, Sergei.'

'You've got a day, by my reckoning. You know where the Russian embassy is: Aleksandr Barayev Street. You'll be safe there. We can get you out of here, start making sense of things.'

'This isn't the cold war.'

'You don't need an ideology to defect, just a life. I was sorry to hear about Hugh Stevenson.'

I grabbed his arm as he got up to leave. A bottle fell from the table and smashed. People turned.

'What's happened?' I said.

'The question I'd be asking is: what hasn't happened? Why are *you* still alive?'

I pulled him back into the booth, got my fingers around his larynx. His protection detail moved in.

'What's happened to Hugh Stevenson?'

'I'm trying to save you,' he gasped. I released him. He gathered himself together, then walked out, followed by his team.

FORTY

I searched online for news of Stevenson once I was out of the club. A BBC report had been published two hours ago: *Body found on heath identified as senior government official.*

> The body of senior Foreign Office official Hugh Stevenson was spotted by a jogger on Hampstead Heath in the early hours of Tuesday morning. It is believed his wallet and phone were missing. The area, a notorious cruising spot, has seen two violent robberies in the past week. A police spokesperson has said that there are no immediate suggestions of any connection, but individuals are being warned to stay away from the area after dark. A government spokesperson has said that a full investigation is under way and it would be inappropriate to comment at this time.

Cold-blooded bastards. I felt the wind knocked out of me. Ruthlessness like that spelled desperation. I looked around, and the absence of any visible company seemed threatening in itself. *The question I'd be asking is: why are you still alive?* Then the absence filled with guilt. I saw Stevenson in the library, where I'd first met him, flapping the pages of a newspaper as if in endless irritation. Over a long career, there were only two other individuals for whose death I felt directly responsible, but they happened in the course of authorised operations; I could offload some of the guilt. Not here.

Tom Marsh had tried calling twice in the last hour. I went to a public phone box, exhaling with relief when he answered.

'You're okay?'

'Just.'

'When did you last speak to him?'

'I spoke to him the afternoon before he was killed.'

'What did he say?'

'He asked if I'd had any email contact with Joanna – he was interested in an IP address.'

'Which IP address?'

Marsh gave it. It was the IP address for KS internet café, Kiber Sports: Joanna's last known location.

'That's an internet café over here.'

'Well, Hugh seemed to think there was more information we could get out of it. Asked about hacking in, whether I thought you had.'

'Whether I had?'

'Yes.'

'You think he didn't trust me?'

'He was trying to establish what was going on. Listen, Hugh was killed less than a couple of hours after speaking to me, not at night like the papers are saying. I spoke to his partner, Sunil. He said Hugh had a taxi booked to go somewhere.'

'Where?'

'Cording House, St James's Street.'

I could picture St James's Street: grey-stoned Georgian blocks between Piccadilly and Pall Mall. According to Marsh, Cording House was currently the headquarters of a company called Talon.

'It does defence technology – research and development. Used to be part of the government's Defence Evaluation and Research Agency. Still comes up as List X.'

I'd heard of Talon. It was one of several companies created in the early 2000s, when the government privatised its defence research. List X contractors were those approved to handle classified governmental material, with sufficient in-house security of their own. Which made sense if they used to be a governmental department and were still supplying tech to the UK military.

'Any idea who he was going to visit?'

'No. Apparently he knew someone with information. Someone he trusted.'

By the time I got back to the hotel, they'd finished searching the place and departed. I found two listening devices and dismantled them. I went up to the top floor of the hotel and brought up a number listed for Talon Inc. But I had no idea what I'd say to whoever answered. A company like that would be stuffed with individuals close to government and intelligence. Hugh could know any number of them.

I called Stefan. He had checked into the St Regis Hotel, next to Astana airport. The political situation had rendered flights scarce but he was well positioned to grab one at any sign of trouble.

'We need more on the internet café she used,' I said. 'It's her last known location. She was in there a while. I want to know what she did on that computer aside from contacting me. The search history was wiped but I reckon they might be monitored by the owners, in which case there will be records on the central system. Their security cameras don't work, if that's any help.'

'I can take a look.'

I searched for more information on Stevenson's death. There was nothing online. A few stories speculating on his intelligence service connections had vanished.

Meanwhile, overnight, a lot of accounts had appeared making anti-Chinese comments. About two hundred of them, mostly in

Russia, some in Kazakhstan. Aliya was on a Sinophobic jag of her own: Chinese companies buying up Kazakh land, Chinese men stealing Kazakh women, Chinese dams diverting water from Kazakh lakes. Who was steering her? Vishinsky? Russia using residual Kazakh prejudice against the Chinese to ensure their own grip on the region wasn't supplanted?

She linked to aerial shots of prison camps in Xinjiang, supposedly housing thousands of ethnic Kazakhs. There was an interview with a man in Almaty.

My wife went to China in 2016 and hasn't returned. A year and eight months have passed since then and we have had no word from her. We've just recently found out that she's in a re-education camp. I'm begging our government, our Ministry of Foreign Affairs, to return the mother of my children. We're living in a kind of hell at the moment.

I switched the laptop off, lay back on the bed and saw Stevenson walking towards the lamplight and the pond. I felt the darkness returning. The only way of staying sane in this job was to remain detached. Other people's tragedies defeated that or rendered it psychopathic. The stupid game, Joanna called intelligence work. You involve people, telling yourself it's under control, draw them in.

I could still feel Aliya's kiss. I sat up again, opened the laptop and went back into her phone, planning to wipe all traces of myself. I would take a look first, though, after the effort of gaining access. *Lord, let me be pure, but not yet.* I began with text messages and WhatsApp. Friends, social occasions, advice to one girlfriend about a break-up, plans for a holiday. Eighty-one entries in the address book, fifteen landlines, sixteen addresses outside Astana, none overseas. In images: a crowd around a table in a restaurant, a young Kazakh woman with a baby. Aliya's parents and grandmother. I activated the camera. It was dark, the phone face down on a surface. I reversed directions, selfie-mode, got a blade of ceiling fan. I kept the visuals open in the corner of the screen, put headphones on and activated the microphone. Listened to what sounded like crockery being set down, then her parents' voices.

Seventeen anodyne videos. I watched through them all: someone's baby, a friend's birthday party, a 360-degree view of mountains. No sex. It was all so generic I started to wonder again if she was real.

I checked the sent file. A lot of people didn't realise it stored sent images even when the original had been deleted. I looked through until I got to a view that made me stop.

The Houses of Parliament.

Aliya stood in Parliament Square, Big Ben behind her, smiling and saluting.

23rd April last year.

Similar photos beside the Thames, in a London park, Chinatown. A view from a hotel window across the London skyline. Then one inside the hotel.

It showed a large hall, with tables lined up. Old paintings and busts and dried flowers. The tables were laid out with what looked like conference packs, lanyards. No name or sign was legible to suggest the nature of this event.

I went in to her messages and scrolled back to April; there were several to a girl called Sabina.

I've arrived.
Still don't really know what this is about!
They've asked us not to use our phones while here. No pictures! See you when back!

The cutlery of her home clinked. The family conversation involved Semey: how many dead, what the protest meant.

The image from her phone camera moved as Aliya picked it up. I killed the connection. A minute later my own message light blinked.

Good night, Toby. Thank you for this evening. See you soon. x

London.

Smartphones embed GPS coordinates in each photo they take. The information is stored as metadata embedded in the photo files themselves. All you had to do was view the file's properties and look for it.

I opened the hotel jpeg, went to Info, clicked on the GPS tab. Latitude and longitude coordinates appeared in the header. Lat – N 33.00, 56.00, 17.82, Long – E 19.00, 9.00, 39.85. I entered the coordinates into our mapping software and arrived at the Millennium London Hotel, Earl's Court.

I gave them a call.

'Hi. I don't know if you'll be able to help me. I attended an event at your hotel in April last year, 23rd April. I need to speak to the organisers but have lost their contact details.'

'What event was it?'

'I can't remember the exact name.'

'Hang on ... We had several events that day.'

'Could you read them out?'

'Asperian Retirement, The Association of Vice Chancellors, Worldwide Media.'

'Worldwide Media, I think.'

She gave me a phone number, but it didn't connect when I tried to call. There were a lot of 'Worldwide Medias' online but none that seemed more dubious than any other marketing company.

Why London? I wondered. It seemed to point towards whoever was behind this, but there was a range of options: UK government, a UK company, an outsider trying to make it look

310

like that. Plenty of Russians in London. Plenty of offices of global companies.

Hacking a hotel was easy enough. You could just email as a current supplier, a guest, or a wedding planner, with malware-infected specs attached. A conference would leave plenty of traces.

I sat on the edge of the bed, handling one of the listening devices, thinking through options. Then I looked at Aliya's photograph of London again, then at videos of the shooting in Semey going up and getting taken down.

FORTY-ONE

People in the crowd had guns. That was the first deflection used by officials in Semey: Salafi jihadists running amok. It attracted widespread derision, cracking the surface of Kazakhstan's usually respectful social media. The President, as ever, played a smarter game, announcing an immediate investigation and calling for unity. He identified a spiritual crisis in society. WhatsApp and YouTube were down. Tumblr had vanished amidst claims that the platform hosted pornography.

In photos on surviving message boards you could see volunteers tending to the wounded in what looked like a mosque, padding around in socks, oxygen cylinders and plasma bags set up between stone arches. People had formed human chains in front of Semey's police station, while solidarity protests erupted in three other cities. This was it: the point of no turning back. I felt that dizzying, glorious fascination of being there; seeing what happens when the limits of what is possible are breached. Spring again. I used to hear the chants in my dreams: *The people demand the fall of the regime*. It was slicker in Arabic but still had something wistful about it, even when there was hope – something measured and legalistic. Chanted by people who hadn't chanted before, spreading across Tunisia, Egypt, Libya, carried by a shared language, the language of the Koran, suddenly become a vehicle for this democratic virus.

News of Stevenson's death had gained a note of caution: *Question marks over intelligence officer's murder.* That would turn the heat up. One Astana news site had reported an incident at Khan Shatyr's indoor beach before the story was taken down.

Sirens outside.

For the sake of not keeping still, I went for a drive.

I drove past the Kiber Sports café. There were police vehicles parked outside. It looked like it had been broken into. So we'd been beaten to it, I thought. I wondered who had the data. That was a precious lead gone.

I continued past the places you might expect protests in Astana: the main square, government buildings, Bayterek. In the long, landscaped park that stretched from Bayterek to Khan Shatyr, the committed had turned up, in clusters of eight or nine, wrapped against the cold. I recognised a handful of individuals from Elena Yussopova's flat. They held up handwritten signs and two laminated prints showing a man and woman's faces. Riot police stood across the road, hands behind their backs. No sign of Yussopova herself.

But it only made the absence of other protests conspicuous. A city without a past does not really have a population; everyone is dependent on keeping the fantasy alive. It felt like being swaddled in one man's dream, which was a generous way to describe dictatorship but had some truth here.

When I logged in to Aliya's phone, I could see her also searching for protests. She'd caught the bug. Where and when are people meeting?

I logged out, sent a text message:

Awful news about Semey.
Really awful. Did you get back ok last night?
Yes. Can I see you later?
Of course.

Will be in touch. Stay safe. I wrote: Keep clear of crowds, then deleted it. A message came in from Stefan. He was still stuck in the St Regis waiting for a flight. He had something I might be interested in.

I drove over to the airport hotel. Stefan answered, looking unslept and unshaven.

There was a hard drive on the carpet, connected to his laptop, the beige case of the PC it had belonged to beside it.

'Is that what I think it is?'

'That's right.'

'You took it?'

'I couldn't sleep so I went out. The door was practically open. They have everything on here. This must be her, right?'

On the screen of his laptop was a Google search history from the time Joanna had been in the internet café. It included the search strings: *Elliot Kane*; *Elliot Kane Kazakhstan*; *Elliot Kane MI6*. There were also four different cover names I'd used on operations.

'She's trying to see if you're out there, what you're up to. Less than a minute later someone goes to the Earth Explorer site.'

He showed me: the user checked through a series of sites that let you search recent satellite imagery: Digital Globe, the European Space Agency, finally Earth Explorer, which gave you access to NASA's Land Data feeds. In each, she typed in the same coordinates.

'She's trying to get up-to-date imagery of a particular region,' Stefan said.

I punched in the GPS coordinates she'd been searching. They took me to white spaces in the east of Kazakhstan. I heard Shomko's voice – *I saw them studying a map, talking about the possibility she went east* – then thought of the chain of events he had suggested: before disappearing, she stole a Chevy Equinox.

I looked at the imagery again. What I had taken for blank had a faint pattern visible: roads, that appeared to have faded. I cross-checked with Google Maps, then official Kazakh maps. Neither recorded anything for the area. But, zooming in on satellite view, I could make out right angles suggesting man-made structures.

'You think she's there?' Stefan asked.

'Something is. Can you check to see if anything with a nearby geotag has been uploaded? Photos, video, anything.'

My phone screen lit up. It was Callum Walker. I didn't answer. I considered speaking to Aliya, asking straight out what was going on, what took her to London. Instead I studied the photograph of Joanna that Reza had sent through, feeling increasingly sure this connected to the location in the east. Ten minutes later, Stefan said, 'It's wrong.' He had the satellite images up again.

'What's wrong?'

'The weather doesn't fit current reports.' He showed me two current weather reports. 'I think someone's hacked the feed.'

'What about local uploads?'

'Nothing at all. Not even a phone call.'

'Someone's trying to hide something.'

'They've succeeded. This is advanced cyber. The people trying to hide something are state-level, possibly military.'

I clicked 'directions' on Google Maps: 240 miles.

'Google doesn't allow for people trying to kill you on the way,' Stefan said.

FORTY-TWO

I filled the tank at a petrol station with a supermarket attached, then filled two spare jerrycans. I estimated I could cover 240 miles in six hours with my foot down. I bought a new shirt, eight litres of water, three days' worth of food, and spare batteries. I put the gun under the seat.

The only plausible destinations in this direction were Pavlodar and Karaganda, although it was still insane to be driving across the desert. Karaganda had a football stadium and a power plant. Pavlodar had Sary-Arka airport 14 miles to its south. I went online and bought a plane ticket to Istanbul, then kept going east.

A Toyota Yaris passed in the opposite direction, seemed to slow. I watched the mirror as it continued away from me. Then I left the last construction sites behind and plunged into a landscape like a white sea. The city receded behind me – civilisation, other humans – the elastic stretching until the view in the mirrors was as empty as the one through the windscreen, and I was alone.

Desert rules: beware men flagging you down. Give lorry drivers a wide berth – most are wrecked on crystal meth. Don't lose the road: it was level with the desert either side, no barriers, no lights. An old Soviet road, potholed, bleeding into the landscape. I focused on its line. There was something comforting in being able to see endlessly in each direction. I had escaped, for now. I had no idea what I was heading towards.

A few miles further and the road became white gravel. A rusted line of containers stretched along the horizon. I passed one dust-coated lorry marked Dong Feng, driver expressionless behind shades. Around 2 p.m. I saw a settlement a couple of miles to the east. They cropped up at intervals along the railway: track gangs, who might try to rob you, but would possibly sell you some stale food and black-market fuel. The railway itself was invisible but would be a single track carrying cargos of oil and gas from the Caspian to Druzhba on the border of China. I could smell the diesel fumes when I opened my window a crack. After another five miles I could see the oil tanks themselves, stained black and smeared with rail grease.

The railway veered away, replaced by mountains alongside me, then the mountains retreated. No landmarks apart from the road itself. Sometimes that vanished beneath snow and I had to check coordinates and pray. I'd read of intrepid Roman travellers who had reached these parts trying to navigate by the stars like sailors. I'd been trained in astral navigation but it was a long time ago and I hadn't had to call upon it recently.

Any variation meant a lot: small shifts in gradient, the appearance of a ruined fort on the horizon, occasional nomad tombs: domes a few metres high, made of well-preserved mud brick. Then the gradual appearance of low blunt mountains to the east, striped in bands of pink and grey. The snow thinned, and I realised the dirty white landscape beside me was salt. A hunter near the Uzbek border had once told me about centuries-old corpses brought up perfectly preserved.

I made out the horsemen ten minutes before I reached them. Two figures, rugged as the land around them, leading horses visibly starving beneath blankets. They seemed inexplicable, and you had to remind yourself this was the scale of their world.

They came over when I stopped. The horses were gaunt, ribs

vivid. I greeted them in Kazakh and explained where I was going, asked if there'd been any trouble. They shook their heads.

'Where have you come from?' I asked.

They had come from a village 30 miles to the east, looking for pasture. That was the only trouble they were aware of: starvation. I drove on, wondering what they knew of the country around them. If there was a war, would they realise? There would be signs and portents; people like me passing through their emptiness, loaded with a meaning we carried away with us. The hunter I'd met in the south of the country ten years ago had spoken as if the Soviet Union still existed. He knew that England had once invaded India, that the English were bloodthirsty, but wasn't convinced the country still existed. Events reached them like the light from dead stars.

I didn't pass any other vehicles. The road surface was reasonable. I had five hours of daylight left. The nearest town was over 100 miles away. At 3 p.m. I passed a 12-ton China Transport Shipping lorry crashed on its side, a day's snow on it. The windscreen was cracked but not by a bullet. Jiangxi plates, straps for the canvas sides hanging loose. Beyond it, pylons thickened across the landscape towards a town as if catching it in a web.

I checked the GPS. I was heading in the right direction. Heading into gulag territory. Dostoevsky, Solzhenitsyn. Kok-Terek, where Solzhenitsyn had been locked up and where he was released into exile, lay 30 miles to the east. There were towns around here where men freed from the gulags had settled, too exhausted to go further. Or unwilling, for reasons that never quite clarified for me, but made me think of Solzhenitsyn's advice for survival in the camps: let go of the idea that your life ahead will be anything like the one behind. A new range appeared on the horizon, all grey shards. Then I hit a problem.

Two vehicles appeared in the distance, parked across the road. I touched the brakes. There was still half a mile before I reached them. One was a black Subaru Outback, the other a UAZ minibus of the kind you see being used as dirt-cheap public transport. They'd seen me. There was nothing else around for miles.

They had radios and possible backup and would most likely be armed. I'd driven almost six hours and wasn't inclined to turn around.

I advanced slowly, stopping 20 metres short of the checkpoint. The closer you were, the fewer options you had. I left the engine running. The signals on my phone indicated they were using radios, but not police band.

Three men climbed out of the Subaru. One of them, the oldest, was in a heavy ankle-length winter coat. The other two wore desert fatigues under fur-trimmed bomber jackets and carried Kalashnikovs. They moved with the stiff caution of men who are bored, cold but prepared to kill you if it comes to it. The older man was craggy, thick-featured, with an unpleasant stare. A black-handled pistol nestled in his holster.

He approached my window shaking his head and wagging a finger. Then he saw my face and peered closer. 'No further,' he said in Russian.

'Why?' I asked. His men stepped either side of my vehicle.

'Papers, please.'

I handed over my papers, gave my story about the flight and showed the e-ticket on my phone.

'I need to get to Pavlodar,' I said.

'The road's closed.'

I offered money. The captain rejected it sullenly, like someone taunted. Which meant there was a big old chain of command beyond them. It had them scared. One of the younger men wore a ten-inch hunting knife on his hip. That wasn't a style I'd seen in Kazakhstan. It would have looked more at home two or three countries further south.

I steered the car around, making a show of irritation, and wondered what I'd encountered. The mixed uniforms and weaponry suggested a militia. The younger men had the determined eyes of insurgents. I drove half a mile back until they were out of my rear-view then turned off-road. According to the map I could loop them. If I went a mile east I could rejoin the road beyond the block, unseen. I could also lose my bearings and never find another road again.

I marked my GPS position and set off. After twenty minutes of rough driving I found myself back at something approximating a path, but it was not the same road. I'd gone wrong somewhere. According to the GPS I was getting closer to my destination, but I wasn't going to get there over raw desert. I had half a tank of petrol left. I swigged some water, got out and checked the tyres. There was a faint pall of smoke a mile or so away.

After ten minutes' driving in the direction of the smoke I found another track. It was heading towards a cluster of makeshift buildings. There was a chance I was about to be robbed, but I didn't have much choice. I continued, past a starved-looking dog chasing a carrier bag, into a herdsmen's village. The houses were low and misshapen: rough walls of mud bricks, occasionally plastered over and painted white; small windows; roofs of corrugated iron weighed down by bricks. A grotesque parody of a nomadic camp: winter cattle sheds had been built from whatever lay to hand – fragments from dismembered trucks, old tyres, rusted bedposts.

The smoke led to a shack. Two men lay among empty vodka bottles beside a stove filled with ash. They looked up at me as if I was a hallucination not worth responding to. Past the shack was an adobe house behind a fence made of flattened drums that, according to their markings, had once held sodium chlorate. I walked around to the back, past an ice-encrusted water tank to a pile of scrap metal. No one responded when I called.

I was leaving when I felt eyes on me. A girl, nine or ten years old, appeared among the scrap.

'Hello,' I said. An identical girl appeared. They were twins, clothes faded and patched beneath their coats. One whispered something to the other and they giggled. I searched my pockets and gave them a protein bar. Then the mother appeared, saw me and began scolding them.

I showed her the map on my phone and asked where we were. It was too cold to be outside, she said, and invited me in.

The home had a warm, damp, close smell. Wall-hung carpets hid the dirt. Furniture was a double mattress and cushions. An antique sewing machine took centre stage. A stove poked its chimney through the roof. A man's boots hung off a nail along with a rusted horse bridle.

The woman heated a samovar. I felt that code of hospitality, lost in the developed world, with no knowledge of what it might mean to be dependent on strangers. I would never forget the men and women who had invited me into their homes and offered tea: in Aleppo, Afrin, Shatoi. It was the code of the sea, an obligation to help vessels in distress, and an Islamic tradition, a religion of the desert; the knowledge that the absence of hospitality was death.

'The weather is changing,' she warned as the tea heated. 'Where are you going?'

'Pavlodar,' I said.

'Not tonight,' she said.

She asked where I was from, what on earth I was doing here, and I gave my story. The girls poured the tea, watching me openly.

'Hello,' one said in English. 'How are you?'

'I'm very well. How are you?'

They laughed. 'What is your name?' the other said.

'Toby. What is yours?'

I didn't get an answer.

'They are learning English,' the mother explained. She brought out what I thought might be an exercise book but was a pamphlet from Saracen Oil and Gas Exploration in English, Russian and Kazakh. *Investing in Communities*. There were pictures of Kazakh engineers in protective eyewear, fields spewing fire, the management school in Astana.

The girls read some words out loud, then looked up at me smiling.

'Who gave you this?' I asked.

She passed a hand through one of her daughters' hair, mimed cutting it. 'The men who came.'

'People who cut her hair?'

'Just a little.'

'A sample?'

'Yes.'

What were Saracen doing passing through here, running tests? Light was fading. I finished my tea, checked the map again. I tried to give them some money as I left. The woman refused, then shyly took it.

'You are crazy. You should not go further.'

The girls cleared the cups away without taking their eyes off me. I said goodbye, they waved and I saw that both had an extra finger on each hand. It jutted out, slender and perfectly formed, like a second stalk beside the little finger.

They giggled again. I smiled. I walked past the rusting scrap and the old sodium chlorate barrels.

Half a mile outside the village, signs appeared on either side: *Agriculture banned*.

Desert secrets. Sodium chlorate was used in the mining of uranium. North-eastern Kazakhstan was used for an atomic-bomb programme for forty years. They were still testing bombs as the Berlin Wall came down. Moscow men would make a trip to watch the mushroom clouds. Locals had been exposed deliberately as guinea pigs. The steppe was a laboratory, riddled with unfissioned plutonium.

Trees appeared ahead: a dark canopy of Scots pine on emaciated-looking trunks. But just inside the woodland, the road had been blocked. Square slabs of wood lay across it, painted white with signs nailed into them: *Danger. No entry.*

The signs looked new. I got out of the car, listened, checked for footprints, empty bottles, cigarettes. Then I checked for sensors, cameras, landmines.

The blocks were heavy, but I managed to work a solid branch beneath them and use it as a lever to roll each one a couple of times. That was enough to squeeze the car through. I stopped on the other side, got out and rolled them back, flattened the snow where they'd been moved.

Trees closed in, the spectral white trunks of aspen and birch among the pine. Then they opened out and I glimpsed a small dead lake. A decrepit jetty reached into mud. I checked the map: nothing for 120 miles. Then I cleared the trees and saw the outskirts of a small town.

FORTY-THREE

There was only one road in and it went past the concrete ruins of a guards' post: a booth with broken windows, struts in the ground beside it where a barrier would have rested. Every piece of metal that could be lifted had been stripped from the place. There had been a fence once. The roof of the booth itself had been prised off.

Two slender, red and white striped factory chimneys rose up a mile out. Closer than them were three apartment blocks, hinged into shallow V shapes, pocked with hundreds of dark windows.

It had been a closed town, one of those the Soviets considered too sensitive to have people moving in and out of freely. Abandoned for a couple of decades by the looks of it. Which made the fresh tracks of a vehicle with deep tread and 10-inch-thick wheels seem curious.

The blocks came into focus as I drove in, windows smashed, faded murals flaked from the end walls: a woman with arms aloft before a globe; two miners, one with Slavic features, one Kazakh. Silver water pipes snaked above the ground. The ice that ran down from them formed a low, opalescent curtain, waist high. It was minus 3, but the wind straight off the steppe took another 10 degrees off. I was worried about the car. I'd seen them stop functioning at higher temperatures than this and had no idea what coolant or anti-freeze was in use, if any. Without transport I had a lot of snow and ghosts for company.

I drove further in, slowly. Two red-brick buildings the size of churches had collapsed into themselves, filled with piles of their own bricks. Trees grew above and through the buildings. The water pipes wound between them, scattering lagging across the ground.

In the centre was a town square. I got out of the car, pulling my scarf tight, sealing myself into my jacket. Walked past a town hall, a school with cracked plasterwork the same colour as the snow, into a park with a playground and a sculpture: a sphere of blue and white oxidised copper beside a bearded man in a suit. I cleaned the plaque at his feet. *Igor Vasilyevich Kurchatov. Nuclear physicist.*

I laid a gloved hand on a roundabout and it turned, smoother than I'd expected. Every blank window seemed to watch me. I wondered how far I was from another living human.

You reached the factories before the mine: two roofless chemical plants, stripped like carcasses. One brown-bricked factory more intact. Squares of late sun decorated the floor inside like glowing fire pits. Fixings remained where the machines had been. Nests filled the corners, black pellet-like droppings across the floor from bats. Turbines and gangways had been left to rot. There was an office in the corner with a jacket hanging on a peg, rusted circuit boards from a computer on the floor.

Beyond the factories, indentations preserved the direction of a narrow-gauge track running towards the mine. I returned to my car. It started. I had no idea where I'd get to beyond the factory, but I wanted to find out. I followed the traces of the old track until the town disappeared behind me. Then a warning sign appeared, this one bright and startling, placed on a gate in the road in the past few weeks: *Danger. Private Property. KazMunaiGaz.*

It was getting dark, the white disc of sun sinking. Clouds moved fast, as if getting out of the way of the approaching night.

I entered woods again, my petrol light came on. I refilled from the canister. The trees blocked the rising wind at least. I needed headlights now but was reluctant to use them. Then my phone lit up: radio frequencies ahead. Military radios.

I stopped, unwound the window and listened, then reversed slowly into the trees, positioning the car so that passing head-lights wouldn't illuminate its reflectors. It was bitterly cold once out of the car. I could make out faint light ahead: pervasive, artificial, paling the sky above the trees. I set my phone to pick up radio activity, pocketed the knife and tucked the gun into the back of my waistband. Whatever lay ahead, it connected to Joanna's visit here, and her subsequent disappearance.

The road felt conspicuous. I continued deeper into the woods until I was out of sight, but close enough to the road that I didn't lose it entirely. I could hear vehicles half a mile ahead. Forty miles from the Russian border, I estimated. The signals pattern on my phone showed layers of radios. Then the trees were inter-rupted by a chain-link fence and I heard Russian voices.

I crouched, then reluctantly flattened myself on the ground. Torch beams came closer, snow crunching between boots. There were five of them, bulky with black combat gear – the pouched tactical vests of special forces, assault rifles with mounted night sights. No insignia that I could make out. Vehicles had Kazakh plates. Kit was carefully generic. But these weren't local farmers.

The steps stopped. My fingers were already throbbing ago-nisingly with the cold, my body starting to shake. I needed to move but the noise would reach them. I needed the cover of some other sounds. None came. Two of them spoke a language that wasn't Russian. It took me a second to place it as Serbian. That was unexpected. I was considering a run for it when there was a crackle from their radios; they adjusted their kit and walked on.

I waited a moment, then eased into a low crouch, trying to

still my shivering and stop my hands from going numb. They'd wandered away from the site. I moved towards it, following the fence to a gate with another KMG warning sign but no guards.

It was another fifteen minutes stumbling through trees before the gradient afforded a view. Floodlights lit a flattened square of compacted mud half a mile across, cleared for a drill pad. Bright yellow diggers looked small beside it. Security guards patrolled with sniffer dogs. To the east was a pit large enough to bury a five-storey building. Pipes and cables waited to be laid, stacked beside two holding tanks bearing the Saracen logo. Around the edges, unlit, you could see the ruins of the old mine: a mountain of grey waste, the rusting towers of the extraction plant. A new road ran from the site to a complex of temporary buildings, port-acabins with gleaming black GL5 patrol vehicles beside them.

The level of development suggested there was something special about this site. I didn't have time or warmth to search for it now. I headed back towards my car, hit a problem.

Five men stood around it, the Russians and Serbs, quiet now, scanning the surroundings with their weapons up as one of them radioed details. The boot was open, more men approaching through the trees. I stepped back.

Their own patrol vehicle was parked a few metres away, closer to me than it was to them: a light cargo truck, mud-coloured canvas over its flat bed. No one had stayed with it. I took a few steps closer to the truck, saw keys in the ignition. One of the men looked up. I climbed into the vehicle as he raised his gun. They all turned in my direction. I prayed that it accelerated fast.

'Hey!'

I turned the key, slid low. Bullets pinged off the front engine. I began to drive, straight at them at first, which caused some temporary disruption and blinded them with the headlights, then I dragged down the oversized steering wheel and circled away. Shifting gears was a fight, but the horsepower felt good.

Once on the road I floored the accelerator. I took turnings when I could, lost but glad to put several miles between myself and the Russians. Twenty minutes later I was still so focused on threats behind that I didn't see the Toyota Cruiser speeding towards me, less than a second from a head-on collision.

FORTY-FOUR

They reacted slower, which meant I was the one who steered off-road. I crashed into trees, wrenching the wheel, managing to avoid one trunk, slamming into the next. I almost broke my ribs on the steering wheel, came to a stop. The wheels were stuck.

Three balaclava'd men appeared in the headlights, Kalashnikovs pointed at my windscreen. I raised my hands. One of the men tore the door open and I was dragged out, forced to the ground, pockets emptied. My face pressed down into the snow as I tried to imagine various ways this could unfold and kept arriving at the likelihood of death. It felt too soon, rushed, and with this came rising panic, and then a faint, accompanying awareness that I needed to keep control of myself if I was going to have any chance of surviving.

I was lifted to my feet. Four men now, two in camo fatigues, two in a mixture of nondescript khaki and civilian clothes. I could see narrower Kazakh eyes behind the balaclavas of the khaki men. The lead camo fatigues wore grey gloves and sounded Syrian. He was the jumpiest, the one I was most cautious about, scarf pulled up to his eyes, shoulders hunched, combat jittery.

He turned and called: *Hna.* Another man appeared from the trees, unmasked. *Hna.* Here.

Arabic.

The new arrival had broad, blunt Slavic features, blue-eyed, a fair beard beneath his chin encrusted with ice, but moustache shaved. All of which said Chechnya. The sharp, unmistakable scent of unwashed fighters cut through the cold. No alcohol on their breath. Weapons held professionally, kept angled down when they spoke to one another, movements controlled, pupils undilated. No visible radios: an underground crew, guerrilla-smart. I took a proper look at the weaponry. Kalashnikovs and AR-15 assault rifles. I couldn't tell if they were the Chinese copies or the real thing.

The Chechen barked orders in Arabic without taking his eyes off me: 'Check the vehicle, check the boot, check the road.' The choppy, guttural language sounded startling among the snow. When he spoke to me he used Russian, which was understandable as I'd just been hauled out of a Russian military vehicle.

'Get down.'

I was forced back to my knees, the barrel of the AK ground against my temple, told to put my hands on my head. The flash eliminator at the end of the barrel dug into my forehead. Was this the Islamic Movement of Kazakhstan? It wasn't unusual to come across men who didn't know who they were fighting for that week. Deals were made several ranks higher, sometimes countries away. My phone was torn out of my pocket then thrust at me. I entered the password, watched out of the corner of my eye as he tried to scroll through with gloves on. I tried to decide which cover story was least likely to get me shot immediately. One of the Kazakhs was going through the truck. He spoke in faltering Arabic to the Syrian. There was a debate along the lines of: should we kill him or take him? It was my lucky day: my hands were bound behind my back with duct tape, and I was marched to their vehicle, a blue Toyota Cruiser with roof rack, where I was offered the boot.

The only other time I'd ridden in a boot it had been voluntary, and got me across the border with Kashmir. That boot had been larger and more recently hoovered. I rested my head on a coil of old rope and believed I was going to freeze to death before we got anywhere. When the car started I jammed my feet against the metalwork to stop myself being bounced too hard. Kept thinking through cover, feeling out any remote possibility of surviving the night.

After thirty minutes we pulled over ruts. I was hauled out and a bag came down over my head. We entered somewhere heated, which felt like a reprieve in itself. The bag came off.

We were in a brick-walled farmhouse. I was put in a side room with a concrete floor and a small barred window. Twenty minutes later another vehicle stopped outside and my cell door opened. I looked up to see a man in his fifties or sixties, hard-looking, Syrian or possibly Iraqi. He had a nickel-plated Kalashnikov slung over his shoulder. His hands were gnarled.

While the rest of the men explained finding me, I pondered this multinational get-together. Chechens got around; in Syria, at least one vicious rebel crew – Jaish al-Muhajireen wal-Ansar – was Chechen-led. You found Chechen Islamists wherever there was the opportunity to fight Russians – especially since Russia had gained the upper hand at home. And Russia had pushed plenty of its own Chechens into Syria to fight for Assad. Same war, different country. Many of the Islamists joined IS.

It made some sense that they'd head north again.

This territory was home to several criminal gangs, some with jihadist connections. I wondered if they were involved. I could see how Russians encroaching on Kazakhstan would be a provocation to them. I could see how jihadists encroaching on Kazakhstan would be a provocation to the Russians. Could see, with sickening clarity, why they'd cut my throat with nonchalance.

A rifle butt slammed into my face. I thought it might have broken a cheekbone and experimentally moved my jaw and checked my sight. I was intact for now. I was made to squat with my back against the wall, thighs parallel with the ground, while the boss questioned me: *Name, commanders. Which unit, which battalion? Why no uniform?*

'You are Russian.'

'English.'

'The jeep—'

'I stole it.'

'What are you doing here?'

In training you're told to ride out the first few hours, when the situation's new and everything's terrifying. But then things become known and it's not always uplifting.

'Where is the man you took?'

They seemed to think I was involved in the abduction of one of their men. I wondered who was. I had nothing for them. I'd stumbled into a war zone, it seemed, but was playing catch-up. We kept going around in circles. *Why are you here? What are your plans?*

After a while the questions stopped. A new length of rope was looped around my hands and tied to a bolt in the wall. A guard was left to watch over me, one of the youngest of the men. I hadn't been fed or watered, which meant they were probably intending to kill me. They wouldn't spend a second night here, and I was a travel liability.

An hour passed. I stretched and relaxed as far as my restrictions allowed, recited poems in my head to keep alert and conscious. I listened to the voices of my captors and let them carry me to various points of the globe. I was back in the Caucasus Mountains, two years into my career; a dream job, among the tribes, up in the clouds and jagged white peaks, told to establish a picture of gang operations. I was shown how to chew certain flowers against altitude sickness. I watched my shadow cast up into the morning mist half a mile in height. My official brief involved establishing hierarchies, but these people didn't do hierarchy, they did blood feuds. That was their life. And the only way to step beyond the endless, innumerable tangle of feuds was to establish yourself as *abrek*. Russians translated the word as 'bandit', which missed the sense utterly. The *abrek* were outcasts, gathered high in the hills, forbidden to work the fields or engage in business. They survived alone, feared but respected. These were the men I was trying to reach. I outlined the anthropological phenomenon of the *abrek* in a detailed report sent to the Central Asia desk in London, for which I was informed that I was not at Cambridge any more. It elicited a smile, even now.

A spade hit the frozen soil outside. I listened to the clink and shuck of its blade. The darkness began to soften. My guard stepped out of the room and I watched his shadow on the bare concrete floor as he knelt and prayed. *Fajr*, dawn prayer. A time worth marking. I tried to remember all the different calls to prayer that had interrupted my sleep in various countries; all the men I'd watched praying: complacent ones, desperate ones, ones who did not know they were about to die. His shadow pointed to the front of the house, which meant Mecca was in the opposite direction to my barred window. That was south-west then; at least I had my bearings. There was something unusual about his muttered prayers, and after a while I realised he was praying in Dari. A Dari like that spoken in West Afghanistan, cut off from Kabul by five hundred miles of mountains. I thought of the deep blue lakes of Band-e Amir, and the pristine Panjshir Valley, and the people there, serene and welcoming as the landscape, as if environments worked so transparently. I watched his face when he returned.

'From Herat?' I asked, trying to rustle up what remained of my own Dari.

He looked suspicious.

'It's a beautiful place.'

No answer. From West Afghanistan to Kazakhstan: that sounded like a heroin route. I thought through the various warlords who controlled the trade.

'Can I stretch for a few seconds?' I asked. 'I can't feel my legs.'

He kept the gun on me as I got to my feet, bent my body left and right to stretch the spine. A vehicle pulled up outside and there were new voices: talk of firefights, low ammo, faulty radios.

Around 6 a.m. I was untied and marched out. They'd dug a shallow grave. Given the conditions, it was more trouble than I was worth. Eight men stood around and I scanned for the weapon intended to kill me. No one had a knife out; no camera ready to film. One of the new arrivals, arm in a bloody sling, came and looked at me. He wore the uniform of a Kazakh border guard.

The situation started to make hazy sense.

I was led to the edge of the grave, hands still bound. The sky was a washed-out blue. In its half-light you saw the spindly fence around the farm buildings, dividing a hazy, infinite pallor. Borders. One man controlled the roads all the way from Balkh in Afghanistan to Kazakhstan's border with Russia. I had sat on a carpeted floor with him, toasting our friendship with fermented camel's milk.

'Kneel.' My knees touched the cold ground. The Chechen raised his gun.

I said, 'Akan Satayev.'

'What?'

'I know Akan Satayev. I've worked with him.'

The Iraqi boss came over. 'What are you saying?'

'I was at his wedding two years ago in Aktobe. Akan's. I met him through General Abdul Dostum. I imagine you came here via Mingdon, on the Uzbek border, under Akan's protection.' I didn't expect anyone to believe me; I just needed to make any potentially wrong decision too risky for them to make.

'What are you doing here?'

'Tell Akan it's Christopher Bohren. The British want to help.'

The safety catch eased down. Someone lifted me to my feet, and I found myself eyeball to eyeball with the boss.

'You lie.'

'You've got half the Russian army coming in,' I said, switching to Arabic, which got his attention. 'Low ammunition, bad radios. How long are you going to last? Let me speak to Akan.'

The senior men consulted. I was made to go through my story once more, before the buttons of a satellite phone were punched.

I don't know what was said. After five minutes I was begrudgingly given a blanket, driven again.

FORTY-FIVE

I was spared the boot this time. We drove in a straight line east, by my estimation. After 20 miles or so there was a change of vehicles. I was blindfolded, passed over to someone with a different grip, led over broken branches for a couple of hundred metres to a car with good heating and leather seats. We drove for what felt like an hour. Then I was pulled out.

Ten metres of tarmac underfoot, into the warmth of a building with a smell of bleach. I was led down a long flight of stairs through two doorways with beaded curtains trailing over me. Someone unknotted my blindfold.

I stood in the basement dining room of a restaurant with plastic vine leaves over the ceiling. Akan Satayev sat at the furthest table watching me. I was shoved into the seat facing him.

His hair had greyed, eyes dark. He wore a cashmere coat over a creased jacket, and a white shirt that wasn't fresh today. A rich man who hadn't slept in his own home for a while. We'd both aged less than we deserved. His career had clearly done better than mine, although, until last week, he was more likely to be the target of an assassination. Hence the missile-proof basement, I imagined.

Satayev had started out as a regular mid-level thug. His family was heavily involved in the transportation of heroin and lapis lazuli. He became boss, expanded the empire a little, gained some notoriety for extortion and kidnappings. Then the

Kazakh President had trouble with Cossack gangs who wanted the North Eastern region transferred to Russia. Satayev was given carte blanche to get rid of them, which he did, ruthlessly. That handed the Satayev family not only regional power but control of the smuggling route across the border.

Afghanistan is the world's biggest producer of heroin. Russia's the world's biggest consumer. In between the two lie Uzbekistan, Turkmenistan, Kazakhstan, depending on your route: 100 kilograms of raw opium cost a thousand dollars in Osh. In Moscow you could sell it for fifteen times that, more again in Western Europe. Labs around Moscow processed it into heroin. Smuggled into Sweden by boat, then all over world, the epidemics raging meant big money. I'd spent a lot of time beside the US-built Nizhny Pyanj Bridge that connected Afghanistan and Tajikistan, getting blind drunk with border guards, but not so blind I couldn't see the bulky sacks coming through on the backs of Satayev's trucks. From Tajikistan, the heroin and opium should logically pass through Uzbekistan, only the Uzbeks are paranoid, hate their neighbours, and so actually pay border guards to do their job. Which meant Kazakhstan was good traffic.

Satayev got filthy rich. And like any business person who finds themselves sitting on several million dollars he expanded. Guns, oil; most of all, he controlled men. His money funded the armed wings of various criminal enterprises in Iraq, Afghanistan, Kyrgyzstan and Kazakhstan. He was a blissfully unidealistic fulcrum of several shit-storms, which made him as appealing to MI6 as he was to anyone else. His routes were precisely those along which NATO wanted to move armies. So I set up shop beside the historic Jayma bazaar in Osh – buying cheap cotton for a fictitious textiles company – and in less than a month I was sharing boiled sheep's head and negotiating pay-offs.

Like a lot of barely literate, power-hungry criminals he had an instinctive grasp of international diplomacy. It had been a while since his name did me any favours. He might decide to kill me anyway but there was a shred of comfort in being killed by someone who knew at least one of my lives.

'A ghost,' Satayev said.

'It's good to see you, Akan.'

'Are you sure?'

He studied my damaged face. The wars and deaths since our last meeting had carved a depth behind his eyes. He retained some of that aura of the rich, of moving through the world in a slightly slicker substance, but there was a gravity there, a melancholy that I associated with military figures more than with criminals or businessmen, both of whom could go a long way without knowing the names of those killed on their behalf.

My phone and gun were on the table. The table's polished black surface reflected the plastic vine leaves above us so that they seemed to reach up like pond weed. A decent restaurant suggested some habitations nearby. I considered the scale of the place, the distance driven – a town between Semey and Pavlodar.

One guard stood to the side of Satayev. Another took the doorway, gun on me.

'It looks like you have trouble,' I said. 'Maybe I can help.'

'You were sent to find me?'

'To assess the situation.'

The vagueness was reassuring, it seemed. He ordered my cuffs removed and sent the guards away with orders to bring water and tea.

'Is this a good place to talk?' I said.

'That is why we're here.' The drinks arrived. He stirred a sugar cube into his tea.

'What do the Russians want?' I said.

'What do you think?'

I let this ride, curious.

He continued: 'There have been drone strikes on my men, my vehicles.'

'From across the border?'

'We think so. Russians closed the border, set up checkpoints. Said they were a "local militia" defending ethnic Russians against fanatics. Bullshit. They have seized my relatives, my money. There is no law, nothing.'

I let his outrage at lawlessness pass.

'So you got some jihadis,' I said.

He dismissed the word. 'I don't believe you've become that naive.'

'Do they belong to the Islamic Movement of Kazakhstan?'

'I've never come across any such group.'

'Where did you get the guns?'

'The usual places.'

'You're using Chechens and Syrians as hired muscle. That's an unfortunate look. It's not going to win you friends.'

'Who would you like me to use? Or shall I tell the Russians that Block Nine is all theirs?'

'Block Nine?'

'What do your bosses say to that? Is the UK government backing Saracen?'

'I don't know about Block Nine,' I said.

Satayev looked puzzled. 'Why do you think Saracen are here?'

'Tell me.'

'Because it's big. Their big new discovery.'

'How big?'

'According to their estimates, around 30 trillion cubic feet of gas, over 5 billion barrels of oil.'

I stared at him in astonishment as my brain did the calculations. If what he was saying was true, it was the biggest discovery of the last twenty years. Satayev, at least, seemed sure of the numbers.

'You've seen data?' I asked.

'I've seen data.'

'Where did you get it?'

'Friends in Russia.'

'Where did they get it?'

'Stolen from Saracen. Hacked, leaked, I don't know.'

'I need to see that data.'

'Of course – if you're in a position to help. Saracen have been buying up every square kilometre of land around. They use front companies, but we're not stupid. Nor are the Russians. You could have saved yourself a lot of trouble by speaking to me in the first place.'

He reached into his pocket and tossed over a dog tag: four digits, no name. The numbers given to soldiers by the Russian defence ministry usually have a single letter of the Russian alphabet followed by a six-digit number. Russia's PMCs – Private Military Contractors – only had four.

'Sigma Group,' I said.

'You know them?'

They'd turned up in Ukraine aiding the separatist forces of the self-declared Donetsk and Luhansk People's Republics. Then we picked up the same men in Syria, fighting on behalf of the Syrian government. Their chief mission was capturing ISIS-held oilfields. A former special forces brigade commander was in charge, and the company was named after his old call sign; he headhunted elite troops, some from the Russian army's *Nefte polk*, the Oil Protection Regiment created to protect Chechnya's oil infrastructure, some *Spetsgruppa A*, a counterterrorist sub-unit of special forces. The company was registered in Argentina, offices in St Petersburg. By our estimations it controlled over six thousand men. They got good pay. In return, they signed ten-year confidentiality clauses, handed over their phones, received a nameless dog tag with a four-digit number. I handed it back.

'Private military. Possibly used as cover for Moscow, possibly more renegade.'

Sigma had a Serbian unit that had cropped up briefly in Palmyra. That startled the GCHQ listeners initially, especially those who'd been around in the Nineties. Like the West, the Kremlin had become keen on the PMCs as a way of lowering official casualty numbers – but the situation wasn't without friction. When US air strikes ended up killing a lot of Sigma men attempting to capture a Kurdish base last year there were accusations that information hadn't been shared by Russia's Main Intelligence Directorate – suspicions that the defence ministry might have been hostile towards private entities conducting a major operation without its approval.

The scale of things made sense now: the information warfare, the cultivation of Zhaparov, the *Agentsumpf*. It was possible that a lot of the information warfare online was Sigma-produced. I knew they had advanced cyber capabilities; there'd been run-ins over signal jamming and electronic warfare with both the US and China when Sigma deployed in Sudan. Did mercs do social media now? Brave new world. It looked like Akan needed help, which was fortunate for me.

'Who else are you speaking to from the UK?' I asked.

'No one.'

'You have contact with GL5?'

'Informal.'

'They pay you so they can operate here.'

'Yes.'

'And when did the Russians arrive?'

'Six days ago.'

Just after Joanna had gone missing.

'Have you come across an English woman?'

'No.'

'Do you still have contact with Jan Jágr?'

He looked surprised to hear the name. Jágr was a former military translator from Slovakia. He ran an air-freight company based in Namibia, with two Ukrainian-registered Ilyushin-76 cargo aircraft originally designed for delivering machinery to remote areas of the USSR. The hulls were sheathed in lead to deflect bullets, and he managed to land them almost anywhere. More important, he was a master of paperwork, with a web of thirty or forty front companies under his command, re-registering aircraft every couple of months. This was the way he'd survived three decades as a priority for Interpol. Still, I had to get him out of German custody in 2015, so he owed me a favour.

'You can contact him?' Satayev asked.

'I can try.'

'We need communications equipment, ammunition, satellite pictures and radio interception. But until I have the roads back, I cannot throw money around. I cannot fight the Russian army out of my own funds. They are already raping, cutting throats, stealing homes.'

'I can get you what I can.'

'That is all you'll say? After I saved your life?'

'I need to speak to people.'

'How do I know you have anything to do with anything?'

'You know me, Akan.'

'You disappear from the scene, cut all ties, then turn up again in a Russian truck. Explain to me why I have saved your life.'

'Speak to Saracen, tell them you've got a Vectis employee here.' I gave him a number to call. He walked off. I was left watching the vines in the tabletop and feeling the tickle of the gun on me. So I'd been picked up by a new militia. More men with nowhere left to go except into new zones of conflict. Army of exiles. The future: swarms of mercs and militias chasing each other around the globe like weather systems, a constant rumbling in the

342

background as we lock down air-conned shopping malls, and wait for the coffee to run out.

Satayev came back ten minutes later. I don't know who he spoke to, or what was exchanged, but he seemed open, keener.

'They say you should go back to Astana.'

'Who does?'

'Saracen.'

'Is that right.'

'I said I'd help.'

He told me about jets I could use, then we talked supply routes for equipment. I said I could get small arms to Uzbekistan. Moving them on was the difficulty.

'Taraz airfield,' I suggested.

'We don't have access to it any more.'

'Sigma got it already?'

'Yes.'

Things were moving fast, and strategically.

'On the ground then,' I suggested. 'Tashkent to Shymkent to Taraz.'

'Maybe. We can try. What about Reza Nikfar? Are the Americans with you on this?'

'This is a different situation to last time, Akan. I need you to understand that. I may not be in such a strong position.'

'Yet you are in a position to endanger your life and be saved by me.'

My pose was convincing, and had kept me alive so far, but it wasn't a roleplay I could back out of easily.

'Saracen have given me their guarantee,' he said.

'Then we need to be clear on styles: no suicide bombs, no beheadings. No bearded men on YouTube waving rifles.'

'I understand.'

Did he? We exchanged secure means of communication. I asked where I was.

343

'Glukhovka.'

'Where's that?'

'North-east. I can arrange a flight to Astana. I have contacts in Astana who can collect from you.'

I was a hostage, essentially. But it was the only way I was going to get out of here. And I'd been in Satayev's jets before. They had coffee machines. Things like that can help you feel immortal.

'Checks at the other end?'

'Not for an internal flight. Not with my set-up. I have jets in Semey or Pavlodar. Pavlodar is probably safer right now.'

'What's the news from Semey?'

'Twenty dead. More protests.'

'Twenty dead?'

'So it seems.'

'I'd like to take a look.'

'It's on the edge of going very bad.'

'Give me an hour in the town. I heard it has a Dostoevsky museum.'

'A Dostoevsky museum?'

'I thought I'd check it out while I'm in the area.'

FORTY-SIX

My belongings were returned, although the gun had no bullets. I was led out. Glukhovka was pretty much just a crossroads, with a petrol station, the restaurant and not much else apart from six blacked-out armour-plated SUVs scattered across the frozen mud.

One of them took me to Semey. Two men sat up front, with an AK-47 propped between them. The driver chainsmoked, glancing in his mirror at me then looking away instantly when our eyes met. The dashboard clock said 8 a.m. We drove back into barrenness: snow and rock. I checked my bruising in the rearview mirror. I looked rough.

Block 9 was a supergiant, the largest class of field, with 1 billion or more barrels of ultimately recoverable oil. Fewer than forty had ever been found, and two-thirds were in the Persian Gulf. People hunted hard, but for years the word was that there were no more out there. I did the maths. Even if the estimates were optimistic, it was vast. Thirty trillion cubic feet of gas, 5.5 billion barrels of oil: that would meet Europe's energy needs for years to come. All buried 50 miles from the Russian border.

I messaged Walker with an update and he rang back. 'We got a call from Akan Satayev.'

'What did you say?'

'We told him not to kill you. What took you east?'

'Block Nine, it turns out. You didn't mention it.'

'It's incredibly sensitive. Are you able to get here?'

'I'm sure I'll find a way.'

The more oil around, the less I trusted people, and my trust levels had been minimal to start with. But the hardest question was whether you could trust yourself. I thought through the exchange with Satayev and felt the ice of Christopher Bohren hardening around me again.

I fell asleep, and when I woke Semey was visible on the other side of the Irtish river. Ten a.m. on the dashboard. The town looked innocent enough, in the way of medium-sized towns: snow-crested, a scatter of older buildings among the concrete, arranged between the river and the mountains behind. A suspension bridge crossed the river towards it. Population 300,000. No sign that twenty of them had been shot dead in the last forty-eight hours. I wanted to assess which way the wind was blowing. Whether they were ready to join Russia, who was steering this, how far they were prepared to go. Call it habit.

We crossed the bridge, above lumps of ice floating downstream. The town was called Semipalatinsk until 2007: seven-templed city, named after the ruins of a Buddhist monastery. By the time they decided it was time for a rebrand the name meant nothing but nuclear tests. I'd met a nurse in Moscow who used to work in Semey's central hospital and remembered terminally ill children running around the wards pretending to be radiation.

Now Semey was metamorphosing again.

I told the driver to stop once we'd crossed the bridge. I could already see police vehicles parked on the main road. It would be wiser to approach on foot. The men refused money. As soon as I was out the driver pulled a fast U-turn that left me wondering what I was heading into.

I kept to back streets. The few who were out and about were moving quickly, nervously. Patrols of men, military and police, appeared every other block. Most shops were closed, phone signal intermittent.

The main public square had been taped off, with teams of armed police at each corner. The ground had been hosed but broken glass glinted in the cracks between paving slabs. A block away I found a café open beside a small frozen park. A stone Lenin rose up above the cold shrubbery of the park, right arm thrust out as if seeking to shake hands. Most of these monuments had vanished over the last two decades, usually removed in the dead of night, and I wondered what kept this one here. Proximity to the Motherland? Distance from brave new Astana? I ordered coffee and a hot pastry, took a seat in the centre so I could see the windows but would be mostly obscured from those looking in from outside.

I warmed my hands on the coffee, then sipped, my insides contracting in surprise. I ate the pastry slowly, then I ordered more food and another coffee. Events of the previous twenty-four hours repeated in my mind, with stabs of dread, interwoven with a sense that I was still walking in Joanna's footsteps. When I had caffeine and carbohydrates inside me, I focused on the view.

The patrols were a mix: local police, Ministry of State Security, Kazakh army. I wasn't inclined to get involved with any of them. Enough escaping death for one day. I brought up a map of the town on my phone, checked the routes out, the location of the police station, the university. According to conversations around me, four bodies had been released to the relevant families. There were ongoing disputes over the rest: relatives were being told that their loved ones' bodies wouldn't be released until they signed waivers. Relatives had been arrested. A funeral scheduled for tomorrow morning had been cancelled. A mix of ethnicities had been killed.

I assessed how easily the paving stones would come up. What other ammunition was there? No loose bricks, hardly any street furniture. I finished my coffee, walked up Lenin Street, past a T-34 tank on a plinth which turned out to be a monument to Kazakh independence. Small memorial stones lined the pavement, inscribed with the names of local military heroes. At the end of the road was a shabby department store. I went in, bought two rainproof jackets in green and black, a clean shirt, a black hoody, a grey baseball cap, a small backpack, then shaving kit and concealer cream from the pharmacy. At the shop next door I bought a disposable phone and pre-paid card.

I spent a moment circling back alleys to make sure I was alone, then headed up Dostoevsky Street to the rundown edge of the city, past the apartment blocks rising from the snow. Set back, as if removed from the present, was a log cabin, its shutters and window frames painted green. A small sign at the front announced the museum, with a picture of Dostoevsky and a list of prices. It looked closed, but the door opened when I pushed and an old woman stirred in the half-light. She tapped a price list taped to the desk in front of her. I paid 300 tenge, took a ticket and walked in.

It was empty. In the first room, a display of photos showed a dirt village, more wooden houses similar to this one, a horse in the street. I watched the reflections on the glass, listened for the drop of coins, the printing of a ticket. No one entered.

They'd reconstructed a bedroom, sitting room and study. Simple but solid furniture, a chintz print, matching armchairs, bouquets of flowers. In the study was a walnut writing desk with photographic reproductions of the writer's notes amidst stationery, as if he'd just got up. I tried to imagine him here. My movements were followed by a second woman who'd appeared, solid and suspicious, remnant of the Soviet Union's weaponisation of nosy grandmothers. I considered the study dutifully, just reverentially enough, and thought of various other unlikely museums I had used as refuge and counter-surveillance.

In the final room was an exhibition about his time in the gulag: portraits of prison labourers, quotations from *The House of the Dead*. Murals traced his journey through suffering to religion. What had Dostoevsky written? *If they drive God from the earth, we shall shelter Him underground.* I wiped dust from the window and gazed out across an empty square to the mint-green Tatar mosque.

No one waiting, no one watching. I changed into my new clothes in the first-floor toilet, binned the old ones, and used the concealer to cover my bruising as much as possible. The gift shop contained an odd assortment of memorabilia: Dostoevsky's works in multiple languages, postcards of the building itself, then general Kazakh souvenirs – boxes of chocolates, etched glass ornaments all bearing the yellow and blue of the Kazakh flag. You could buy pictures of Nazarbayev, of Astana's skyline, and flags themselves, cheap nylon on plastic poles.

'How many flags do you have in stock?' I asked. I had to repeat the question a couple of times. The woman on duty showed me the wholesale box. I checked the supplier.

'Do you have more?'

'One more box.'

'Okay, thank you. The exhibition was fascinating.'

I cut south again, in the direction of chanting. There were coaches parked on back streets, blocking them. The passengers were men, all between the ages of eighteen and thirty-five or so, with military-style haircuts. Content to hold back for now. I walked past, listening to the accents, checking the shoes. Accents were Russian, footwear mostly combat boots. I kept moving. A few minutes further on, I found a crowd of thirty or forty locals across the road from the main police station, young and old, many of the elderly in conservative dress, white headscarves, fur hats. It was ethnically mixed. Flames licked from a brazier. Twenty police stood cold, looking reluctant, across the street from them. It was the old women who led the chanting, fists in the air. Placards had photographs of young men and women pasted on.

I walked on past the university. A thin crowd of students braved the cold in front of the gates handing out flyers. I took one, checked the names. The image from my piece accusing Zhaparov's anti-terrorist forces.

A plump, bespectacled student appeared to be in charge, wearing a thick tweed jacket as if dressed for premature responsibility.

'I am an English journalist,' I said. 'John Sands. I work with Reporters for Human Rights.' I waved the flyer. 'I've worked with Kaisha Atakhanova and Timur Bekmambetov. What happened?'

'They're in Dolinka prison.'

'Both of them?' I said.

'Two days ago.'

'For Christ's sake.'

I tried to read the crowd. The anti-Russian signs outnumbered pro-democracy ones. *Fuck Putin. Hands off Kazakhstan.* On one placard, I glimpsed a portrait of Raiymbek Batyr, my Kazakh warrior, on horseback. The faces were all Kazakh.

'What are people saying in England?' he asked.

'They're concerned, but not as engaged as they should be. We need to get images to them, stories. Who fired? Do you know?'

'We don't know anything for sure.'

'What's your plan?'

'We are arranging more protests. We will resist the curfew. There is no going back now.'

'How are you communicating?

He showed me some of their software and techniques.

'For tonight,' I said, 'If you're organising protests, download GatewaySMS. They'll cut the internet again but you'll still be able to communicate with anyone in the group. And it's secure.'

I made sure he understood what I was talking about. He grasped the concept enthusiastically.

'Thank you.'

'What do you want?' I asked. 'At the end of this?'

'Justice. That is all.'

'Have you thought about using the flag? Maybe the colours in it. Doesn't the blue symbolise peace and unity? You're proud of Kazakhstan. You want to defend it, defend Nazarbayev's legacy, for everyone. The Western press understands that.'

'Maybe.'

'Any famous people supporting you? Celebrities?'

'Not openly.'

'Okay. Keep in touch.' I didn't feel optimistic for them, and wondered if they knew they were on a frontline.

'Please, tell the world.'

I went to shake his hand and he hugged me.

I found Satayev's armed guard a mile west of the city centre, as promised. It was a ten-minute drive to the airport. As we drove, I experienced the faint, flickering promise of redemption: this could be the good revolution I was owed, the one I'd been waiting for. The one that was going to go right.

Which should have been a warning sign.

Semey airport was small and low-tech. A side gate opened for us, well-rehearsed men averting their eyes as we drove straight onto the smooth tarmac of the runway. We passed helicopters and one IL-76 cargo plane, rolled right up to a crisp white forty-seat Tupolev jet, just as the cockpit lights came on.

Once on board I was given a drink and code for the wi-fi. There were others travelling – three well-dressed men, none of whom spoke to one another, one of whom might have been a discreet chaperone. They glanced at me but seemed unfazed by my bruised face. A pilot with gold teeth shook our hands. A free newspaper told me the President was making efforts to address concerns around the country: long-serving men had resigned, though not Zhaparov. Independence Day was coming up on 16 December and would be an opportunity to show the world that Kazakhstan stood united.

When we were in the air, one of the men gave me a folder. 'From Akan.'

Inside was a copy of a document from GRU's Asian Directorate, carrying the *CEKPETHO* stamp for highest-level classified: Lt General Grigory Tanayev, to Anton Kirkorov, head of the Russian Federation Ministry of Energy. Timeline: 19:07, 25 November. Topic: Block 9 estimates.

The intelligence came from an agent named SERENADE. It consisted largely of stolen hyperspectral data, translated into 3D sections of the Earth, veined with dayglo pinks and blues.

This was the dream, that with equipment sensitive enough – with the ability to read the near-infrared spectral band – you might get a sniff of something to which your rivals were oblivious. Down beneath the abandoned Soviet tools, the skeletons of loyal comrades, in among the Miocene fossils: five billion barrels of light sweet crude. It was calling out to change history.

At the bottom of the computer imagery it said *Property of Auracle Inc*. Someone had stolen it off Craig Bryant's company, given it to Russia.

FORTY-SEVEN

The flight gave me time to think. I spent a lot of time studying the GRU report, piecing together a variety of potential chronologies. The one I wanted to counter: she chases Bryant; she sells the data. I kept seeing that CCTV, Joanna getting into the car, which I tried to analyse with a cool objectivity that I didn't feel.

Would Vishinsky trust her? If this was a long game, perhaps; if she'd been working for him for years. Meaning I would have been lied to for years. I dissected the past twelve months: my op closed down; her disaster in Turkey. Memory comes into its own when you've been betrayed. I saw details I hadn't even seen the first time around. I thought through an interpretation of my life in which Joanna was working for Moscow: our relationship, its feints and circumlocution. Vishinsky had a file on us. She was tasked with getting close to me. She resisted. Finally, she was going to invite me over to the other side. I would have been good. I would have been tempted. Caracas. *We'd need money.*

Or it was all very carefully constructed bullshit. Oldest psyops in the book: get departments to tear themselves apart over moles. You don't even need to penetrate, just sow doubt. The Russians were old hands at that. It might have been what got Hugh Stevenson killed. My immediate mission was clear: stop their incursion.

My gut instinct: this was Vishinsky's idea of victory. Joanna had been working against him in some way since Turkey. Perfect

Vision, whatever it was, represented that attempt. Vishinsky had ensured both Six and Vectis turned against her, closed down the Shefford operation. He not only destroyed her but who she was, her reputation. I knew he would make sure she was aware of this: her disgrace in the eyes of those who loved and respected her. Perhaps she was being made to watch it from her cell.

The image I needed to understand was Aliya's: the one of the Millennium London Hotel. I had a message from Aliya, sent while I'd been detained: How long are you in Astana? Let me know if you want another coffee. Got something for you. Nothing from Reza Nikfar; no lead on 4,000 kilograms of stashed explosives. Although it seemed I wasn't the only one who felt an attack coming.

We dipped towards Astana and the intercom came to life, the pilot clearing his throat and informing us that it was minus 8 on the ground and there were roadblocks around the city. The time was 3.15 p.m. Beneath us, two C-130 military transport planes sat fatly on the airport runway, a line of 50-ton army trucks parked along the perimeter fence.

Touchdown was smooth. We exited via a lounge with car magazines and a white leatherette sofa. No passport control, no DV camera in the face. I was met by a GL5 Mercedes, with Walker in the back. I got in. We started heading around the outskirts of the city.

'What took you east?' Walker asked.

'I was following a lead.'

'And you found Akan Satayev.'

'He found me. So did Russian special forces on Kazakh soil.'

'Definitely Russian?'

'Russian, Serb. Probably Sigma Group.'

'We're going to the Saracen HQ. They need to hear what you saw.'

I played along. I was being invited into the heart of a company

whose actions threatened to provoke a Russian invasion. I
needed to know what they were planning.

'The President is terrified of upsetting Moscow,' Walker said,
after another moment. 'That's our problem right now.'

'Does the Oil Ministry know how big it is? Over five billion barrels?'

'As of yesterday, it seems. They're asking 8.9 billion dollars.
Saracen have secured credit up to eight. They're trying to get
it within that. Money's not the biggest problem. If they get the
Conqueror field for eight they've got a bargain.'

'Conqueror?'

'That's what they've named it.'

'Jesus Christ.'

We passed striped office complexes, emerald towers, clouds
held in glass, moving around corners.

'Can I ask,' he said, cautiously, 'did you have any suspicions
about her? Ever?'

'No.'

We pulled up in front of the Saracen HQ. There was already a
wall of four armoured black Lexus limousines with motorbike
outriders waiting.

'I want you to meet Robert Carter,' Walker said. 'I told him
you know what's going on.'

Armed guards searched my pockets, ran a scanner around
my body then waved us through. Everything was calm until we
got to the sixth floor, where over sixty Saracen personnel were
working phones and computers. I was brought up to speed as
we marched through, past geological surveys and dense spreadsheets. Experts across Saracen's divisions had been ordered
to abandon everything else and number-crunch the bid. The
European Investment Bank had their own people coming over
to conduct a feasibility study. On the plans I saw, wells stretched
out in all directions once they got underground, thousands of

feet long, running to multiple reservoirs. Tight oil: light crude held in shale, which meant digging deep and fracking.

A meeting with the President and the head of KMG was lined up for 8 a.m. tomorrow. Two hundred more GL5 contractors were set to roll into Kazakhstan by nightfall.

I was shown into a glass-walled side office with framed pictures of flare stacks and six tense individuals standing around a table of contracts. Lucy Piper was there, typing, one phone between ear and shoulder, one flashing on the table beside her. She raised an eyebrow by way of greeting. I was introduced to Jill Friedman from the European Bank, Ahmad Suleiman representing the Qatar Investment Authority. Carter stood at the back, arms crossed, bristling. He had a rugby player's build and a drinker's flush to his face. He had taken a big gamble and was a presidential signature away from breaking the casino. I recognised him, seeing him up close, and knew I'd been in his company before, but couldn't think where. His lawyer and chief negotiator stood beside him, sixty-something, thinning white hair, tight-jawed. This was Ronald Steiner, who I'd heard about in Iraq: go-to man for oil contracts. He looked furious.

Walker was playing an audio file off his MacBook: two men talking in what sounded like a car, a debate in Russian about the term *pon-yatino*. From people's expressions, he'd played it a few times before. A translator was struggling.

'A *pon-yatino* is like an understanding, rather than a written agreement.'

'So which is stronger?' Steiner wanted to know. The men on the recording, I gathered, were the head of Kazakhstan's state energy company and the Russian Minister for Oil and Gas. Saracen had extraction rights on any new discovery, but it seemed the Kazakhs weren't compelled to grant those rights unless certain criteria had been fulfilled. The criteria were spread across the table alongside intel on Gazprom's proposed offer, and satellite images of the region with military activity circled.

The voices continued:

'No Western company.'

'No. He is clear.'

'He understands. It is unacceptable.'

'You have spoken to …'

'To Putin, to his people. They say this has always been the position.'

'Always.'

Steiner hit pause.

'The field or the line is unacceptable?' he asked.

'Both, I think,' the translator said.

I was trying to figure out what the line referred to, when I saw it. Among the paperwork on the table was a map showing a proposed route for a pipeline. It ran west from the field to Aktau, under the Caspian to the terminal south of Baku in Azerbaijan. From Baku to Erzurum in Turkey, up through Bulgaria and Romania to Austria. Plans came courtesy of Bechtel Engineering. They were costed. Either a team of hundreds had worked overnight or there were longstanding ambitions in play.

'You've been up to the drill site?' Steiner asked. It took me a second to realise I was being addressed.

'Just returned.'

'How does it look?'

I talked them through the situation, indicating that these were highly trained fighters coming in. I mentioned the local support Saracen might need to draw upon, alluding to Akan Satayev without actually using the words 'heroin-trafficking warlord'. When I'd finished, Steiner clicked a mouse and a map appeared on a wall-mounted screen: Kazakhstan divided horizontally by a meandering dotted line. It took me a second to realise what I was looking at, then I felt sick.

357

'These are the regions we think the Russians would go for: Akmola, Pavlodar, East Kazakhstan.'

I followed the dashed line that signified the Russian border sinking south.

'Those regions mostly have forty to fifty per cent ethnic Russian population. Then there's West Kazakhstan and Kostanay which are less clear.'

Piper waved her phone, cleared her throat. 'Sir Mark Jameson from the Foreign Office is on the line.'

'Get him a copy of this,' Steiner said, gesturing at the map as he gathered his papers. 'I want him to see this.'

The Saracen crew moved as one towards the secure communications area, followed shortly by the others, leaving Walker, Piper and myself. We all stared at the map.

'The Crimea rerun narrative is strong,' Piper said, eventually, managing to sound level-headed. 'We let Russia get away with that. Not again. This is a challenge to the world.'

'Where did you get the map?' I asked.

'Analysts. Does it fit what you've seen?'

'It fits a nightmare. Why exactly is Robert Carter on the phone to the Foreign Office?'

'Saracen want guarantees, backed up by military commitment if Russia oversteps the line. They're in conversation with the EU as well, with regards to the pipeline. People are up for this,' Piper said. 'It's a game-changer.'

'I really wouldn't push the pipeline-to-Europe angle,' I said.

'Not up front, no,' Piper agreed. 'In-house perhaps, for Westminster. Energy security.'

'The whole project cuts Russia off from Central Asia.'

'Should we shed tears?'

'They won't let it happen. They never do. I can tell you at least three similar schemes in the last ten years, all of which led to a protracted conflict and no line.' I stepped closer to the map and traced the new border with my finger, then down into the empty spaces. There were few population centres. An army could gain a hundred miles with a single battle.

'Apparently the military base in Omsk has become lively,' Walker said. 'A couple of hundred ground forces from Russia's Central Military District arrived in the last few hours.' He seemed phlegmatic, the SAS man in his comfort zone. 'Russia's Armenian bases have also lit up. Same with the airfield near Bishkek. And we're getting repeated reports of Russian civilians arming in Kazakhstan. GL5 are holding twenty of them who came near the site: possibly Sigma, possibly amateur local protection units.'

I didn't want to dwell on the legal sensitivities of a private security contractor holding twenty Kazakh citizens. I concentrated on the big blank map.

'If they make a move it will be fast and on the ground,' I said. 'Government buildings, roadways, telecom cables – they'll have them within hours.'

'We're preparing for that. Lines open with both Kazakh military and China. GL5 have some advanced capability: the means of blocking radar and electronic jamming. They're monitoring.'

'China's invested too much to let Russia march in,' I said.

'What are you thinking?'

'Any annexation would cut their new Silk Road in half. That's our biggest asset.'

'For sure.'

'What about the other 'Stans? Who would they side with? Could they turn against Russia?'

'We're hearing positive noises. Certainly Uzbekistan and Kyrgyzstan would be reluctant to fall in line with Moscow, if it came down to it.'

'Find out what kind of loans Russia has given this place, and then how much China's put in. Most war is debt collection. See who's left out of pocket.'

Walker agreed, collected his papers and went to speak to his own analysts. I was briefly alone with Piper and her press releases.

'Whose idea was it to call the field Conqueror?' I said.

'Not us.'

'You should try to find something local, something Kazakh.'

'We can try.' Piper thought. 'This is about independence, right? Local strength. What could be more independent than selling your oil to Europe?'

'When you've got five thousand miles of border with Russia, that's not a joke. Eight billion pounds: a flagship for the Kazakh economy, the largest-ever foreign investment in Kazakhstan. Money from this deal will keep the peace, keep Kazakhstan at the heart of international values and progress. And Gazprom don't have the tech. They won't get it out of the ground.'

'Are you sure?'

'I've no idea. But it sounds right. This is fracking, horizontal drilling, new advances. Show diagrams, flag up old Russian kit. Get photos of dead herons from Gazprom fields. Russia will be ready to exploit environmental issues. Spin Conqueror as a clean-up operation. This isn't wilderness, it's a brown site. We're going to leave it in a better state than we find it. We'll clean up the groundwater, dispose of the radioactive tailings. Then get the British Prime Minister over here on Independence Day. Now or never. Gold fountain pens.'

She stared at me, unblinking, tongue pressed against her teeth.

'That's a big ask.'

'What you get the man who has everything is moral approval. The President doesn't need more money, he needs to look good in the eyes of the world, so he can hand it all to his daughter and people still cheer. It can be twenty-four hours in and out.'

'I'll put out feelers.'

Walker returned with paperwork. 'Kazakhstan owes Russia five billion for arms sales alone. Then there's about three billion in cash-for-oil financing: pre-pay deals.'

'China will have more,' I said.

'China's loaned this place fifteen billion in the last two years. Mostly through joint ventures.'

'Jesus,' Piper said.

'That's how they colonise,' I said. I'd been expecting a lot, but not that much. You look in the accounts book and the whole thing's floating on thin air. It's a shell game, and then something threatens to bring it down, some little thing, and the tanks appear.

'It makes it pretty obvious,' I said. 'There's no way Beijing would let Russia invade.'

Walker handed me the report. The China Investment Corporation had issued 60 billion dollars in bonds to underwrite construction in Kazakhstan. They needed to make a profit of 20 million yuan every day just to pay the interest and operation costs.

'You know, the Chinese refer to the Russians as the warring nation,' I said.

'I hear you,' Piper said, writing this down.

'Do they try to hack us?' I asked.

'The Chinese? Only about ten times a day.'

'Put the annexation map on the system, take the security off.'

'I'm not in a position to do that,' she said, more like a disclaimer than a fact. 'But I'll pass the suggestion on.' Her phone rang. She checked the screen and got to her feet. 'You can still make the party?' she asked me, heading for the door.

'The party?'

'Galina's birthday. Tonight.'

'Sure.'

'Will you get a chance to shave?' She was serious. I nodded. She slipped me what I thought was a flash drive but turned out to be a tube of concealer – 'for your injuries.' I nodded. Then she was gone.

Walker said, 'People are asking about the local support on the ground you mentioned, as a temporary measure for keeping the field secure. How much of a politically acceptable option is Akan Satayev?'

'He's the only option.'

'How many men does he control?'

'I think he's got two or three hundred in the area now. And it's a clan system, with alliances: each of those men can bring in thirty or forty more. There are gangs in Tajikistan and Uzbekistan that ultimately answer to Satayev. They can be protecting Conqueror in days.'

'What would he need to work with us?'

'A few hundred thousand, I reckon. Get his trucks moving, crossing borders, his men equipped, confident that they've got backing. In the longer term, with the field, it may come down to giving him a cut of final profits.'

'There's no way he's getting final profits,' Walker said. 'But keep that channel open.'

'He'll need reassurances. Concrete ones.'

'You know more about that side of things than I do. There are options. Keep him onside if you can.'

'Sure.'

He glanced outside the office, then shut the door, locked it, turned to me. The mood had changed. I let him work his way out of the silence.

'We know she pursued Craig Bryant. All Carter knows for now is that there was a leak of some kind, somewhere along the line. They want to sue Auracle.'

'That's going to get messy.'

'We're going to make sure it doesn't. We're going to bury the whole Joanna thing. Understand?'

'No, I don't understand.'

'Are there any other copies of the footage showing Joanna in Vishinsky's car?'

I felt myself thrown off-balance. My muscles tensed, and I glanced across the room for objects I could use as a weapon if it came to blows, wondered how much of his training Walker remembered. Where did he get that information? Shomko? From taps on me? There was no shortage of ways.

'Your pisshead police officer needs to forget he ever saw it.'

'And the computer-generated clip I showed you? What has that got to do with spying for Vishinsky?'

'What's it got to do with anything? What are you really doing here, Elliot?' He was too cool, too experienced for all-out anger. And he held cards. 'Both you and Joanna have been on a caution list since 2010, with some heavy question marks by your names. Security Branch are very, very keen to speak to you right now, as you can imagine. So be thankful you're in here and not Belmarsh. I may be the only one still willing to trust you.'

It was possible, but the feeling wasn't mutual. If he didn't trust Joanna he didn't trust me. Manage the immediate situation, I thought: Russian incursion, a possible bomb in Astana. Then get out.

'Do you know where she is?' I asked.

'Moscow, I expect.'

'I was hunting her for you.'

'I don't remember asking you to come over here. Joanna Lake's seen in a car connected to Vladislav Vishinsky on Saturday the twenty-fifth. Over the next forty-eight hours there's huge Russian activity: flights booked, meetings arranged, money transferred. The first troops move down to the Kazakh border.

We've checked imagery from the last week down to minutes and hours. Vishinsky arranges an emergency meeting at which he presents data to Gazprom. And there's a payment of half a million dollars into a Cayman Islands account Joanna set up the previous month.'

He produced the last fact with a flourish, and enjoyed watching me hesitate.

'How do you know?' I asked.

'We know.'

'That's my point. She's a trained officer. You think she sets up a visible account in the Cayman Islands?'

'Elliot, do you really think it's impossible she'd do this?'

'She'd do it better. This is being handed to us.'

'So why didn't you tell us about the footage from Lieutenant Shomko?'

'Why would I trust you?'

Walker sighed. 'The phone line's secure,' he said. 'Sigma troops have begun taking hostages. Call Satayev, tell him we need him. Unless it turns out you do favour Moscow. If so, I'd find a way of moving there.'

He walked out. I picked up the phone, called Craig Bryant instead. I was surprised that he answered. He sounded like he'd been drunk but sobered by my call.

'Toby, what's happened?' he said.

'Why? You okay?'

'The company's had some problems.'

'What problems?'

'Big problems. You struck me as a guy who might hear things. Have you?'

'Nothing. I don't understand.'

'Shit, Toby. You work somewhere like this and you know it's not going to be Houston, but I'm not equipped to operate in a jungle.'

'A jungle?'

'We spoke about that woman, Vanessa. Ever hear anything else?'

'The documentary maker? You think she caused you problems?'

'This town, Toby ...' It sounded like he dropped the phone. I heard him shuffling around, then his voice returned. 'Are you going to the party later?'

'Maybe. Are you?'

'If I don't make an appearance people will talk.'

'What will they say?'

'They'll say I'm not there. See you later, Toby.'

I studied the annexation map, then social media: a burning building, the first clips of refugees, cars laden with mattresses and furniture and mirrors. It looked like Bosnia to me, but the licence plates were Kazakh. I went to the window. The dome of the Presidential Palace shone blue through the snow. The Triumph of Astana muscled into the horizon beyond it.

I called my contact for Jan Jágr, the Slovak arms dealer, and once the contact had called back I spoke to Akan Satayev.

'Jágr's on. If you can find somewhere for a plane to land, he can get you the equipment you need. My people can cover the cost.'

'And for us?'

Satayev named his price: 1.5 million dollars in cash, hand-delivered to his man in Astana.

'I'll ask. If they do agree, that's going to take some time.'

'The Russians are not taking their time. More men are coming in every hour.' He lowered his voice. 'They have spoken to me. They have reached out.'

'I'll see what I can do.'

I left a message for Walker:

1.5.

When I tried to leave the HQ it turned out I needed an escort: the lifts were pin-code entry. I was searched before I entered them, my phone checked for photos. I watched Carter march back from his call with the Foreign Secretary, poker-faced.

I thought of the *Herald Tribune* clipping I'd seen at Elena's: *Both rivals and shareholders claim he has paid well over the odds on a quixotic and personal mission*. Lucky gamble, I thought. Choosing Kazakhstan as the place to drill, buying up Saracen, billions of his own money thrown in. The chips were stacked high, the ball spinning.

I looked at his face and tried to think where I'd met him before.

FORTY-EIGHT

Six hours to party time. I looked a mess. At the Ramada Plaza they seemed surprised to see me.

'Mr Bell.'

'How have things been?'

'All very fine here. We have an oriental buffet in the restaurant tonight, if you are interested.'

I went up to my room and stood there in the light of the TV holding a crumpled shirt, Semey on the TV. I glanced across the faces in the angry crowd, and thought of my experiences there. Thought of Akan Satayev and his men, who weren't on the TV yet.

No answer from Stefan when I called him. Marius in the Evotec office answered, told me Stefan had messaged to say he was booked on a flight a few hours ago. I hoped he was well on his way, enjoying the complimentary G&Ts.

'One other thing,' Marius said. 'You asked for alerts on "Catalyst"?'

'Yes.'

'He sent us an email tonight: said he'd intercepted someone or something about an issue regarding Catalyst attending a party tonight. Does that mean anything?'

'He said Catalyst was going to be at a party?'

'Someone said that. Stefan picked it up.'

'Galina's birthday party?'

'I've no idea. Stefan couldn't get hold of you, but wanted us to pass the message on.'

'I need the exact message.'

Marius read it out: 'If you speak to EK, tell him that Catalyst will be at party tomorrow. People are concerned re issues arising. More details to follow. He'll understand.'

I wished that was more than half-true. Marius believed the information had come from a phone or computer Stefan had gained access to, but he'd refused to give details over an open line.

'Any idea when he lands?'

'No.'

'Any suggestion what the "issues" are?'

'That's all we've got.'

'Okay. Would you tell him to contact me as soon as he's on his phone?'

'Will do.'

The party had gained a new edge of significance. I watched the clip of myself and the Central Asian man again, to ensure I had his features memorised, as if I hadn't been dreaming them each night for a week.

I shaved. I went to the Kerulen mall and bought a new shirt and tie. On my way back I told the taxi to stop early and walked to the river. It was getting dark but there were lights on the ice, music playing. People sledged down the sides, others skated in the centre. I wondered how they knew when the ice began getting too thin; who told them it was time to stop.

The front drive was full of cars when I got to the Marriott, the hotel lobby thick with bodyguards. I went through three security checks to get to the lifts, then had to share them with half of Gazprom's board.

The 38th floor was packed. Suits and gowns, pyramids of

champagne coupes, everything – everyone's consciousness – inconspicuously centred on the President, who stood at the back of the room talking to the Chinese Foreign Secretary. Banners declared that Saracen Oil and Gas Exploration wished Galina Nazarbayev a happy birthday. There was a Kazakh flag and, beneath it, the Saracen logo. I squeezed among diplomats and spies, looking for my Triumph companion, equally alert for Cherenkov, and for representatives of the British embassy. I found Lucy Piper looking wired. She needed help with Carter's speech.

'Something Kazakh, a quote or something.'

'Abai's their national poet. He's quotable.' I pointed her towards some lines. She scribbled the name and walked off, already Googling. I took a drink as it floated past.

The optimism on display was impressive, as if a deal could be willed into existence through sheer decadence. The banners, the waterfall of champagne down the stacked coupe glasses, the *moelleux au chocolat* birthday cake. How much love can go unrequited? Saracen were putting a determined face on things. Every situation changes.

All the intelligence services had gathered, checking the President for IV drip scars, tremoring, slurs in his speech; noting who he spoke to, who he avoided, checking the demeanour of CEOs, engineers, financiers and go-betweens, men and women whose lives had become devoted to the carbon molecules of buried plankton, the energy from three-hundred-million-year-old sunlight.

It was all going smoothly, I thought. Galina sang two songs by Céline Dion with a world-class pianist who had apparently insisted on ten grand for every hour spent on Kazakh soil; Piper introduced me to journalists and I told them Kazakhstan was a peaceful country at heart – 'We have homegrown terrorists in the UK, you know, and nowhere's going to become a liberal democracy overnight.' I met rich people and heard myself saying: 'It's a family-run Swiss school but it follows the British National Curriculum so it's probably your most *British* international school.' Guests swayed with bonhomie. A lot of the newcomers had been drinking hard since the flight over. Fireworks exploded outside, unannounced. A Tajik warlord flinched. So did the Deputy Defence Minister and a security officer from the British embassy. Then everyone loosened their ties and began to do shots.

I met Anastasia two drinks into the evening. She came by way of Bryant, who lunged out of the crowd, tie loose.

'Toby!'

He had two women with him this time.

'Toby, can I introduce you to Olga and ... ' He looked to the other woman for help. She wore a dress of gold sequins.

'Anastasia.'

I noticed her Moscow accent, and her eyes. *There you are*, they seemed to say, which was how you seduced someone. Her blonde hair was cut into a bob that framed clear features. She had the assured good looks of escorts and honeytraps. I don't know where Bryant went. Anastasia and I ended up on a sofa.

'So, an Englishman in Astana. You are either rich or here to get rich.'

'I am here to see history being made,' I said. 'To broaden my mind.'

My companion looked sceptical. She touched a hand to her necklace as if it might protect her. Her cocktail was down to slush. She smelled of Miss Dior and was being watched by a man at the bar wearing a concealed handgun.

'People from England come here for business.'

'This is a young place,' I said. 'There are not many of those. Once or twice in a lifetime, if you're lucky, you get to see somewhere being born rather than dying.' I gestured at the room. 'This is the future.'

'The future's drunk,' she said.

As if on cue, the UK's Secretary of State for Business, Energy and Industrial Strategy roared with laughter, followed a few seconds later by some unsteady Chinese pipeline engineers and a man with a greasy smile who did PR for the Kazakh government.

'And you?' I said to my companion. 'What brings you here?'

'I am a translator.'

'A noble career.' If there were Russians trying to seduce me, I wanted to know. If she was innocently attached to Russians, with potential access, I was equally curious. I leaned closer. 'I'm glad I met you,' I said. 'I was slightly dreading this whole thing. I have a suspicion that you're one of the more interesting people in the room.'

She studied my face, then leaned back into the sofa. I considered my next move. The party was going to seed. Sushi congealed on platters, and condensation from the ice buckets had made a soggy carpet out of brochures about renewables. A raucous foursome from KazMunaiGaz, the state energy company, were raising toasts by the bar. They knocked into the gunman, oblivious, but he didn't react. The holster was strapped crossways under the man's jacket; he was overweight and kept his jacket buttoned, which meant it was tight on his back when he turned. He wore the gun on his right hip, making him sit twisted on his stool. The holster suggested a licence, someone official or well connected, as did getting past the scanners downstairs. He used the mirror behind the bar to watch the crowd. The local offices of Chevron and Merrill Lynch had turned out in force, as had representatives from the French and German embassies.

Robert Carter made his speech, sweating hard, coloured lights reflecting off his face.

'In the words of Abai, your excellent national poet, Kazakhstan should be a convivial meeting place of Russia, the West and

371

Islam. Ambitious, perhaps but, as I believe he also said, "A clever man can set fire to the snow."'

Polite laughter rippled. The President said something to the UK Minister. Galina beamed and would have clapped if she hadn't been holding a glass of champagne. Carter smiled gratefully.

There was more applause as he finished, then a toast to Galina, the birthday girl. I watched the Russians to see if they toasted and they did so unreservedly, downing the Veuve Clicquot. The President himself moved away from the stage and everyone went back to their previous conversations.

Bryant was talking to the Chinese. The Head of Extraction for the Italian oil firm Agip was nearby, sharing something on his phone with the man who ran the central bank. But no one was conspicuously hustling. The mood was carefree. Outside, snow thickened in the air, to the extent that I wondered if we were all going to become trapped, and how that would pan out. But for now all were drunk and we could stop pretending that power was anything other than ridiculous good fortune. Almost 11 p.m. and there was the lightheaded hilarity of getting away with it.

Anastasia checked a silver iPhone then dropped it in her bag. She transferred her gaze to the room. Bryant caught my eye and winked. The man at the bar saw this, checked Bryant, turned back to the mirror. He had tan lines from wraparound sunglasses.

None of this was how I'd manage an assassination.

'I bet, when you were studying, you did not want to interpret for these people,' I said. 'You wanted to translate literature.'

Anastasia glanced across the crowd. 'Yes.' She conceded this in a tone of inevitability. 'But there is no security in that. Here, that is what people care about. My family need me to earn money.'

'A country only truly develops when people stop caring about their family,' I said. 'That is what developed means.'

She raised an eyebrow, considering this.

'Come with me,' I said. I took her hand and helped her up, leading her to the windows. 'I also like languages,' I said. 'Did you know, the Germans call this *Lichtarchitektur*: the architecture of light.'

Glass towers shimmered. A block away, on the side of the KazInvest offices, a pale-skinned woman twenty floors high repeatedly lifted a Samsung 7 to her ear and smiled. Her face lit the canvas roofs of three troop carriers parked beside the building. I lifted my phone and took a photo of the skyline.

'And one of us,' I said.

She stiffened. 'I hate photos.'

'Come on, something to make my friends in London jealous.'

Anastasia rolled her eyes, but flicked her hair away from her face compliantly and leaned in. 'So many photographs,' she muttered.

In the bathroom, I locked a stall and put the image through facial recognition. Four separate names came up, three nationalities. I thought of the message Stefan had picked up: *Catalyst will be at the party*. It was time to get out of here.

I passed Galina in the corridor on my way back, Lucy Piper adjusting the zip on the back of her blue Versace cocktail dress.

'Toby, have you met Galina?' Piper said. 'Galina, this is one of my stars: Toby Bell. A true English gentleman.'

'I've heard about you,' Galina said. She reached towards me. I moved forward so we could shake hands without the dress being torn from Piper's hands.

'This is an honour,' I said. 'I thought your singing was amazing.'

'Thank you. It's been a wonderful event. Am I right that you were involved in arranging it?'

'Hardly. But I'm glad you're enjoying it. Your father is looking well.'

She smiled, as confident in her father's immortality as the rest of the nation. 'He is well. He is well, thank God.'

'And next year, perhaps, we will have the honour of seeing you on television again.'

'Maybe.'

'You must do it. You're such a natural. It would bring a lot of joy to the people of this country.'

She beamed. Bryant appeared from the main room. Galina sashayed past him. Piper gave a cursory nod at the American and leaned towards me, speaking low.

'Some of us are going back to the Palace. Moving now. Come with us, she'd like that.'

It was an electrifying invitation. Piper disappeared back towards her entourage and Bryant was left grinning at me.

'Hear about the jet?' he said. 'What are they going to get her for Christmas, for Christ's sake?'

'I'm not sure they celebrate Christmas.' I began moving past Bryant towards the main room, trying to calculate how to get my coat from the cloakroom while avoiding my honeytrap.

'I'm getting us some shots. You'll have one. Or are you busy?'

'I'm busy.'

Bryant kept grinning. On the far side of the main bar I could see Anastasia waiting, toe tapping the air; a woman conscious of sitting alone in a room of drunken men. A woman with a job to do. She exchanged a glance with the gunman, who got to his feet, adjusting his jacket. Bryant headed to the bar. I cut back through the crowd, saw Anastasia moving in my direction.

'Toby.'

'Anastasia, I'm so sorry. I've got to run.' I slipped her a business card. 'Dinner? Can you forgive me? Have you been to La Primavera?'

I could see Galina's entourage moving. They were going down to the convoy. It looked like the President was already downstairs. Piper came up to me. 'Ride with us. Galina says it's all good.'

Anastasia had a hand on my arm.

'You are going with them?'

'I've made a promise. I really am sorry.' I kept moving. At some point, presidential security would kick in, I thought. Or she could come to the palace, kill me there. That would be chic. The entourage had gone by the time I made it to the corridor. The lifts were blocked by a crowd of oil execs. I went for the stairs.

Someone followed. I heard the door slam, footsteps behind me. Then a man's voice, English.

'You forgot this.' It was the gunman. He held up a wallet. It wasn't mine. He sounded well spoken, which wasn't the comfort you'd expect. I thought through the various options for incapacitating him: eyes, throat, knees. Then it became irrelevant.

The explosion shook the building. I found myself on the floor beside the wall, in the dark, thinking: that sound, the one that gets you in the stomach. A car bomb. Thinking: I'm alive. The President ...

I got to my feet. There was plaster over my skin. I continued down the stairs, checking myself for injury. I was okay. I'd been lucky.

I'd been saved.

Screaming began on the seventh floor. Windows had blown in from the fifth floor down. Then I was stepping over debris, over a car door. A woman's bare arm lay on the third-floor carpet, severed at the shoulder, bracelet still on.

Dust filled the reception. The heat of the explosion lingered. There was no front wall. The central spine of the revolving doors had become implanted in the wall. A car lay on its roof beside a stump of the lobby's fountain. One security guard sat on the floor, back against the reception desk, gun out, no right leg beneath the knee.

A few dazed, dust-caked figures wandered in the snow outside. Thick smoke plumed from two burning cars, turning the snow black. I made out a 20-foot crater in the driveway's tarmac, halfway between the hotel's entrance and the gates to the street.

The security staff who had survived were coming to their senses, trying to clear the area. More often than not there was a second bomb. Sometimes the second bomber waited for the emergency services to arrive. I couldn't see any unattended vehicles. The first sirens were approaching.

Saved. I turned back, thinking I might see my guardian angels emerging from the dust. There was a woman in shredded evening wear, blood down her chin, mouth working silently. I gave her my coat before continuing into the storm.

FORTY-NINE

I stumbled away from the scene through a cloud of black flakes, gripped by a sense that I should have known. I heard the screams of two women. The first emergency vehicles tore into the hotel grounds, almost hitting me.

A minute later I was still walking, starting to shiver with early-stage hypothermia. I flagged a car beside Lovers' Park. The driver was agitated, seeking information rather than a fare. The sirens were endless now; a troop carrier tore past us. I could still smell synthetic materials burning, and see the smoke plume in the light of adverts.

'What happened?'

'A bomb.'

'I must go home. I can't drive you.'

'I just need to get to somewhere where I can be indoors.'

He took me to a Ramstor all-night supermarket. I found a coat on the rails and put it on and crouched in a corner, warming my hands. My phone rang. I couldn't move my fingers. Eventually I managed to answer the phone by putting it on the ground and using my knuckles. It was Piper in a state of high anxiety.

'You're alive. Jesus Christ. Where are you?'

'A supermarket. What do you know?'

'Nothing. I'm in a car somewhere around the Northern Lights complex. We've been stopped at a roadblock. We're trying to get to the Saracen offices. It's just ... It's going to be a holding situation. Until we know how this is going to play out.'

'Nothing's going to hold.'

'No.'

'They'll try to pin this on us,' I said.

'I know.'

'Who's alive?'

'The President's critical. He's at City Hospital Number One. Galina's also at the hospital. She might be okay.'

'This is fucked. How did they drive up to the hotel?'

The line went. I checked social media for IMK, Twitter feeds for Al-Nusra, ISIS in Central Asia, Hizb ut-Tahrir: no one claiming credit for the attack.

The art of an assassination is controlling what happens next. That's not the sole prerogative of those responsible; they've just got a head start. On Russian media they were cutting between footage from Astana and a story about a GL5 maritime patrol vessel caught illegally patrolling in the Caspian: *In the last five or six hours a Russian coast guard patrol rammed and water-cannoned a boat belonging to a UK-registered private security company – a 183-foot vessel with a crew of 14 and a helicopter pad.* The contractors had been arrested; they showed men in GL5 uniform sitting on the ground, hands on their heads like drug runners.

All domestic flights were grounded. The first 'convenient for Saracen' posts had appeared less than twenty minutes after the attack. Oil was up five points, FTSE closing just as Saracen started to lift.

I saw a store security guard watching me from the end of the aisle, speaking to two men in GL5 uniforms, then realised they were talking about me. The contractors walked over.

'We've been instructed to get you somewhere safe,' one of them said.

'Where would that be?'

'Everyone's convening at the Saracen headquarters. We may have to get out of the country.' He sounded Australian. I said I'd make my own way. They were having none of it. We went out to where a Nissan 4×4 was waiting.

The guards were silent as we drove, eerily calm, the man in the passenger seat cradling a semi-automatic. He looked South East Asian. Inside the vehicle were steel lock boxes for weapons, medibags, an axe affixed to the back of the driver's seat. There were chemsuits and atropine autoinjectors: antidote for nerve agents.

'Know anything about the patrol boat in the Caspian?' I asked, to get a reading of them, at least; their tension, their accents. 'Is this true?'

'We can't comment on that,' the driver said.

'Are you guys in the Caspian?'

'No comment.'

The business district was crawling with riot police, sniffer dogs, busy within the red and blue flashing lights. Only speed, visible weaponry and a uniformed gravitas kept us moving. Piper called again.

'Galina's conscious. She was still in the hotel when it happened. The bomb went off beside the President.'

'There was a battalion of security at the hotel. How did they get that close?'

'I don't know.'

We sped up. I was about to ask Piper about the security setup at the hotel, then it occurred to me that GL5 must have been involved somewhere along the line. I said I'd speak to her at the office and hung up. My chauffeurs faced frontwards, unmoving. The doors were centrally locked. I reached down and clicked the release for the hand axe, then checked we were on the correct route. We arrived at the Saracen offices a few minutes later, which didn't feel like a huge relief. I was hustled past security barriers to the lift where, to my surprise, we went down.

Doors opened directly onto a bunker office, one half of which was crowded with forty staff. The other half, through a glass partition, was a conference room with a large oval table. Both ends had multiple TVs showing CNN, BBC, Al Jazeera, Russia's Channel One – plus screens carrying maps and satellite feeds of the various fields. The lift kept chiming, Saracen executives arriving from the party in their evening wear, faded by ash. Medics had set up a small first-aid station in the corner. Piper had a list of names, hammering the phones, checking off all employees and members of the trade delegation who were in the area. Some of the Kazakh staff were crying.

I went over to a live satellite feed of the Conqueror field and tried to see activity. Nothing, which was ominous in itself. The Sigma battalions were preparing, I felt sure. Piper hung up and came over. Tiny specks of glass glittered in her hair.

'We've got a plane on stand-by to evacuate the delegation, soon as we know it's safe to get there. Trying to get clearance to fly.'

'Where's Callum?'

'On his way. I just spoke to Galina. Obviously she's not in a good way psychologically, but her injuries are superficial. She wasn't at the front when it happened.'

Through the panic and confusion, the trained officer in me still felt the need to brief those in a position to act.

'There's no succession plan. There's nothing to guarantee she ends up in charge.'

'That's what we're worried about. This went live a few hours before the bomb.' Piper showed me a website on her phone: an organisation called Corruption Watch, based in Helsinki, had come into possession of data hacked from Galina's financial adviser: emails concerning a BVI-registered shell company used to buy a 23-metre yacht and three properties in London.

Someone had got footage flying over a mansion: tennis courts and a boating lake, a chain of interconnecting pools, some sports cars and a helipad. The cover was off the pool, furniture out. It had been filmed in summer. Someone had waited for the right moment.

'We can get it onto the second page, at least. That may be all. Same accounts pushing photos of Galina with Carter at the party last night, and a story about Galina wanting to take Kazakhstan into NATO.'

It was on at least three reputable sites. Her photo was placed beside one of the NATO Secretary-General. *It is unlikely the invitation to begin accession talks will appear anytime soon, but the meeting indicates Galina's willingness to reorient the country her father has steered for so long ...*

'That one appeared about an hour after the bomb,' Piper said.

A lot of Kazakhs had begun demanding free elections: bots, calling out for representation. *The Kazakh people deserve to choose!* They had memes: ballot boxes with the Kazakh flag on the side and a cartoon of Galina stealing a map of the country behind the backs of grieving citizens.

'Get pictures of Galina injured,' I said. 'She's a hero now. She survived an attempt on her life. Remind people that democracy's divisive and what we need now is unity. Make it clear that any free elections would be won by Islamists. Point towards Egypt.'

'Okay.'

'So we're going to let Galina unite Kazakhstan and steer us through this difficult time. Emphasise that she's a victim of last night's attack. Get pictures of her injured face. Everything needs to be about her now. Continuity.'

'We can't get access to the hospital.'

'They didn't get access to the party but they've got pictures of it. Photoshop something.'

Politics has two speeds: glacial and crisis. Crisis is a storm in which all the little laws are up in the air, the dice of history tumbling. You have a window before reality congeals again. Hours, sometimes minutes.

By 3 a.m. they'd managed to assemble all the big names. Those in Kazakhstan stood around a conference table in the corner office. Their London colleagues streamed in on a video screen. I recognised Charlene Hayes, who used to chair the Joint Intelligence Committee. I also recognised John Weston, former British ambassador to NATO and the UN. Walker led with the intel he'd received.

'The President's dead. That's confirmed. The bomber's believed to be Samat Baysufinov – Kazakh, from Shymkent. Twenty-eight years old, no known affiliations.'

He hadn't been flagged by the services. Used false papers to hire a Mercedes 220, attached fake diplomatic plates, drove up to the front of the hotel past six hotel security and almost twice as many members of the presidential guard. That was insane, and suggested inside support, which was currently a high-priority line of investigation. Nine minutes to eleven, Baysufinov parked a few metres away from the entrance. The President went downstairs at 11.03.

Forty-two injured, seventeen dead. If I'd made it downstairs thirty seconds earlier it would have been eighteen.

'Do we have a group responsible?' Weston asked.

'Not yet.'

People kept one eye on the TV screens as it hit: *Reports coming in of a bomb* ... Normal broadcasting ceased. Kazakh channels, KTK News and Channel 31, cut to visibly distressed presenters. *The President is reported to have been injured* ...

Someone had to say it. In the end it was Hayes.

'Who's going to be giving the green light now, when it comes to Conqueror?'

'It's not clear.'

'We're going to have to move carefully,' Piper said. 'We know Galina's been supportive so far. Obviously this will ruffle a lot of feathers. And we don't want to seem to be taking advantage.' Something caught in her voice. It sounded wooden. She turned to me. 'Thoughts?'

'This is going to plunge their economy into crisis,' I said. 'That's our opportunity. Objectively speaking, they need this deal now more than ever. Show them UK investors standing firm. We won't be cowed, Kazakhstan won't be cowed.'

There were nods. I felt like I was watching myself from a distance. Everyone agreed to speak again in an hour. I took Piper aside, removed some of the glass from her hair. She looked at me with a strange smile.

'Toby, are there any aspects of Vectis that I need to know about? What you do, what's going on?'

'What do you mean?'

'I mean aspects of Vectis that I *shouldn't* know about.'

Walker arrived before I could think of an answer.

'Zhaparov is directing pretty much everything, as far as we can tell.' He had signals intelligence. 'The head of the Kazakh Defence Force is on his way to the anti-terrorism HQ. There are calls from Zhaparov's advisers to senior figures in the Kyrgyz, Uzbek and Russian governments, all made less than an hour after the bomb. The calls lasted five to ten minutes, enough to get guarantees, establish details, chains of command.'

'And China?'

'Expressing concern.'

'That's screaming fire,' Piper said, as if we hadn't just had our inconclusive exchange. 'For Beijing.'

'We have a fairly strong indication that there's going to be another attack in Astana,' Walker said.

'What kind of attack?'

'A bomb. That's all I know.'

'Who's feeding you this?'

'Reliable sources.' He wouldn't say more. I wondered which of his friends in Six were slipping him this information, and why.

The story hit international news at 5 a.m. *Word of an alleged terror attack at an event attended by Kazakhstan's President* ... Statements from world leaders scrolled across the screens. Nothing yet from Kyrgyzstan, with its Russian bases. Nothing yet from Tehran. Mass arrests had started under Zhaparov's instructions. The official Russian statement: *Nazarbayev was a pillar of stability in the region and Russia will do everything it can to preserve peace and security for the people of Kazakhstan.* Which meant it was ready to invade.

I logged in to the VKontakte account of Aslan Cherchesov, my Russian seaman, checked his military friends. Leave had been cancelled. I posted: *Can't believe leave's cancelled. Going to miss my girlfriend's 21st birthday. Where are you being sent?*

A hush fell across the headquarters. I looked up and saw Zhaparov on the screens. He stood in the lobby of Astana's Parliament House, surrounded by senior military.

'The President is in a very critical condition. I want the people of Kazakhstan to know, we will stop at nothing to catch those responsible. Nowhere on earth will be safe. They will see what happens when the Kazakh people stand together.'

Zhaparov declared a state of emergency. Vladislav Vishinsky stood in the crowd behind him. Walker touched my arm.

'Come with me.'

Was this it? I wondered. Was he leading me to some form of incarceration or worse? I considered running. In the end I pocketed a biro on the way, as a last-ditch form of defence.

We walked the length of the ground floor to a door that opened into a gym. No cameras. One shaven-headed individual guarding a scratched brown briefcase. The man departed with a nod at Walker. The case sat there beside a rowing machine.

384

'It's what he asked for,' Walker said. 'There'll be another million in his designated account if the field's in GL5 control this time next week.'

I lifted the case by the handle. It was heavy. I sat on a bench, lifted it onto my lap and slid the locks. The money was portioned into clear bags of several thousand dollars, a mixture of bank-fresh and used notes, both with plain seals.

'I've arranged guards,' Walker said.

'We need to keep it light.'

'I get that. You can appreciate our concern.'

I called Satayev. He called me back within a few minutes.

'We're in a position to help,' I said.

'We are ready to fight. But people need to hear your government say they are with us.'

'I've got what you asked for. I'm not doing this on behalf of the government.'

'I understand.'

'It's the truth this time. I need you to know that.'

I told him how much money I was about to deliver and he relaxed.

'Take it to my colleague.'

'Someone you can trust? This is a big delivery.'

'He is my righthand man. I will give you the address.'

'Go for it.'

He gave me an address in the Triumph of Astana.

FIFTY

Apartment 601. No name. I was told to buzz, say I had a delivery, get the lift straight up.

Satayev ended the call, and I was left staring across the gym equipment. I was being swept along by something. This was my last chance to escape, I thought, but I knew I was kidding myself. That moment had long passed. I wanted to know what story I was in.

Walker had arranged a driver. He put a tracker on the case, the size of a memory card. Morbid curiosity kept me moving.

The dawn was dreamlike and fragile. People huddled at the bus stop in the grey sunrise, looking at phones. There was heavy activity around the government district, tactical vehicles containing special forces driving in. A city in shock. Viewing it through tinted glass didn't help shake the sense of travelling through a dream. Towards a dream.

I kept the case on my lap as GL5 drove me there, but that made me self-conscious so I put it on the seat beside me as if it was just another load of paperwork. I had an earpiece that connected to GL5 high command, a discreet microphone on my jacket. The vehicle would be tracked on satellite. None of this helps you feel secure. As a rule I don't handcuff briefcases to my wrist: it's blatant, and arms get severed for a lot less than 1.5 million dollars. Still, you never get used to carrying that amount around.

We turned north. The Triumph appeared. I felt a heavy,

sleep-deprived wave of dread. Something was making sense in a way I could only associate with impending death.

'I want to walk in on foot,' I said, trying to keep some kind of control on the situation.

He shook his head. 'That is not possible.'

We entered the building's shadow. Barriers for the underground car park sank into the ground and we sped down the ramp towards a lot of high-end vehicles under neon.

There was a lift in the underground car park, with its own armed guard.

'I think I'll be okay from here.'

'We'll stay by the car.'

The lift took me up to the ground-floor reception where I had to cross the lobby to another set of lifts. These lift doors opened to reveal a gleaming interior of polished brass and mirrored walls. I stepped inside, reflected to infinity – me and 1.5 million dollars rising through the building, asking myself why I was still alive.

The doors opened on a long corridor, five doors in each direction. Number 601 was the furthest to the left. The beige carpet absorbed all sound.

I knocked. The door opened. He wasn't in the dark suit, but it was him – the man in the clip. He wore a white shirt, open at the neck, sleeves rolled up, beltless black suit trousers, leather slip-ons. He glanced at the case.

'Come in.'

He asked me to take the battery out of my phone. The place was over-carpeted and overheated. I followed the corridor to the room where I had supposedly been filmed.

It was the same room: same view, same cupboard with mirrored panels. The rug had gone and there was a new sofa: brown where the one in the clip was pale. A TV was on: shots of troops marching. *The assassination opens up a Pandora's box as*

Russia, China and Turkey contest for control of the region. An emergency summit had been called in Brussels. The first crowds had appeared across Kazakhstan, holding images of Nazarbayev.

'We must be quick,' he said.

I glanced up to where a camera might be. I couldn't see anything, or anywhere you'd hide one. I walked over to the mirror, ran a thumbnail over the crack, then stood back and looked at myself in it. I had the case gripped in my hand.

'Who are you?' I said.

'A friend of Akan Satayev.' He watched me curiously.

'I don't work with people I don't know.'

'You don't need to work with me,' he said.

'Do you know who I am?' I asked.

'Akan says you can be trusted.' The man wanted this over, but was cautious. He didn't offer a drink. Someone wanted me here, I thought. I checked the view from the window. 'We don't have long. Show me what you have.'

I lifted the case to the coffee table, slipped the locks and nudged it towards him. He checked a couple of the blocks then went and made a call, moving stiffly.

I looked for papers, post, anything with a name, pressed the pedal of a bin in the corner but it was empty. I picked up a jacket slung over the arm of the sofa and retrieved a receipt for a Visa card in the name of B. Golovkin. Golovkin, if it was him, remained in deep discussion in the kitchen. He spoke in Arabic. I heard the words 'two hours' and 'cleaning up'. I messaged the name to Reza Nikfar, picked up an open laptop beside the table. No folders or documents saved, just news streaming: Turkey had stopped a Russian ship from passing through the Bosphorus Strait. NATO vessels from Spain and Italy were moving towards Georgia. Saudi Arabia had described Kazakhstan as a friend, and any threat to the country's independence and integrity as unacceptable.

There were Chinese troops at Khorgos. The ruble had sunk to 59 per dollar.

West united in warning to Russia. Territorial integrity is the foundation of international law.

The man returned and nodded.

'Okay. Now we move forward. Akan will be in touch.' He took a packet of cigarettes from his pocket and tapped one against the box. That was when I saw his fingernails. They were blackened and stunted – where they'd grown back at all. It meant someone had seen fit to remove them at some point. Time spent in the hands of those people explained the care with which he moved, the unblinking eyes. I imagined seeing him through bars, without the suit, in Kabul's Policharki prison, in Baghdad's Karrada district hellhole. What else did it explain?

'How long have you lived here?' I asked.

'I don't live here.'

I returned to my reflection in the mirror: the bruising, the new coat I'd stolen. You start operations in control, you end up looking like you're on the run. Reza messaged back: Golovkin = high alert. What do you know? Call me.

I returned to the case, picked it up and walked out.

'What are you doing?' he said.

FIFTY-ONE

I got into an open lift and hit the button for the ground floor, hearing Golovkin's steps approach. The doors closed. The feeling I had was that I'd spent a long time in a dream someone had subjected me to, and I was ready to walk out now, and that was going to involve punching through doors. I had a message from GL5: the car was ready in the basement car park. Confirm delivery. I crossed the ground floor to a doorman who held the doors open for me and my case as we walked out.

Then I ran.

I took the tracker out of the case, threw it into the back of a pickup waiting at traffic lights, and kept going. Half a mile south I stole a boxy old Honda Civic from beside the university. I threw the case on the back seat, put another mile between myself and the Triumph.

An unmarked car screamed past, 50 miles per hour with a siren on and someone sitting in the back, head bowed. Police were everywhere now, stiff with live rounds. They'd turned the adverts off on the sides of buildings. Main roads were being used by the military. My instinct was to get out of the city. I kept to the back roads and sank low in my seat, cut towards the airport.

I called Reza as I drove.

'Who is Golovkin?'

'Elliot, you're on an Interpol red notice.'

'Issued by who?'

'The States.'

'Under what name?'

'Your own. If you are actually Elliot Kane.'

A Red Notice was an instruction to locate and provisionally arrest an individual pending extradition. It was issued by Interpol when a member country had produced a valid national arrest warrant.

'I've been set up.'

My phone vibrated. I had an alert from Cognizance, the facial-recognition app, which meant a face resembling my own had shown up online. I groaned.

'Are you back working with Akan Satayev? Is that what this is to do with?' Reza asked.

The phone buzzed again. I took vibrate off.

'I'm not working with anyone. Who's Golovkin?'

'One of the twenty or so cover names used by Serik Ten. He's the money man for ISIS in Central Asia. His name just came up in connection with the truck that took the explosives to Astana.'

Everything was coming into focus. The CGI clip showed me consorting with a terrorist linchpin: MI6 stirring Central Asia against Russia.

I was the catalyst.

'Serik Ten was seen two months ago in the company of Ibrahim Al-Salhi,' Reza continued. 'The bomb-maker who brought down the Raffles Hotel in Doha. We have an individual in custody talking to us. He says there will be a vehicle-borne attack in Astana today, targeting civilians. Can you confirm that?'

'I don't have that intelligence personally.'

'People believe you do.'

'This is verified?'

'We identified seven Kazakh terror cells allied with the bomber. They've gone underground as of two hours ago – a surge in electronic chatter, then total silence. Something's about to happen.'

I said I'd call back, then braced myself and checked what the facial alert was bringing up. Online I'd gone viral. *Police release footage of British citizen accused of conspiracy to provide resources to a designated foreign terrorist organisation.*

Bohren crossing the lobby of Jeddah's Waldorf Astoria; Bohren on security cameras in the vaults of Singapore's FreePort.

Russian sites: *Who is Christopher Bohren?* Me in Queen Alia, crossing the departures hall, a red circle around my head like a halo. Then a more blurred shot at the GL5 compound. *Questions must be answered regarding Bohren's connections with GL5, the private contractor now suspended from all security work at UK military and governmental facilities . . .*

I stopped the car, checked the case, took out a wad of cash and ripped it open. I checked for watermarks, metallic thread, ran my finger over the print. I wasn't convinced, but others might be. I threw it onto the back seat. Another call came in: Marius from the Evotec office, sounding uncharacteristically tense.

'Where's Stefan?' he said.

'I thought he was on his way back to you.'

'He never got the flight.'

'You're joking.'

'We got word via contacts: he was flown to Moscow. Russia thinks we were involved in hacking them on behalf of China.'

'You're kidding me.'

'Critical infrastructure in Russia went down a few hours ago – Sberbank, Lukoil, Rosneft: all hacked. China's Cyberspace Administration was taken down in return.'

'By the Russians?'

'Not by us, that's for sure.'

'I'll get you Stefan. I'll sort this out.'

'We can't work with you any more.'

'Leave it with me.'

I put thoughts of Stefan's probable interrogation out of my

mind and checked Aliya's Vkontakte account. It was still putting out messages. She had moved on from conspiracy theories about the President's death to encouraging Astana's citizens to gather in memory and defiance.

She was encouraging people to meet at Independence Square.

I logged in to her phone, looked at her London photos again, then checked the phone's current location. It came up as the Eagilik bookshop, Kenesary Street. According to social media, people were gathering there in preparation for a march or memorial or protest of some kind: no one seemed entirely sure which.

Individuals were spilling out by the time I arrived, some with candles, others placards. I saw Aliya, pulled up alongside her, opened the passenger door.

'Get in.'

'Toby?' She looked terrified. Her companions stared.

'I need to speak to you.'

'I know who you are.'

'I doubt it. Please, get in.'

'You are Christopher Bohren. You work for MI6.'

'Close. You're in trouble, Aliya. I need to know why you went to London.'

Now she felt the heat of her friends' attention, just as I did. Others were watching. It was a tense morning and my presence wasn't making it any more comprehensible.

'Please.'

She got in.

'Aliya?' a young woman with a candle said.

'It's okay.'

I began to drive.

'I want to talk to you about Worldwide Media,' I said. 'I want to know what's going on.'

'I can't.'

'Yes you can.'

393

'Let me out.'

'In a minute.'

'This is what it was all about. Café Corso . . . '

'Not all of it.'

She sat frozen, silent, while I drove. I didn't want a scene in the car. I wanted her somewhere isolated.

When we got to the motel she panicked, tried to grab the wheel. I stopped the car, persuaded her again that I wasn't the threat, that she needed me to save her, which was sounding less convincing by the minute. She stayed in the car while I paid for a room. I bought a bottle of vodka from the shop. We went into the room and I set the vodka down, fetched tumblers from the bathroom and gave her one.

'Have a drink.'

'You kissed me.' Aliya shook her head. 'Drive me back,' she said. 'Please.'

'I will drive you back. Now, or any time you want. But I am concerned about what you're involved in, and I think it might place you in danger. Look at your last posts: you're tweeting about another bomb. Is that going to happen? How do you know that's going to happen?'

'It's nothing to do with me.'

'But it is. I think it is, other people will think it is. That brings danger to you and your family.'

Her glass whistled past my head and smashed against the wall. She went for the door, then changed her mind and came at me, slashing my face with her nails. I got hold of her wrists.

'Look in the case,' I said. I turned her towards the case. She hesitated, then opened it and stared at the money. 'Ten minutes,' I said. 'Explain why this is nothing to do with you, and tell me who it's to do with. Then I drive you back with as much money as you want.'

'Who are you?'

'I'm the one who's going to stop you from being arrested. I can get you out of here. But I need you to trust me.'

I poured her a drink in the remaining glass, then took a swig from the bottle. She sat down on the bed, holding the glass, staring through it to the dirty walls, finally knocking it back.

'I did what they told me.'

'Who?'

'Worldwide Media.'

'What do Worldwide Media do?'

'They said it was about helping with social media, encouraging real voices. Opening Kazakhstan up.'

'What happened in London?'

'It was like a job interview. They paid for me to go. I was recruited.'

'To do what exactly?'

'Write for them. They wanted young people in Kazakhstan. They'd read my blog. They said they were looking for young people who knew the local perspective – music, events, celebrities, places, customs. Kazakh and Russian.'

'Who else did you meet while over there?'

'Lots of people. Other organisers, other people being recruited.'

'How many being recruited?'

'Around twenty of us.'

'What ethnicity?'

'A mix.'

'And the people in charge? Where were they from?'

'I don't know.'

'What accents did they have?'

'English.'

'Were they staying at the hotel?'

'I don't think so.'

'Did you ever visit an office?'

'No.'

'Receive any correspondence with a company address?'

'No.'

I put on a bedside lamp and turned off the neon tubes. We were talking now, and I needed her to continue. I needed to arrive at a point where I understood who was behind this, and what they wanted. I topped up her glass, then asked Aliya to lead me through the whole experience from first contact. She took a breath and began to speak.

They'd arranged a travel visa for her. She flew British Airways, via Helsinki. Picked up at Heathrow by a woman called Natasha, who was accompanied by two men, neither of whom was introduced to Aliya. She'd spent five days total in London. Most of the recruitment and training was handled by Natasha and a man around the same age as her, who called himself Mark. Aliya described him as slick and energetic: he spoke about social media, building profiles, persuasive writing. No conspicuous security was visible during her stay, though she was accompanied on outings, which they took as a group, and they asked her not to bring her phone to the training sessions.

'What else did these sessions involve?'

'They wanted to know about me: what languages I spoke, what I cared about, what my passions were, how I felt politically. Did I think representations of Russia were fair? What are hot topics in Kazakhstan? I did some written exercises: short pieces about news stories they showed us.'

'Then what happened?'

'I got the job.'

She had signed a non-disclosure agreement but no official contract. That was the last time she met anyone involved in person.

I asked her to talk me through the protocols they'd arranged. The first thing she did each day was to switch on an internet proxy service, which hid her IP address, then she accessed an encrypted cloud-storage service. It contained instructions from Worldwide Media: files uploaded with material, wiped after seven days. She followed the instructions; money appeared in her account.

'Some of it's just translating news articles from English to Russian. Or they ask me to leave comments on news sites.'

'They tell you what to say?'

'I'm allowed to say what I want. They sometimes send me graphics and videos to use; sometimes ideas and articles they want me to think about, suggestions about which websites to post on.'

'All under your name?'

'No. I have other names.'

'Tell me about them.'

She told me about Maria Zagitova, who was very anti-Chinese, and Sabina, a housewife in Shymkent who concentrated more on traditional Kazakh values. She wrote in Kazakh. The third identity Aliya controlled was a fortune teller named Cantadora. She passed on advice from the spirit world, often regarding sex or relationships, sometimes dieting, occasionally geopolitics. She believed the future lay with Russia.

I passed Aliya my laptop and asked her to show me the dropbox. She hesitated, then logged in to a Boxcryptor online storage account.

'This is just the last few days.'

It was enough – more than forty files. I copied the lot. Then I read a few.

Then I stopped.

Russia's idea of a secure border is one with Russians on
both sides.

My words to Joanna.

I scanned through the bullet points. There were other ideas I remembered from our conversation.

> – For several years, figures close to Putin have been agitating for a more aggressive foreign policy to the south as well as to the east.
>
> – Kazakhstan is an attractive prospect to Russians nostalgic for the territorial reach of the Soviet Union.
>
> – Invasion itself would not present a problem for Russia's military. Kazakhstan's limited forces of some 70,000 could not offer significant resistance. Seizing their 'rightful' portion of Kazakhstan would bring Russia substantial resources and enormous geopolitical advantages. It would also gain control of China's border to the west, thereby getting a monopoly of control over China's energy imports and any manufactured exports that pass west through Kazakhstan.

Beneath the terse prose, it was Joanna's voice, I felt sure. I took my phone out, accessed my encrypted files and found the image of Joanna taken from the mall CCTV.

'This woman,' I said.

'That's Natasha,' Aliya said, staring at the image, puzzled.

'This is definitely Natasha?'

'Yes.'

She sounded certain, and calmer now; it was my turn to deal with bewilderment.

'What was Natasha's role, exactly?'

'She runs the company. She was in charge.'

I sensed a lot of pieces falling into place, without being able to see what shape they formed just yet.

'What did you think it was all for?'

'I thought it was to generate clicks, drive traffic. Why else?'

I checked the latest file, dated Monday. Aliya was being

prompted to tweet about people protesting. Encouraging them. Announcing the gathering in Independence Square.

'Why this gathering? What do you know?' I asked.

'Nothing. I need to get out of here.'

She topped up her glass, drank again. Then she asked if I had cigarettes. I went to buy some from the front. When I returned she had vanished.

So had the case with the money.

No sign of her in the car park. I checked the road. She was nowhere to be seen. There was nothing to suggest she'd been abducted. My laptop remained on the bed. She must have hitched a lift. Good luck to her, I thought. I hoped she was going to use that money to get herself and her family as far away from here as possible.

The dropbox was still open on the laptop. The zip file within it contained twenty or so links, suggestions, articles and academic papers. Now I could hear Joanna's voice in the instructions. The latest set of instructions included a map showing areas of Kazakhstan that Russia might annex in an invasion, identical to the one I'd seen in Saracen's offices.

I ran a reverse image search online and it came up attached to a paper by a professor at Southampton's School of International Relations. 'Russia's Southern Front'.

The writer was a Professor Romas Kleiza. He came up online: Lithuanian-born, expert in Cold War history. A quick browse gave me a sense of Kleiza and his career. Not the world's most success-ful scholar – he had one book to his name, *World Without the West*, regarding a plot by Russia, China and Iran to dominate the next millennium – but popular with right-wing think tanks and anti-Russian lobby groups. I recognised him as the expert who'd been on TV pontificating about Islamist terror in Central Asia.

There was another map he'd created: *June 2030. Political struc-tures after NATO.*

Poland was misshapen, its eastern regions absorbed into the Russian Federation. Same with Estonia. Ukraine had disintegrated entirely. Turkey was pocked with Russian bases. So were Syria, Libya and Egypt.

A lot of Western countries lay in fragments, broken rocks on the shoreline of a great sea: Central Asia and the Middle East, including the Gulf states, divided between Russia, China and Iran. Symbols indicated their ports, airfields, shipping routes, oil and gas pipelines. As a bloc, they controlled 90 per cent of energy and trade to Europe.

According to his website, the map had been used at a conference, 'Approaches to the New Russia–China Threat', put on by the Eurasian Futures Foundation.

The name rang a bell.

A lot of his work, apparently, had been made possible by the generosity of this foundation. EFF, as it styled itself, had been active between 2013 and early 2018, funding conferences, journals and books, and supplying quotes, statistics and opinion pieces to the media. Then it closed down. Even their website was gone.

I had a look to see who had supplied the Eurasian Futures Foundation with their money. The name that came up was Robert Carter.

Robert Carter, it turned out after a few minutes browsing, had put millions into EFF, alongside likeminded business leaders and philanthropists. The establishment of the Foundation was recorded in the press as another front in Carter's lobbying war. To celebrate the occasion, the *Spectator* ran a think piece under his name.

We're told NATO is coming apart, EU defence pacts are in tatters, and the West, defeated in the Middle East, will now bow out gracefully from affairs on our very own doorstep. For new powers are on the rise. Well, some of us will not stand by as the two most autocratic, undemocratic and merciless regimes gang

400

up to make liberal democracy a mere memory. The cynical alliance between Russian and China is the greatest threat we face. Their machinations, combined with America's absence, is bad news for the free world. It is up to all politicians and diplomats to ensure the twenty-first century won't turn into the Sino-Russian century.

Then I knew where I'd seen him. He'd been at the event where I'd first met Callum Walker.

I thought back to that night, which had been a memorable one in and of itself. Wilton Park was an eighteenth-century mansion in Buckinghamshire, used by the Foreign and Commonwealth Office for strategic forums, mostly focused on international security, bringing together big names from politics, business and academia. It had originally been commandeered as a site to interrogate German prisoners after the Second World War. I was thinking about this as I arrived and saw the place.

Helicopters on the lawn; inside the house, a sweeping staircase, an ornate room with Greek gods painted across the ceiling. Beneath the gods, international political figures, former heads of banks, energy companies, retired military.

Talks were self-regarding, centred on fantasies. Fantasies of Russian schemes and capabilities, of our capacity to respond, and visions of various futures in which it was too late. With the décor and candlelight, the whole thing felt like a strange form of court masque, an attempt at decorating power with ideas. It was a waste of my time, and I wondered why Alastair Undercroft had suggested I attend. After the final speech I moved to the bar, feeling superstitious and wanting to clear the foggy visions away with whisky. I was looking forward to getting back on a plane to Kurdistan. I met Callum Walker. His eyes were bright with drink. His business card was in my hand when I next sat down.

I checked Google's cached pages for archived versions of the

EFF website, then Wayback Machine, which preserved old or deleted websites. The Eurasian Futures Foundation website was there. It listed events, sponsors, speakers, attendees. I was scanning down names when one caught my eye in the list of sponsors: Talon.

Hugh Stevenson had been on his way to their offices when he was killed.

I called the number for Talon. A receptionist answered.

'I believe someone at your company wants to speak to me,' I said. 'I'm not sure who. My name is Elliot Kane, and I believe they want to speak to me about Hugh Stevenson. It's urgent, and I'd appreciate if you could identify the relevant employee.'

I thought I sounded insane. The well-spoken woman on the other end remained polite. She said she'd see what she could do. I didn't believe her. I gave a number to call.

My phone rang in less than two minutes.

'You know I can't tell you much.' It was a woman's voice, rich, soaked in decades of power. I could hear birds chirping in the background.

'Who is this?'

'You don't need my name. Hugh suggested you might call. He said if anything happened I should speak to you. You have to understand, I am not part of the privileged circle. But I was at the initial meeting. At the Foreign and Commonwealth Office, 1st March 2014.'

'What happened?'

'I was told it was going to be a closed conference on Central Asian policy, put together by the Eurasian Futures Foundation. There was an astonishing array of figures present: the Foreign Secretary and Chief of Six, the army chief of General Staff. There were representatives of the NATO Psychological Operations Working Group, individuals from Sweden, Finland and Croatia. Robert Carter, of course, along with the CEO of British Energy, the chief executives of Fortune Capital, Shell, Deutsche Bank.

Then a lot of foreign policy think tanks, Washington and Brussels as well as UK.

'Eurasian Futures had arranged a presentation. We were shown data and forecasting on Central Asia, on Russian leadership and Central Asia, a set of scenarios that could unfold. All incorporated loss of Western influence, financial losses of billions, a complete shift of global power. Robert Carter had intelligence regarding a meeting in August between China, Russia and Iran. He claimed that Russia persuaded its allies that the West had become politically incapable of coordinated military response, and he believed they were about to take advantage of this to establish joint control of the region. More broadly, we lacked the means of responding to their psychological operations.

'He presented data that showed Russian dominance of online media in more countries than not, said the effects of this would only be fully understood in the coming years. The argument made was that we needed to step up our own offensive psyop strategy urgently, before it was too late. The British government needed to take these warnings seriously. It was now or never.

'I detached myself, so to speak, when they began talking about invading Syria and Iran. We would need Russia distracted etcetera. That was when I decided they were fantasists. Now I believe they had alliances within the MOD and beyond, in the States: individuals who backed a more aggressive foreign policy.'

'How high up do you think it goes?'

'I don't know. I raised objections in the meeting. I was closed out. So I can't say with certainty how things proceeded. I know Robert Carter bought Saracen a month later. Saracen hired the intelligence company, Vectis. Their founder, Callum Walker, had been one of the more positive voices at the meeting.'

'Walker was there?'

'He was there. I've no doubt his connections within the Secret Intelligence Service helped win initial support for whatever unfolded. The government did spend millions, I've heard. My own acquaintances were able to share that much. No other information came my way until six months ago when those acquaintances suggested my instincts had been right. The PM got cold feet, balked at the scale things had grown to. Perhaps they hadn't realised that Kazakhstan was part of a much bigger play. You can imagine the government's response to that. We can't risk starting World War Three: thoughts along those lines.'

'And then people moved out of Six,' I said, as the pieces came together.

'Quite an exodus. The big names associated with the project seemed to feel their time in state intelligence had come to an end. They went off in a sulk. Robert Carter ensured that most of them had a soft landing.'

'Joanna Lake?'

'Lake, yes. She moved to Vectis.'

I went to the motel window, stared at the car park as my mind reeled.

'Do you think it *was* closed down?' I asked.

'What do you mean?'

'Did they jump ship or just change ship?'

'I see.' There was a long pause. 'I wouldn't want to speculate. I've probably said all I can for now.'

'I appreciate it.'

'Hugh was a good friend.'

'Mine also.'

She rang off. Olivia Gresham had messaged: Is this real? Reza Nikfar: Call me. I returned to the car and began to drive back into the centre. I called Reza first.

'Got a possible ID for the attacker,' he said. 'We're looking for Emad Sabri, Iraqi from Anbar province. Seventeen years old. Usual story: parents killed, spent time in prison, came out angry and possibly disabled. Next seen in Raqqa, learning how to take apart an AK-47. His brother was arrested last year, but Emad must have had some decent training as he's been off-radar since entering Kazakhstan.'

'Where's he going to bomb?'

'That's the question. Would be nice to answer it before he does.'

I closed my eyes, tried not to see the aftermath of a suicide bomb: the body parts, the children, the bones through skin.

'Listen, Reza, you said Joanna Lake put you on to this attack in the first place when she called. I think she'd just seen the plans – I think she'd accessed something that told her what was going to happen. She judged that it had gone too far. She was going somewhere to try to stop it.'

'You think she got there? She got involved with terrorists?'

'I don't know. You've got the cell number she rang you from; you may have her last location.'

'Give me fifteen.'

'Five.'

'Five.'

Gresham was still trying to get through. I answered.

'Where are you?' she said.

'Astana.'

'You're on the news.'

'Ignore the news.'

'Are you okay?'

'No. What have you heard about the situation?'

'The President might be dead.'

'The President is dead.'

'What about the deal?'

'Up in the air.'

'I'm hearing five billion barrels, I'm hearing three billion, then zero billion; I'm hearing a line into Turkey, then people saying that's a no-go. Others telling me the field's sixty million years out, and the oil's gone.'

'Who's saying that?'

'Smart people. Apparently there's been drilling around Block Nine for years. The fossils coming up are Cretaceous rather than Miocene – so say people who know about these things. It's clay all the way down.'

'Saracen have new remote sensing technology,' I said.

'Auracle.'

'Right.'

'Start-up snake oil. No one had heard of Auracle or their drones until two years ago. Now they've vanished off the face of the earth.'

'What do you mean?'

'Try calling them.'

'I will.'

'Are you really on a wanted list, Elliot?'

'So it seems.'

I promised I'd message with an update asap and hung up. I was a few blocks east of the Special Economic Zone. I could do better than calling them. I turned the car around and headed for their office.

Astana's citizens were out in force. Many carried flowers or wreaths. I passed two satellite broadcasting vans, then heard the first chants. At the corner of Independence Square I saw the crowd: two thousand or so men and women drawn together by shock. Police lines protected the governmental palace. Military groups waited beside armoured vehicles at the corners of the square. Taking up positions: Zhaparov's national guard, balaclavas covering their faces, fingerless gloves on assault rifles.

Three security police waved me away. I turned east, kept going, into narrower, poorer back streets, turned another corner and saw two black Land Cruisers, ten black uniforms. A man was down on the snow, clutching his face, eight more individuals with their hands on their heads, noses pressed to the wall.

An open doorway led into a tatty prayer hall with overlapping rugs on the floor, a speaker on the wall, prayer books in a case by the door. I checked the uniformed men. They looked sharp, well equipped, with Glocks and MP3s. Looked like Zhaparov's personal unit.

I reversed fast, circled back to the gates of the economic zone. Two guards kept uneasy watch. They asked for my pass.

'I'm visiting Auracle.'

'Gone,' one of the men said. 'No visitors today.'

I talked my way in by virtue of being a white European and passing them my last handful of cash. Besides, it wasn't a day for excess propriety.

The businesses were housed in identikit warehouse-style buildings and it took me ten minutes to find Auracle's unit, not helped by the fact that their signage had been removed.

The door to the office was locked but no alarm went off when I smashed a back window. Inside, it was bare bricks and trailing cables beneath empty desks. The desks were askew, bins filled with shredded paper. A whiteboard had been smeared. The small kitchen contained bags of unused stationery and stacks of plastic cups. In a back room was a snub-nosed drone with its wings off.

I sat down in a swivel chair at an empty desk.

'They have software that can tell you how long a relationship will last,' she said.

'What does that allow you to do? What are we, marriage guidance?'

'It means, theoretically, if you wanted a relationship to end, you could run the program backwards and see what steps would engineer that outcome.'

My phone battery was low. I brought up real-time satellite imagery of the Kazakh border with Russia. This was what

Joanna had been doing in the internet café, I realised now: watching the creep of war. The hacked data showed her something that had got out of control.

Imagery was vague; Russian troops were more than capable of going invisible if they chose. There were no more updates from Aliya in Astana, or her other personas. No reply when I messaged her, which was understandable. I logged into her phone, switched the mic on, heard a crowd chanting. She had joined the protest. She could have chosen safety and she chose history.

I tried Walker, then the Vectis office. Both lines were dead. I stood at the window and stared out at the corrugated walls of the industrial estate. According to local news, Zhaparov was due to address the Independence Square crowd in an hour, flanked by senior officials from Russia. He was branding it a mass vigil, an attempt to keep the square occupied by grief rather than anger: *Kazakhstan united against terrorism.*

In 2014, ISIS published instructions for building and deploying vehicle-borne explosives. They encouraged targeting mass gatherings. They advised on components that weren't going to trigger security tripwires, and suggested waiting to construct the device until just before the operation for maximum discretion.

Police had seized a laptop containing research on fuel-air bombs along with a detailed satellite image of Astana and surveillance photographs of public squares.

Fuel-air meant thermobaric. Thermobaric explosions were unlike anything else. Mix in enough petrol with your military-grade explosives and you got a second blast wave as the air itself caught light, sucking up all the oxygen. Most forms of defence were useless; the fuel cloud flowed around objects and into structures. What tended to kill people wasn't just the pressure wave but the subsequent vacuum, which tore lungs apart.

In a crowd like Independence Square, there would be more than five or six hundred in the kill zone.

But how would you get the vehicle through? No parked cars, area checked by sniffer dogs, airspace closed. Blocks on every approach road. I sat on a swivel chair in the abandoned office, hearing the peace outside. I made a fist of my left hand then opened it and stared at the scar.

Reza called.

'We have the last location of Joanna's cellphone.'

FIFTY-TWO

The location was two miles out of the city. I coaxed the car to seventy miles per hour, prayed that its wheels would hold on the icy road.

The coordinates led me into nothingness: salt flats as far as the eye could see. I considered the possibility that Reza's readings were out, or even that GPS signals were being scrambled, which wasn't unheard of during states of emergency. A mile later, as I was about to turn back, I saw something.

It looked like a village in the distance, with low, brown buildings. As I got closer I saw it was a cemetery, mud tombs surrounded by a low metal fence. Not a soul in sight.

I left the car by the fence and walked in. Graves were snow-capped, some domed, others square mausoleums of stone or clay. That was what had made me think it was a town. The graves were carved with images of camels and swords and inscriptions in Arabic. Poles jutted out of the snow, tied with bundles of horse hair. A low tree in the centre shrieked with coloured rags that had been wound around its dead branches.

Families had cleared snow from some of the graves. A path had been dug to a small brick mosque with barred windows and a crude water pump beside its door. A few hundred metres behind the mosque were the low concrete ruins of a collective farm.

I knocked at the door of the mosque, then turned back towards the cemetery and considered my next move. A few hundred metres to the right of where I'd parked there was a glint of what looked like water. Which was impossible. I walked over. As I got closer I saw it was something hard, reflective: a panel of grey metal. I kicked it with the toe of my boot. I thought it was a car door, and wondered how it had become detached, then realised it was the car's roof and it hadn't.

Heart thumping, I went back to the mosque, knocking hard on the door. When no one answered I pulled on the handle and it opened. I walked in, looking for a shovel. A figure moved. It was an old man, head shrouded, face sunken. A caretaker of some kind; scared.

I tried various languages before realising he was deaf. I mimed digging, then pointed out, towards my car. That did the trick. He disappeared into the shadows and came back with an ancient-looking spade. He followed me, and seemed curious when I started digging.

The Chevy Equinox sat in what must once have been a hollow. There was a ridge of earth on at least two sides. These would have obscured the car from the road, but also left it exposed to the east – the direction that the snow had blown in – and had served as a trap.

After ten minutes digging I had the top of a window. I crouched to try and see through but it was too dark inside. The caretaker watched as I dug furiously. I shone my phone light through the glass, couldn't see anything. When I had another few inches of window exposed I took the shovel and smashed the glass in.

The car was empty but for a laptop and the contents of a first-aid kit spilled across the front seats. Down by the pedals was a nylon pouch used for carrying a spare box magazine for a handgun. The grey fabric of the driver's seat was bloodstained. There was blood smeared on the window and the door handle.

411

The caretaker called out. He stood between the car and the cemetery, waving for me to come over.

A few metres away from him, I saw the fabric showing through the snow.

I dug with my hands, not minding that they went numb in seconds. I uncovered strands of hair, then skin, clearing the snow gently around her closed eyes. Joanna lay on her side. The snow remained pink around her right arm where she'd bled from beneath a shoelace tourniquet. Her lips were parted, frozen.

I crouched with my face to the exposed skin and felt the illusion of warmth. The caretaker muttered a prayer in Arabic. *O God, forgive our living and our dead . . .* Yes, I thought. I'd heard that prayer too many times but the words had never felt so necessary. The stupid game. She knew that and she'd kept playing. I saw the girl at the recruitment interview, climbing through the window and out of her life. I had loved her then. I couldn't remember why we had waited. Why had we let them rob us of our lives?

Some pins remained in Joanna's hair, the ones that had fastened the wig. I took a hairpin and pocketed it. I touched my lips to her frozen cheek because that was what I wanted to remember doing. A unique intelligence had gone from the world, a dangerous, discontented one that involved some knowledge of me, and that was gone too. I didn't want to leave her here. I thought of people I had encountered in Abkhazia, exiles from a flurry of war who had dug up the corpses of their relatives to bring with them, all shrouded in tarpaulin on the back of a pickup truck. Who was going to collect Joanna Lake? Not Vectis. The embassy, perhaps. I imagined her loaded onto a plane, unloaded tactfully on British soil. A spy's repatriation: anonymous, unmourned.

I returned to the half-excavated Chevy, retrieved the laptop. It was the one I'd seen her use on the mall CCTV. The battery was dead. I looked around, thought of her last minutes here.

Terrified? Surprised by an incongruous euphoria? Still fighting, I thought. Where was she trying to get to?

I pointed towards the abandoned farm buildings at the back. 'Anyone there?'

The caretaker shook his head. Then a thought occurred to him. I saw his sunken eyes come to life. He said something about ambulances.

'Ambulances came?' I tried both Russian and Kazakh. He lifted a hand as if to say 'Wait', went into the mosque and returned a moment later with a torch. He guided me towards the farm.

Blades of abandoned threshing machines lay around – dismembered combines, tractors. An air of desolation hung over the place. We went through to a long, breeze-block shelter, with rusted doors sealing it shut. The chain that had sealed them lay on the floor. The caretaker gestured for me to help him pull the doors open, and they scraped over the concrete.

The darkness inside was undiluted. He clicked a torch and pointed it. Hessian bags, more rusted metal, a stained floor. Then, in the furthest corner, a pile of medical kit: stretchers, a wheelchair, a drip stand, dressing pads, boxes of latex gloves.

There had been an ambulance here. It had been stripped; even the seats had been ripped out. There were also approximately forty canisters of petrol lying in a pile. The petrol would have been transferred to breakable containers, probably mixed with nails or other shrapnel. I estimated the volume of an ambulance as around 400 cubic feet, which would hold a horrific amount of explosive power.

My phone rang as I ran back to the stolen Honda. Number withheld. I answered.

'Elliot, this is Suzanna Ford. We understand the various complexities of your situation. Right now we're focused on preventing this attack. I'm sure that's your priority too.'

I got in the car, started the engine.

'He's using an ambulance,' I said. 'That's all I know. What resources do you have to stop it?'

'I've got a four-man team here. We're equipped.'

'That's not going to do it. Track me.'

'Elliot—'

I called the number on Cherenkov's business card. He answered.

'I have what you want,' I said. 'We need to be quick.'

FIFTY-THREE

He told me to head straight to the Russian embassy. I was stopped 10 metres before the gates by three men in Russian military uniform, one with a pistol drawn. Joanna's laptop was taken, along with my phone. I was patted down, steered down a driveway, pushed into the building.

Embassy stucco, pastel walls, pictures of Putin. Cherenkov sat in a reception room with oil paintings of forests, a prissy suite of antique furniture and one incongruous computer. He welcomed me without taking his eyes from the screen. He looked unslept but smarter than usual, the sleeves of his white shirt rolled up, absorbed in clicking his mouse. He turned the monitor towards me. It contained multiple images: more CGI versions of the room in the Triumph of Astana; me and Serik Ten; then me, Joanna and Serik Ten. Then low-quality images from other locations: my body on the ground with a spread of blood across my shirt; Joanna hanging from a belt in a toilet cubicle. Me and Joanna unconscious in the front seats of an SUV.

'Sit down.'

'Where's Stefan?'

'He's fine. He gave us this. I thought you might want to see.'

'We've got minutes before another attack. It's vehicle-borne, using a stolen ambulance. Target's Independence Square, I reckon.'

Cherenkov took a second to digest this, then relayed instructions to the men around him: communication channels to open, combat preparations to initiate. The guard showed him Joanna's laptop and Cherenkov nodded. It was passed to a second man, a technical specialist of some kind in civilian clothes who took it out of sight.

Door locked. Just the two of us. A well-upholstered interrogation room.

'Perfect Vision's a large-scale psychological operation, set up to hit back at Russia,' I said. 'Developed by MI6 after you invaded Ukraine. The idea's to inflame issues between you and your allies, China in particular. Kazakhstan's being used for that.'

Cherenkov absorbed this information expressionlessly.

'And the oilfield? How long have they known about Conqueror?'

'There is no Conqueror. No oil. Just an attempt to get Russia muscling into Kazakhstan, to set China on the defensive, introduce a crack in that special relationship. Get Russia mired in Central Asia again, distracted from the Middle East, discredited among the 'Stans. My theory is that it wasn't originally intended to go this far. What started as an attempt to sow discord gathered a momentum of its own. Some people were wise enough to try and close it down, but there's no monopoly on starting wars any more. When the British government got cold feet it just got moved into the hands of people with more resources. A lot of people left MI6 around that time. Vectis soaked them up. Robert Carter and his billions kept the operation afloat.'

'And you?'

'I'm proof that it's real. You know what my presence means. You know my history. I suspect they kept all this from Joanna. She got uneasy about what was going on. She would have known she wasn't being given full access to the scheme, so she used Ruslan Batur to hack in. Then she saw clips of me. Tried to save my life, and paid the price.'

'You really don't think she knew?'

'No.'

'I have to say, you played your part well.'

'Ruslan Batur was shot by GL5. They would have shot her too but she escaped. The files she saw also contained information about a planned attack, the final straw that forces Russia's hand. She almost got to the explosives.'

'And the attacker's using an ambulance?'

'Yes. Loaded with two tons of plastic explosives. He's probably on the move now.'

A guard returned, spoke to Cherenkov; he showed him a laptop with a satellite image of Astana. Cherenkov instructed him to bring up a connection with Moscow and got to his feet.

'There's one other thing you should know,' I said.

'What?'

I hesitated.

'MI6 have been running a top-level agent in the GRU for six or seven years. The codename's MADRIGAL. Rumours are that it's Vladislav Vishinsky himself. I don't have proof of that, but Vishinsky met Callum Walker in Moscow in 2005.' I improvised. 'This agent's valuable enough to Six that they refuse to close him down. He's protected. I thought you should know, in case it makes what happens now more complicated for you.'

'Vladislav Vishinsky?'

'Or someone in an equivalent position.'

'There's no one in an equivalent position.' Cherenkov stared at me. 'You expect me to believe that?'

'Maybe. I don't know what to believe any more.'

'Stay here.' He called the guard back to watch over me. We were sitting there, admiring Putin, when I heard a commotion; voices at the front, some speaking English. My guard hesitated, drew his weapon and went to look.

I followed.

About twenty GL5 contractors blocked the road in front of the embassy. The men wore helmets, draped in webbing and pouched vests, AKs and MP5s at the ready. Cherenkov was in heated discussion with their team leader, voices raised. The British-accented GL5 boss seemed to be saying that it wasn't safe, the Russians should stay inside. That wasn't going down well. No one stopped me getting close enough to hear.

'You have no jurisdiction,' Cherenkov said. But nor did he. It was quite a stand-off. Then Walker appeared.

He climbed out of an armoured SUV, moved through the GL5 officers, pistol in his right hand. He approached me cautiously, as if I was the one who was armed. 'Come on, Elliot. Let's go.' When he was a couple of feet away he lowered his voice. 'This was what she wanted, what she spent years building.' And, when he was even closer: 'I tried to keep you out of it.'

I leaned in and whispered, 'Thank you.'

Then I drove the base of my right palm into his face so that the cartilage of his nose crumpled. He began to fall. I gripped his wrist and unhooked the gun from his fingers, pulling him up by his thin hair and ramming the barrel of the Browning into the side of his skull. Blood streamed down into his mouth and he spluttered. His hired backup froze, staring. I turned to Cherenkov.

'Go,' I said. 'Do it.'

But it was too late. More trouble pulled up with a screech: a crew of ten British SAS in two Land Rovers. They jumped out, taking up combat stance. Suzanna Ford appeared from among them. She saw me and Walker.

'Elliot. We can take him off your hands.'

'Please do.'

Ford gestured to her men. They approached, one eye on the Russians, one on the GL5 contractors, and grabbed hold of Walker. Then, before I knew what was happening, Cherenkov had bundled me into a car and it was already moving, a glimpse of Suzanna Ford in the mirrors giving chase, yelling for him to stop before running back to her own team.

FIFTY-FOUR

I was in an armoured Mitsubishi Outlander filled with military communications systems, a compact signals intelligence suite and four Russian special forces officers dressed in civilian clothes but operation-ready. I saw a couple of AK-12 assault rifles, stun grenades, respirator kits and a sniper rifle. There were headsets and a blocky laptop monitor. They had the special forces habit of looking as unlike soldiers as possible. The driver was unshaven, gloved hands on the wheel, earpiece in. Beside him sat a malign-looking figure with a ponytail and webbed body armour over a denim jacket. The sniper sat behind mirror shades in the back beside a signals operator with a tactical data link system, involving a headset, mic and two screens on a portable box. It looked like they had a quad drone up.

Cherenkov briefed them on the situation. He brought up a feed on the laptop.

'Know if the bomb involves chemicals?' he asked me. 'Gases? Radioactive materials?'

'I don't know. Try not to cause panic over the radio; we need to keep the streets clear. Have you got access to Emergency Command?'

'Possibly.'

We headed into the centre. Cherenkov had a live feed of the square: it was packed edge to edge with people. They were still pouring in, holding candles and posters. The man who was working the data link touched his ear piece, checked the laptop screen, said:

'Look at that.'

He prodded the screen. The roof markings made it conspicuous from the air: one ambulance, heading north. It was ten minutes from us and less than half a mile from the square.

'It has its lights on, moving fast.'

'We've got about four minutes,' I said. The Mitsubishi accelerated. I checked the map again.

'He's going to circle and come from the east,' I said. 'That gives him the longest run-up. Either Akhmet or Jumeken. There's no obstacles on either. He'll get up to ninety miles per hour. We need to reach him before that.'

The driver muttered curses in Russian. Radios crackled. Moscow wanted to know what was going on. Cherenkov was struggling with his Kazakh counterparts.

'Yes, I am FSB. Russia. The situation is live ... '

'It's already inside most security checks,' the signals operator said. 'I don't see any further blocks between it and the square, until you get to the guards around the square itself.'

'What defences do they have?' I asked.

'Crowd-control barriers. They wouldn't stop a push bike.'

We tore down the deserted streets, Cherenkov desperately trying to radio various Kazakh commanders, but it was clear he didn't have the authority to get his message taken seriously.

'Evacuate the square,' the driver said.

'You'd need to evacuate more than half a kilometre,' I said. 'People will go straight towards the ambulance. They'll block the road.'

'He's just crossing the M-36 into the centre,' the man with the satellite feed said. 'It's at Sarayshyq Street.'

'Get them to close the street down.'

After another minute of frustration Cherenkov took the phone from his ear and swore.

'I can't establish the chain of command,' he said. 'We're on our own.'

'Target now on Alash Highway.'

'We can cut him off on Respublika,' I said. It was an optimistic, high-risk suggestion. The driver checked his map, swung the car to the right.

The city centre had emptied entirely. The PA system from the memorial service echoed across its streets. We were conspicuous. Four Kazakh troops, heavily armed, waved us down. We ignored them. They released safety catches, caught a glimpse of us and became uneasy. We all exhaled when we we'd gone past without shots fired.

Then the ambulance appeared ahead.

'There it is.'

There was a silence, save for the clicking of three safety catches.

'Go easy,' Cherenkov said.

'How easy?'

We narrowed the gap between us. Either of the next two turns could take him to the square. I could see the crowd through gaps in the buildings. The street tightened ahead. I thought we could block him at least, but we'd have to move fast.

'Don't panic him.'

'He's stopped.'

'Shit.'

'They've stopped him.'

I tried to see what was going on. There were barriers in front of the ambulance, blue uniforms: a checkpoint of some kind. The ambulance's sirens blared, its lights making the scene pulse. Cherenkov got on the radio and tried to ascertain if the Kazakh soldiers ahead knew who they'd stopped.

Our driver twisted in his seat, staring through the back window.

'We're blocked,' he said.

The Kazakh troops had tailed us and now parked two armoured personnel carriers a metre or so behind our vehicle. They got out, shouting, pointing assault rifles in our direction. The ambulance was also boxed in now, vehicles on three sides, the crowd on the fourth. Speeches continued from the stage. This was it, I thought. He was going to detonate.

I don't know what sparked the panic. There was no shortage of potential causes.

'An attack!' someone shouted. It was followed a second later by an order over the tannoy: 'Please evacuate the square in an orderly fashion.'

People began to run. They filled the side road.

'Fuck.'

The only people unfazed appeared to be the men in charge of the roadblock.

'Jesus Christ, they're going to let him through,' Cherenkov said, as the first barrier was pulled aside.

'They've got no idea.'

We climbed out of the vehicle. The Kazakhs behind us had their weapons ready. They stepped closer, six paramilitaries, then they lifted their weapons and ran. The Russians took up position behind the doors of the Mitsubishi. I stepped aside. Then they were past us.

'Maybe they do,' Cherenkov said. The crowd parted as the Kazakhs swarmed the ambulance. They took up positions around it then, at a hand signal, three men smashed the windows. I heard two shots, then two more. Then a second's silence before the crowd began to scream.

Everyone ran. We were pushed back a block by terrified individuals and roaring Kazakh soldiers. Other troops arrived and

I glimpsed British faces in the chaos: Suzanna Ford, her SAS detail. She locked eyes with Cherenkov. The leather-jacketed officer beside her had a gun, low but intent, focused on the Russian intelligence officer.

Ford was reading the situation, reading me. She beckoned me closer. I took a step.

'Good work.' She nodded in the direction of the ambulance. When I failed to react, she said, 'We collected her body. I'm sorry, Elliot. If it's any consolation, we're holding Callum Walker. Going to need a full debrief from you, but you'll be protected.'

Cherenkov caught my look of scepticism.

'The invitation's still open, Elliot. Moscow for Christmas. You'd be treated well.'

'Maybe next time,' I said.

He stepped back, eyeing Ford and her gunman.

'I mean it,' he said. 'Keep my card.' Then he disappeared into the crowd.

Ford winked. 'Welcome back, Elliot,' she said. 'We'll get a brew on the plane.' She turned to the SAS team and began coordinating our own evacuation. They studied a handheld device with a map on it. I walked back towards the ambulance, against the flow of the crowd, curious to see the seventeen-year-old martyr, then lost interest and walked into the square instead. The ground was littered with placards. I passed on through, keeping an eye out for Aliya, then I was on the other side and still walking.

FIFTY-FIVE

No one tailed me through Astana's freezing back streets. I cut north, flagged down a car, ended up at the train station. I bought a third-class ticket to Beyneu, near the border with Uzbekistan, picked up a loaf of bread, some biscuits, two bottles of local vodka. I bought some more gloves and a hat.

The train was modern, but the cheap carriage felt Soviet-era as it filled with farmers and traders, women who sat down amidst bags of produce. Those who made the journey regularly settled themselves with blankets, the initiates stiff and staring at the small windows. I checked their hands and nails to see if they matched the clothes. I passed my vodka around. They shared lamb and flatbreads doled out of newspaper, the assassination smudged to whorls of black and grey. I told them I was from Belarus, which was as exotic and distant as England to them, but less worthy of attention. I said I sold electronic equipment, and was visiting my wife who was in Tashkent with her family, and was ill.

China's troop movements were on hold. The BBC showed Russian APCs rolling back from the Kazakh border. I had a message from Reza, curious about what had happened to Vishinsky: Suddenly off-radar. Call me. I deleted the message, then dropped my phone out of the window onto the tracks below. I saw Joanna's serene death mask and felt, in some small way, I had completed the journey she had been trying to make.

Bukhara, in southern Uzbekistan, had a tenth-century mosque rumoured to be built on the remains of a Zoroastrian fire temple. I'd always wanted to visit. I'd been told that a Sufi sect survived in the area, still worshipping God by staring into flames. The city had once been a great centre of world civilisation. I knew of a remote border crossing on the Zhanaozen–Turkmenbashi road where you could cross into Uzbekistan on foot.

Around midnight the train stopped, troops boarded it and marched through, searching for something or someone. I felt torchlight in my face, and when it continued onwards I imagined the moment as a kind of benediction. We moved off again and five minutes later passed a lit platform with one guard holding a signal flag. A sign said *Koshoba*. You could see the scattered lights of oil derricks a few miles away. My companions fell asleep on each other's shoulders, and I relaxed into the violence of the train, the relentless shudder of metal as if it had to drill through the space ahead of us.

I wanted to see the fire temple and Bukhara's fortress that had once contained a vast library of ancient manuscripts. From there onwards was straightforward: two nights in Dushanbe in Tajikistan, where forged paperwork would be available. Then keep moving south and east, through the world's deep places: Kashmir, maybe Nepal. I would fix myself, regain equilibrium, until the day came when I looked up, met someone's gaze and they looked away. It would turn out that they'd been asking after me. That night I'd unlock my room and the man would be sitting there, white and well spoken. 'Elliot, excuse the intrusion, rather hoped you'd be able to lend a hand.' No introduction is necessary. 'Not much money in it,' he explains, 'but you might find it diverting. Needs someone like you: a field man.' And I'll show some reluctance before agreeing, mainly out of curiosity. Just to see, I'll tell myself. What else is there to do?

ACKNOWLEDGMENTS

Thanks to:

Matthew Plowright, Tom Nuttall, Gulliver Cragg, Olga Nikonchuk, Yulia Erlykina, Stephanie Cross, Calum Murray, Thomas MacManus, Kuralay Kabdeshova, Rahat Tuyakbaev and his friend behind the bar, Clare Smith, Veronique Baxter, Judith Murray, Rana Feghali, Joanna Lillis, Ranjan Balakumaran, Neil Arun, Robin Forrestier-Walker, N. B. Ray, The Young Roots team, and one individual who has asked to remain anonymous.

Very special thanks to Suzie Kim Jihyon.